CONTENTS

SOME RANDOM REFLEXIONS*

It is useless expecting a writer to explain his own work. "Read my books—it's all there," is what Chekhov used to say on such occasions. And this represents my views entirely.

So I shall limit myself here to a few general reflections on my writing and a brief outline of my life. There is little point in giving a detailed autobiography as this is already the subject of my work *Story of a Life*. Six volumes covering some forty years from early childhood up to the beginning of the thirties have already been published, and I am still working on the later periods.

I was born in Moscow on May 31, 1892, in the family of a railway statistician living in Granatny Alley. My father was a descendant of the Zaporozhye Cossacks who fled to the banks

---

* These notes by Paustovsky, which are reproduced here in slightly abridged form, provided the introduction to an eight-volume collection of his works published by *Khudozhestvennaya Literatura*, Vol. 1, Moscow, 1967.

of the River Ros near Belaya Tserkov after the suppression of the Sich. This was where my grandfather, who had formerly served in the ranks of Nicholas I's army, lived with my Turkish grandmother.

In spite of his profession which called for a sober assessment of things my father was incurably romantic and nonconformist with the result that he never stayed for long in any one place. After Moscow we moved to Vilno, Pskov and finally to Kiev where we settled more or less permanently.

My mother, the daughter of a sugar factory clerk, was a strict, overbearing woman.

Our family was a large one, composed of highly different individuals but all artistically inclined. We liked singing, playing the piano, debating and were passionately interested in the theatre.

I went to the 1st Kiev grammar school.

The family broke up when I was thirteen and after that I had to find a way of earning my own living and paying for my education. I managed to struggle along by coaching, a rather arduous job.

In my last year at school I wrote my first short story which was published in the Kiev literary magazine *Ogni*. This was in 1911 as far as I remember.

After leaving school I studied for two years at Kiev University and then got myself transferred to Moscow University and came to live in Moscow.

At the beginning of the First World War I worked as a tram driver and conductor in Moscow and later as a medical orderly on trains for the wounded both in the rear and at the front.

In 1915 I moved to an army medical unit and worked with it during the long retreat from Lublin in Poland to the town of Nesvizh in Byelorussia.

Then I happened to get hold of an old newspaper which reported that both my brothers had been killed on the same day in different parts of the front. I went home to my mother who was living in Moscow at the time, but found it impossible to settle down there for long and set off on my wanderings again. First I went to Yekaterinoslav and worked at a metal factory, then at the Novorossiisky factory in Yuzovka, and after that in the Nev-Vilde boiler factory in Taganrog. I left the boiler factory in the autumn of 1916 and found work in a fishing artel on the Azov Sea.

It was in Taganrog that I began writing my first novel *Romantics* in my spare time.

After that, shortly before the February Revolution I returned to Moscow and became a journalist.

My character both as a writer and person developed in Soviet times and it was this factor which determined the whole course of my life.

I was in Moscow during the October Revolution and saw many historic events between 1917-19, hearing Lenin speak on several occasions and living the hectic life of a newspaper correspondent.

But the itch to move soon got me again and I went back to my mother who was now living in the Ukraine again; I saw some turbulent events in Kiev and then left for Odessa. It was there that I came into contact for the first time with a group of young writers: Ilf, Babel, Bagritsky, Shengeli, Lev Slavin and others.

But my "wanderlust" would not let me be and after spending two years in Odessa I went to Sukhum and then to Batum and Tiflis. From Tiflis I travelled to Armenia and even got as far as northern Persia. I returned to Moscow in 1923 and worked for a few years as an editor in the Russian Telegraph Agency. During this period my work was beginning to appear in print.

My first "real" book was a collection of short stories entitled *Meetings in the Open Sea* (1928).

In the summer of 1932 I began writing *Kara-Bugaz*. There is a fairly detailed description of my work on this book and several others in *The Golden Rose*, so I will not go into it here.

After the publication of *Kara-Bugaz* I gave up all my other jobs and ever since then writing has been my single all-consuming, and sometimes agonising profession, but one which I love with all my heart.

I continued to travel a lot, even more than before. Since then I have been to the Kola Peninsula, lived in the Meshchora woodlands, travelled all over the Caucasus and the Ukraine, and along the Volga, Kama, Don, Dnieper, Oka and Desna, on lakes Ladoga and Onega, been to Siberia and the wonderful regions of northwest Russia—Pskov, Novgorod, Vitebsk and Pushkin's estate, Mikhailovskoye.

During the Great Patriotic War I worked as a war correspondent at the Southern Front and also moved around a good deal. After the war I again travelled extensively. In the fifties and early sixties I visited Czechoslovakia, lived for a while in Bulgaria in the delightful small fishing towns of Nesebur (Mesemvria) and Sozopol, travelled all over Poland from Krakow to Gdansk, sailed round Europe, visited Istanbul, Athens, Rotterdam, Stockholm, Italy (Rome, Turin, Milan, Naples and the Italian Alps), France, particularly Provence, and England where I went to Oxford and visited Shakespeare's birthplace, Stratford-on-Avon. In 1965 due to my chronic asthma I spent a fairly long time on the island of Capri—that enormous rock set in the warm crystal-clear waters of the Mediterranean and covered with a riot of fragrant grasses, resinous Italian pines and cascades of tropical bright red bougainvillea.

My impressions of all these journeys and the people that I met, all very different and all interesting in their own way, have provided material for many of my stories and travel sketches ("Beautiful Bulgaria", "Amphora", "The Third Meeting", "Fleeting Paris", "Channel Lights" and others).

I have written a fair amount in my time, but I still feel that I have a lot more to do and that certain aspects of life can only be fully understood and described by a writer when he has reached a ripe old age.

In my youth I had a passion for the exotic. In the dull Kiev flat where my childhood was spent I was constantly surrounded by the whispers of

9

an exotic world conjured up by the force of my own young imagination.

These whispers carried the scent of a yew forest, the foam of Atlantic breakers, the rumble of tropical storms and the ripple of an Aeolian harp.

But this brightly coloured exotic world was simply the figment of my imagination. I had never seen a dark yew forest (with the exception of a few yew trees in the Nikitsky Botanical Gardens), or the Atlantic ocean, or the tropics and I had certainly never heard an Aeolian harp. I did not even know what it looked like. It was not until years later that I read about it in the memoirs of the explorer Miklukho-Maklai. He built a harp frame out of bamboo around his hut in New Guinea. The wind made a blood-curdling howl down the hollow bamboo and terrified the superstitious local natives so much that they never interfered with his work.

My favourite subject at school was geography. It provided objective confirmation of the fact that there were exotic, far-away countries. I knew that my poor, unsettled life of those days would never give me the opportunity of seeing them. My dreams would obviously never come true, but I went on nourishing them all the same.

My state of mind could be described quite simply as a mixture of delight in the world of my imagination and sorrow that I could not see it. These were the two sentiments that predominated in my early poetry and first immature attempts at prose.

With time I abandoned my love of the exotic with all its titillating, extravagant glamour and indifference to simple, ordinary people. But its golden threads continued to weave at random in and out of my stories for many years to come.

We often make the mistake of confusing two different concepts, the so-called exotic and romantic. We substitute the purely exotic for the romantic, forgetting that the former is only one of the external forms of the latter and has no independent content of its own.

The exotic as such is divorced from real life, whereas the romantic is firmly rooted in life and feeds on its rich sap. I abandoned the exotic, but I did not abandon the romantic and never will. I will never renounce its purifying fire, its compulsion for human warmth and spiritual generosity, and its constant quest.

A person with a romantic disposition will never be false, ignorant, cowardly or cruel. The romantic element is an ennobling one. There are no reasonable grounds for renouncing it in our struggle for the future good of mankind or even in our everyday life.

The exotic element is, of course, present in *Romantics*, *Glittering Clouds* and many of my other early short stories. I did not think it necessary to revise these works later. They bear the imprint of my outlook on life at that particular stage. But I did not break with the purely exotic without any inner conflict, and this process formed the subject of a short story entitled "Sea Vaccination".

The final decisive factor in this break was a visit to the Moscow planetarium. It had only just been opened and the architect Sinyavsky took me to see the first demonstration of the artificial firmament. Like everyone else I was enchanted by the spectacle.

We came out of the planetarium late on a dry October evening. There was a smell of autumn leaves in the streets. Suddenly, as if for the first time, I caught sight of the vast sky above throbbing and pulsating with stars. Wisps of light clouds were floating on high but they did not obscure the stars. The dark autumn air seemed to enhance the brilliance of the heavens.

At that moment everything I had written appeared as unreal as the sky on the concrete dome of the planetarium with its artificial stars. At first it had been impressive, but now I realised that it lacked depth, air, volume and fusion with the vast world around it.

After that evening I destroyed several of my more flamboyant and artificial short stories.

In the course of later life, however, I realised the simple truth that everything we do, however trifling it may be, is of some use to us. My youthful passion for the exotic was responsible to a certain extent for training me to search for and pick out the colourful and sometimes even bizarre elements in my surroundings.

Ever since then I have been aware of an additional source of light glimmering albeit faintly alongside reality—a slight touch of romantic fantasy. Like a small beam of light in a painting it illuminated details which would otherwise perhaps have passed unobserved. And this made my inner world the richer.

This slight intrusion of fantasy helped me in my work on *Kara-Bugaz, Colchis, Black Sea* and other stories.

My craving for the exotic was over and I was striving to replace it by authenticity and simplicity.

However a comparatively short time ago I was again compelled to revise my ideas on the exotic. This happened on a cruise round Europe.

Our boat left Odessa and ploughed for two days through the greyish deserted waters of the Black Sea clouded by the overcast sky above. A trail of foam was forming behind the stern and seemed to be drawing after it a flock of sea gulls, their red feet tucked beneath them.

Thick grey mist enveloped the horizon. It did not begin to lighten until we approached the Bosporus and then the wild mountains of Anatolia covered with black forests broke through the haze.

The boat made a steep turn and entered the Bosporus.

Suddenly we were confronted by a picture which was like a rich old stage set of a country by the sea. Here and there patches of peeling gold mingled with new touches of fresh paint. In the fiery sunset this riot of mountains, old towers, minarets, cliffs, arcades, castles, lighthouses, olive groves, sails, wild roses, ancient sypresses, masts and yards looked like a deliberately heightened festive scene invented by some indefatigable light-hearted artist.

Dozens of feluccas brightly coloured as parrots—crimson, yellow, green, white, blue and black with golden stripes along their sides—were sailing towards our ship leaving a trail of foam behind them.

13

We dropped anchor opposite the toy town. In the evening the windows of the houses lit up and the lights flickered through the dense foliage.

From the deck I could see a narrow alley disappearing up into the mountains. All along it was covered by a dense, almost black curtain of grape vines twined round supporting sticks. The large ripe bunches of grapes hung down low over the alley. Walking along beneath them was a little donkey with a torch round his neck. It was an electric torch and gave out a strong light.

This town was the gateway to Istanbul. Strains of haunting music drifted from the terrace of a small coffee house perched up high over the water. Young Turkish girls in light-coloured dresses were leaning on the rails staring at the gulf. Their faces looked very pale through the binoculars. A scent of oleanders wafted from the shore. In the darkening sky the half-moon gave out a faint light like the cupolas of the innumerable small mosques.

The whole scene seemed unreal and reminded me of my early day dreams. But it was real nevertheless.

At last I managed to realise that I was actually looking at the famous Bosporus, that the person standing on the deck was me and that somewhere out there in the darkness lay the ancient land of Asia Minor, the legendary city of Troy, and the Hellespont.

The more I feasted my eyes on things which had previously existed only as exotic pictures in my imagination, the clearer it became that this world, now translated from the realm of fantasy into real life, was far more interesting, significant and, I would even say, magical than I had imagined it to be.

From then onwards this discovery remained with me all through the journey—through the Aegean with its solemn procession of pink islands trailing along the horizon, on the Acropolis which looked as though it were made of wax nibbled away by bees, in the Straits of Messina where the air is blindingly blue, in Rome where a withered carnation lay on the Raphael's simple, severe grave in the Pantheon, in the Atlantic, in bustling Paris and the Channel where our ship was greeted on all sides by the old bells of the floating buoys ringing out through the mist.

I think that one of the most distinctive features of my prose is a tendency towards romanticism.

This reflects my character, of course. It is ridiculous to expect anyone, least of all a writer, to renounce this tendency. Anyone who makes such a demand does so through ignorance. With a few rare exceptions the seeds of romanticism are planted deep in all spheres of reality and human activity. They may be ignored or crushed, or else given the opportunity to grow, embellish and ennoble man's inner world with their blooms.

Romanticism is inherent in everything, particularly in learning and knowledge. The more a person knows, the fuller is his perception of reality, the closer he is surrounded by poetry and the happier he becomes.

Ignorance, on the other hand, makes a person indifferent to the world, and indifference is like a cancerous growth in that it develops slowly but surely. For the indifferent person life soon becomes bleached and faded, vast layers of it

15

withering away, until in the end he is left alone with his ignorance and pitiful sense of well-being.

True happiness is above all the lot of those eager for knowledge, the dreamers. And I am very pleased that after the heated controversy among critics not so long ago romanticism has resumed its rightful place in our literature.

In this introduction to my writing I am trying to follow my own development and take stock of it (for my own benefit as well), defining those factors which led to the birth of this or that work.

It is vital to know the motives which govern a writer in his work. It is the power and integrity of these motives which already determine the recognition of the writer by the public or its indifference or outright rejection of his work.

The desire to know everything, see everything and to take part in all sorts of events and clashes of human passions made me long for an unusual profession. It had to be linked with this seething richness of life.

But did such a profession exist? The more I thought about it, the more quickly I rejected one profession after the other. They did not promise full freedom. They did not embrace life in all the fullness of its drive towards development and variety. There was a time when I seriously thought of becoming a sailor. But shortly afterwards the urge to write excluded everything else.

Writing combined all the most attractive professions in the world. It was an independent, courageous and noble vocation.

But at that time I did not realise that writing also demanded an enormous expenditure of time and energy, that even the smallest grain of truth concealed by the author from his readers was a crime against his own conscience for which he was bound to pay dearly.

The writer becomes a part to all human joy and suffering. He must possess his own independent view of the world, staunchness in battle, lyrical power and the ability to commune with nature, to say nothing of many other qualities, such as simple psychological stamina.

The decision was made. The future became clear. The chosen path turned out to be a wonderful, though very difficult one, and during the many long years which have passed since then I have never once been tempted to abandon it.

My life as a writer began, as I have already mentioned, with the desire to know and see everything. And it looks as though it will end on this note as well.

The poetry of travel blended with unadorned reality has produced the best possible fusion for writing books. Traces of my wanderings can be found in almost all my stories.

At first it was the South. *Romantics, Glittering Clouds, Kara-Bugaz, Colchis, Black Sea* and a number of other stories, such as "Labels for Colonial Goods", "The Lost Day", "The Expert Yachtsman", "Dark Blue" and a few others.

My first visit to the North—to Leningrad, Karelia and the Kola Peninsula—completely overwhelmed me. I came to understand its deep fascination. My first experience of the white nights over the Neva did more to deepen my understanding of Russian poetry than dozens of books and many hours of reflection on them.

I realised that the concept of the North stands for more than just the quiet beauty of its landscape. It is also Pushkin's poem *Friend of My Hard Days* written in the solitude of the Pskov forests. It is the brooding cathedrals of Novgorod and Pskov, the slender magnificence of Leningrad, the Neva seen through the windows of the Hermitage, the chanted epics, the calm gaze of the women, the black conifers, the sparkling mica of the lakes, the white foam of the bird-cherry trees, the smell of bark, the blows of the woodcutters' axes, the rustle of pages read at night when the dawn is already rising over the Gulf of Finland and Blok's words are ringing in one's head:

> *One dawn*
> *Has stretched its hand to another*
> *And, sisters of two heavens, they weave*
> *A mist, now pink, now blue,*
> *And in the sea a dark drowning cloud*
> *Shoots from its eyes in angry death throes*
> *Flashes of light, now red, now purple.*

I could cover many a page with these vague associations which give such a clear picture of the North. The North captivated me more strongly than the South.

There is, perhaps, not a single artist who has succeeded in conveying the mysterious silence of a damp northern night, when each drop of dew and the reflection of a campfire in the meadow lake will suddenly evoke a shy, profound love for

Russia that makes your heart thump painfully. And you want to live for hundreds of years to be able to see all this northern beauty which is as pale as a field daisy.

The North inspired such books as *Charles Lonceville's Fate, The Lake Front, The Northern Story* and such short stories as "Lump Sugar" and "Brief Encounters".

But it was Central Russia which turned out to have the most productive and beneficial influence on me. This happened fairly late on when I was nearly thirty. Of course I had been to these parts before, but my visits had always been brief, passing ones.

It occasionally happens that you see a path across the fields or a little village on a hillside and all of a sudden you know that you have seen it somewhere before long ago, perhaps even in a dream, and it became overwhelmingly precious to you.

This is what happened to me with Central Russia. I fell under its spell immediately for the rest of my life. I became aware of it as my true native land and felt a Russian to the very core of my being.

Since then I have known nothing closer to me than simple Russian people and nothing more beautiful than our land.

I would not exchange Central Russia for any of the most famous, fantastically beautiful spots in the whole world. Now I remember with a smile my youthful dreams of yew forests and tropical storms. I would give all the splendour of the Bay of Naples with its riot of colour for a willow bush wet from the rain on the sandy bank of the River Oka or the winding little River Taruska on whose quiet banks I often live for long spells.

My life is now deeply bound up with this bush and the cloudy sky blinking with rain, the smoke curling up from the villages and the damp meadow wind.

> *I have returned to my own people.*
> *My gentle, brooding land. . . .*

I found the greatest feeling of simple, ingenuous happiness in the forests of Meshchora. The happiness of being close to one's native soil, of inner freedom and concentration, of hard work and sweet contemplation.

I owe most of my works to Central Russia. It would take too long to list them all, so I shall mention only the main ones such as "Meshchora Country", "Isaak Levitan", "The Tale of Forests" and the cycle of stories "Summer Days", "The Old Boat", "A Night in October", "The Telegram", "The Rainy Sunrise", "Cordon 273", "In the Heart of Russia", "Alone with Autumn" and "Ilyinsky Waters".

It was in Meshchora that I found the pure unadulterated language of Russian country people. I do not wish to repeat myself, so I will not dwell on the subject here. I have described my views on the Russian language in *The Golden Rose* in the chapter entitled "Diamond Language".

The reader may find it strange that the author of this article is concentrating on the external surroundings in which the action of his works takes place, without saying hardly anything about his characters. It is impossible for me to evaluate my characters objectively and therefore I find it difficult to discuss them. Let the reader judge them for himself.

I can only say that I have always shared the life of my characters and always tried to show their good features, to reveal their true nature and their uniqueness, which is not always immediately apparent. It is not for me to judge whether I have succeeded in doing this or not. I have always been at the side of my favourite characters, sharing their joys and sorrows, their conflicts and worries, their success and failure. And as strongly as I loved all that was truly humane in the most insignificant and mediocre characters, I hated stupidity, ignorance and baseness in people.

Each of my books contains a collection of many people of different ages, nationalities, occupations, temperaments and actions. Consequently I am somewhat surprised by the accusation of some critics that I draw my characters sketchily and without any real interest. Clearly there is some confusion here between compressed characterisation and sketchiness.

Well, all this is easy enough to put to the test. Just take any of my books, even from the autobiographical cycle, and have a look at the characters who inhabit them.

I used to be interested in the lives of famous people and tried to find features which they had in common, those features which made them stand out as the leading representatives of mankind.

Apart from separate works on Levitan, Kiprensky and Taras Shevchenko I have written stories, sketches and parts of novels on Lenin, Gorky, Chaikovsky, Chekhov, Lieutenant Schmidt, Victor Hugo, Blok, Pushkin, Hans Christian Andersen, Maupassant, Prishvin, Grieg, Gaidar, Charles Coster, Flaubert, Bagritsky, Multattuli, Lermontov, Mozart, Gogol, Edgar Allan Poe, Vrubel, Dickens, Grin and Malyshkin.

But most of the time I have been happy writing about simple unknown people, artisans, shepherds, ferrymen, forest wardens, buoy keepers, watchmen and village children—my bosom friends.

I owe a great deal in my work to poets, writers, artists and scholars belonging to various ages and lands. I will not attempt to mention them here but they range from the unknown author of *The Lay of Igor's Host* and Michelangelo to Stendhal and Chekhov and there are many of them.

But most of all I am indebted to life itself in all its simplicity and significance. I was happy enough to witness and take part in it.

In conclusion I should like to repeat that my development as a writer and a person took place in Soviet times.

My country, my people and the new truly socialist society which they have created are the noble masters which I have served and continue to serve with each fresh word.

Konstantin Paustovsky

COLCHIS

The Wild Cat

To him who shall destroy a cat, death.
An ancient Mingrelian law

The wind swept a handful of dust and dry rose petals through the *duhan* windows. The palms began to sway, their green leaves fluttering nervously. They made a sound like the gritting of teeth. The smoke from the chimneys raced low over the flat streets of Poti, drowning the fragrance of falling mandarin blossoms. The frogs in the town square stopped croaking.

"It's going to rain," said the young engineer, Gabunia.

He looked moodily out through the window. A sign which had been whitewashed over said: "Have a Bite".

The rain was moving slowly up from the sea. It spread over the water like heavy smoke, torn by white flashes—screaming sea gulls.

"It pours down two hundred and forty days a year," Gabunia added.

"Fiery Colchis," muttered Lapshin. "One scientist calculated that every year the earth gets ninety cubic kilometres of rain. I reckon that all ninety fall right here."

Gabunia was not impressed.

The *duhan* keeper, a fat Gurian, wheezed asthmatically. Nothing in the wide world interested him: not the engineers lingering over their dinner, nor the old man with the staff, Artem Korkia, sitting glumly at an empty table, nor Becho, the self-taught itinerant artist, nor even the approaching rain. He was depressed by the heat and his gloomy thoughts. He kept driving away the flies from the sticky wineglasses and occasionally fingering the beads of his abacus.

Becho was doing a remarkable oil painting on the *duhan* wall. The theme of his painting had been suggested by Gabunia. It showed the Colchis of the future, when fragrant orange groves would bloom on what were now broad stretches of warm swampland. Golden fruits glowed like electric bulbs among dark foliage. Pink mountains steamed like smoke-crowned conflagrations. White steamers advanced through luxuriant growths of lotus blossom, and little boats carried women and girls in holiday attire. Mingrelians in felt hats and riding breeches banqueted in the groves. And an old man in a Circassian coat, his long, curly hair framing the face of Leonardo da Vinci, stood with his arms outstretched towards this childish landscape.

"Where'd he get hold of Leonardo?" Lapshin asked.

Gabunia flushed.

"From me," he said. "Why not?"

Lapshin shrugged his shoulders.

Slow raindrops beat heavily on the pavement. The *duhan* began to fill up with people seeking shelter from the rain. They dropped their eyes as they greeted the *duhan* keeper, embarrassed because they did not order. They all looked with interest at Becho's painting.

A buzz of admiration passed from table to table. The people clicked their tongues, amazed at the skill of this mild and unassuming man.

Noting the general enthusiasm, the *duhan* keeper sulkily dumped some cornmeal porridge and fried fish onto a plate, and poured a glass of tart wine. This he handed to Becho. It was the artist's daily wage.

Becho rinsed his hands with wine, and ate his meal. Then he sighed and sat back, with closed eyes, resting. Taking in the murmured praises, he thought to himself that the *duhan* might be co-operative, but just the same the boss was cheating him. The food wasn't anywhere near what had been agreed.

The rain grew louder, drowning the voices of the people in the *duhan*. Water poured noisily through rainpipes and pounded against closed windows. There was a hurried pattering of raindrops on walls and signboards, like the hammering of a myriad tiny carpenters and tinsmiths.

The monsoon was blowing—the southwest wind. It swept the clouds before it like a herd of grey sheep, driving them against the wall formed by the Guria Mountains.

Another sound rose gradually to join the splashing and pattering, the whispering and gurgling, all the frivolous water sounds. It was a heavy drone of human voices, of guttural cries.

The people in the *duhan* flocked to the windows. A drenched throng was coming down the street. Little boys ran at its head. Behind them strode a tall grim man with a gun slung over his shoulder. His eyes glittered fiercely. He carried a furry black animal, swinging it proudly by the tail. Blood and raindrops dribbled from its muzzle.

A little old man darted out of the barbershop next door to the *duhan*. His face was covered with lather. Blobs of lather spattered his grey Circassian coat. He touched the animal, and recoiled.

"*Rambavia!*" he cried. "You've shot a wild cat, *katso!*"

The crowd roared. The hunter entered the *duhan*. He threw the wet, slippery animal to the *duhan* keeper. The wineglasses tinkled. The whole room shook to the thud of the heavy carcass on the counter.

The *duhan* was now packed. People were shouting as though life and death were at stake.

The bringer of the animal brushed the raindrops from his face with the palm of his hand. In dull, stern tones, he said to the *duhan* keeper: "Buy the skin, manager."

A hush fell over the crowd. Not a word must be missed in this extraordinary deal! A deal in the skin of a wild cat—perhaps the last wild cat ever to be shot in Colchis' swampy forests.

The *duhan* keeper turned his yellow eyes on the beast. He did not say a word. A young girl with a hen under her arm and a bunch of roses in her hand climbed onto a chair to get a better view. The hen stopped pecking at the rose petals. It squawked and tried to flap its wings. Then old Artem Korkia shouted, brandishing his staff:

"Curses on your head, *katso*! You've shot a cat. In the old days, the punishment was death."

"I beg your pardon," said the owner of the animal, scowling darkly at Korkia. "I beg your pardon for contradicting my elders. Only this is not cat."

The crowd gasped. Only now did it realise that the beast was actually not a wild cat. It looked more like an enormous rat, this furry carcass lying on the counter.

"What is it, then, if it's not a cat?" demanded Korkia, perplexed.

"For God's sake, what's your hurry?" yelled the hunter, in barely suppressed fury. "Use your eyes!"

Gabunia and Lapshin elbowed their way to the counter. The creature was a strange one. Its powerful hind paws had yellow webs. Its long, hairless tail hung almost to the ground.

The crowd was at a loss. All eyes were fixed expectantly on the *duhan* keeper. But he maintained a sullen, wheezing silence.

It was then that Vano Akhmeteli made his appearance. Vano was a post-graduate student of the Fur Institute. He strolled easily through the staring crowd, as though he were crossing a deserted square. Close on his heels came Grisha, the little militiaman, with his whistle in his hand.

Vano strode up to the counter. He lifted the animal by its tail. Grisha blew his whistle and started pushing back the crowd. Some people were stubborn, and he shouted at them, ridiculing their curiosity:

"I suppose you'll die if you don't see! Don't be so inquisitive! It makes me laugh to watch such foolish people!"

"Where did you shoot it?" Vano asked the hunter, drawing together his shaggy brows.

"At the Turkish Canal."

"What's your name?"

"Gulia."

"Well then, Gulia," said Vano quietly, "you've killed forbidden game. You'll get two weeks in the cooler for it."

Gulia snorted in disgust. Then, with a terrible glance at Vano, he muttered:

"Rats' watchman! Will you put me in jail if I kill a frog?"

"Don't get excited, *katso*. They'll let you talk in court. Grisha, take him to the station."

The crowd followed Grisha and Gulia out of the *duhan*. The hunter was fuming. Again he carried the animal by its tail; but his erstwhile pride was gone. The animal's head bumped along the wet sidewalk.

The rain was subsiding. It came down in a fine drizzle.

Gabunia, Vano and Lapshin remained in the *duhan*.

"What sort of creature was that?" Lapshin asked.

"Don't you know?" cried Vano, feigning surprise. "Argentine nutria, from Rio Negro."

"Pardon my ignorance," returned Lapshin icily. "I never was a zoologist, you know. My subject is botany."

"You specialise in the humid subtropics. Seems to me you ought to know."

Gabunia tried to turn the conversation, which threatened to develop into a quarrel. Every time Vano and Lapshin met, there were sure to be sharp words. Vano disliked the young botanist for his shaggy American suits and elaborate manners. It seemed to Vano that the botanist held himself above Soviet affairs, like some puffed-up foreigner.

Rudeness always distressed Gabunia. He was very shy. He was a tall man, with the yellow film of malaria clouding his ever-smiling eyes.

"Nutria," he said flushing, "is the most quarrelsome beast in the world."

This announcement was received with complete indifference. Vano threw Gabunia a bitter glance.

"When you drain the swamps and turn Colchis into those wonderful groves Becho's painting," he said, "the nutria will die. You're the chief nutria killer. They need jungles, not lemon groves. How can I help feeling bad about it?"

They all looked at Becho's painting. The rain had stopped. The sunlight came down through the magnolia trees, and the foliage turned it into a greenish haze. In this soft light, Becho's painting appeared to Gabunia in an entirely new aspect. He felt a desire to touch the heavy oranges.

"Feeling bad about what?" he asked abstractedly.

"About the work I've put in," Vano replied. "I've spent two whole years on those damned beasts. I supervise their breeding. I hate to think of all that work thrown away. And it's a shame about the jungle, too. Your excavators have scared the wild boar away. Even the jackals are running off to the mountains."

"And good riddance to them!"

Lapshin left. He would have liked to ask Vano how Argentine nutria came to be living in Colchis; but he refrained.

He found the world around him an unpleasant place. He did not like this flat, swampy country with its fanciful name. He did not like the warm, protracted rains, the muddy rivers rushing seaward at express-train speed, the wooden houses built on piles, or the *duhans*, where he was served tepid wine that tasted of castor oil.

It began to drizzle again. The sun disappeared. And, as always when it rained, the town was suffused with odours—odours so intense that one could all but touch them. There was the soft fragrance of the eucalyptus, the clinging perfume of roses, and the tart lemon smell that crinkled your finger tips. But this lasted only until the first gust of the monsoon. When the wind came rustling through the orchards, turning up the leaves and filling the streets with dust, everything would change. The scented vapours, the source of headache and indolence, would be dispersed by an acrid sea breeze.

Gabunia took his leave of Vano, and went out into the street. The Rion was roaring wildly, rocking its bridges, rolling its liquid clay to the sea. Gabunia walked slowly in the direction of the harbour. Malaria had even affected the way he walked.

He reflected that it was his own soft nature that made things so awkward for him. He always tried to avoid any talk with Vano. He could not rid himself of an altogether irrational feeling of guilt in regard to Vano, because he, Gabunia, was draining the Colchian swamps, digging canals, rooting up the virgin forest, burning the jungles where the nutria bred.

The animals had been brought from Argentina, by no means an easy task, and released in the Colchian swamps to breed. For two successive summers, Vano had been watching their acclimatisation. He told wonderful tales about their precious fur. In the West, he said, it was all but worth its weight in gold.

They multiplied rapidly. Nobody ever saw them, however, except for Vano and a few Mingrelian hunters, who described the beasts as inveterate fighters. Nutria will battle for days and nights on end, and always to the death. They are extremely timid, and ordinarily no man can come within a hundred paces of them; but when fighting they lose all sense of fear, and a man can easily approach and pull the combatants apart by their tails. The battle is always begun in the same manner, each beast making for its rival's jaws and attempting to break the teeth. Nutria can stay under water for five full minutes without coming up for air.

Gabunia found it hard to understand how Vano could devote himself to these repulsive creatures.

Vano's study of the nutria often kept him in the swamps for months on end. He came to love it and began to sing the praises of the Colchian jungles—of the airless, liana-twined forests, the stagnant lakes, the wild, putrescent, malaria-ridden vegetation.

Vano called the Colchian forests tropical, though the trees were almost exclusively northern alder and rhododendron. It was a strange inter-mingling of North and South. The alders grew with fantastic rapidity. In three years a fresh clearing would become impassable forest.

Gabunia sensed Vano's unexpressed hostility to the draining project under way in Colchis. Vano frankly rejoiced at the slow pace of the work, which was held up by malaria, floods, and rains, and the excavators getting stranded in the swamps.

Gabunia knew that, sooner or later, Vano would have to be faced. And yet, he sometimes felt a twinge of pity as the excavators pushed step by step into Vano's land of legend. For they rent the lianas, bailed the water and the dark-gold carp out of the lakes, and drove the wild boar and the nutria to the sea. They left a wake of ugly ditches, mounds of sticky clay, and rotting stumps. The forests of Colchis stood knee-deep in water. The slimy soil afforded but scant root-hold for the trees. To fell a tree, the workers had only to throw a chain around it, and pull. This was per-fectly safe. The trees never dropped all the way to the ground. The thorny lianas, thick as a man's arm, would catch and hold them. The forests had a dense undergrowth of buckthorn and clematis, bramble and fern.

It was stupendous—the vigour of the vegetation. The clematis climbed trees and snapped their trunks like blades of grass. The bramble seemed to grow as you watched it. A summer would add another six feet to its height.

No grass grew in these forests. They were dark and airless. There were almost no birds. Instead, there were bats. Dormant, impassable, the forests stood veiled in a mist of warm rains.

When a wind blew, the dark forests would suddenly turn the colour of mercury. The alder leaves, turned up by the wind, were a silvery grey on their undersides.

For countless days, months and years the forests had murmured and swayed, rolling waves of dull silver. And Gabunia could well understand Vano's anger. He, too, felt sorry, at times, that the forests must go.

Engineer Kakhiani, head of the Colchis draining project, took a much simpler view of things. He had no eye for the forests, or the lily-covered lakes, or the countless creeping rivers in their green tunnels of foliage. All this was scheduled for destruction; it was but an obstacle, standing in his way.

Kakhiani thought Vano a young fool. A careless shrug and grunt were his only response to Vano's fervent pleas in defence of jungle and nutria. Kakhiani's lips were set in a bitter grimace that never relaxed. It came from too much quinine, people said. Kakhiani would chew up the bitter pills unhurriedly and gulp it down without water.

Any regret for the fate of these virgin forests, for the fate of that which belonged to the past, was a feeling completely alien to him. He believed that Nature, when left to herself, was bound to decline and degenerate. In support of this thesis, he would languidly cite the works of prominent men of science.

As for Gabunia, Kakhiani considered him a capable engineer, but one too inclined to dreaming. "Engineering romantic", he called him. Kakhiani was always cross when he chanced upon a volume of Mayakovsky or Blok in Gabunia's room.

"The only real classics," he would say, "are mathematics. All the rest is hot air."

Vano's only sympathiser was the old engineer Pakhomov, the author of imposing schemes for the draining of the Colchian swamps. Bending over his blueprints, Pakhomov would sometimes declare with a sigh:

"I'm glad I won't live to see it finished. Really, I am. After all it's a pity to destroy Nature."

But he would go right on to plot a new network of canals through the virgin forests he had just bewailed, and his pencil would tap the desk in triumph as he exclaimed:

"There! Another two thousand hectares for citrus plantations. Not so bad!"

The old man had his peculiarities. It was he who had talked Becho into adding Leonardo to the painting on the *duhan* wall.

"What are you thinking of, friend?" he demanded reproachfully. "Painting Colchis' future, and leaving out the world's first drainage and irrigation engineer—Leonardo da Vinci!"

Becho glanced at him suspiciously.

"Leonardo was an artist," he protested.

"That's beside the point. He was a wonderful artist, but he was also a great engineer."

It was after the conversation that Becho asked Gabunia for a picture of the great Italian.

Pakhomov's name was closely associated with the mysterious new word, *colmatage*. This word designated a system of swamp drainage that people talked about as they might of a flight to Mars, or of transforming the Sahara into a sea. It was fantastic. But more about that later.

Having occasion to be in town for two days, Gabunia, who was in charge of construction of the main canal in the Chaladidi forest, now wandered through the port in search of Captain Chup. Chup was the port inspector. Gabunia wanted him to send a couple of sailors out to run a dredging machine at the canal.

Frequently as Gabunia visited Poti, the town and port impressed him ever anew as places quite outside the ordinary. And so it was today.

Evening fell as Gabunia walked about the port. The wharves smelled of crabs and sea slime. Signal lights hung low over the restless waves. The surf beat a doleful refrain against the breakwater, a sleepy lullaby.

Over the town the clouds had gathered again. The street lamps lit them dully from below. Frogs were bellowing in the swamps.

Gabunia skirted an iron warehouse, and found himself on a broad wharf. Here he stopped for a while. The *Abkhasia* was entering the harbour. She had come from Batum. Mirrored blue stars contracted and spread with the rise and fall of the water alongside it, merging with the white glare of the ship's reflected lights. The *Abkhasia* was like a hollow crystal, lit from within.

She hooted. The sound was low, but wrathful. Colliding with the low-hung, cloudy sky, it spread out and out, like slow circles over water. The echo called sadly back from the Chaladidi forest, and then returned once more, now barely audible, from the Guria Mountains.

The *Abkhasia* swung heavily around. The port grew noisy with shouts, the sound of running water, children's laughter, and the rumble of windlasses.

Veteran anglers savagely drew in their lines, heaping invective on the infernal ships that spoiled their fishing.

"White Hair"

A young woman got off a steamer, late that night, leading a little girl of about seven by the hand. The steamer was a freight and passenger boat. It gave off a stale adour of hides and oil that you could smell a mile away. Making fast to the pier, it put out its lights and relapsed into silence.

The woman stopped beside her valises and looked about her with an anxious frown. There was nobody to be seen. The other passengers, three or four Mingrelians, had made off with a light, almost dancing step into the darkness, evidently in the direction of the town.

Water splashed on every side. The sea droned in dull indifference.

"How do I get to town?" the woman asked the darkness, hoping that someone might hear; but no answer came. The little girl sat on a valise, looking up at her mother with fearful eyes.

Christophor Christophoridi, a ten-year-old shoeshine boy, walked through the shadowed port. He carried a bamboo fishing rod, and also his box of brushes and polish.

Christophoridi was an inveterate angler. He liked to fish by night, when he could appropriate the place beside the winking beacon—the best spot for scad. The dampness kept him shivering, and his lips would grow so stiff with cold that by morning he would lose the gift of speech. But he bore every trial with magnificent fortitude.

Christophoridi was in a hurry. He could only fish until eight o'clock in the morning, when he must drop in at the homes of the port employees —Captain Chup, the cashier, the pilot—and polish their boots. That left him a bare three hours. His professional visits done, Christophoridi would station himself at the bus stop in the port, where he would earn perhaps two rubles in the course of the day on shines. This was a little frequented, and therefore unprofitable stand. Christophoridi had chosen it because of the insuperable urge that drew him to the sea.

Though Christophoridi was in a hurry, he paused outside the little house where Chup lived, and peeped in through an open window. The house stood just off the jetty, in the most deserted section of the port. When there was a storm at sea, the spray would fly in at the captain's windows.

There were three people inside. They sat puffing out thick clouds of tobacco smoke over the table, which, despite the late hour, was set for tea. Christophoridi knew them all: Chup, engineer

Gabunia, and a lanky English sailor known in the port as Sima.

He had missed his ship when it sailed from Poti, and now he hung around the town at a loose end. When asked, "Who are you?" he would reply in English, "Seaman". Chup had turned that into the Russian name Sima.

"Who's that outside?" Chup shouted ferociously.

Christophoridi turned and ran. From a safe distance, he shook his fist at the window. He was not afraid of Chup, but he did expect some trouble. Chup could not tolerate anglers roaming the port at night. Then Christophoridi heard a child crying, and a woman's voice said:

"Don't cry, Yolochka. We'll find somebody right away."

Christophoridi moved towards the voices. A quick-witted lad, he understood at once that the woman must be a stranger to Poti, who had arrived on the night boat. The bus to town, he knew, would not be running for another four hours, and there were no cabs at night.

Christophoridi decided to speak to the woman. He felt sorry for the little girl. At a loss how to begin, he sang out:

"Shine your shoes?"

"Silly boy!" returned the woman, laughing. "Who ever heard of shining shoes at night?"

And so the talk began. The woman was delighted. What could be better, in a strange and deserted port at night, than to meet a shoeshine boy—and an angler, too, at that? Fishing makes people good-natured and talkative; and shoeshining brings its disciples a great store of practical information. There is no need for an inquiry office in a town with a good crop of shoeshine boys.

Christophoridi, besides his valuable qualities as shoeshine boy and angler, had the additional gift of enthusiasm. The woman's helpless situation inspired a torrent of wonderful ideas. But what could he do to help? It was three kilometres to the Black Sea Hotel, in town. He could never drag her luggage that far.

His meditation, however, was brief. A few slow drops came down, heralding the rain that in Poti precedes the dawn.

"Wait here—I'll be right back," said Christophoridi, and disappeared, leaving his box of brushes and his fishing rod at the woman's feet.

He ran as fast as he could to Chup's. Breathless with excitement at the extraordinary events of the night, he panted out his story to the captain. Chup grumbled something about his house not being a waiting room. Then he got up slowly and said, with a menacing glare at Christophoridi:

"She can stay here till morning. I'm on duty all night anyway. Show us the way, youngster!"

Christophoridi led the captain and Gabunia to the pier. The captain argued with Gabunia all the way. Gabunia wanted to leave, but the captain would not let him go.

"I never knew how to deal with silly women," he muttered, and demanded that Gabunia stay till morning. In the end, Gabunia agreed.

The woman was rather bewildered. Two men seized her valises and led her off towards what seemed to be the jetty. The roar of the sea grew louder and more insistent with every step. Christophoridi trotted along behind, so pleased he had to whistle. He had decided to follow events to their conclusion. There was no conversation to speak of, because the wind from the sea and the gravel crunching underfoot made hearing difficult.

The woman walked as in a dream. She still seemed to be on boardship. The earth rocked with the rustling of the wind in the acacias.

As in a dream, she entered the little white house, where the copper barometers all indicated "variable", and a white clipper model with a gilded bowsprit swung just below the ceiling.

A tow-headed sailor in a loose blue suit rose to his feet as she came in, and shook her hand, and then the little girl's. His grip was so hard it made their knuckles crack. The little girl began to cry.

Then the sailor squatted in front of the child. He made a funny face, and began singing raucously some silly English foxtrot tune, clapping his hands in time. He was trying to soothe her tears. And the little girl laughed, though she did not understand.

That broke the general tension. The woman got into conversation with Gabunia. Christophoridi, in search of a pretext for staying on, went off to the captain's kitchen, where he dug up an old pair of boots and attacked them furiously with his brushes. He brushed until the boots shone so brightly that they made him blink.

As Christophoridi worked, he listened. From the woman's replies to Gabunia he learned that her name was Yelena Sergeyevna Nevskaya, that she was a botanist (Christophoridi knew what a botanist was), and that she was going to work at the subtropical experimental gardens in Poti. After the child had been put to bed, the grown-ups sat down to tea.

And the things they talked about over their tea made Christophoridi lose all his interest in fishing. The captain found him in the kitchen in the morning, surrounded by a ring of worn-out shoes that seemed to be coated with Japanese lacquer. They were shoes the captain had long since been intending to throw away; only now they looked like works of art. Christophoridi did not regret his wasted labour and polish. The talk he had heard that night was worth a good dozen tins of the very best blacking.

After the woman had hung up her hat and raincoat and settled down at the table, Chup said good-naturedly, looking into her tired young face:

"So you've come to stay in our blessed Colchis? Fine! And what will you do here?"

"I'm a specialist in tea, but out here I'll be working on everything that grows. Mainly, eucalyptus."

"Eucalyptus—that's nonsense," said the captain. "Tea, now—that's another matter. I've specialised in tea, so to speak, myself. Hundreds of tons of it I've brought across the seas in my day. Look!"

The captain pointed to the hanging model.

"Let me introduce you. That's the tea clipper *Begonia*. The world's last clipper. I sailed on it for three years."

Sima grunted admiration. Nevskaya looked up at the clipper. Gabunia noticed the peaceful calm of her tired eyes, and her heavy, reddish-chestnut hair.

Chup was a very talkative man. He considered talk the best form of relaxation, and would often say to his numerous friends:

"Let's have a rest and a natter."

Gabunia was certain Chup would yield to temptation now. And sure enough he did.

"I suppose," he said, "you think the old man's lying, and all the clippers disappeared ages ago? That they did. I don't deny it. But one clipper—the *Begonia*—went on plying between Ceylon and England right up to the war. It was a tea clipper, and it certainly was a beauty! Every trip, we gave it a new coat of lacquer, and it always glistened as if it had just been washed.

"We were an eyesore for the captains of the rotten, filthy coalers. They'd signal to us: 'Pick up your skirts before we soil it, angel face!' 'Tea club lickspittles,' they called us. We were hated in every port. And why? Hold on—I'll be getting to that.

"We freighted tea from Colombo to London. A special brand of tea—the world's most fearful brand, to my way of thinking. 'White Hair' it was called—Pekoe. You specialise in tea. You'll understand. Tea is supposed to be best when it's had a good long journey. While it's travelling, it gains strength and fragrance and delicacy. They say time has to do with it, and air, and warmth. There was good reason why 'caravan' tea was considered the best, here in Russia in the old days. It travelled over a year by caravan from China. And while it was travelling third grade turned into first. Isn't that true? You see, I know something about it too."

Sima began to snore, with his head on the table. Chup pulled the sailor's cap down until it almost covered his nose, and said to Gabunia:

"Be a good fellow, take him out to your place and give him a job. He missed his ship, and he doesn't want to go back to England. He's a good sort, only he seems to be a bit stupid. And untalkative."

"All right. I'll take him. Go on about that clipper!"

"Well, it was just that about tea that kept our clipper sailing. It belonged to the Leslie Tea Company. Most of the Leslie tea was shipped on metal steamers. But let me tell you, tea absorbs odours as fast as blotting paper soaks up ink. On the steamers it lost its fragrance. It absorbed the smells of iron and coal and skins, of rats and stagnant water—all the junk you can find in the hold. That tea—the steamer tea—was sold to the general public. But for the connoisseurs, for the gourmands, blast 'em, tea was shipped on a wooden clipper.

"We didn't smell of rats. We smelled of palm wood and jasmine. Honest to God! Why jasmine? Because they put jasmine blossoms, and camellia, and laurel in the tea to give it fragrance. Our sense of smell was as delicate as a fussy woman's. We left a wake of perfume behind us, and the steamers we met would yell, 'Phew! Give us air! There's Captain Frey again, taking his floating barber's shop to London!'

"But that's not all. Company orders were to

sail from Colombo to London all the way around Africa, instead of using the Suez Canal. We never hurried. The idea was to keep the tea on its way as long as possible. But they certainly charged money for that tea, when it did arrive! Now you can understand why we were despised in every port.

"We carried the best brands of tea, and one of them was 'White Hair'. Every time I look at Gabunia, here, I remember that tea. Not because of the grey on your temples, Gabunia. That comes from thinking too much. You're only thirty-two, I know.

"Now, how did I come to find out how the 'White Hair' got its name? Listen—it's interesting.

"In Ceylon, once, I missed my ship, just like Sima here." The captain pulled Sima's cap still further down over his nose. "What was I to do? Dead broke, and nothing to eat! While I was waiting for the *Begonia* to get back, I took a job as an overseer on Leslie's tea plantations. All the workers were natives, mainly women."

The sound of brushes in the kitchen stopped. Evidently Christophoridi was too carried away by the captain's tale to keep up his pretence.

Dawn was breaking. The sky above was as green and vast as an ocean. Chup glanced through the window.

"It's so calm," he said. "Beautiful! Well, it was there I learned what colonies are, and tropics. Ever since then I have hated the tropics. It gives me a sour taste even to think of them.

"You wake up at dawn. . . . The air makes you feel younger every minute. Gurgling brooks, and some sort of devilish flowers on the trees, the size of soup plates, and monkeys hanging by their tails, dropping things onto your head. Fertility and wealth. The smells alone could make a man a poet.

"And so, you wake up and see a great sun shining over the tropical groves. And then you hear the sound of rods on flesh, and women crying, and the overseers' rough voices, and you see the children gnawing coconut husks. And you begin to boil inside, till your head almost splits with anger.

"They say the tropics are paradise. Who says that? Don't believe such fools! The tropics are hell. Nights drowned in tears, that's what the tropics are! Sometimes you see a native's face go grey, and he grits his teeth, and you'd think he'd let fly at the overseer's jaw. Only he can't clench his fist. That's a disease they have out there. 'Rubber fist' it's called. The heat, and the fever, and the inhuman labour drain every last drop of strength. I could force open the strongest native's fist with my finger and thumb, without any effort. That's the tropics for you!

"Well, I was put to work on a plantation where they grow the 'White Hair' brand of tea. The tips of its leaves are whitish, true enough.

"One day, on that plantation, I came across a grey-haired woman. She was huddled up on the ground, crying. I asked her what was wrong. It turned out her husband was sick, and she couldn't go home to take care of him, for fear they'd sack her or beat her. I helped her up, and then I saw how young she was. No older than you. I told her, 'Go home. I'll take the blame.' She kissed my hand. 'Master,' she said, 'you don't know what those bosses do to us! Even the tea turns white, watching our torment. Even the tea! And that's why we call it 'White Hair'."

Chup fell silent.

"But where do I come in, *katso*?" asked Gabunia. "What's the connection between that tea and me?"

"The connection is this: on account of you, I've stopped hating the tropics." Here Chup turned to Nevskaya, and went on, with a nod at Gabunia: "This man is creating Soviet tropics in our parts. That I can understand. The same wealth, the same fertility, but allied with freedom and purpose. There's an aim worth working for!

"I met Pakhomov the other day. 'Listen, Chup,' he said to me. 'You don't understand a thing. Yes, we're draining the swamps and creating a new tropical region in their place. We're planting oranges, lemons, ramie, tea, and all the rest. We're rooting out malaria and lining the sea coast with health resorts. That's all very well. But that's not the main thing. The main thing is, we're creating Nature anew for a people whose labour is free. We shall make our tropics prosper as those bosses of yours never dreamed they could. We'll prove the power of our epoch here, and it will be far beyond your wildest imaginings.' Good for Pakhomov! He's a grand old man!"

Gabunia stood up. He had to catch the noon train to Chaladidi, to get back to his canal.

Morning had come into its own. Stevedores were shouting, windlasses screeching. The bus sounded its horn. A sea gull swept past the windows, screaming hoarsely.

Nevskaya looked up, with a wan smile. Her eyelids were heavy. She was fighting painfully to keep awake.

"Look here, botanist," said Chup ferociously. "Why not stay right here till you get permanent quarters? It's no sort of life in a hotel, with a child on your hands. I've got two rooms here. I'll put you up in one of them. And Christophoridi can take care of the little girl for the time being. He played nursemaid to his own sisters when he wasn't much more than a baby himself."

"Are you really in earnest?" asked Nevskaya. "I must admit I'm so tired I can hardly sit up straight."

"We're leaving now. Just make yourself at home, and welcome," said Chup, blushing.

Gabunia and Chup went away, taking Christophoridi with them. Nevskaya went into the other room, where her little girl lay fast asleep, and dropped wearily onto a couch.

Sima woke up. He yawned, pushed back his cap, and said, in English:

"Ladies and gentlemen, the show goes on!"

He looked around. There was no one in the room, but he could hear the even breathing of the sleeping woman and child. Then he tiptoed to the kitchen, took a brush from the corner, and set about sweeping the floor. Now and then he would balance his brush in the air, or whirl it around his head like a steamer screw, exclaiming softly:

"Ladies and gentlemen, the show goes on!"

Gulia the Hunter

When man entered the jungle, solitude
joined him at his fire.

N. Tikhonov

The grim hunter, Gulia, sat beside his fire,
talking to his dog. The dog was on the verge of
an attack of malaria. It lay shivering, the tip of
its tongue caught between its teeth. Its yellow
eyes were fixed on its master.

The jungle lay around them. Day was drawing
to a close, and the strange hush that precedes
evening made the dog's ears ring. It twitched
them nervously. The ringing was like the drone
of advancing mosquito swarms.

Impenetrable thickets overhung the lonely
shores of Lake Narionali. Here and there a dark
hornbeam, or a few curly mulberry trees, had
taken root among the alders. The yellowing
lianas were studded with long thorns, like
roosters' spurs. Evil-smelling ferns grew,
luxuriant as nettle, in the deep shadow beneath
the trees.

"I beg your pardon," said Gulia to his dog,
"but I'm an honest hunter. I'm no Menshevik."

The dog wagged its tail.

"May the whole world spit if I don't get even
with that young upstart," Gulia added malevolently. "A ten-ruble fine for a dirty American
rat! Ten rubles in a rat's maw! 'You poached,' he
said in court. 'You poached on this beast.' He
called me by a bad name, 'poacher'. Ugh, friend,
and what's a poacher? 'Poaching means hunting
forbidden game,' the judge explained. I know
myself what poaching means. That Vano, he said

I ought to get a hundred-ruble fine and two weeks in jail."

Gulia spat disgustedly.

"Two weeks for a stinking rat with no hair on its tail! Even me, I laughed right out in court. I laughed so loud, the judge looked up and asked militiaman Grisha, 'What's wrong with him? Did you bring him to court drunk?' Then Grisha said, 'He can't stop laughing. He thinks he's in a cabaret, instead of a courtroom.'"

Gulia got up.

"'It's no laughing matter,' the judge said, 'when you've shot a beast from the American River Rio Negro. Do you know how much they're worth? A hundred dollars apiece, or two hundred gold rubles. I'm telling you the real truth, like I'd tell my mother. You're an ignorant man, Gulia.'

"'I beg your pardon,' I told him. 'Of course, I never learned to read. But I'm the best hunter between the Supsa and the Hopi. Which of you can go out to the Nedoard Canal at night, and come back alive? Not a single one! Which of you knows what rivers run black, and what rivers run red? Which of you can shoot a wild boar at Horga, or catch a wild cat without getting your eyes scratched out? Not a single one! Gulia can go anywhere the water snake or the minnow can. Watch what you're saying!'

"Then Vano had to barge in, and he stuck a dagger right through my heart. 'I see,' he said. 'You're the best hunter between the Supsa and the Hopi where your pocket's concerned. Only I want you to be the best hunter where the Soviet state's concerned.'

"What could I say to this puppy? 'Hold your tongue, you wretched fool,' I yelled. I jumped up to hit him, but the militiaman grabbed me. He said you're not allowed to fight in court. If you want to fight, go to the bazaar!

"They all yelled and shouted, and they were going to lock me up for a month. Then Gabunia came in, the handsome young engineer, son of old engine-driver Gabunia from Samtredi, and he made such a speech in that court...."

Gulia fell silent. For a long time he tried to recall Gabunia's wonderful speech. It hovered on the fringe of memory, like a persistent mosquito, but Gulia could not catch it. He sighed, and took up his gun.

"Anyway, he said what he said! 'You ought to use your head,' that's what he said. 'I'm draining the swamps, and pretty soon there won't be any place for those American rats to live, and they'll all die out. So why do you sit in judgement on this poor man, and not on me?' That's what Gabunia said, the young Bolshevik—may he live to be a hundred. 'Why punish,' he said, 'when the Party says, teach? Give him to me. I shall find a use for him.' And if it hadn't been for Gabunia, I'd be in jail right now, like the thieves that steal in the bazaar. Let's be going, *katso*."

The dog got up and followed its master, swaying. Gulia pulled a neatly folded paper out of his pocket, opened it, and held it up to the light. Had he been literate, he would have read the following:

"For the attention of the topographer Abashidze. The bearer is Gulia, the hunter. You can find no better guide for the Colchian swamps. Gulia knows the most inaccessible spots. He should be of invaluable assistance in mapping the central swamps and forests. Gabunia, construction chief of the main canal."

Gulia put the note away and strode into the forest. He was heading for the ruins of the Roman fortress. The swamp had half absorbed the crumbling walls, and they were overgrown with moss. It was a good place for wild boar.

What Gulia had said in court was true. Nobody knew the jungle as he did. But he did not know how to express himself. Spending his days and nights tracking game and sleeping by smouldering campfires, floundering through swamps and whistling at prowling jackals, he had forgotten the art of conversation. He talked animatedly only when he was alone or with his dog.

Gulia's wife had died some twenty years ago. He had no children. While his wife was alive— that was before the Revolution—he had worked the land. Like everyone else, he would spread river mud over his land for fertiliser, and plant sweet corn in the swamp. And then, when the rivers overflowed their banks, he would row out in his leaky boat to cut the flooded corn, as reed is cut in lakes.

Dry soil was very scarce. Gulia fought his neighbour in the courts for twelve years over a bit of land the size of a small room.

Life dragged on, slow and full of trouble. Every year brought the dread of new taxes. Every year some of the villagers, and some of the buffaloes, died of the fever. Every year, the lonely village was drenched in icy water that came rushing down from the accursed mountains. And just before the Revolution the whole village was wiped out by the fever. That was nothing unusual. Gulia himself remembered seven villages that had been wiped out during his lifetime.

The sole survivors, Gulia and Artem Korkia, tied black rags to the mouldering porches in token of mourning, and went away to Poti.

The village dogs wandered off. Some went wild in the swamps, and others begged in the bazaars of Poti and Senaki. Gulia picked up one of these dogs, hired a gun from the *duhan* keeper, and became a hunter.

He was always away in the swamps, and life passed him by. People joined collective farms. An electric power station was built on the Rion. But the swamps lay desolate and airless still, and stagnant water filled every hollow over scores of kilometres.

Then came engineers and workers, with excavators, and Gulia learned that the days of the swamps were numbered. Forests of mandarin and lemon trees would be planted in their place, and the new land would receive a new name: not Mingrelia, but Colchis.

Who can resist the temptation to make fun of the ignorant? Artem Korkia kidded Gulia. "A Colchis," he said, "is a collective farm where the women do all the work, and drive out the men—especially lazy good-for-nothings like you. Ours will be the first Colchis in the Soviet country." Gulia believed what he said, and worried over it. How could one doubt an old man who in his youth had been known to drink half a keg of wine at one go?

When Gulia discovered that he had been kidded, he had the impulse to go call Korkia a fool, right to his face; but he did not go, for Korkia was his elder by ten years.

Pushing on towards the fortress, Gulia thought to himself: "Where will I go when the swamps are drained?" Then he recalled Gabunia's note again, and determined by all means to get a wild boar and give it to the young engineer. Blood for blood, injury for injury, service for service—such was Gulia's simple code.

He had been back in the jungle for two days now. Strange things surrounded him, but he paid them no attention. To him, the jungle had lost its mystery.

He knew the muddy, rushing waters of the rivers: the Rion, the Tsiva, the Hopi. They rolled to the sea along high beds, built up in the course of centuries. They flowed at a higher level than the surrounding lowland, and when their water rose (in the Rion alone, it rose more than a hundred and fifty times a year) they would overflow their banks and flood the jungles, transforming the country into a vast, turbid lake.

Gulia sometimes wondered: "How do the rivers come to flow higher than the swamps, as if their beds had been built by man?" Nor would it have helped him to see the crosscut of the country that Gabunia had charted. Here it was clearly shown that the chief rivers of Colchis flowed on high embankments, while between them lay "thalwegs"—huge lowlands, into which the rivers' superfluous water overflowed.

But after all, is every river as insane as the Rion and the Hopi? Gulia knew dozens of little rivers, flowing almost without current—clear, pensive streams, that barely seemed to move. Dense thickets overhung their banks. When Gulia sped along these rivers in his boat, bright afternoon was sometimes grey as dusk, for the treetops met over the water, forming a heavy tent of foliage. These rivers were not fed by the mountains. They took their water from the jungle, and carried it lazily to the sea.

The engineers called these rivers "parasites", and "malaria victims". Parasites, because they fed on water that was not their own: the overflow from the Rion and the Hopi; malaria victims, because their current was so slow—like the gait of a man whose strength has been sapped by the fever.

The sea blocked the warm water in the swamps. The land was flat as a sheet of paper, and the thickness of a sheet of paper was sufficient measure for its elevation above sea level. The little rivers had not the force to discharge their waters into the sea. The breakers beat them back. And the rivers turned reluctantly aside, flowing along the coast until they found some quiet inlet where the sea would at last accept their waters.

Gulia detested storms at sea, especially at the period of the equinox. The sea would roar so furiously that he could hear it even in the jungle. It would seem on the very point of breaking over the coast and launching its dark waves upon the alder forests, smashing and felling the trees. And the rain would pour incessantly over this drenched, unhappy land.

Storms ended in floods. The breakers would cast up mountains of sand at the river mouths. And the little rivers, unable to break through, would stop in their course and flood the land.

Such a flood would continue until the water rose higher than the sand barriers the breakers had cast up, until it washed the sand away and escaped to the sea, blanketing the waves with mud and slime for many a league from shore.

After a flood, the country would look as though it had been daubed with some grey ointment. Trees, lianas, and buildings would be coated with viscous slime. But this would soon dry and drop off.

Gulia had his own ideas about flood prevention. The mouths of the rivers, he knew, were so thickly overgrown with alder that the current was greatly weakened. The bush should be cut, to give the water way; but nobody ever thought of that, and Gulia said nothing. Nobody asked him. Nobody ever asked him anything. Such foolish people!

Gulia sighed. Gabunia was the only one who had ever asked him anything. Gabunia had asked, that day in the courtroom, whether Gulia could guide a group of workers through the swamps. Of course he could! And then Gabunia had written the note.

Once more the thought of the courtroom brought the angry blood to Gulia's cheeks. He would have to get even with that puppy, Vano!

Evening had fallen when Gulia came out at the ruins of the Roman fortress. The low walls, built of huge blocks of stone, had sunk deep into the earth. Within them lay a little bog, overgrown with rushes and yellow flag.

Gulia built a fire, and supped on a dirty hunk of cheese that he took from his bag. Bats flew back and forth, back and forth overhead, in measured sweeps, as though suspended by invisible threads. The dog lay on its side. Now and then it would lift its head sharply, snapping at the flittering bats as though they were flies.

Dark night spread through the jungle, beneath a sea of stars. The whine of the mosquitoes died. Some creature sighed and gurgled in the swamps. The last faint glow faded over the distant mountains.

The fire smoked and crackled. The dog slept, its lax skin twitching. Gulia sang to make the night more cheerful. At dawn he must visit the wild boar at their watering place.

Suddenly the song broke off. Gulia reached slowly for his gun, and poked his dog. For the first time in all his years of wandering through the jungle he was afraid. A cold sweat broke out on his brown cheeks. His hands shook.

His eyes were fixed on the little bog inside the fortress. Among the thickets of flag, barely visible in the starlight, he saw a human arm and hand.

The dog growled. Hardly knowing what he was doing, Gulia took aim and fired. A finger disappeared from the hand. The dog sprang into the bog, and returned with the finger in its mouth. It laid the trophy at Gulia's feet. The finger was large and white, and delicately shaped as only a woman's can be. Gulia touched it. It was made of stone.

Then Gulia went into the bog. For a long time he stood looking down at the strange apparition.

A liana shoot entwined the wrist, like a dark, taut vein. Gulia took the hand in his. He encountered the coldness of marble.

Squatting, he dug into the soil with his knife. A woman's face appeared: straight nose, and parted lips. He lit a match. Mould lay thick on the heavy braids twined around the stone woman's head.

Gulia wet a bit of rag in the bog and rubbed the dirt from the statue's head and shoulders.

The darkness had thickened. Gulia brought a brand from his fire to light up the statue. The radiant countenance of a Roman goddess met his gaze, staring at him through rounded marble eyeballs. The fire lent it life. The marble woman smiled.

Gulia sprang to his feet and cursed. He cursed the jungle and the statue, the nutria and Vano Akhmeteli. Fate was mocking at him. The jungle was flouting the old hunter. A ten-ruble fine for the nutria, and insults from a raw cub in court, and a stone woman instead of wild boar.

The devil only knew what those city people might take into their heads to do! What if they dragged him to court again, for the finger shot off the statue? Gulia had been poaching again, they would say. That it was he, Gulia, who had done this thing, of course, no one would doubt. No other Mingrelian would venture out to the ruined fortress.

Gulia fingered the bullet groove on the marble hand. He was hot and sweating with anger. Collecting dry branches, he heaped them furiously onto the statue, until it was hidden from sight.

At daybreak it began to rain. Gulia's fire

hissed and spluttered. His eyes smarted with the acrid smoke.

Gulia got up and spat. He plodded towards the Rion. His rain-soaked felt hat and woollen shirt smelled of dog. His legs ached with the dampness.

There were no boar. It looked as if that devil's brood of excavators had driven off all the game.

The forest was still. It seemed to Gulia that the trees all turned their heads, peering after him anxiously. As always, the stinging rain came obliquely from the sea. It lashed at Gulia's face, and trickled down his chest and back. An attack of malaria was beginning.

Gulia came out on the bank of the Rion. As a thousand years before, the accursed river rolled its muddy waters to the sea. Gulia drank of the Rion's water, and spat. Sand gritted on his teeth. The water was tart and sour, and did not quench his thirst.

The river was swollen, rushing seaward on a level with its banks. The smaller islands seemed to float along. Gulia noticed one islet on which he had spent the night a month before. It had shifted downstream about a hundred paces.

Moaning and shivering, he crept into the bushes where his boat was hidden.

He did not look back. Only when embarked did he turn to shake his dark, scrawny fist at the jungle. He could no longer curse. His blue lips twitched, and sobs rose from his throat in place of words. It was then that Gulia realised why the trees had turned to look after him. This had been their sad farewell to the last of the hunters, as he left the jungle forever.

But perhaps the trees had not turned at all, and it was just delusion—delirium? What did it matter? Gulia shrugged impatiently.

Two hours later, topographer Abashidze found a hunter lying on the ground near his house at Chaladidi village. The hunter was writhing in the grip of a frightful attack of fever. A lean dog stood licking his cheeks. Abashidze drove the dog away and bent over its master. Groaning, the hunter pulled a note from his pocket and handed it to Abashidze.

"All right, Gulia," said Abashidze, when he had read the note. "We'll make a topographer of you. Only now you'd better come in and go to bed."

Gulia tried to smile, but his lips twisted into a grimace of pain. He staggered to his feet and followed Abashidze into a wooden house, where all the walls were hung with blue maps.

Rion Mud

Paleostom lay on the outskirts of the city. It was a lake of green water, blanketed always with a thin layer of mist. Dark plane trees towered above it, and sea gulls dipped and screamed the whole day long.

Nevskaya had hired a boat to take her to the colmatage workings, across Paleostom.

As the boat skirted the workings, she caught the odour of river slime, and the sound of water gurgling through sluices. Behind low dirt embankments, overgrown with willows, the new soil of Colchis was coming slowly into being.

Having made time, at last, for this long-planned outing, Nevskaya came determined to learn from Pakhomov what was really meant by colmatage.

She asked the boatmen to draw into the bank, and sprang lightly to the top of the embankment. The sultry air smelled of sun-warmed sedge.

She soon caught sight of Pakhomov, and walked towards him. The old man stood beside a nearby sluice gate, frowning down at the water that poured through the wooden duct. A little man, with a shock of white hair, he looked a veritable sorcerer.

"You promised a long time ago to tell me about your work," said Nevskaya, smiling shyly.

Pakhomov glanced at her with troubled eyes.

"The water's running clear again," he said unhappily. "It's the devil's own job!"

Nevskaya did not understand. A huge, shallow lake lay before her, side by side with Paleostom. It was walled in by dirt embankments, and thickly overgrown with reeds. Water flowed slowly from this lake, through wooden sluices, into Paleostom. What did it all mean? And why was Pakhomov so upset about the water running clear?

"Don't blame an old man if you get bored, then," Pakhomov grumbled. "You see, there's hardly anyone that really knows about Colchis, even if you take people who've done quite a lot of reading. Some think it's in Greece, and they're simply astounded when they discover it's part of the Soviet Union. I call that a disgrace. One thing I like about Pushkin is that he knew

60

such things. Remember the lines: 'From the drear Finnish crags to Colchis' fiery strand'? But enough of all that." The old man waved his hand.

"This flat seaside country about us—this is Colchis. It's very young, only two hundred and fifty thousand years. Before that, there was nothing here but an inlet of the Sarmatian Sea. The rivers bring huge quantities of mud down from the mountains, especially when the snows are melting. The Rion dirties the sea for almost two hundred kilometres out. Every year, it washes away ten thousand million cubic metres of fertile soil.

"The sea is receding from Poti almost visibly. Every year the coast line advances six metres. Do you know the old Turkish fortress in the city park? It was built by the Sultan Murad in the sixteenth century. In those days it stood right by the sea. The waves washed against its walls. But now it's quite a way from the coast to the fortress.

"The whole country is swampland. Why? First of all, there's no slant. And then—the everlasting rains, and the river floods.

"The country's as smooth as a plate. Even at the foot of the Guria Mountains, it's only two metres above sea level, and out here at Poti it's less than a metre. In fact we're practically living on the water.

"It's the swamps that cause the terrible monotony of plant life. Look for yourself: alder, alder, nothing but alder, blast it! And a little hornbeam and beech. If it weren't for the mountains on the horizon, there'd be no way of telling Colchis from the swamps around Pinsk. Why, there is sundew in these swamps. Yes, indeed, the very same sundew that you find in the Arctic tundra. And they talk about tropics!

"Why should the plant life be so poor? You're a botanist. You know better than I do that trees need at least a metre of dry soil. And where's it to come from this metre of dry soil, when the whole country's soaking wet? So nothing grows but swamp junk.

"Colchis has a climate like southern Japan, or Sumatra. Plenty of warmth. And yet it's a malarial desert, in the full sense of the word. Something like the tropical penal colony at New Caledonia. If it weren't for the swamps, we could beat Java and Ceylon, for all their fertility and wealth. Well, then, the swamps have to be drained.

"Splendid! That's just what we're doing. Near the mountains—at Chaladidi, for instance, where Gabunia's working—there's a little slant, and the swamps can be drained by ordinary canals. There the rivers can be kept in bounds by putting up dirt embankments. That's all in the primers. But it can only be done in Gabunia's section. Here, it's impossible. There's no slope to speak of, and canals won't drain anything but the top layer of the soil—a useless twenty centimetres or so. In other words, we've got to find some other way of drainage. What way? Why, colmatage."

Pakhomov paused to roll a cigarette, glancing sidewise at Nevskaya.

It was very pleasant here, on the bank of Paleostom she found. The mist and the sun created a landscape of silvery, transparent beauty.

The wind blew in Nevskaya's face in swift light gusts, like a mischievous child.

"What's colmatage?" Pakhomov continued. "It's the drainage of swamps by flooding them with water from muddy rivers. A sort of technical paradox. Colmatage drains the swamps, and at the same time it builds up a thick layer of new, fertile soil. Here's an example for you. We put up embankments around this swamp, and dug canals to it from the Rion. We kept the sluices closed till the water in the Rion was at its muddiest—real liquid clay. Then we opened the sluices and flooded the swamp with water from the Rion. And on the opposite side we built another row of sluices, so we could let the water out into Paleostom when the mud had settled. Simple, isn't it? The mud settles, and we let the clear water go. Then we flood the swamp with muddy water again, and so on and on. That's all there is to it. The soil keeps building up, at almost no cost. And without this new soil, there can't be any question of subtropics here. There's nothing but sphagnum and young peat under the water in the swamps, and that won't grow anything but alder. Colmatage makes wonderful soil. The mud is magnificent. Stick a broken fig branch in it, and in four months it will yield fruit.

"The Rion carries twice as much silt as the Nile. The Nile was always considered the world's muddiest river. It carries a kilogram and a half of silt in every cubic metre of water. The Rion carries three! The land that was flooded by the Nile nourished a mighty civilisation. But the wealth of plant life we're going to have in Colchis is something the Egyptians never dreamed of. There's twice as much phosphorus and nitrogen in our silt as in theirs.

"Well, that's about all. There's nothing more to tell. In five years we've built up a layer of soil a metre and a half thick. It will be used for growing oranges and lemons."

"Well, then," said Nevskaya, "I don't understand why the clear water should upset you. Isn't that as it should be? It means all the mud has settled."

"That's just what's wrong about it," returned Pakhomov. "The current should be stronger, so only the bigger particles will settle, and the finer stuff run off into Paleostom. Fine silt is bad. It makes the soil heavy."

Confined though it was to bare essentials, Pakhomov's explanation of colmatage made the world seem so full of interest and wonder to Nevskaya that she almost wished she might make time stand still.

Nevskaya was a botanist, and had trained herself to mental discipline; but hers was a nature inclined to stirring generalisations. She saw colmatage not simply as a new method of draining swamps, but as something more significant: man's complete power over Nature; the creation of a new face for the land.

She smiled to Pakhomov. Her voice, as she called to the boatmen, rang out distinct and clear; yet it did not mar the hush of the warm lakes around her. When she fell silent, she could hear the drone of bees.

"Give me a lift to town," said Pakhomov. "I ought to be getting home."

They had a long walk through the outskirts of

Poti. The streets here were paved with pebbles from the seashore, and hairy pigs wandered about, with forked sticks tied around their necks to prevent them from pushing through fences into the vegetable gardens.

Somebody called to them. It was Kakhiani. He was sitting on the porch of one of the wooden houses, with a pile of blueprints. His mother was busy in the vegetable garden. She was wearing the dark, muslim trimmed bonnet that is the traditional headwear of married Georgian women.

"Hold on, comrades!" cried Kakhiani. "Can't you stop a minute? I heard a real beauty today. I was on my way to the port in old Shaliko's cab, and he said to me: 'Do you know what I think, Comrade Kakhiani? Ten years from now, the steamers won't need any beacon to find our port at night. They'll steer by the fragrance of the lemons!' Poetry, poetry, wherever you go. No getting away from it! Even the cabmen are turning into poets. A new Hafiz on every hand! Why don't you come in?"

Nevskaya joined Kakhiani's mother in the vegetable garden, and helped her draw a pail of water from the well. The old woman was washing some bunches of huge green leeks.

"What beautiful leeks," said Nevskaya, sniffing at the luscious white bulbs. "They do look tasty!"

The old woman smiled, but did not answer. She did not speak Russian well.

From Kakhiani's, Nevskaya went to the experimental gardens. It was twilight when she finally set out for home—one of those Poti evenings when lights seem to hang suspended in mid-air without any support. There had been no rain for two days.

The streets were like the shady walks of a park. Lamps glowed white in the wooden houses, set on high piles. Crumpled roses carpeted the pavements. Buffaloes, their heavy horns thrown back, drew squeaky carts over the fading petals.

Blue evening hung over the sea and glittered in the windowpanes. Through the orchards, over dusky street corners and thorny hedges, shone the piercing light of the beacon, like a bright planet caught in black nets of foliage.

Coming up to the house, Nevskaya caught sight of Christophoridi. He was catching bunches of leeks that came flying out of the kitchen window, and Yolochka was dragging bunch after bunch to the shed. Chup was in the kitchen cursing as he flung out the leeks.

"Congratulations!" he shouted to Nevskaya. "Now you've got enough leek to last till next year's harvest. Wait! Don't come in! Let me air the place first."

"What's up?"

"What's up, eh? When you live in a country, you ought to know its customs. Did you praise anybody's leeks?"

"Why, yes. Kakhiani's mother's."

"There you are! Just as I thought!"

It turned out that cabman Shaliko had driven up about two hours before and dumped ten huge bunches of leeks on the kitchen floor. There had been no one at home but the children. To Christophoridi's queries Shaliko had deigned no reply but:

"Quiet, *bicho*. It's a present from mother Kakhiani."

Nevskaya hung her head. Forgetting the old custom which obliges Mingrelians to make a gift of anything that pleases a guest, she had been so incautious as to praise these beautiful leeks. And here was her punishment!

"This is nothing," said Chup, to console her. "Just an innocent trifle. Sometimes it's much worse. In tsarist times, Mingrelia belonged to the Dadiani princes. First-class drunkards and layabouts. They drank and feasted till they had nothing left to their names. Even the beds were gone. But when guests arrived, they just had to show off. They'd make their guests gifts of horses. Only the horses belonged to the peasants. The Dadianis had no horses left. The peasants would keep their mouths shut, and wait for the guests to leave. They'd catch 'em at the boundary of the Dadianis' land, and take the horses back. And while they were at it they'd beat those guests into ribbons, so they wouldn't be in any hurry to visit the Dadianis again."

They had to put so much leek into their roast lamb for supper that night that they could never have eaten it up, had not Sima come to their rescue.

Sima was only in town for a day. He was working under Gabunia, at Chaladidi, running an excavator.

He gave them a spirited demonstration of the excavator's work, whistling, clicking his tongue, and rattling imaginary chains. Yolochka stared at him, fascinated.

That evening they learned that Sima's real

name was Jim Birling, that he had been born in Scotland, and that he had almost gone down, one day, in the wreck of the steamer *Klondike.*

To prove it, Sima pulled down the neck of his jersey and showed three blue lines on his chest, like three huge exclamation marks. But how they had come to be there remained a mystery. Sima fell asleep at the table, as usual, and nobody disturbed him.

The Foehn

Chup rubbed the bright, hairy leaves between his finger tips—and hastily pulled his hand away. The skin smarted as though he had seared it with a red-hot iron. He swung his arm back and forth, and cursed. Damned Japanese nettle!

He thought the pain would pass quickly enough, but it grew worse and worse. It seemed to be creeping into the very bone, seizing his fingers in a merciless iron grip.

Then Chup began to worry. He strode quickly through the gate, out of the plantation. Only now, glancing back over his shoulder, did he notice the faded sign: "Attention! Do not touch leaves with bare hands!"

"Stupid woman!" thought the captain of Nevskaya. "Why didn't she warn me?"

But at once he stopped short, flushing. How could he, an old sailor, talk about a woman like that? Had not he himself asked to come with her to Supsa, on his free day, to visit the plantations of this idiotic tree? Well, then, he had no one but himself to blame. Nobody had forced him to come.

Chup was not only talkative, but inquisitive.

Nevskaya had told him of the test plantations of the Japanese varnish tree. The sap of this tree is made into splendid lacquer. Neither time nor damp can dull its sheen, and fire is powerless to crack its surface. Chup remembered the Japanese boxes he had seen. They were coated with lacquer made from the sap of this tree. It was hard as transparent steel.

He had also learned from Nevskaya that this lacquer is used in shipbuilding, to coat underwater parts. That had caught his interest as a sailor. And so, when Nevskaya and Lapshin planned their trip to Supsa to visit the plantations of the varnish tree, he had asked them to take him along.

The pain was getting worse. Chup thrust his hand into his pocket and went out onto the road. The dusty Ford stood dreaming in the thin shade of some old acacias. Neither Nevskaya nor Lapshin were anywhere to be seen.

The captain got into the car and sat down to wait. He glanced at the sky, and it did not please him. There was no wind, but the air was growing steadily hotter. A reddish mist hung over the mountains. It looked like soapy water. There had been no rain for four days.

"Hope we don't get a foehn," the captain thought, and sighed.

The devil's own climate in this country! All year round it rained and poured. All year round it was as hot and damp as a Chinese laundry. But once in a while the foehn would begin to blow, and it would seem as though torrid Arabia, land of simooms and deserts, had been transplanted to Colchis.

"Looks like a foehn getting up," said the captain, as Lapshin came up to the car. "We'd better get started."

Lapshin made no reply. Throwing open the hood, he began fussing with the motor.

"Snooty devil," thought the captain. The hand in his pocket was growing heavier and heavier, as though the veins had been filled with lead.

"Do you know what the foehn is?" he asked.

"It's a wind," said Lapshin. "Why should an old sea wolf like you get worried over such trifles."

"If you get caught in one, you'll find out soon enough."

Nevskaya came up, and got in beside the captain. Lapshin took his seat at the wheel. He put on his goggles, and they were off.

A hot breeze struck Nevskaya's cheeks, and caught at her hair. Vibrant, impatient, the car sped on towards the huge white clouds that blocked the horizon.

The clouds approached with dizzy speed. They stretched and grew, reaching up to the sky like mountains. All at once the car burst into them. It raced on, noiseless now, over a heavy carpet of acacia petals.

The clouds were a forest of ancient acacias. White petals beat against the windscreen, and swirled skyward behind the car.

The trees rushed up and past, up and past, like a wild, white flurry of snow. There was no air to breathe, only the sweet, heavy fragrance of the blossoms.

"Wonderful!" cried Nevskaya.

Lapshin put on more speed. The petals made it difficult to see. The sun hung dull above the white-crowned trees. It seemed to move together with the car.

Something snapped in the motor. Lapshin stopped the car and ducked under the bonnet. Nevskaya and the captain got out and sat down on a fallen acacia trunk. For some time they did not speak. The sun blinked at the zenith, its white glare turned to crimson.

"It's a regular Turkish bath," Chup grumbled. "This climate belongs in Asia!"

Nevskaya disagreed. She said that Colchis had a splendid climate. Many a spot in the subtropics got less warmth. There was no winter to speak of. The summer lasted six months, and plant growth continued all year round. What more did he want? The village of Codor, on the Rion, was the warmest spot in Europe.

"You don't say!" returned Chup, in mock amazement. "And to think I never knew!"

"The temperature here is very even," Nevskaya continued severely. "There are no sudden jumps."

"Except for the exceptions."

"What exceptions?"

"The foehn will start blowing in half an hour or so, and then you'll see. I wonder how you're going to protect your subtle plants from winds like that."

"Subtle plants" was the captain's term for all subtropical vegetation.

"We'll plant protective belts of tall trees."

Chup grunted his disbelief.

"If you're so interested in the climate," said Nevskaya, "you ought to have a talk to Lapshin. He's studying the microclimate."

71

"What on earth is that?" the captain mumbled.

He was not interested in any sort of climate just then, be it normal, or micro, or that of the devil in hell. His hand was smarting as though it had been flayed.

"Ready!" called Lapshin.

"It's very simple," Nevskaya explained, as she and the captain got into the car. "Climate depends on all sorts of small things. It can vary within a radius of a hundred metres. You needn't grunt. It's true. This forest has a climate of its own, and the swamps five kilometres away have one of their own, too—entirely different. The climate in a hollow isn't anything like the climate on the surface outside the hollow. And that's what we call microclimate: the variations in climate over short distances. It's very important, especially for 'subtle' vegetation."

"Interesting," Chup muttered. He pulled his hand out of his pocket. The cloth, pressing against it, made the pain unbearable.

Nevskaya glanced at him, and cried out in alarm.

"What's happened to you?" she demanded. "Look at your hand!"

"I got stung by those nettles."

"What nettles?"

"Those Japanese things of yours."

"What do you mean?" she cried. "Why, there are signs everywhere in Georgian and Russian. I didn't think you were such a baby! It's dangerous!"

"Think I'll lose my arm?" The captain was sulky with pain.

Leaning forward, Nevskaya shouted to Lapshin:

"He's burnt his hand on the Japanese tree. We've got to get to town as fast as we can."

Lapshin looked back at her, with a quick flash of his motoring glasses, and stepped on the gas. His shaggy jacket creased heavily across his narrow shoulders.

The car dashed out into the open, leaving the acacias behind. And just then the foehn swept down.

The captain ducked quickly, seeking shelter behind the driver's seat. Nevskaya turned her head back, for the wind gagged her mouth and nostrils as though with scorching cotton.

Through a whirlwind of red dust she saw, to remember always, the cruel descent of the foehn upon the acacias. At one swift blow the blossoms were swept from the trees, like vanishing soapsuds—an ocean of fluttering petals, borne upward into an unseeing sky.

The wind advanced with such force that vacuums seemed to arise in its path. There was nothing to breathe. Hot dust rushed, hissing, to fill the vacuums.

Huge columns of dust raced past. Lapshin could not see the road.

"We'll have to go back to the woods," he shouted, slowing down and turning to his passengers. "It's calmer there."

"We can't go back!" cried Nevskaya. "Don't you dare turn back!"

Lapshin shrugged in submission. Silly woman! Why make so much fuss about a burn?

The car could barely push its way through the

scorching wind. Chup cursed under his breath. The dust blinded him. His hand was swollen and stiff, and his heart thumped heavily—not in his chest, but in that blasted hand.

Chup had been through the foehn before. Fighting down his pain, he turned to Nevskaya. "The dust will soon stop," he told her. "Don't let it bother you. The temperature's much worse."

Nevskaya did not understand. What did he mean by the temperature? She touched his sound hand, thinking he might be feverish. But he shook his head and explained:

"It's not that. I'm all right. Can't you feel the temperature going up?"

Then Nevskaya realised that the wind was steadily growing hotter and hotter. A wild thought flashed through her mind: if this went on much longer, they would all be burnt to ashes. The wind would consume them, as it consumed the foliage on the trees.

Their mouths grew parched and they began to feel thirsty. A red murk seethed above at a dizzy height, surging ever and again to the sun. Each new gust of wind tossed the sun about, like a child's ball. Now it would disappear, now shine again—a blood-red disk above the furious current of murk.

The captain glanced at the sky.

"Sixty metres a second," he muttered dully.

"What's that?" shouted Nevskaya.

"The wind up there—it's racing at sixty metres a second. Worse than a typhoon! The foehn will raise the temperature twenty-five degrees before an hour's out."

The dust subsided, and Nevskaya found herself looking out over a strange, new country, illumined as though in the glow of a distant conflagration.

The horizon was veiled in brick-red murk. A yellow light hung over everything. Only in the time-faded paintings of the old masters had Nevskaya seen landscapes such as this.

One of the back tyres burst. Lapshin stopped the car, and mopped the sweat from his face and neck. Pulling off his jacket, he dropped it to the floor.

"We'll burn up," he said, peevishly hitting the side of the car. Cracked by the heat, the paint came off at his touch. "It won't be a minute before all the tyres are gone. They never were any good, anyway."

"How far is it to town?" asked Nevskaya.

"Ten kilometres."

Nevskaya recalled the details of the road. Two kilometres along the coast, with the waves splashing up at the wheels—there was no other road; then the ferry across the River Caparcha; and after that, a full seven kilometres to town.

"Turn down to the sea," she told Lapshin. "We can get into the water. There's no surf, and the wind's blowing off shore. The water will save the tyres."

"Well, let me catch my breath," said Lapshin, shrugging.

Nobody spoke. They had stopped near a clump of alders. The foliage was shrivelling, darkening before their eyes. The fiery wind stripped away the leaves and carried them to the sea. The captain moaned. If only he had a drop of water, to moisten his hand!

Nevskaya sat very still, watching the alders being stripped of their leaves.

As they came out on the grey sand of the shore, the car skidded violently. Another tyre had burst.

Lapshin gritted his teeth, cursing to himself.

He had begun to hate the captain and Nevskaya —to hate them because they sat idle, while he choked on gasoline fumes and worried over the engine.

He cursed the very name of Colchis, and caught himself reflecting maliciously that the planned subtropics would never materialise, that the first foehn would reduce the lemon groves to dirty ashes.

Turning, Lapshin looked back at Nevskaya with hatred. Her face was pale, her answering look no less resentful than his. A blue spark flashed in her eyes.

"Just like a cat," thought Lapshin. Aloud, he said, with an ill-natured smile:

"We're wasting our efforts."

"Think we won't make it?"

"Of course, we won't."

The red murk swept out over the hot, purple sea. On the horizon it thickened, its colour deepening into black. The sea was deserted.

Not far from the Caparcha, the third tyre burst. The car could go no further. They left it behind, making their way slowly towards the ferry on foot.

Nevskaya was worried. Suppose the ferry were on the far bank? The ferrymen would never bring it over in such a wind.

The foehn had turned the earth to stone. Dark cracks zigzagged across the surface. That morning, on the way to Supsa, the soil had gurgled wetly under the wheels of the car.

Walking at Nevskaya's side, the captain tried to fight down his pain and talk. To comfort her, he lied about his hand, saying that it was not hurting so much now.

And here he made an unexpected discovery: that this was his first glimpse of the real Nevskaya. He had always conceived of women scientists as poor, sickly creatures, sapped by overstudy and quite devoid of femininity. Due, perhaps, to this deep-seated prejudice, he had never had a real talk with Nevskaya, had never even looked at her with interest.

He watched her now in astonished admiration, not unmixed with gratitude. With new eyes he saw her pale, determined features; her light step, quickened as by vexation; her dark, resentful eyes, and the lock of reddish chestnut hair that fell across her dust-grimed cheek.

The Caparcha, at last. Wind tossed foam and spray above the water. Nevskaya breathed a deep sigh of relief. The ferry was on the near side. But there was not a soul to be seen.

The captain bathed his hand, and the cool river water brought relief.

"Well, let's be going," said Nevskaya cheerfully, approaching the ferry. "The oars are here."

Lapshin stared at her blankly.

"I never thought," he said calmly, "that the foehn could drive people mad so quickly. It isn't usually till the second day that groundless irritation sets in. On the third day, people start picking quarrels, and on the fourth the foehn stops blowing and mental equilibrium is restored. That's what the local people say."

"What do you mean?" Nevskaya demanded stiffly.

"That it's impossible to get across. At best, the ferry will be swept out to sea. At worst, it will go under."

"And what do you propose we do?"

"Wait."

"We can't wait!" she cried. "You know yourself what the consequences may be."

Lapshin shrugged his shoulders.

"Ask the captain," he returned. "He's had more experience of this sort of thing."

Chup looked at the river. The risk, of course, was great.

The water was rolling seaward in great brown waves, foaming and roaring. The riverside bushes, prostrate before the wind, lashed the waves with their branches.

Chup forgot his hand. He remembered only the old traditions of the sea, the splendid laws of storm and shipwreck. When a ship is sinking—women and children first! How could he put a woman in danger on account of a burnt hand? To hell with his hand. It would be all right. And so he said:

"The crossing's dangerous. We'd better wait. My hand's much better now."

"You're lying, Chup!" exclaimed Nevskaya hotly. "Why? Your hand is blue. We're crossing right away."

"All right then," Chup replied, too taken aback to protest. "We're crossing right away."

Nevskaya turned to Lapshin, with a brief:

"Come on!"

Lapshin did not answer. He wiped his arm over his face, and the shirt sleeve came away black.

"He can't row," said Nevskaya, glancing at the captain. "I can hardly manage it alone. Everything depends on you."

"I'm not going," replied Lapshin quietly.

Nevskaya turned white.

"Coward!" she cried, the tears rising to her eyes. "Now I know what you mean when you talk about scientists' 'superior morality'. Let's get going, Chup!"

Lapshin turned and walked slowly away in the direction of the abandoned car. He was actually whistling.

Nevskaya and Chup pushed the heavy boat from shore in silence. The captain muttered, looking after Lapshin:

"He can go to blazes!"

Nevskaya rowed. Chup rowed too, with one hand, biting his lip to keep from moaning.

The riverbanks whirled before them like a grey merry-go-round. The wind whistled and caught at the oars, trying to pull them free. It carried off Nevskaya's beret, and her reddish hair blew loose, a flaunting pennant.

The waves beat heavily against the low wooden sides. With his bad hand, Chup bailed out the water. Nevskaya was soaked to the skin. Her every sinew was tensed in superhuman effort.

"Where does she get such strength from?" the captain wondered.

He kept a watchful eye on the mouth of the river. It was drawing rapidly nearer. He could see the beating breakers, the seething surface.

"We mustn't get swept out to sea!"

Nevskaya's head was spinning desperately. She bit her lip until it bled. A gust of wind tore the oar from her hands. The boat rocked. The captain glanced at the bank. The trees were bowing low in terror before a new and still more furious blast.

"We're done for now," the captain muttered.

Nevskaya was blinded by the spray. But she managed, somehow, to rescue her oar, and went on rowing.

Time dragged on endlessly.

Glancing over his shoulder once more, the captain found that the shore was very near. He saw the ferrymen's shanty on the bank, and two fishermen standing in the river, up to the knee in water. One of the fishermen held a boat hook.

When the hook caught the side of the boat, the captain shouted to Nevskaya:

"We're safe!"

He had forgotten his hand entirely; but once they were safely on shore, the pain returned.

A young fisherman in shorts looked at the captain ironically.

"What's the matter, *katso*?" he said. "Gone a little crazy with the wind? You've got the looks of a sailor, but you act like a fool. And a woman with you, too."

"Drop it, friend," said the captain, clapping the fisherman's shoulder with his sound hand. "Come and visit me at the port. *Shashlik* and new wine. We'll celebrate the rescue."

The fishermen laughed.

"When the wind drops, bring that fellow over," said the captain, pointing to Lapshin, who was working over the car.

"All right!"

They set out for town, walking along the coast, where the grey dunes sheltered them from the wind.

For some time Nevskaya did not speak. Suddenly, she turned her face away and began to cry. Chup was at a loss. He cursed the foehn, because it brings on hysteria. It was blowing with undiminished force.

Again a strange landscape lay before them. The soil was dry and scorched, as though by fire. It occurred to the captain that he had seen just such a louring, slatey sky before an eclipse of the sun.

The orchards of Poti appeared in the distance. The foehn had not affected them. They were protected by tall belts of plane trees.

"Listen," said the captain. "They'll bring him over. What does it matter if he does go hungry a day?"

"Don't be silly, Chup! He can stay there three days, for all I care."

"Then what are you crying about?"

"Because I was scared."

This was more than Chup could understand. He decided to say no more, and held his tongue all the way to the hospital. Once safely there, he began to curse again, heaping invective on the Japanese varnish tree.

A Football Game

The bamboo at the experimental gardens began to flower. The first signs of bloom robbed Nevskaya of her peace. Bamboo flowers only once and then dies.

Lapshin remained unperturbed. Since the incident on the Caparcha, he had spoken little to Nevskaya. He smirked disdainfully when her name was mentioned. He thought she was silly to get so upset. The process could not be stopped. The bamboo was doomed. Hence, it was silly to worry about it.

The captain came to the gardens to have a look at the flowering bamboo. His hand was getting better, but it was still bandaged. He brought Yolochka and Christophoridi with him.

Entering Nevskaya's bright workroom in the little wooden house at the gardens, the captain found another visitor—Sima, come to town to get some spare parts for his excavator. He had brought a note from Gabunia, inviting Nevskaya and Chup to Chaladidi to see the canal.

The windows were wide open. Outdoors, in the dazzling morning light, a fresh, clear breeze ruffled through the trees. Blossoming vines drooped their cold white spray over the windowsill.

The breath of damp earth and vegetation, the sweet fragrance of mimosa, reminded Chup of his days in Madagascar with Rozhdestvensky's fleet. It brought back the dizzy aroma of fruits in the Eastern bazaars.

Yolochka and Christophoridi ran off to play under the trees. The experimental gardens were a huge, shady orchard, brimful of wonders. Christophoridi rubbed young lemon leaves between his palms, and sniffed ecstatically.

A thick column of smoke rose to the sky over a bonfire of last year's magnolia leaves.

Christophoridi invented a game. He was a tiger and Yolochka a huntress. He hid among the undergrowth, snarling and snapping at leaves in tigrish fury, crouching in readiness for tremendous springs. He grew so absorbed in the game that he forgot the troubles that were bound to follow. His mother would be sure to scold because he had earned so little. He'd have to ask Chup for another fifty kopeks, or the old lady would give him no peace.

Christophoridi snarled and snapped, until he almost cried. He had caught at a leaf of the camphor laurel, and his very jaws ached with its bitter pungence.

The sunlight poured through the branches in jets of green, like water running through the openings in a sluice gate. A medicinal odour of roots rose from the soil. Porcelain rhododendron leaves lay like starfish among the grass. The bamboo rustled its ribbony leaves, and the sound was like the crystal twitter of tiny birds. The ragged leaves of the bananas squeaked with the effort of the rising sap. The cryptomeria needles smelled like a hundred pine ships smeared with yellow resin.

The eucalyptus turned their heavy, sweating leaves edgewise to the sun. Christophoridi avoided the eucalyptus. They gave no shade.

Among the Kazanlik roses, Christophoridi caught a fuzzy beetle. The beetle got very angry, shut up in Christophoridi's fist. How loud it buzzed! Christophoridi showed it to Yolochka.

Then, making sure there were no grown-ups about, they broke a little piece of bark off the cork tree, to make Christophoridi some floats.

The light and shade, the murmuring foliage, the drops of dew that fell on his swarthy arms,

6*

the glad sounds of the sea, the clouds rising straight to the zenith like diamond vapour, filled Christophoridi's heart with rapture. He turned cartwheels all the way down the central path, shouting crazily, "Shine 'em right! Shine 'em bright!"—and ended by tumbling into a geranium bed.

After that, Christophoridi's spirits subsided. The crushed geraniums might mean serious trouble. He took Yolochka by the hand and led her towards the office, where voices could be heard through the windows.

There was an argument going on inside. The first voice Christophoridi recognised was Lapshin's. Christophoridi did not like Lapshin. His shoes, enormous red-brown Oxfords, were torture to shine. Christophoridi just couldn't get hold of the right shade of polish.

"Colchis has nothing in common with the subtropics," Lapshin declared. "The annual temperature is too low for many of the tropical fruits to ripen."

"Nonsense!" said Nevskaya. "The annual total in the subtropics comes to three thousand degrees. In Colchis, it's as much as forty-five hundred. What's the point of such cheap scepticism?"

"It's impossible to discuss anything with you. You're rude to everybody."

"I apologised to you after that day on the Caparcha, though I was entirely in the right. Let's not bring it up again."

"Your botany's a Chinese puzzle to me," put in Chup, to turn the conversation.

Nevskaya smiled.

"In vegetable life," she said, "everything is

simple. For tropical fruits to ripen, they have to get a definite amount of the sun's heat in the course of the year. At least three thousand degrees. Fluctuations in temperature don't matter so much. You can counteract them by smudging the trees—it's always warmer in the smoke—or by hot water bags, for the more delicate plants. For the winter, you can wrap them in sacking. The main thing is the year-round total. I can't understand what Lapshin's arguing about. He knows very well we get more than enough heat."

"I'm not arguing. I'm only permitting myself to doubt."

"The professor permits himself," retorted Nevskaya, laughing. Struck by a mischievous idea, she went on: "Well, suppose we make a check. It's far from cold in the south of England, for instance, in spite of the fog and rain. The annual heat totals something like three thousand degrees. What do you think: is there any tropical vegetation there?"

"There isn't, and there can't be," Lapshin replied.

"Here's an English sailor," said Nevskaya, nodding at Sima. "He won't lie. He doesn't understand what we're arguing about. Let's take him out into the gardens and ask him what trees grow here that he knew in England."

The captain translated. Sima bared his strong, yellow teeth in a grin. Yes, of course, he had been to the south of England, on the Isle of Wight, and he'd be glad to satisfy "my lady's" request. He wondered how much "my lady" had bet Lapshin.

They went out into the gardens. On the way, Chup sternly impressed it upon Sima that it was out of place to call people "my lady" in the Soviet Union. Sima readily agreed. After that, he called Nevskaya "comrade".

The captain looked around in astonishment. It was hard to believe that the recent foehn had not harmed all this luxuriant vegetation. But Nevskaya pointed to the belts of eucalyptus and plane trees, which had protected the gardens from the scorching wind. Eucalyptus trees do not fear the foehn.

Sima strode along with his hands in his pockets, whistling carelessly, as if to say that nothing could surprise a sailor.

The tropics! On the island of Trinidad Sima had smashed a café window with lemons, because they wouldn't let a Negro sailor in. He knew the tropics. He knew everything: the ugly periscopes of submarines, and the taste of corn bread, and bloody fights with the police, and life-or-death football games, and false papers, and strikes, and the "long prayer". The "long prayer" was a block of holy stone that weighed half a ton. It was used for scrubbing the decks on sailing ships.

Sima had never been really surprised in his life until he got to Colchis. Here the captain who worked as port inspector—according to the international traditions of the sea, he should have cursed Sima sky-high—this captain took Sima in and fed him for over a week. On the Soviet ships that came into the port of Poti, Sima saw forecastles that lacked nothing but fresh flowers. After seven days he was given a job, and the young engineer, Gabunia, shook his hand and spoke to him as an equal. The most surprising thing about this country, to Sima, was the way everyone spoke to him as an equal, even educated ladies.

Sima walked through the gardens, whistling. He spied a bed of leeks, and smiled. That was an old acquaintance. When he reached the blossoming bamboo, he stopped short, spat loudly, and made a strange sound with his tongue, like the crack of a whip.

"Crikey! That grows on the Isle of Wight," he said.

"Ridiculous!" Lapshin protested angrily. "A nice joke you've dragged me into, with this sailor of yours. Is that what you call scientific proof?"

"He's right," said Nevskaya. "There are bamboo groves in the south of England."

Lapshin was furious. First Vano had made him out an ignoramus, and now this woman tried to do the same. If it wasn't nutria, it was bamboo.

"There's nothing to get so angry about, Lapshin," said Nevskaya amicably. "Any good scientist can learn a great deal about his subject from people he regards as ignorant. You should be more careful."

Lapshin shrugged and turned back to his microclimate laboratory. Nevskaya returned to her workroom. Sima left, too. He had to catch the train to Chaladidi.

Chup stayed in the gardens with the children. On two weeks' sick leave, he could spend his time as he wished.

Standing beside the bamboo, Chup shook his head. It was clearly doomed. Memories of Japan came back to mind, and Chup told the children about an incident in a little Japanese port where his steamer had put in for a load of rice.

The lookout woke Chup at dawn. Something had happened in the town, he said. He could hear shouts, and women crying. Chup went ashore. It looked like a fire. People were running towards the outskirts of the town. The men shouted curses, and the women clasped their children to their breasts. There was no sign of flame or smoke.

Chup followed the people, and soon found himself in a bamboo grove. Then he saw that the bamboo was flowering. It had blossomed during the night.

That day Chup learned that whole groves of bamboo grow from one single root, and after blossoming, these huge areas all die at once. Bamboo, both to the townspeople and to the peasants of the nearby villages, served not only as building material, but also as food, for the Japanese eat the young shoots. The flowering of the bamboo is a great calamity in Japan.

"And so you see, kiddies," said Chup, "there's a story to every tree."

At length the captain and his charges set out for home. On their way out of the gardens they dropped in to say goodbye to Nevskaya. She was sitting at a table covered with little heaps of seed.

"Incidentally," said the captain, "you say that fellow"—this was his name for Lapshin—"that fellow studies the microclimate. And what do you do?"

"I select plants for Colchis. Plants vary, just like human beings. There are cranky plants, and weak ones, sturdy plants, and plants that hate the cold. There are plants that demand lots of water, and others that suffer when it's damp. There are northerners and southerners, greedy plants and plants that yield generous fruit, lean plants and stout ones. When you sailed on long voyages, I'm sure you must have been very careful about picking your crew. It's the same thing here. Types of plants have to be selected like the members of an expedition. A single fool or sniveler is liable to spoil everything. Right now, I'm looking for the best type of eucalyptus."

"That's just what I..." the captain began; but he did not finish. Loud shouts sounded suddenly in the street, arresting his attention.

Christophoridi darted out of the room. The captain stood listening intently. The shouting continued. Was it anger, or enthusiasm? The captain hurried out.

A football game was on a piece of wasteland just outside the gardens. In accordance with an old Poti custom, one team was made up of bachelors, and the other of married men. In such games, passions always ran high. The bachelors would mock and sneer at their married opponents. The married team would play in sullen silence, but at every possible opportunity—rules or no rules—a married toe would meet up violently with the back of a bachelor knee.

The players had gathered in a knot. Among them, Chup caught sight of Sima. The sailor, besieged by the married team, was swearing in English. The bachelors were defending him.

Militiaman Grisha quickly established order, and the discussion proceeded more peaceably.

The trouble had started over nothing. Sima had stopped to watch the game. Growing enthusiastic, he had joined the bachelors' team, when one of their forwards sprained his ankle, and had scored them three goals. Then the married team had raised a row, and demanded that the whole match should be replayed. Someone had struck a blow. Someone has called someone else a bum.

Chup pushed through the crowd to Sima, took him by the arm, and led him away. Sima was hot and grimy. He breathed like a winded horse.

"Mr. Birling," said the captain, furiously polite, "does it strike you that you've missed the only train to Chaladidi? In Soviet Russia people differentiate between the time for work and the time for playing football. I recommended you to Gabunia, and I'm ashamed."

Sima's neck turned scarlet. He muttered something unintelligible, and turned off into the first side street. Once around the corner he stopped, lit his pipe, and began to think. He decided to set out on foot, in the hope of reaching Chaladidi by morning.

Nevskaya was absorbed in her work with the seeds of the eucalyptus. There on her table lay the future of Colchis. Minute kernels, brought from across the seas—repositories of wondrous, almost miraculous, qualities. Fragrance, healing juices, hard and indestructible timber, the beauty of inflorescence, and the bitterness of fading bloom.

Since her arrival in Poti, Nevskaya had read a number of Lapshin's articles on botanical problems. These articles gave a headache. Their writer had no understanding of essentials. He fussed over petty detail with the tedious precision of an apothecary. He had no vision of the future, no understanding of plant life, whereas Nevskaya felt that plants, like people, demanded love and insight.

Lapshin shrank from independent thought, from untrammelled scientific interpretation. He was precise beyond all bounds. He had no imagination. He was that worthless type now happily dying out—a scientist by trade, not by vocation.

Lapshin's writing was long-winded and dull. His manner of talking was duller still: the mincing, emasculated language once regarded, among an older generation of scientists, as a mark of superior culture. He looked down upon everyone who had less knowledge than himself, and made it his business to emphasise such people's insignificance at every opportunity.

When Nevskaya had finished his articles, Lapshin asked her what she thought of them. She did not answer at once. The next day, she brought him a volume of Pushkin, and pointed to a line in one of the poet's letters:

"Inspiration is no less essential in geometry than in poetry."

Lapshin made no comment.

Bending over her eucalyptus seeds, Nevskaya often thought of the work that she could write about this splendid tree. Who had devoted such study as she to all two hundred species of this "tree of life"? Who was more fitted to describe their multitude of extraordinary qualities? This was a labour of which she had long been dreaming.

Nevskaya regarded the eucalyptus as the most valuable of all tropical plants. Small wonder the British called these trees the gem of the forests!

In Colchis, eucalyptus became fine, seven-metre trees two years after planting. They grew at an incredible rate. Some old trees were as tall as Cologne cathedral—a dizzy height of a hundred and fifty metres.

In breadth, too, they grew at an unparalleled rate. Nevskaya had recently measured the annual rings on an eucalyptus stump. Not one was less than three centimetres thick.

It was almost frightening—this tree's extraordinary vital force, the wealth and scope of the qualities that made it valuable to mankind. A five-year-old eucalyptus yielded more timber than two-hundred-year-old northern firs and spruces.

The timber of the eucalyptus is considered indestructible. It does not decay. It is never infected by grubs or borers. Eucalyptus piles in sea water are as fresh after thirty years as on the day when they were driven in. The eucalyptus railway sleepers last twice and three times as long as ordinary ties. Eucalyptus wood is stronger than oak or walnut.

Nevskaya recalled Chup's tales of sailing ships with eucalyptus masts. Never a squeak had been heard from such a mast, even in the frightful storms that rage between the fortieth and the fiftieth parallels—what sailors call "the roaring forties". They only hummed in the wind, erect as though in a dead calm. The most sensitive measuring apparatus could probably not have detected a deflection from the vertical. Yet pinewood masts often snapped like matchsticks in these storms.

"Moscow paved with eucalyptus blocks! How wonderful!" thought Nevskaya.

The leaves of the eucalyptus are turned edgewise to the sun. There is no shade in eucalyptus groves. This is the best tree for drying swampland. Its heavy, rigid leaves exhale a tremendous amount of moisture. Neither rain nor foehn can harm it, and it will grow on any soil.

Malarial mosquitoes cannot stand the smell of eucalyptus leaves. In effect the eucalyptus gets rid of malaria. Perhaps this is why they call it the "tree of life" in the tropics.

The room grew dark. Nevskaya glanced up to see the time. The clock was ticking busily in the hush of this little house, lost in its sea of vegetation. It was only five o'clock. Then why such darkness?

Nevskaya looked out of the window. A grey-blue cloud hung high over the sea. A slow peal of thunder rolled through the breathless air. A breeze began to blow. The dark tropical foliage, thinly coated with glossy wax, rustled uneasily.

"It's going to pour," said a voice outside the window.

Just then a tremendous forked flash of lightning issued from the cloud, as though a great golden glass had been shattered into a thousand fragments. Brilliant points of light glittered and died among the lemon trees. To Nevskaya they seemed like clusters of dazzling lemons, such as the world had never seen before.

The breeze looked in at the window, setting the curtains fluttering wildly, then raced off again through the gardens. There was a new flash of lightning. The thunder rolled, louder and far more threatening than before.

Nevskaya decided to hurry home. The downpour might last all night.

Walking through the wind-swept town, she thought again and again of that first flash of lightning. It had seemed to show her the future Colchis, bright with a golden, citrus beauty.

At home, Chup told her that rains were approaching. The barometer was falling. But the night brought no downpour. In the morning, Nevskaya set out for Chaladidi, hoping to get back before the rains set in.

The Bust of Lenin

Gabunia sat in his room, absorbed in a volume of Hippocrates. He was writing a scientific treatise on Colchis, and did a great deal of reading on this subject, both among modern geographers and in the works of the ancients: Strabo, Hippocrates, and Homer.

It was Gabunia's contention that the *Iliad* presents an ideal weather map of the period of the Trojan war. Day by day, with punctilious exactitude, Homer describes the movements of winds and clouds. One modern scientist, indeed, has drawn up a table of atmospheric pressure for those legendary times, based on Homer's descriptions, which makes it clear that the Achaean ships were scattered by a cyclone passing over the Archipelago.

"The people who live on the Phasis [the Rion]," Gabunia read, "have a hot, swampy country, wooded, and full of dampness. At all seasons there are heavy rains. The people spend their lives in the swamps. In the midst of the waters they build themselves dwellings of branches. They traverse their lands in boats hollowed out of tree trunks, following the numerous rivers and canals. They drink tepid, stagnant water, made foul by the heat of the sun and replenished by the rains. The winds blow from the south, but there is also an east wind at times: hot, strong, and unpleasant."

". . . Stagnant water, made foul by the heat of the sun," Gabunia repeated, and cursed. How well he knew that water's brackish taste! It was the water, he was convinced, that had given him the fever.

Gabunia got up and threw open the windows. It was very stuffy. A faint scent of vanilla hung in the air. The scent of vanilla always came before heavy rains.

"There's a storm brewing somewhere," thought Gabunia, and turned a page.

Foreman Mikha came in. Mikha's eyes were darting about anxiously and he kept jerking at the folds of his shabby Circassian coat. Stepping noiselessly over to the barometer, he tapped the glass with a yellow finger nail. His eyes narrowed mournfully. The mercury was dropping with steady, inexorable persistence.

"It's going to pour. Do you smell it?" said Mikha, with a crooked smile. It was Mikha's habit to smile on all occasions, even when life was at its worst. This habit had earned him a reputation for reckless daring. "When the water comes down from the mountains, we'll all be swept off the face of the earth."

Gabunia did not answer.

"The redheaded Englishman hasn't come back," said Mikha. He glanced at his reflection in the barometer glass, and added, "This fever's turned me as yellow as a canary!"

Gabunia looked up. At the fifth reach, the canal embankments had subsided by a metre. They must be built up immediately. The men couldn't manage it, of course. The only excavator on that reach lacked an essential part. Sima had gone to town for the part and had not returned.

"What can the men do, when they've all got malaria," the foreman mumbled, wiping his sweating forehead.

The air was heavy and suffocating, as in a great steam bath. Such was this country. Mikha spat disgustedly.

"I know," Gabunia replied.

He was thinking hard. Outside his windows, the forest stood languishing of heat and miasma. The sky was an airtight leaden dome.

Like a heavy sigh, came the faint roll of distant thunder.

"Let me see." With flying pencil, Gabunia began to figure on a page of Hippocrates. "In two hours, the rain should start. In three hours, the water will come down the mountains. Before three hours are up we've got to make that part for the excavator in our camp workshop. Only what are we going to make it of, the devil take it all? Eh? We need some bronze."

Gabunia felt an attack of malaria coming on. The blood whined in his veins, like shrilling mosquitoes. He wanted to get into bed, and pull the blankets up over his ears, and forget about everything.

The first gust of wind passed over the forest. And again the world was silent as the grave.

"All out to the fifth reach, *katso*," said Gabunia hoarsely. "Every living soul, even the women! And we've got to find a lump of bronze somewhere, in a hurry."

"Ho!" said Mikha, shaking his head. "It's seven versts to Chaladidi station. There's a bronze bell there. Say the word. I'll go. I'll pinch the bell as easy as pie."

"Don't talk nonsense," Gabunia told him. "Hurry, now! All out to the fifth reach. Get going!"

Mikha disappeared. An instant later, Gabunia heard loud shouts and a hurried clanging of metal. Mikha was beating the rail that served as a gong, yelling at the top of his voice:

"Fifth reach! Fifth reach!"

The Mingrelian workers came running out of their barracks, heading straight for the canal. Their heads were covered with sacking hoods. Lianas caught at their legs, and slit the leather of their boots like razor blades. Their spades clattered against the tree trunks.

Gabunia dropped fuzzy quinine crystals onto his tongue, and washed them down with water. Then he got slowly into his stiff tarpaulin. His face was aflame.

He looked out through the window. A cloud advancing from the west, like a great black wall, hid the sun from view. Smoke curled round the edges of the cloud. It looked like tufts of dirty cotton. The forest was hushed. The deathly stillness rang in Gabunia's ears like the pulsing of slow, heavy blood. His temples ached.

"It must be the quinine," he thought, rubbing his forehead to expel the sodden fever thoughts.

"What can we do? The workers can't manage it by half. There is nobody but Mikha. Abashidze's gone off with Gulia and some workers to explore the swamp along the Nedoard canal. If they get caught in the rain, they're done for."

Only two people in authority left: he and Mikha. Mikha was a coward. He was thought a hero, because of a war-time episode, when he had fired a rusty Smith and Wesson at the German warship *Goeben*. The *Goeben* steamed into the harbour and opened fire on the town from its big guns. Panic began in the bazaar, where Mikha was selling tobacco at the time. Mikha pulled out his revolver and fired seven shots at the armoured cruiser. His bullets could not even reach the ship, which was standing at a cable's length from shore. Mikha was simply crazy with fear. He thought he was defending himself.

By some fluke of chance, it was right after Mikha's shots that the cruiser ceased fire and put out to sea. From that day on, all Poti regarded Mikha as a hero. But Gabunia knew that Mikha was an arrant coward, and not to be depended on. He had only offered to steal the station bell as an excuse for getting out of the forest onto higher ground. The station would not be flooded.

And that redheaded Englishman must have got drunk in town, and got stuck somewhere with the new part for the excavator.

"And here I stand wasting time!" Gabunia started. It seemed to him that an hour must have passed in inactivity. Actually, his thoughts had occupied no more than a minute or two.

"The workshop, first of all. Where can I find some bronze?"

A hot pain shot through Gabunia's leg bones, and sent a shudder up his spine. He staggered out to the porch.

He glanced to the west. Impenetrable murk hung above the forest. The trees were pale with fear. The alder leaves had lost their colour. Far in the distance, the earth heaved and groaned. An ominious rumbling approached, as if the oceans were marching on Colchis. A wild flash of lightning stabbed the swamps.

Gabunia's teeth were chattering. His head began to shake. An icy cold crept slowly, slowly to his brain. The shivers! It was this he feared worst of all.

Darkness was falling rapidly, but not a single lamp shone in the barracks. The workers were all at the canal.

Gabunia set out for the workshop. Somebody called his name. He looked around. The darkness was thickening. The wind had sprung up again, driving before it flocks of grey clouds and dry leaves.

Gabunia pressed his hands to his head, forcibly suppressing its tremor. He peered into the murk, and breathed a sigh of relief. It was Nevskaya. Her boots were slashed by lianas, her waterproof torn. She was breathing heavily.

"I was afraid I wouldn't make it from the station," she said. Then, with a nod at the advancing cloud: "I just can't bear to look at it. It makes my blood run cold."

Gabunia smiled weakly.

"You'd better go to my place," he told her. "That barrack over there, with the aerial."

"You've got the fever," said Nevskaya. "Why isn't there anybody around?"

"They're all at the canal. I'm afraid the embankments may go. The excavator's out of order. That idiot Sima got stuck in town with a part we need. I'll be back in a minute. You picked a bad time to come."

Gabunia noticed the sudden stiffening of Nevskaya's lips. He realised that he had hurt her feelings. How untimely and foolish!

"Go straight inside," he told her, almost shouting. "Wait for me there. I'll be right back."

Nevskaya turned away. Her brows were knit, and her lips trembled. Did that lanky youngster think she couldn't work in time of danger just as well as anyone? Ridiculous Caucasian chivalry!

She stopped beside the barrack to look at the canal—a broad ribbon cutting through the virgin forest, fifty kilometres long. The water reflected a heavy sky, banked high with clouds.

A bird flew past, with a wailing cry. It flew so low that its wing brushed Nevskaya's shoulder. The bird was hurrying to the mountains, seeking safety from the storm.

Nevskaya went indoors. A spirit lamp was burning in Gabunia's room, spreading a bluish light. Nevskaya looked around. Books, barometers, heavy swamp boots, maps. A small bust of Lenin on a rough wooden shelf.

A window banged to, then swung open again. The forest swayed and murmured. The treetops were bent by the wind.

Gabunia came in. A nervous tic distorted his features. His cheeks were ashen grey. His eyes glittered.

"Listen," he said. His speech was rapid and indistinct. "Only a hundred Mingrelian workers. . . . Yes, only a hundred workers, and you and me, to save all this section of Colchis from flood. Not another soul . . . in tens of kilometres . . . even more. . . . The excavator's out of order. . . . All we have is our hands. There isn't any bronze. The sailor can't get here now. It'll start to pour in ten minutes. Can you hold out?"

"If you didn't have the fever, you wouldn't ask such questions," returned Nevskaya mildly. "There's nothing to be afraid of. Everything will turn out all right."

Gabunia laughed sourly.

"Nothing to be afraid of?" he asked. "I must say, I like your confidence! Well then, let's get going."

There was a flash of lightning. The swift glare caught the bust of Lenin, on its rough wooden shelf. Lenin's eyes were screwed up in the faintest smile. He was looking quizzically at Gabunia.

Gabunia clutched at the edge of his desk. He was faint and dizzy.

"Bronze!" He spoke so low and huskily that Nevskaya heard only a hoarse sigh. "Bronze! What a fool I've been!"

He seized the bust, and laughed aloud. Nevskaya watched him anxiously. She was afraid he had gone mad.

Outside there was wind and darkness, and a light drizzle of rain. The downpour was still delayed.

"It's got to be melted, cast, and turned. That will take more than three hours, but there's nothing else we can do," said Gabunia slowly,

101

gently fingering the bust. "He'd have done the same, in my place."

"Who'd have done the same?" asked Nevskaya.

Gabunia did not answer, but strode quickly out of the room. He went straight to the workshop, and dropped the bust carefully into the glowing furnace.

The two Mingrelian mechanics glanced at Gabunia and turned away. The fire threw a flickering light on their clouded brows.

Gabunia issued brief orders. The part must be prepared and brought to the excavator, come what may.

"Ho!" said the elder of the mechanics, nodding. "We'll take care of it, comrade. Don't you worry."

As though released by the mechanic's words, the rain came rushing down. It poured from the sky in even sheets, with the dull roar of a waterfall. At twenty paces nothing could be seen.

Gabunia turned back to the barrack for Nevskaya, spluttering and choking in the tepid, bitter water. The wet soil was slippery underfoot. Gabunia cursed. It seemed to him that the Black Sea had risen to the skies, to come pouring down on the earth for forty days and forty nights.

Nevskaya sat waiting for Gabunia. The rain drummed on the roof and poured in ink-black torrents down the windowpanes.

Nevskaya lit the oil lamp. The telephone rang. A voice cried excitedly in the receiver:

"Qualoni calling! The water's coming down the mountains. It's something fearful. Have you got the fifth reach manned?"

"Yes, yes!" shouted Nevskaya, but there was no reply.

She hung up the receiver. From this moment on, she realised, they were cut off from the outside world—Gabunia, his workers, and herself, a tiny handful of humans lost among the swamps and forests. No help could reach them.

The storm raged on, growing steadily wilder. Its voice dropped to an ever lower pitch. Now and again the clouds would flash up with a grim reflection of lightning, and thunder would roll, stumbling over the mountain peaks.

It took Gabunia and Nevskaya half an hour to get to the fifth reach.

Pitch darkness. The roar of the storm, and the guttural shouts of the workers. No lanterns. There was a searchlight on the excavator, but the excavator was out of order.

They worked by sense of touch. They wheezed and spat, and shovelled like soldiers entrenching themselves under scathing enemy fire. There was no earth, no air, no sky, no forest—nothing but slippery, primeval chaos.

The canal roared furiously. Gabunia lit his flashlight and directed its ray to a measuring rod stuck into the bed of the canal. The water was rushing past in great, turbid waves. It carried broken trees and uprooted stumps.

"Mikha!" cried Gabunia. "How's it rising?"

"Two centimetres a minute, *katso*," called Mikha, through the darkness. He sent a dim flashlight ray down the side of the canal. The water was two metres below the top of the embankment.

Gabunia made rapid calculations. An hour and a half, and the water here would overflow, wash away the embankments and pour into the forest, making a dirty lake of all that section of Colchis known as Horga.

If only the rain would not get any heavier!

Gabunia was trembling with cold. The water streamed down his tarpaulin coat, and squelched in his boots. He pulled off his cap and threw it away into the mud. Soaking wet, it was only an oppressive weight on his head.

Nevskaya did not know how much time passed before she heard the strange rumbling and hissing in the canal. She flung earth with her spade with the same obdurate fury as the workers around her. The hair falling over her face made it hard to breathe. She brushed it back with a clay-grimed hand. The clay made it stick, and things were easier for a while.

She heard the strained breathing of the workers, the clatter of spades, the heavy impact of wet earth, Mikha's shouts and Gabunia's swift, guttural orders. Sometimes the wind and rain drove straight against her, and she slipped and fell into the liquid mud.

The water gnawed at the embankments, and all the work seemed in vain.

And suddenly, that ominous, seething hiss in the canal. Gabunia turned his light on the measuring rod. The foam-covered water was rising tempestuously.

"It's a boom!" he yelled. "The driftwood's caught!"

He plunged headlong to the wooden boat sliding, erect, down the clay side of the embankment, as little boys slide down ice hills in the North. Mikha dashed after him, with a few of the workers.

"Axes!" Gabunia shouted.

The Mingrelians worked on, never pausing. The boat tore loose and disappeared into the darkness.

"If only they manage in time! If only they manage in time," muttered Nevskaya, savagely flinging earth.

The water mounted. A belated flash of lightning cut the murk.

Nevskaya glimpsed the grey oceans pouring down from the skies, the workers, clay-besmeared, ankle-deep in water—the fierce current licking at the embankments. She thought she saw water pouring over the top in several places.

A long roll of thunder passed from the sea to the mountains. It shook up the sky, and the rain grew still heavier. Somewhere far off, the workers sent up a shout. A black shadow ran past, feet squelching loudly in the sticky clay. A young boy working at Nevskaya's side threw down his spade and burst into tears.

"He's gone! It's no use!" a dull voice cried.

Axes sounded down the canal. Gabunia and his men were breaking up the boom.

"What's up?" shouted Nevskaya.

"Someone fell in," answered a voice in hasty Russian. "He's gone. Work, girl. No time to talk!"

The men's breathing was heavy as the death rattle. The earth stuck to their spades like glue. Nevskaya's head began to swim.

She heard Gabunia's voice. He had returned. He was speaking cheerfully to the workers, actually joking! The boom was broken, but the water continued to rise.

Gabunia climbed to the top of the embankment. The water flowed twenty centimetres from the rim. Gabunia listened intently, hoping that the rain might be growing lighter. But it roared on as before.

Gabunia walked slowly along the embankment, until his foot caught in a slight depression. Water was running through it. Every thought disappeared but one: here, here was the spot where the embankment would give!

"*Habarda*!" shouted Gabunia. "Mikha! Call the men up here! Quick!"

Mikha came running up, and fired a shot into the air—the emergency signal. The workers hurried to Gabunia, lashing out with their spades at the clinging lianas that barred the way.

Gabunia turned his face towards the invisible sea, whence the storm had descended. He clenched his teeth, and shook his fist in the darkness.

"I'll stop you yet, you devil," he said, and laughed. The malaria muddled his brain, and he was near to delirium.

The workers were rapidly filling in the breach. Mikha fired again, a few paces away. He had found a second breach, deeper than the first.

"It's no use," Gabunia muttered, straining to pull his feet free from the sucking clay. He could not walk. He swayed, and crashed down into the liquid mud. He tried to lean on his arms. They slipped and would not hold him. With a last desperate effort, Gabunia tore himself free. But his legs would not obey. He lay flat on the ground and cursed. The fever tossed his limbs as the water in the canal tossed the floating driftwood.

"They've all got malaria. . . . Heroes," he murmured, as his eyes closed. "Mikha didn't let me down."

He heard a third shot. Somebody stumbled against him, and cried out. He thought it was Nevskaya. His breath came in hoarse gulps. His mouth was full of clay and dirty water. Somebody lifted him to a sitting position.

Then he heard desperate yells, and the heavy squelching of many running feet. The embankments had given, he thought indifferently. Now the wet clay would suck him under, and the water would bury him.

He opened his eyes, and started violently. A blinding white star was moving towards him from the forest, with a clatter and clanging of iron.

The searchlight!

Gabunia staggered to his feet. He did not notice the gentle supporting hands that helped him up. He stared at the star and wept. He was not ashamed. The malaria and this insane night had sapped his strength to the core. Anyway who could see the tears when his face was so smeared with clay?

The excavator crawled rapidly towards the fifth reach. Great mounds of clay collected on its treads. It rattled its chains and rumbled like a battery of heavy guns. Its dazzling searchlight blazed far aloft.

There was a hiss of escaping steam, a tremendous roar of exertion.

The workers made way. The gigantic scoop passed swiftly overhead and discharged its heavy load of clay. The breach was stopped.

The workers' ecstatic shouts drowned out the din of the storm.

Gabunia saw uplifted arms, pale faces, streaming tarpaulins. He saw an old Mingrelian reach out trembling hands towards the machine. He saw Sima—stripped to the waist, his jaws clenched, and a crimson seam cutting across the three dark spots on his chest. Sima's muscles swelled with effort as he worked the levers. His face was changed beyond recognition: the cheeks pale, the skin stretched taut over bulging jaws, the eyes but narrow slits.

For one brief instant Sima dropped the levers to wave his hand in greeting. Without the shadow of a smile, he cried in English:

"Hullo! Ladies and gentlemen, the show goes on!"

The workers swung their spades. The work went on with renewed energy.

The Mingrelian mechanic jumped off the excavator and joined Gabunia.

"The Englishman beat us to it," he said. "He came running out of the woods like a mad jackal, and started up the machine. I tell you, *katso*, I don't know how he got here. Half naked and bleeding all over!"

Gabunia smiled. And suddenly, he heard—silence. He felt the stillness before he realised its cause.

The rain had stopped. An unearthly hush hung over the forest.

Gabunia staggered and lost consciousness.

The Last Flood

Frosted bulbs glowed at the port radio station. A cricket-like chirping issued from the set. The operator frowned and twitched his shoulders irritably, transmitting a message from the chief of the port:

"The Rion and Caparcha have overflowed. Their waters have joined and deluged the town. Only the port remains unflooded. The water is rising. It is almost a metre high in the streets. Send ships and flotage at once to rescue the population."

Chup shrugged his shoulders. A furious storm was raging outside. Black waves dashed over the jetty, buffeting the Greek-steamer that tossed at anchor in the harbour. A pouring rain rattled machine-gun fire on the corrugated iron warehouses.

What ship could hazard the voyage from Batum to Poti? What flotage could the chief of the port have in mind? Even ocean liners would fear to venture out in such a storm.

Chup was out of sorts. He had had a crazy day. Christophoridi had not shown his nose since morning, and Yolochka was all alone. Chup had given her a story book, but he knew very well that she was not reading. She was afraid, and now and then she cried. The captain shivered when he thought of it. How could she help being afraid, with the elements rowdying it right outside the window? The house was barely out of reach of the beating waves.

"Just wait till I get hold of you, you little rascal!" thought the captain, recalling Christophoridi's desertion. He sighed. The devil's own day! On his way to the radio station, he had come across two snakes. Driven by the flood, the creatures had sought refuge in the port. They hid among the piles of manganese ore.

Chup hated creeping, crawling things of every kind, especially snakes and toads. He could not even bear the sight of pickled lampreys. Next thing, he supposed, the wild boar from the swamps would come galloping into the port!

"Well, how's the chief?" asked the operator, his message dispatched. "Getting nervous?"

"He's all right," Chup replied. "Keeping his pecker up."

Chup had yet another worry. A felucca loaded with mandarins had smashed up against the breakwater that afternoon. The only person on board, an old Turk, had been promptly rescued. He was a cantankerous old fellow, this Turk, and his accident had sent him off his rocker. He demanded that Chup send a boat out to salvage his mandarins, which were dancing on the waves all over the harbour. He swore he would drag Chup to court for their loss.

The sailors on the Greek steamer tried to catch the mandarins, throwing out pails tied to long ropes. Their ship made Chup think of a floating tavern, it was so filthy, and smelled so of mutton and coffee. Tossed by the waves, it kept tilting up its squalid, scuffled deck.

Chup disliked Greek ships in general, partly because they were dirty, and partly because their sailors had such a passion for inappropriate colour schemes. On a sky-blue smokestack they were liable to slap down a huge scarlet rose, perhaps a whole garland of roses. In any case, those Greek smokestacks were always daubed with some kind of festoonery or other. The only thing lacking was Cupids. They drove Chup wild.

Sailors, did they call themselves? Lemonade vendors!

The telephone rang. Chup picked up the receiver. A report from the manganese pier. No light showed from the winking beacon at the end of the jetty, where the waves were leaping over the barrier with feline ease.

Chup pulled on his black uniform coat and went out. Was there to be no end to his troubles? Suppose some fool ship tried to enter the harbour at night, to get out of the storm? With the beacon not working, it might miss the passage and land on the rocks.

Repairing the light now would be next to impossible. The first wave would swamp any boat that tried to approach the jetty.

Chup went out to the end of the pier. The beacon was alight. He watched it for some time. It went out and gave no light for more than five minutes. The proper interval between flashes was ten seconds. Obviously, there was something wrong with the mechanism.

Then the light began to flash again, just as it should. And then again it went out. What devil's work was this?

Raising his binoculars, he saw a human figure crouching on the banistered platform just below the light.

Chup really lost his temper. The whole port was going to the dogs! What was anyone doing on the beacon? There could be only one explanation. The fellow had gone out to the end of the jetty, and got so absorbed in something there ("Wonder what anyone could find so interesting on the jetty, with a storm on," thought Chup.) that he had

failed to notice the increasing agitation of the sea.
When he turned to go back, he had found the
waves surging over the jetty behind him and the
road to land cut off. And so, for safety, he had
climbed the iron ladder to the beacon platform.
The waves could not reach him there. The
figure on the platform was small, a veritable
dwarf.

"Who the devil is it?" Chup muttered. "Does
the damn fool want a shipwreck to his credit? It's
a disgrace to the port!"

Be that as it may, however, the fellow had to
be taken off.

There were only two skiffs left. All the rest
had been sent to town to help the population.
Chup took one of them and headed for the beacon, with two sailors at the oars. All the way out
he cursed the "thrice-deadly Caucasus", with its
endless rains and all the problems of working
there.

With great difficulty, the boat was brought up
alongside the beacon. The captain, cursing like
mad, pulled a shivering, whimpering Christophoridi down from the platform.

"You little rascal! Killing's too good for you!
Fishing again?"

Christophoridi shivered and cried. The captain
took him home, gave him dry clothes, and poured
a stiff dose of vodka down his throat. Then
he ordered the boy to put the kettle on, and
left.

Christophoridi was still whimpering. He had
spent eight hours on the beacon, eight hours that
were to remain one of his life's most fearful
memories.

He had gone fishing early in the morning. The scad rose to his bait as never before. The harbour was calm, but behind him the sea was roaring. After a while, the spray began to fly over his head. He scrambled to his feet. And then he saw the waves cascading over the jetty, at the point where it turned sharply in towards the shore. There was no way of escape. Christophoridi was cut off entirely from the world.

He was afraid. He was frightened by the tumult of the waves, by their seething fury. They seemed determined to wreck the jetty and make short work of Christophoridi.

He climbed to the platform of the beacon, where the lamp protected him from the spray. The storm was deafening. He had never known the sea could raise such a furious din.

Leaving Christophoridi with Yolochka, Chup returned to his duties in the port. Soon afterwards he climbed into a motor launch and set out for town.

The water was rising. The power station was dead, and the town lay in darkness. Only the green lights in the port were shining. They hung over deserted piers overgrown with grass and dotted with puddles of salt water.

The launch had to fight its way across the central fairway of the Rion where the water was humped high, as though over the back of some gigantic serpent. Puffing and sputtering, it turned down the inundated streets.

Quiet reigned in the town, despite the flood. Most of the houses stood on piles, so that only a few families had needed to be moved from their homes to the cathedral.

It was the cattle that had given the greatest trouble. Cows and horses had had to be dragged to the upper floors of the houses—a risky operation, that caused no few tears from the townswomen and no few curses from the sailors sent to their assistance.

The rain grew lighter. High-wheeled carts floated down the streets. The water lay motionless, carpeted with leaves and petals. Frogs croaked on windowsills and fence posts. They sprang into the water when the motor launch came flying through the flooded avenues.

A fat fish leapt out of the water by the "Have a Bite" *duhan*. The captain regretted that he had left Christophoridi behind. What a time the boy could have had, fishing out of his own bedroom window!

The town presented a picture hardly to be believed. The water glittered and played in the glare of the launch headlights. Fish darted to and fro beneath the surface, and roses nodded above. Light waves washed up against dark windowpanes.

Kakhiani called to Chup from one of the windows, and asked him to look out for Pakhomov. The old man had rushed off to the colmatage workings as soon as the flood began.

Day was breaking when the launch reached the colmatage district. The workings stood like a fortress, surrounded on all sides by water. The sluice gates were open. The embankments stood only a few centimetres above the flood but they were unharmed.

Pakhomov stood near the first sluice gate, with a group of workers. He looked out over the boundless, muddy lake that spread to the very horizon, looked out over the deluged land, and smiled.

"What are you smiling about?" asked Chup. To himself, he thought: "Queer bird! What a time for smiling!"

"The embankments have held," replied Pakhomov. "The workings aren't damaged. But I'm afraid it's hell out at Gabunia's, in Chaladidi. The current there was something fierce."

"Yes, it must be pretty bad," the captain mumbled. He felt uneasy at the thought of the two children, all alone at home.

Pakhomov refused to go back to town. He pointed to the sun rising slowly through a blanket of fog. The land flashed white beneath it, a land transformed into a great lagoon.

"What a sight!" he said. "It's a pity, really. A month from now we'll bring the canal through the dunes, and floods will vanish forever from the country's chronicles. You're witnessing the last flood. Mind my word!"

"All I can say is, thank goodness," Chup returned. "Cast off, boys!"

Yolochka did not sleep for ever so long. She sat up in her bed, reading the story book Chup had left her. Christophoridi was fast asleep in the kitchen, warm and snug under a blanket and an old coat of the captain's. He was snoring dreadfully.

Yolochka read a story about a young girl who went to visit an old toymaker. The toymaker's room was so small that the train of the girl's beautiful holiday dress could not get in.

The toymaker was blind. He said to the girl:

"I can tell that you are smiling, and I know that joy awaits you. I wish I were not blind. Then I might look into your happy eyes, and rejoice."

A fog horn shrieked hysterically from the Greek steamer in the harbour. Yolochka jumped and began to cry. Mummy had been away since yesterday. Chup was gone. And besides, she was so sorry for the poor toymaker. Why did he have to be blind?

Yolochka buried her face in the pillow, and cried and cried. And finally she fell asleep. She dreamed that the sun came into her room, only then it wasn't the sun at all, but a young girl in a glittering dress. And the train of her dress just couldn't fit into the room. It murmured silkily outside the open door. And the girl said, in Mummy's voice:

"I'm so grateful to you, Chup, for taking care of Yolochka. I've never known a man like you!"

Through the open door the murmuring sea shimmered in an ever changing pattern of blue and green, like a peacock's tail.

An Eye for an Eye

Nobody could accuse Vano Akhmeteli, postgraduate student of the Fur Institute, of cowardice or irresolution. When Vano learned that topographer Abashidze and his men had set out to chart the Nedoard canal, he made up his mind to join them there.

It was around the Nedoard canal, the most dangerous and impassable spot in the jungle, that the nutria should breed best. There were thick growths of rushes there, white water lilies, and yellow flag—the nutria's best-loved foods.

Vano had never been to the canal. This, he felt, was sheer neglect of duty: not a single word, in all his reports, about the very finest nutria district!

He decided to head for the canal from the direction of the railroad. He was sure he could make it, as the recent foehn had dried the soil.

He left town on foot, equipped with a compass, a gun, and a map of his own making. In his knapsack he carried four days' supply of food.

Just outside the town, he was overtaken by Sima, the redheaded English sailor. They strode on together for several kilometres, talking mainly with the help of their hands. Then the sailor turned off towards Chaladidi.

Sima showed Vano some copper engine parts he was carrying. He whistled and clicked his tongue, and did his best to imitate the movements of an excavator. Vano understood. The sailor must be working at Gabunia's, running an excavator.

"He's a queer sort," Vano reflected. "What makes him tramp thirty-five kilometres on foot when there's a train tomorrow morning?"

They parted friends.

Vano took a boat across the Rion, and plunged into the jungle.

The air hung dense and stifling, tangled in the branches of the trees. The swamps exhaled sourish, stupefying odours. The earth rocked underfoot. Tall hornbeams shuddered from root to crown at Vano's footsteps. They frightened him. It seemed as though they must come crashing down.

"You're going to root up all this, and burn it," said Vano, addressing an invisible Gabunia.

117

When a man finds himself all alone in the forest, he will often talk to himself, or whistle, or sing, or break dry twigs from the trees with a swinging stick. The sounds he makes seem to create a broad defensive belt around him.

In the midst of the swamps, Vano came upon a half-obliterated trail. He followed it. Every now and then his feet would sink deep in mud; but he kept strictly to the rule old hunters had taught him: not one step off the trail! Treacherous quagmires spread their poisonous green on either side.

Sometimes lianas would catch at Vano's pack. He would have to slip the pack from his shoulders and hack it free with his knife. The crooked liana thorns were too strong for his fingers.

Towards evening Vano reached the bank of the canal. He gave a shrill whistle of pleasure. It was only three kilometres, now, to the point where the canal spread out into a lake. That was where the nutria bred.

Vano decided to rest. The air had grown thick as strong, fresh tea. It had to be pumped into the lungs with painful effort.

Vano dropped his knapsack, then stiffened suddenly to attention. An artillery volley rumbled in the west. He glanced at the sky. There were no clouds.

Another volley, louder than before. Vano's heart began to thump, and he cursed himself for being a coward. Quickly, he climbed the nearest alder.

It was no reassuring vista that spread before him when he reached the top. Cloud was piling up, far over the sea, slashed by darting lightning, as black marble is slashed with silvery veins. A cool, fresh, rainy breath reached Vano's nostrils.

Vano climbed down. What was he to do? There was no use turning back. He could never make the nearest village before the rain came down. Gabunia had told him once about the ruins of a Roman fortress, somewhere along the Nedoard canal. Perhaps those ruins would offer safety against the flood.

Flood was inevitable. As soon as the downpour reached the mountains, Colchis would be deluged by thousands of muddy torrents.

Vano made up his mind to push ahead, though he had no idea where the fortress might be. Sitting still was impossible. A queer feeling gnawed at the pit of his stomach.

He set out. The path was lit by frequent flashes of lightning. The cloud crept slowly, ominously eastward. Now and again the thunder rumbled forth, dull and protracted, like gigantic tigers roaring from the depths of the forest.

Never had Vano felt so helpless before the dread majesty of that which was taking place in the heavens.

He stopped frequently to look up at the cloud, hoping that it might avoid the canal. But each time he realised with growing alarm, that the cloud was coming straight for him.

It was a dull, heavy black, dripping tangled shreads of smoke, dust, and rain. At the horizon it thickened into impenetrable night.

Every new flash of lightning sent a shiver down Vano's back. He wished the rain would come. Jackals were laughing and crying in the thickets.

Vano saw a white ball of flame shoot past,

sweeping the treetops. A light smoke seemed to be rising from the foliage.

Pressing up against an alder trunk, he yelled. A peal of thunder split the sky in two. But Vano heard the sound of his own voice, and it calmed his fear. He decided to call once more.

He shouted. A faint human voice responded. Vano took it for an echo. He shouted again, and again came a familiar voice in answer. Vano thought he recognised Abashidze.

He strode rapidly down the path, shouting again and again. Each time, the answer sounded nearer.

It was very dark. The rain had not yet begun in earnest. Only now and again a heavy drop would strike against the foliage. Vano whistled and shouted. His fear had vanished.

All at once the answering voice sounded very close, just a few paces ahead. A human figure appeared, vaguely outlined in the darkness. Lightning flashed, and Vano recognised Gulia.

"A-a-ah," said Gulia grimly. "So it's you. The rats' watchman!"

Vano did not answer.

Gulia strode closer.

"Why so quiet?" he went on. "Why don't you say something? In court your tongue tripped like a bird in a cage."

Vano forced himself to speak.

"What do you want?" he asked.

He would have liked to slip the gun from his shoulder, but realised that that might be the end of him.

"The old folk say, an eye for an eye," returned Gulia hoarsely. "The old folk teach us the right way to live. What do you think about that, youngster?"

Lightning flashed again, and there was a peal of thunder. Vano saw Gulia's keen, gaunt features, and the mocking gleam in his eyes.

"Gulia!" he said, trying to smile. "What do you want of me, Gulia? The engineers have come, and things will be bad for you and me. They'll chop down the forests. You're a hunter. Your livelihood will be gone. And me—all my work will be wasted. I've fussed over those blasted beasts for three whole years. You and I, *katso*, we mustn't quarrel."

Gulia was silent. Vano's heart thumped heavily.

"Why should a wise man pick quarrels with fools," said Gulia at last. "You're a fool. I don't give a damn about these rotting forests. I'm no hunter now. I'm a working man. The old folk teach us the right way to live. And the young folk, too. Only not your kind. Why are you trembling, *katso*? You wanted to lock me up in jail, but Gabunia gave me work to do. You thought like a fool, and Gabunia thought like a wise man."

Gulia laughed.

"Why are you trembling, *katso*?" he repeated. "You're afraid. I'm not going to kill you. Come along."

He turned and strode off, leading the way.

Soon they reached the ruined fortress. Abashidze greeted them joyously.

They spent over twenty-four hours in a tent set up on the fortress walls. The rain poured and poured. Water lay on every side, a boundless sea.

Vano was ready to die of shame. He could not look Gulia in the face. The savage hunter had proved wiser than Vano. "I don't give a damn about these rotting forests," he had said. And he was right.

Vano did not notice the passage of time. Dully indifferent, he left the canal together with Abashidze's group. They headed for the Rion.

It took them all day to get there. At every step, they sank deep in the water-logged soil. The workers had heavy measuring rods to carry. The forest was deserted and still. Not a single bird could be heard. All living things had left the jungle. Even the jackals' howls had ceased. Only the frogs leaped from underfoot, and fat water snakes swam lazily through the flooded swamps.

"An accursed spot," thought Vano. How could he have fought to preserve this world of swamps, miasma, and rotting forests, this world of fevers and floods, of corn and bitter peat?

To hell with it! One orange was worth a hundred mangy jackals.

Kakhiani Reports

Writing reports was always hard work for Kakhiani. But once he did send in a report, it was always a model of mathematical precision.

"A violent southwesterly storm," wrote Kakhiani, "washed up a huge wall of sand in the mouth of the river Caparcha, three kilometres from Poti, and dammed the river. At the same time a heavy rain began to fall. It continued for over six hours.

"The rivers Rion, Caparcha, Tsiva, and Hopi, not to mention dozens of minor streams, impetuously overflowed their banks and flooded the entire sea-coast section of Colchis.

"In the city streets the water rose to the level of the first floor. Wild beasts, frightened by the flood, rushed into the town and onto the island where the port is located. The island was not flooded. There were particularly many snakes.

"The flood damaged our drainage projects considerably; but the harm done was less than might have been expected in view of the violence of the rain.

"On the central canal at Chaladidi, the water threatened to wash away the embankments and destroy the results of three years' persistent labour. Thanks to the heroism of the workers and engineer Gabunia, catastrophe was averted.

"The work had to be done by night, and by hand. The only available excavator was out of action for lack of spare parts. An attempt was made to cast the needed parts at the camp workshop, but this failed for lack of time. The situation was saved by the excavator operator, Jim Birling, an Englishman. By night, through the frightful downpour, he brought the parts from Chaladidi station on foot.

"He had to push through the forest. He was wounded by lianas and lost much blood. In spite of everything, however, he brought his machine out to the threatened reach just in time, and set to work with splendid coolness to repair the breaches in the embankments.

"Engineer Gabunia directed all the work, although he was gripped by an attack of tropical malaria. He caught a severe chill, and is now at the Poti hospital with pneumonia. Yefrem Chanturia, a worker, lost his life during the night work.

"The colmatage workings came out with flying

colours. Neither sluices nor embankments suffered any damage. Engineer Pakhomov remained at the workings without a break for some twenty-four hours, directing safety measures.

"A group of topographers under Abashidze had set out for the district of the Nedoard canal. For three days they were considered lost. Searching parties could find no trace of them, as it is impossible to reach the canal without experienced guides. Gulia, the only man who knows these swamps, had left together with Abashidze. Yesterday evening the topographers returned to Chaladidi. With them was Vano Akhmeteli, a postgraduate student of the Fur Institute. They had rescued him in the forest.

"Chief botanist Lapshin reports that the plantations suffered little or no damage.

"I am now taking measures to clear away the sand at the mouths of the rivers, which is one of the chief causes of flood."

Kakhiani frowned as he wrote the last words. The report seemed to him far too poetic. After some reflection, he crossed out the words "impetuously overflowed their banks" and "frightful downpour". There were no other suspicious turns of speech that he could see.

"Damn it all," said Kakhiani. "It's an infectious business—poetry!"

Concerning Insurance Companies

Gabunia's recovery was slow. For several days he was unconscious. All that remained in his memory were the doctor's whiskers, tickling his chest, a cool hand on his forehead; the captain's

124

husky voice, sunk to a whisper, and an endless procession of stars. The stars kept flying past his windows towards the mountains.

Through his delirium, Gabunia struggled to work out what was happening. Evidently, the stars were falling in the mountains like rain. Every night they poured down upon Colchis in a deluge like no one ever seen upon earth. In place of water, the land was flooded with white flame. It rose breast-high, and Gabunia's heart was consumed in fire, and the pain was beyond all belief.

"*Habarda*!" Gabunia shouted. "All out to the fifth reach, *katso*!"

The doctor shook his head. Gabunia's ravings were no good sign.

Again, Gabunia thought he was pushing through the jungle with Chup, towards a blue strip that marked the dawn. The cool breeze of daybreak fanned his cheeks and ruffled his hair. He and Chup were looking for Sima. They could not find him anywhere.

Then Chup dug into his pocket and brought out a safety-razor blade.

"We won't find him in these parts," he said. "We've got to change the landscape."

He inserted the razor blade into the strip of dawn that shone between earth and sky, and turned it like a key in a lock. The sky swung back with a click, and a new land appeared. They were no longer in the jungle. They were on the Neva embankment. White night gleamed over the black water. Bird cherries drooped, shivering, over the iron rail.

Again Chup clicked back the sky, and now they were on a moving steamer, and the water below was gay with reflected lights. A city was piled up on the distant shore. It looked like a heap of old glass. It shone and glittered. Chup whispered in Gabunia's ear that this was Venice, and that here they could buy from smugglers the seeds for an orange the size of a melon, to bring home as a gift to Lapshin.

"The devil take Lapshin," cried Gabunia. He came to and groaned.

He knew that the nightmare would come again and again, before the night was over. It wore him out. He sprang up from his bed to run away from it, and the nurses found it no easy task to press him back to the pillows.

The quinine roared in his ears like the storm. It seemed to him that an unceasing tempest raged over the sea. He stared stupidly at the violet sky outside his windows, trying to understand how could there be a storm, when his eyes were smarting from the glare of the sun?

After the crisis came more bad days. Gabunia felt nothing but weariness, a profound and never before experienced weariness, so that even to whisper or to raise his hand involved exhausting effort.

For the next few days he slept almost all the time.

He was wakened by heavy footsteps. Even before his eyes were open, Gabunia guessed that the person in his room had never had much occasion to walk on tiptoe. One foot would come down, and the floor would creak. A strained silence would follow, broken only by laboured breathing. Then the other foot would be moved, with the same clumsy caution.

Gabunia opened his eyes and saw Sima's broad back in the doorway. The sailor was leaving. He balanced painfully on his toes, and the back of his neck was red with effort.

On the table by Gabunia's bed stood a blue tin box of pipe tobacco—Sima's one and only treasure. Gabunia knew how the sailor valued this tobacco. He smoked it only once a day, contenting with ordinary makhorka the rest of the time.

Gabunia did not call to Sima. A lump had risen to his throat, and he could not speak.

Next day, towards evening, Nevskaya came in. She brought Gabunia a new fruit grown at the experimental gardens. Feijoa, it was called.

Gabunia tried one of the dull, light-green ovals. It tasted of pineapple and wild strawberries.

"It smells of the tropics," he whispered. "Delicious!"

The feijoa smelled of the light summer breeze that blows from the sea in early morning or an orchard after the rain.

"This is a rare fruit," said Nevskaya. "It contains a great deal of iodine, and it could be used to treat sclerosis."

She talked absently of one plant and another, watching Gabunia all the time. A piano sounded upstairs, probably in the doctor's rooms. Nevskaya paused to listen.

Gabunia closed his eyes. He knew the melody. It was Lisa's aria, from *The Queen of Spades*:

There came a cloud, a thunder cloud. . . .

Nevskaya rose quickly, bent for an instant to smooth back Gabunia's damp hair, and left. In the doorway she turned and nodded silently.

Next day there was something of a row in the hospital. Chup and Sima came to see Gabunia. Something had hurt Sima's feelings, and the tall sailor seemed on the point of tears. His eyes blinked, and his breath came heavily. He was very annoyed.

Though Gabunia did not know English very well, he gathered, from Sima's stream of complaints, that the trouble had to do with an insurance company. Most of what Sima said, however, seemed to be crazy nonsense. And he called Mikha all the bad names he could think of.

Chup translated. It appeared that Sima had been unable to work for several days after the flood. His chest and arms had been badly torn by lianas when he pushed through the forest to the canal, and these scratches had swollen and begun to fester. Sima had stayed in town for five days, visiting the clinic for treatment.

On his return to the canal, Mikha told him that he would be paid for those five days out of the insurance fund. Sima called Mikha a bandit, and began to swing his fists. This wasn't England, he yelled. If anyone tried to bring the rotten English system here, he'd smash their face in for them.

Mikha turned tail and fled. Sima yelled on. Nobody had the right to insure Jim Birling without his consent. Insurance was a fraud and a cheat.

"He must have been under the influence," Chup added. "Maybe he'd had a pint of vodka."

Sima understood, and the blood rushed to his face. His life at sea had taught him the meaning of "vodka".

"No, no!" he cried, shaking his head in denial.

128

He pulled his jersey down and pointed to the three blue spots on his chest.

"That's what I got from your insurance companies," he said. "And it's enough for me. I don't want any more to do with any insurance company in the world."

And Sima told the story of the spots.

Before the war, Sima had enrolled as steersman on the steamer *Klondike*, sailing between Liverpool and Newfoundland, where, as every sailor knows, you can always expect storm, fog, and icebergs.

There is a beacon on Newfoundland called Lightwest. From a distance, it looks like a sailing ship, head on. It has a wide base and a squat white tower.

"That beacon was a wonderful place for wrecks," said Sima. "Captains would head straight for it, and land on the rocks. Then they'd write in their lying logs, 'The accident was caused by fog. The lookout took Lightwest beacon for a sailing vessel.'

"But that was all a fraud. They all knew perfectly well what Lightwest looked like, and they used it to wreck their ships without getting in trouble. What for, you ask? Why, because it's the custom in the West, to insure a ship that's on its last legs, then freight it with rubbish and take it out and sink it, to get the insurance money.

"We called the captain of the *Klondike* Dung Beetle, because his clothes were always filthy. He never brushed his pants in his life, and if anyone told him, he'd say, 'What do you think I am, a nigger, to brush my own pants?' Well, this Dung Beetle landed the ship with a bang on the rocks at Lightwest, and thought he'd pulled it off brilliantly.

"He yelled to the radio room for a SOS. And that was where the trouble started. The radio was out of order. The operator sweated blood, but he couldn't do a thing. Dung Beetle got green around the gills.

"If that wasn't bad enough, there was a storm coming on from the ocean. Next day there was such a wind on our beam the riggings whined, and the pots in the galley raised a clatter. Dung Beetle saw he was in for it, and he looked as grim as death.

"The third day, the operator had a stroke of luck. He got his set fixed and sent off the SOS. Before the fourth day was over, the water was running across the decks. Then there was a frost.

"By evening the ship was a block of ice. The storm was getting worse.

"Next morning a ship came in sight. We all tumbled out on deck and lashed ourselves fast so we couldn't be washed overboard.

"The ship nosed around us for a while. Then it saw it couldn't do the job, and left. After that Dung Beetle got the fear of God in him. He confessed he'd put the ship on the rocks on purpose. He cursed the owner, and asked us to forgive him.

"We were too worn out to beat him up even.

"I lashed myself to the wheel in the pilot house. They dragged me out two days later, when the decks of the *Klondike* were level with the water. Three of the wheel spokes froze to my chest, and I left my skin on them.

"I can tell you, this was the first wreck at

Lightwest that didn't bring the owner anything. Dung Beetle said the same in court as he told us on the ship. He couldn't get out of it.

"After that he changed his job. Now he kills rats in the London port. Walks around with a basket and throws stale bread and arsenic in the rat holes.

"There! And you think after that anyone can make me believe in honest insurance companies? When I was in the hospital after the wreck, I said to myself, 'Well, Jim Birling, if you ever insure your life for as much as a thousand pounds, you'll be the worst fool in the Old World, and the New World too.' I've had enough of it!"

Sima banged the table for emphasis. Chup stared and guffawed. Even Gabunia laughed, for the first time since the flood.

Chup explained to Sima at some length the difference between insurance in England and insurance in the Soviet Union. Sima finally got the point, but at first he would not give in. He kept muttering that you were bound to get in a muddle if you used the same names for different things.

Sima was greatly embarrassed by his mistake, and left very soon. Chup remained with Gabunia.

Gabunia's illness started the captain off on the subject of malaria, and he rambled on and on.

"Under the tsar, the Poti garrison used to die out to a man of the fever every three years. How do you like that? That's what started the soldiers' songs about the 'deadly Caucasus'. Redhead says"—"Redhead" was Chup's name for the doctor—"Redhead says there's a special sort of fever in these parts. Swamp cachexia, they call it. Half

of your Mingrelian workers have it. You know
the way Mikha's always complaining. 'No high
temperature,' he says, 'and just the same they can
hardly walk.' In this cachexia, people's temperature drops below normal. That isn't your trouble.
You've got genuine Poti fever. And no wonder!
Decay all around you, and damp, and heat. It's
like West Africa."

"Have you ever been there?" asked Gabunia.

"Once or twice," the captain replied. "Incidentally, Negroes never get malaria. Malays get it,
and all the other peoples in the tropics. Only not
the Negroes. It's amazing! I asked Redhead why.
He says this parasite that gives you malaria develops inside your body, only it has to have ultraviolet rays to make it grow. But the Negroes' skins
are black, and the rays can't get in."

"You're inventing again, Chup," said Gabunia.
"I like your tales."

Chup gave him a foxy look.

"Inventing, you say?" he returned. "Ask Redhead, then. I won't take offence, seeing you're
too sick to know better!"

"Well, and what comes next?"

"It seems the quinine settles on the walls of
the blood vessels in a sort of thin film, and it
takes a long time to dissolve. The quinine keeps
out the ultraviolet rays. It cuts them off entirely.
The rays can't get in, and the parasites die. That's
why quinine's so effective. I had the yellow fever
myself, you know."

"Where?"

"Some islands in the Pacific. Believe it or not,
but all my memories of those islands are mixed up
with quinine. I swallowed quinine by the tea-

spoonful. I was deaf and half crazy, and I staggered like a drunk. If I ate bananas, the bananas tasted bitter. If I drank water, the water was bitter. My hands were blue. It was almost too much for me to get up from my chair and cross the cabin to my bunk. And the heat was just a fraud, it seemed to me. I knew in my mind the air was hot, but it felt like ice.

"Miasma, aroma, luxuriant growth.... Awful places, if you really get down to it. Degeneration. People stagger around with glassy eyes, groaning and shivering.

"Ugh!

"It's a good thing you're cleaning up this damned malaria country, making a new place out of it.

"In the old days, they fussed around with trifles. At the malaria office they'd stick up sheets of glass around the house, and smear them with glue. Then they'd look to see which glass collected the most mosquitoes. If there were more on the north glass, that meant the mosquitoes came from the north. If there were more on the east glass, the mosquitoes came from the east. Then they'd take their tins of kerosene and make off in that direction, and spray the swamps. Child's play."

Suddenly starting up, the captain exclaimed:

"Well, I've got to be going. I've been talking too much, fool that I am. You need rest and quiet."

Gabunia was sorry to see the captain leave. He would willingly have listened to his talk for hours, and have asked him all sorts of questions about what was going on "out there"—beyond the hospital walls.

Gulia asked Abashidze for some time off to go hunting. Abashidze threw him a suspicious look. His finger tips drummed on the edge of his drafting board.

"The jackal can't forget the swamps—is that it?" he asked ironically.

Gulia seemed embarrassed. He crushed and twisted his felt hat.

"For the last time, *katso*," he said. "I'm telling you the truth, as I'd tell you on my deathbed. It's the last time. There's a thing I have to do. Something very important, *katso*."

"What?"

"You'll soon find out."

"Go ahead," said Abashidze. "But see you get back in two days. We're going to survey the swamps along the Hopi."

Gulia stopped off at the camp workshop. His gun hammer needed repair. Squatting beside the mechanic, he watched the file slide back and forth across the silvery metal.

The glittering steel dust danced in a sunbeam that fell through a crack in the wall. Peering through this crack, Gulia saw the fresh earth of the canal embankment, and that heat-weary forest. Thin, shrivelled twigs drooped earthward from discouraged boughs.

"Ah, friend," said the mechanic. "What things we saw here when the water came from the mountains! Engineer Gabunia brought a bust and dropped it in the furnace. He told us to make an engine part out of it."

"A bust?" asked Gulia perplexedly.

"Of Lenin," said the mechanic, his voice dropping to a mysterious whisper. "They say he brought it with him from Leningrad to Tbilisi, and then here, and he was awfully sorry to lose it."

"What's a bust?" Gulia asked once more.

"It's like a little statue. They call it a bust."

Gulia shook his head. Yes, indeed, he knew. He had seen busts. He recalled the statue of the Roman woman. After a pause, he asked:

"You say he was very sorry?"

"Very, *katso*."

Gulia took up his gun. He paid the mechanic with a bunch of dry tobacco leaves, and left for the forest.

For two days he wandered among the swamps. On the third day he appeared at the "Have a Bite" *duhan* in Poti, and spent a long time in whispered conference with the *duhan* keeper. He had a sack with him, and there was something heavy in it.

It was a sunny morning, and the *duhan* looked festive. The fresh oils gleamed on Becho's painting, and the blue and yellow tints were reflected in the eyes of Gulia and the *duhan* keeper. This gave their conference an air of foxy merriment.

The *duhan* keeper wheezed and argued. He kept reaching out to feel the sack, and shaking his head. Then he and Gulia dragged the sack out to the shed.

Evening found Gulia at the hospital. Gabunia had already begun to walk about his room, clutching at walls and furniture for support.

Gulia entered as softly as a cat. His face expressed profound respect. He stopped in the doorway and bowed low to Gabunia. Dark silver gleamed in his bristly, close-cropped hair.

"*Gamarjoba*, comrade," he said to Gabunia, producing a large bundle from the bosom of his jacket. "Accept this gift from a simple man. Eat and be well."

Gabunia undid the heavy bundle. Within the wrappings lay a boar's ham, gleaming with golden fat. It smelled faintly of tar.

"Thanks, friend," said Gabunia, extending a hand to Gulia. "So you haven't dropped hunting yet?"

Gulia stiffened.

"I've dropped it," he replied. "This is my last boar. When you saved me from jail, I said to myself: 'The last boar you kill in the swamps will be your gift to engineer Gabunia, son of the old engine driver from Samtredi. He made a man of you.' This is my last boar. Death has come to the swamps, and life has come for humans. And there was another thing I wanted to say. The little statue that you had in your room. You dropped it in the fire. Were you very sorry?"

"Of course, *katso*."

"That's just what the mechanic said. Well, don't you feel bad about it. When you can walk again, and you have some free time, we'll go to the swamps for a day, you and me, and I'll show you something worth seeing. The swamps hide it from men. No one has seen it but me."

"What is it?"

"Don't be in such a hurry. You'll see. It's been lying in the swamp a thousand years."

Gulia laughed.

"I was ruler over the swamps," he said, "like

Prince Dadiani used to be over Mingrelia. I was master of the swamps. All I found in the swamps was my own. And this thing is mine too. I want to give it to you, because you're so fond of statues."

For all Gabunia's questions, Gulia would say no more about the thing that lay hidden in the swamp. He only shook his head in silence.

Then he returned to the *duhan*. Artem Korkia, Becho, and a few other friends had gathered there that evening to honour foreman Mikha, the bravest man in Poti. The tale of Mikha's heroism during the flood had travelled rapidly from mouth to mouth.

When Gulia entered, Artem Korkia raised his box-tree staff and cried:

"What's this I hear, *katso*? You've sold your hunting dog!"

"And today I sell my gun, old chatterbox," said Gulia, sitting down beside him. "What's the good of a gun to a working man? What he needs is skilful hands."

The White Feather

Six months ago, Lapshin and Nevskaya had disagreed as to where the new "White Hair" tea should be planted: on hillsides, or in hollows. Lapshin insisted that it should be planted in hollows, where the winds could not reach it. Nevskaya demanded that it be planted on hillsides. In hollows, she argued, it might suffer from the cold.

Test plantations were made both on hillsides and in hollows, and tended with the utmost care.

Their relative progress became a matter of public interest.

In the meantime, Lapshin had another disagreement, this time with engineer Gabunia.

Lapshin was determined to plant lemon groves on the soil drained by the main canal. Gabunia objected vigorously. To his mind, the soil bordering the canal was better suited for ramie.

Kakhiani intervened, and appealed to Moscow. Moscow decided in favour of ramie.

Then Nevskaya remarked that Lapshin would do well to take a refresher course. Lapshin took offence, and stopped speaking to Nevskaya. This woman's assurance was beginning to annoy him. He wished he could find some way of hurting her feelings. An opportunity soon presented itself.

A letter arrived from the Conservatoire inquiring about a variety of reed native to Provence. The Conservatoire asked whether this reed grew wild in Colchis, and whether its cultivation could not be launched near Poti. Lapshin shrugged his shoulders. What use could the Conservatoire have for reed? Across the corner of the letter, in his crabbed hand, he wrote:

"Reply: there is no such reed in Colchis, and never has been."

The letter happened to fall into Nevskaya's hands. She returned it to Lapshin, laying it down on his desk together with a round, dry stalk of the reed in question.

"You're mistaken," she said. "This reed grows wild in Colchis. Here's a sample."

"Yes, but what use is it to the Conservatoire?"

"What use? To be made into clarinets, and bassons, and oboes."

"We have more important business to attend to than toy whistles."

"Isn't music important?"

"Much ado about nothing," said Lapshin. "That's all I have to say about music."

Nevskaya flushed. What philistinism! Yet it came from a participant in the recreation of Colchis—an undertaking of a grandeur that might well have inspired Beethoven's greatest symphony!

Late that evening, Lapshin dropped in at the "Have a Bite" *duhan*. This institution had long since become a co-operative restaurant but the old name still clung.

Lapshin suffered from insomnia. He blamed it on Colchis' steam-bath climate, and on Nevskaya's rudeness which brought him to a state of what he called "nervous irritation". And so he dropped in at the *duhan* for a drink or two, hoping that wine might induce sleep.

The place was almost empty. The *duhan* keeper dozed, owl-like, behind his counter. Becho's painting gleamed in the dim lamplight.

Lapshin paused to examine it. What an utter muddle! As if rhododendron leaves looked anything like that! Why were artists always adjusting reality to suit their own tastes, and what good did it do anybody?

Then he noticed Nevskaya and Gabunia at the other end of the room. Gabunia called to Lapshin, and set a chair for him. Somewhat reluctantly, Lapshin joined them. He felt ill at ease in Nevskaya's company.

To break the silence that had fallen, Lapshin remarked, with a disdainful nod at Becho's painting:

"The more I look at that mess, the angrier I get. Do you call those things lemons? Beer bottles! Or take the leaves. Why, they look like green pottery shreds. And there's never been a steamer on the Rion—it's too shallow. And plant life in Colchis won't ever be half so rich and varied as it's painted here. I can't see why artists are allowed to change things around any way the fancy takes them.

Gabunia smiled. Lapshin turned cold with fury.

"What do you know about it, if I may ask?" he demanded, in a tone that even to his own ears had a repulsive ring. "What do you see in this daub?"

"The future," Gabunia replied. "Incidentally, have you ever read Lenin? And Pisarev?"

"A little."

"Then perhaps you'll recall these passages." Gabunia spoke slowly, almost reluctantly. "Lenin wrote that even the most elementary of general idea contains some particle of imagination. He wrote that it would be absurd to deny the place of imagination even in the most precise of sciences. Without imagination, we could never have had colmatage, and eucalyptus groves would never grow in Colchis.

"Lenin cited Pisarev. And Pisarev wrote approximately this: 'If man could not anticipate, if he could not contemplate in his mind's eye the completed image of that which he has only just begun to create—in that case, I am utterly at a loss to think what motive could compel him to undertake and carry to completion his extensive and fatiguing labours in the fields of art, science, and practical life.' There—I've got it almost word for word, and I was afraid the malaria had killed my memory. And that's the answer to your question. Becho's picture shows the future of Colchis. When I look at it, I want to live in the country Becho has painted. And I'm going to live there, too."

"Very well," said Lapshin. He was very pale. "That I must admit. But how can you justify the discrepancy between the things that are painted on this wall and actual reality?"

Nevskaya looked up at him.

"How justify it?" she asked. "Why, by the fact that all creation begins where stark, dull imitation of the world around us ends. And science is no exception. Nature produces, but she doesn't create. Only man creates."

Lapshin did not answer. He failed to grasp Nevskaya's point.

While the argument was in progress, two violinists from the city park had come into the *duhan*. They sat in silence, at an empty table, softly testing the strings of their instruments.

The light sounds pattered through the room like tiny crystal balls.

Nevskaya was somewhat taken aback by Lapshin's silence and his evident weariness. She feared that her attack had been too sharp.

"Look," she said, with a friendly smile. "You're not very fond of music, are you? But there's an aria I know. That same one—remember?" This last remark was addressed to Gabunia. "And I think, if you could hear it now, you'd understand how greatly you've been mistaken."

Approaching the two musicians, Nevskaya asked them to play Lisa's aria, from *The Queen of Spades*: "There came a cloud, a thunder cloud. . . ."

Gabunia shifted a bottle of wine to the musicians' table.

They whispered together, then, in a movement full of harmony, lifted their violins. The haunting melody woke the *duhan* keeper. He yawned and rubbed his eyes, and turned to watch the players —just a fat old man, whose whole life had been spent behind a counter. A faint smile transformed his flabby features.

The violins sobbed as though their hearts were rent by their own music. Then, suddenly, the sounds broke off. The *duhan* keeper sighed.

"Well, what do you say?" asked Nevskaya.

"Nothing," replied Lapshin. He rose to go. "I don't think music can interest anyone but lovers. But those it does interest will naturally take an interest in anything connected with it. Reeds, for example."

The blood rushed to Nevskaya's cheeks.

"What do you mean?" she demanded.

"Only that you're very sentimental."

"How silly!" said Nevskaya, turning her face away.

There was an awkward silence. Lapshin stalked out, avenged at last. The *duhan* keeper glanced at the door through which Lapshin had passed.

"Not a very nice sort of bloke," he wheezed, scratching his hairy chest.

The "White Hair" tea came up equally well on

the hills and in the hollows. There were some, indeed—among them Kakhiani—who thought the plantation in the hollows the better of the two. The bushes here were sturdier, and bore more leaves. Nevskaya admitted that she had been wrong, and apologised to Lapshin.

Young leaves, still gummy, were gathered from each plantation and sent off to be dried and prepared. They had still to be tested for flavour.

Soon both samples were returned, ready for use. Nevskaya left a handful of each at home.

Chup immediately brewed them both. The very name of the tea brought back the old days, when the sailors on the tea clipper would filch "White Hair" from the hold and brew a greenish beverage, fragrant and delicious.

When Nevskaya got home that night, she found Chup in a state of tremendous excitement. Nevskaya thought Christophoridi must have got into mischief again, and decided to intervene on the boy's behalf. But as soon as Chup caught sight of her, he cried:

"You've beat that old stick-in-the-mud by a mile! Congratulations! I tasted his tea and I feel sick. Boiled broom! Try for yourself!"

He poured Nevskaya a cup of tea. True enough, it had a strange, metallic taste.

"That man's trying to disgrace the Soviet subtropics," Chup declared. "Now try this cup. It's yours."

Nevskaya tasted obediently. She encountered a tart flavour of an entirely different order.

"And they're both the same plant," cried Chup. "They're both 'White Hair'."

What could have caused such a difference in

taste and aroma? Evidently, Nevskaya decided, the reason lay in the fact that the slopes were warmer and less damp than the hollows, where the cool air settled and lingered.

She had made endless observations and had always found a difference in temperature of as much as five degrees between the hillsides and the hollows. During the winter months this difference was particularly marked. The outcome of the tea experiment offered one more proof of the great care that must be exercised in the distribution of tropical plants in Colchis, in view of this sharply differentiated microclimate.

A few days later, the official report came in from Chakva. Lapshin's tea was rated mediocre, Nevskaya's as the very highest grade. That same day Lapshin applied to Kakhiani for his vacation. Kakhiani argued heatedly, but Lapshin was persistent. Kakhiani shrugged his shoulders. He just couldn't understand.

It seemed the human race had no brains left at all. What did the man want? Rest? He could rest where he was without dropping his research. Sunshine? There was more than enough in Colchis. The sea was vast and the air was wonderful. Quiet? That was no problem, especially where Lapshin lived, on the outskirts of Poti. Even the dogs didn't bark. What more could you want! But Lapshin insisted, and Kakhiani yielded. His objections had been chiefly a matter of principle. When Lapshin had gone, Kakhiani muttered to himself:

"If a woman got the better of me, I'd bow low and thank her, old engineer that I am. Hurt feelings—fiddlesticks! As if I didn't understand why he wants some leave! Such a delicate soul! Everyone has his pride. But a man should know when to pocket his pride, and when to flaunt it, *katso*!"

Artem Korkia Makes a Speech

Christophoridi's brushes flew like mad, shining the shoes of a little Mingrelian Pioneer. The Pioneer's name was Soso.

Soso looked down, and saw his own broad grin and new red tie reflected in the gleaming leather.

Soso's grandfather, Artem Korkia, stood leaning on his staff nearby. He kept a watchful eye on Christophoridi, grumbling all the time because he thought the wily Greek used too little polish. But Christophoridi grunted back contemptuously. The less polish, the brighter the shine. What was he grouching about, the old jackal?

Never before had Artem Korkia experienced such triumph. His grandson, little Soso, had joined the Young Pioneers. This, to Korkia, meant the first step towards becoming such a man as Shalva Gabunia, the engineer.

But that was not all. In the name of the Pioneers, little Soso was to deliver public greetings to the learned folk who were working in Colchis.

"Where do you make your speech, wonder boy?" asked Christophoridi.

Soso would have liked to take offence. He thought the question hid a sneer. But he was afraid of the shoeshine boy's hasty temper. He knew there was a catapult in Christophoridi's pocket. And so he held his tongue.

A crowd gathered around the group. Gulia came up. He was dressed like a sailor, in blue jacket and trousers. The old laundress from Big Island came up, too, and, last of all, militiaman Grisha.

Korkia began to shout. How could he speak of such things quietly?

He shouted about the agricultural display the learned folk were opening in Poti, to show the people new fruits and vegetables and other valuable plants. He shouted about the speech his Soso was going to make at the opening of the display. Such a speech! Its equal was not to be found, no, not even in *Pravda*!

"It makes me laugh to hear the old man brag," said militiaman Grisha. "He's illiterate. He's never read *Pravda*!"

Korkia was taken aback, but only for a moment.

"It's a sin to speak like that to an old man," he returned. "I may not know how to read, but this boy of mine can read better than all the militiamen from Poti to Kutaisi."

An argument boiled up. But Christophoridi got tired of the noise, and beat a tremendous tattoo on his box with a pair of brushes. The shouting stopped. Christophoridi refused to take any money for his work. "Free service for Pioneers," he said carelessly, his heart swelling with pride at his own generosity.

Korkia strode down the street, holding his grandson by the hand. This day, washed crystal clear by recent rain, was his own holiday. It was a new sun rising over his fading life.

Words came to his mind, vague, florid phrases, that it would be well to pronounce at the opening of the display. If he had the chance, he would pronounce them. He had the right, as the oldest resident of Horga, where the main canal was soon to be completed.

Before the opening, Nevskaya spent all evening and all night at the display.

There was no one in the rooms but Nevskaya and Chup. The captain talked at first; but Nevskaya's responses lagged. She was not in the mood for conversation. Noticing this, Chup soon fell silent.

Nevskaya examined the fruits and plants, each in its turn, as though she had never seen them before.

Electric bulbs hung low among the branches, like dazzling June bugs, their glaring light softened and tempered by the foliage.

Nevskaya paused to listen. She seemed to hear a faint whispering of leaves, a crackling of twigs, a murmur of earth drinking in welcome moisture.

She knew all these plants, and loved them. She was familiar with their weaknesses and foibles, and had learned to value their riches, latent or obvious—the precious juices created by these silent beings, somewhere deep down in roots and stalks, in bark and blossoms, and ovaries.

They were potent and individual, these juices, as good old wine. Medicinal, aromatic, nourishing, preservative, stupefying, sobering, sticky as rubber, thin as water, greasy, thirst-satisfying—to each its own nature.

An intricate and wondrous process of chemical transformation took place within the plant cells. Sun, air, fresh water, Rion mud, and night—yes, night, for plants cannot live without these hours of darkness—created fruits of dizzy fragrance.

Nevskaya moved from plant to plant, and a great world opened up before her. Human history, geography, the material aspects of civilisation, all were there to be found in the quiet trees.

Bamboo and eucalyptus, pink batatas, sweet and mealy; a Japanese radish that weighed eight kilograms.

Big orange-yellow globes: the grapefruit, reminiscent in taste of both orange and lemon.

The citrus fruits—lemons, oranges, kumquats, mandarins—contain the mysterious vitamin C. When vitamin C is excluded from the diet, scurvy results. That is the disease of polar expeditions. It sets the sick blood flowing from the gums, and weakens the teeth until they come out painlessly at a touch. The slightest movement demands a tremendous effort.

Nevskaya was sorry she had chilled Chup into silence. He might have reeled off many a tale of lost explorers, of the mighty frosts of the polar regions, of scurvy, of Amundsen, Scott, and Ross. And he would be sure to add some fiction of his own!

These plants were true friends of childhood. Was that why the leaves of the Japanese mandarin trees looked so much like children's hands?

Nevskaya stroked the little glistening swellings on the leaves, tender as a baby's palm. This tree is very small, but it bears some four thousand mandarins every year. When it is in blossom, the petals hide the leaves.

Nevskaya bent over the piles of oranges. The coarsest were the Rize type, that the Turks brought over from Trebizond every autumn. Feluccas would rock in the harbour, piled high with unripe oranges, and the boatmen would sell them by the sackful. Then there were California's Washington navels, with their sharp, winey tang, and the tiny kumquats, no larger than walnuts.

The lemons lay on a bed of grass: a cold fruit, clad in the yellow tints of dawn. Nevskaya lifted an American limequat. Through its thin, transparent rind she could see the dark seeds at its heart. This fruit withstands the hardest winters.

Nevskaya was confident that the plant life of the subtropics would prosper in Colchis, even through those rare winters when the snow came down. All that was required was a minimum of protective measures. She knew, from old residents, that it was not so much the frost as the weight of the snow on the branches that killed the delicate growths.

Snow very seldom falls in Poti. But when it comes, this snow of the subtropics is quite a different thing from that known to the North. It falls in great abundance, and the flakes are very thick and heavy.

Nevskaya glanced at her watch. It was past midnight. She asked Chup not to wait for her, and he went home.

She lingered over the bitter oranges. Their blossoms are the bridal *fleur d'orange*, which goes to make the most delicate of essences, oil of neroli.

She did not touch the huge Japanese persimmons, for this carmine fruit, coated with a pearly dew, begins to spoil at the slightest contact. It is made into sugar and cider.

Beside the persimmons lay the modest loquat, which cures kidney ailments. A Japanese varnish tree stood fenced in with wire screening. And then came samples of the wood of the tulip tree. The vertical strata in this wood do not grow parallel, as in other trees, but join and combine in intricate knots and curves. This makes the wood pliant and firm. It is used in making aeroplane propellers.

Nevskaya moved on to her beloved peaches, of every tint from pink to yellow. They reminded her of downy baby cheeks. The juice of one such peach would fill a tumbler.

Her next visit was to the fibre plants. Here she found the slender, unimpressive Chinese nettle—ramie.

Large plantations of ramie had already been laid out north of the main canal. They were mowed twice a year, and every hectare planted with this simple nettle yielded eight hundred kilograms of yellowish fibre, glossy and strong as silk.

Here, too, were the sword-like leaves of the dragon tree. The strongest of the stevedores in the port could not tear these leaves in two. They only sweated and cut up their palms in vain.

Again, there was the gift of that old mariner, Captain James Cook—New Zealand flax.

Chup told wonderful tales about Captain Cook. Fine traditions, it will be found, exert a powerful influence in every trade and profession. And the power of the splendid traditions of the sea became particularly manifest in Chup when he spoke of the great mariners who had combined good sense with unflinching courage, modesty with majesty of action.

Chup could talk by the hour of these men and their histories, confirming Nevskaya ever more strongly in her view of him as a treasure-house of fascinating knowledge.

The subject of Cook had come up after the foehn. Recalling Lapshin's conduct, Chup had said to Nevskaya:

"Lapshin's a scientist. I'm just a layman. Captain Cook was considered an ignoramus all his life. Scientists tolerated him as an able navigator and expedition commander, but they put no value at all on his scientific abilities. What could they expect of a man who couldn't express his thoughts in polished language? Cook knew their attitude. He was a sailor. He never feared typhoons, or ice, or God, or the devil. But he was terribly frightened of scientific men. He stammered when he had to speak to them. Even in his logs, he seldom wrote down what he thought. His ideas seemed to him so clumsy, he was afraid to trust them to paper.

"But now and then, among his notes of winds and clouds, of latitudes and longitudes and ship fumigations, one suddenly comes across some really splendid lines. When Cook was thrusting down into the Antarctic, pushing insanely on through ice and storm—when his crew marvelled at their quiet captain—he wrote in his log that the beauty of these spots filled his soul with wonder and awe."

Nevskaya dwelt long on these thoughts of Cook. How many of the plants she knew were bound up with his name! She glanced across the room at the Australian acacia.

Leaving the fibre plants, Nevskaya passed by

the tung trees, source of an excellent oil, to the geranium beds.

She chafed a leaf, and the pungent odour of geranium oil brought memories of summer days in a sleepy provincial town, with potted geraniums behind thin gauze curtains.

In the old days, geraniums were contemptuously termed the flower of the petty bourgeoisie. Actually, they were the flower of the working-class districts—the only guest from sunny climes that deigned to grace the bitter life of the slums. They were cheap, and they grew luxuriantly even in the most airless of holes and cellars. And because of this Nevskaya's love for them was doubled.

She bent to stroke the plants, once so unjustly scorned. The stalks thrust up, arrow-like, crowned with red fans of blossom. And above them stretched the heavy boughs of the cryptomeria, hung with thousands of tiny, globose cones.

The vegetables breathed of damp earth, the dry cigar tobaccos of sweetish dust. Rice and wheat were piled high.

Nevskaya sat down to rest near the camphor laurels. Her head ached with weariness, and the camphor smell was soothing. She reached out to touch the fruits of the Chinese tallow tree. They were thickly coated with a solid vegetable fat, of which the Chinese make excellent soap and candles.

Colchis, Nevskaya knew, could be made the home of some fifteen thousand types of tropical and subtropical vegetation. The wealth and variety here on display were to her but a distant hint of the country's future.

Her eyes closed, and she slept, until a light breeze floated in at the open window and set the foliage rustling overhead.

The breeze ruffled Nevskaya's hair, and blew into her eyes. Geranium petals fluttered to the floor.

Nevskaya went out into the street. The damp pavements smelled of the sea. A team of buffaloes plodded past, dragging a high-wheeled cart loaded with radishes. The buffaloes turned mournful blue eyes to Nevskaya. The driver was asleep. Water dripped from the radishes.

The streets were deserted. There was no one to be seen but Grisha, smoking a cigarette at his corner post. He smiled at Nevskaya, and raised his hand to his cap in salute.

Slowly the sun began to rise.

Nevskaya made her way to the port, and went for a swim from the breakwater. Now and then a plaintive murmur rolled from end to end of the jetty, as the sleepy waves broke against the rocks.

The water was very cold, and washed away every vestige of fatigue. While Nevskaya was dressing, the first sunbeams streamed obliquely into the harbour, caressing the quiet waters and the rusty sides of a Greek steamer that bore the strange name of *Zambezos*.

Light wisps of smoke rose over the steamer's deck. Sailors were washing by the rail. They laughed and jostled, and poured water down one another's necks.

A shoal of scad warily approached a bunch of seaweed. They hung about in the transparent water, then suddenly vanished in a burst of silvery spray. A fierce, pop-eyed crab came out of the seaweed and scuttled off sidewise over the rocks.

Nevskaya went into the house and woke Yolochka and Chup. It was time to get ready for the opening ceremony.

The opening was set for noon. It brought many collective farmers into town, from Horga, Supsa, Senaki, and Anaklia. Pakhomov came, and Gabunia, with Mikha.

Kakhiani made the opening speech.

"Comrades," said Kakhiani, looking out sternly at the assembled people. "There's a little question I would like to ask you. Which of you has had malaria? Would all those who've had it please raise their hands? There! It's had its turn with every one of you. Only the *bicho* here, the little boy in the red tie, has never suffered from that unpleasant disease.

"What is malaria? It's poverty, comrades! Our parts were poverty-stricken because of malaria. You know yourselves how many abandoned villages there are in the swamplands, whose inhabitants were wiped out by the disease.

"Yet Colchis is the richest of the Soviet lands, the warmest, the sunniest, the most fertile. So say the poets, Shota Rustaveli and Alexander Pushkin.

"But this land is covered with swamps. We're going to drain the swamps and create a new tropical region here. At this display you'll see the first of the plants that are going to grow in Colchis.

"It would be a great crime to use this golden soil (I beg your pardon for the comparison) to grow coarse crops like corn and millet. You've been planting corn and millet all your lives. Now you are going to plant tea and mandarins, lemons and ramie. The seacoast, from Anaklia to Cabuleti, will become a zone of health resorts.

"But the aim of our work is not only to drain the swamps and create a new soil but to wipe out the old swamp vegetation, alder and rushes, and introduce an entirely new plant life. That's not the only purpose of our work, comrades. There is something more: to build up a healthy generation.

"You could never work more than four hours a day. Malaria drained you as we squeeze out a sponge. You lay in your wooden homes and groaned, too weak to lift a hand. Thus it was for centuries, comrades. But it will be so no longer. We shall kill this disease, and apples will bloom on our children's cheeks."

Kakhiani's own cheeks reddened, as he caught himself in this poetic figure of speech.

"We are building up a humid subtropical region. We are creating a new landscape, worthy of the age of socialism. But we must remember, comrades, that Nature cannot thrive without wise and untiring human supervision. We must take good care of the new land, or it will regress.

"The history of our planet offers many examples of Nature's degeneration when deprived of human care. Take this tree right here, that yields such enormous luscious figs. Leave it to its own devices, and in ten years it will degenerate entirely. Its fruits will be tasteless, and no larger than a nut. Every one of you knows the difference between wild and cultivated grapes, or apples. All this is elementary. But some"—Kakhiani glanced at Vano Akhmeteli—"have been very slow in accepting it."

The band played a fanfare. Korkia nudged his grandson.

Soso came forward. His cheeks flushed a tomato red. He said a few words in Georgian: that the Mingrelian children would tend the new trees and groves, and help the engineers to build a happy Colchis.

The child was applauded heartily. Again the band played a fanfare. Christophoridi, lurking in the background, thought he would die of envy.

Then Pakhomov spoke, and Nevskaya. Christophoridi did not understand a word. And finally, old Artem Korkia came out to the front. There was a movement in the crowd.

Korkia bowed to Kakhiani. His lips parted. He thought a while, and said:

"*Madlobeli, katso.* Thank you, man."

Again his lips parted, but no words came. He cleared his throat huskily and held out his box-wood staff to Kakhiani.

He was proud of his staff. He had carved it when he was only twenty. It was stronger than iron. Let Kakhiani use it to the end of his days, and let those days be many.

Kakhiani took the staff and kissed the old man. The band struck up a lively march, and the crowd broke up to examine the exhibits.

In the *duhan,* that evening, Artem Korkia described to Becho and Gulia the wonderful speech he had made at the opening of the agricultural display.

"I came out in front of everyone, and this is what I said: 'I lived all my life in Horga, and every year the water washed away my fields. Twice I was almost drowned in the swamps. I ate nothing but corn bread and cheese. The fever sucked my body dry and stretched the skin taut on my bones. Three of my sons died of the fever.' That's what I said. 'I thank you,' I said, 'in the name of the old! I thank you in the name of our grandchildren and our great-grandchildren! The Soviet state spends so much money to make our lives happier. So much money, *katso*! Machinery, workers, engineers! And brains, they cost no little.' That's what I said at the opening.

" 'My grandson here,' I said. 'He's wiser than his grandfather. The new times gallop like a rider on a fine horse, and we old folk, we may lag a bit, but we hurry after. Because the rider leads us along the right road, and we can't get lost any more.' That's what I said, *katso*. And everybody clapped their hands, and the music played a funny fair."

"Fanfare," said Becho. He knew the old man had not uttered a word at the opening, but tactfully refrained from comment.

"Maybe it's fanfare," Korkia conceded. " 'There's no more moneybags now, nor Mensheviks— the ones that started the trouble out at Senaki. Now a man must be kind to his fellow men.' That's what I told them all, *katso*."

Gulia believed every word. He was astonished. He had been too bashful to attend the opening, and now he was sorry.

"In five days," he said, "Gabunia will open the main canal, and the water from the mountains and the forests will flow into the Hopi River and on to the sea. Gabunia told me to look you up, Becho, and ask you to come to the canal."

"What for?"

"You'll deck out the houses, and paint golden letters on the archway."

"Ho!" cried Becho, smiling. "We'll organise a better holiday than any Dadiani prince ever saw."

"I've got business with you, too, old chatter-box," said Gulia, laying a hand on Korkia's shoulder. "It's a great secret. You and I go out to the canal tonight, and tomorrow we'll make for the swamps. You'll help me do a big job for Gabunia."

"What sort of job, *katso*?"

"Ssh! It's political. You must keep your mouth shut."

Korkia nodded agreement. He was an old man, but well and good, he'd make one last trip into the swamps. Gabunia, son of the engine driver from Samtredi, was worth it. And a political business, too!

The Phasian Woman

Artem Korkia was so overwhelmed by Gulia's mysterious bearing that all the way he did not say a word.

They had been on their feet since early morning. Loading two buffaloes with spades and axes, ropes and sacking, they had plunged into the jungle.

The buffaloes were reluctant to get moving and kept trying to lie down in the swamps. Gulia lashed their grey hides so soundly that the forest echoed, and frightened jackals wailed and laughed far off at the ends of the earth.

Towards noon the hunters reached the ruins of the Roman fortress.

Gulia noticed that the forest had undergone a change. The foliage dropped mournfully, sweeping the ground. It was grey and lifeless. A blazing sun hung overhead.

They squatted on the fortress walls to eat their lunch.

"In the old days there was a fortress here, Artem," said Gulia, munching his cheese. "And in the fortress there was a statue. The statue is still here. It's sunk in the swamp. It's worth a lot of money, *katso*!"

Korkia received this announcement with complete indifference.

When they had eaten, they felled two small trees, squared them down with their axes, and shaped them into runners. The result was the skeleton of a sledge, which Gulia covered with a bed of branches and fresh leaves. Then he harnessed the buffaloes to the sledge and drove them to a little bog, where a pile of dry branches was heaped over the mud.

"What are we going to do?" asked Korkia.

"Dig up the statue and bring it to Gabunia. He's very fond of statues, *katso*."

Korkia liked the idea well enough. They set to work, throwing apart the heaped-up branches, and soon discovered an arm: a delicate, feminine arm, of rosy marble. One finger was missing.

"Jackal gnawed it off, the cursed beast," Korkia muttered, shaking his head. His eyes were round with wonder.

Carefully, they began to dig away the earth around the statue. Soon the head appeared, and then the shoulders. An hour later, in a deep pit, half full of water, the figure stood entirely free. It was a smiling woman, loosely draped in marble tissue.

Korkia had been digging busily all this time, pausing only to catch his breath or to lubricate his palms with spittle. He had been too occupied even to glance at the statue. But now the work was finished. Straightening up, he turned his eyes to the result of his labour, only to start back in horror. He scrambled up out of the pit and backed hastily away.

"Dirty liar!" he shouted at Gulia. "Where's your politics? It's a naked woman!"

"I beg an old man's pardon," returned Gulia with biting sarcasm. "I sincerely beg your pardon, *katso*. A clever man like you shouldn't be such a fool. This statue is worth a lot of money. We'll give it to Gabunia. Go and get the ropes and the sacking."

Too bewildered to reply, Korkia went to the sledge and got the sacking. Gulia scooped water from the bog and poured it over the statue, until the living warmth of the ancient marble began to gleam through the green layers of slime.

Gulia covered the statue with sacking and trimmed branches, and tied the whole with rope. Then the statue was dragged to the surface, with the help of the buffaloes, and laid carefully on the sledge.

The road back was slow. The buffaloes kept stopping. Gulia and Korkia argued all the way, over those intricate and difficult problems: civilisation, culture, monuments.

Gulia did not know how to express the vague feelings that had guided his decision to bring the statue in from the swamps. The canal was celebrating. All Colchis was celebrating. And Gulia felt that this statue would be a fitting adornment to the holiday, an unexpected gift wrested from the swamps.

Night had fallen when they reached the canal. There was a light in Gabunia's window. Gulia tapped softly on the pane, and Gabunia came out.

"Bring a flashlight," Gulia whispered. "Come with me. I have something interesting to show you. I found it in the swamp."

Gabunia said nothing, though he glanced suspiciously at Gulia. He took his flashlight and silently followed the former hunter.

In a thicket just beyond the last barrack, the buffaloes were munching noisily. Korkia stood beside them. His face was pale. He was afraid Gabunia would rebuke them, or, even worse, make fun of them for a pair of stupid old fools.

Gabunia entered the thicket.

"Now!" said Gulia.

Gabunia lit his flashlight. Its silvery rays revealed a marble statue, smiling up from a bed of dark leaves.

Korkia glanced at Gabunia, and stiffened fearfully. The engineer's eyes were fixed on the statue. His brows were drawn together. His face was strangely pale. For a long time he did not speak. At length, he asked brusquely:

"Where did you find it?"

"In the ruins of the old fortress, *katso*," said Gulia. "It's for you. You're fond of statues."

Gabunia threw an arm across Gulia's shoulders.

11-1648

"Thanks, friend," he said softly. "You've realised what many of the wisest men refuse to understand. We'll gather together everything worth while that has come down from former times, and our wealth will be greater than any wealth the world has known. We're very fortunate, comrade. Thank you, Gulia. This thing is too beautiful to belong to any one man. It must belong to all."

Gabunia asked them to wrap up the statue again, and then all three bent to lift it and carry it into Gabunia's room. When the work was finished, Gulia and Korkia, elated, went away to their barrack.

Gabunia sat far into the night, leafing through old books. At last he found the passage he sought, in Arrian, and marked it in pencil. The passage read:

"On the left bank of the Phasis there was erected a statue of a Phasian woman of amazing beauty."

It was evidently this statue that Gulia had found.

The Swiss traveller Dubois de Montperreux, one of the few Europeans who had visited the ruined fortress, set its date at approximately 100 B.C. Hence, the statue was two thousand years old.

Gabunia turned back the sacking and looked into the marble features. Two thousand years had passed over this clear forehead and arched brows, over this smile, imbued with tenderness—that same kindness of man to man of which Korkia had spoken in the *duhan*. Two thousand years had covered the rosy marble with a network of fine grey cracks.

As day was breaking, Gabunia threw open his window. Now and then a bird flashed by among the treetops. The foliage rustled in the morning breeze. Low behind the forest the sun was rising, an enormous, glittering gem.

The room was filled with a mercurial play of light and shadow. A bright ray touched the marble face, and the wind caressed the smiling lips. Gabunia realised that he was looking upon the work of some great, unknown master.

On the tall flagpoles at the entrance to the canal, red pennants fluttered, reaching out to the mountains. The monsoon blew from the west, and the air of this seacoast country filled the lungs with youthful vigour.

Looking at the statue, Gabunia reflected that its forgotten sculptor, two thousand years before our day, had embodied in his creation the spirit of Colchis' wondrous future.

Fireworks in the Forest

What small things will sometimes create a happy mood! A fresh breeze, even if it overturns the vase of bright leaves on the table. A bit of orange peel dancing on the waves. The crunch of gravel, a familiar voice outside the window, and the sky—a blue dome over the quiet sea.

So thought Nevskaya, that early morning. But Chup was inclined to disagree.

Orange peel on the waves was downright indiscipline. Those brazen cooks on the Greek steamers had got out of hand again, dumping their garbage overboard in the harbour.

And the water from the overturned vase had stained the tablecloth.

Gravel squeaked like new leather. If you had bad nerves, it gave you the shudders.

As to voices outside the window, there might be all sorts and kinds. The voice of "St. Anthony's fire", the redheaded pilot, was familiar enough, but it couldn't make anyone particularly happy. The pilot lisped offensively: "Thwing her over! Thtarboard, thtarboard, I thay!"

The sky—well, that was another matter. Only the sky couldn't be called a trifle. The sky—yes, that was really something!

Nevskaya did not argue with Chup. Even his grumbling was a joy, that morning. And the greatest joy of all was the sound of the horn, when car arrived to take them to Chaladidi for the opening of the canal.

Chup came out in dazzling white. The sun caught at the gold braid on his uniform sleeve, and his grey eyes seemed keener than ever above his close-shaven cheeks.

Chup lifted Yolochka to the front seat, beside the driver. Christophoridi preferred to ride on the running board. Christophoridi never once stopped smiling, all that day. And next morning he wondered what made the skin around his lips so sore!

Nevskaya lingered in her room a moment, and the others were all in the car when she came out. The captain saw a greenish glint in the clear puddles left by last night's rain, reflecting the soft sea-green of Nevskaya's dress.

She approached the car, with a rustle of wind-swept silk, and a stray beam of sunlight showed the captain the bright depths of her laughing eyes.

Chup got out to help her in, a thing he had never done before. Her warm, strong hand pressed his, and he sighed. Ah, 'twas a cursed thing, the sailor's life!

Deck, helm, hold, bunkering, and mishaps at sea—life had slipped by while he was busy with such things, and he had never come into contact with such beautiful, smiling women. Not little bourgeois things in striped beach suits, with bright red lacquered finger nails, but women of his own sort: the kind who had battled at the fronts, who worked and sacrificed, whose lives were devoted to the future.

Ah, 'twas a ten-times cursed thing, the sailor's life!

"You've missed it all, you old devil," thought Chup dejectedly. "The young folks have left you behind."

They stopped off at the experimental gardens, and cut a huge bouquet of flowers.

The wind often cast the end of Nevskaya's green scarf against the captain's cheek. He trembled at these light blows, as at the touch of well-loved fingers.

Nevskaya laughed all the way. What delighted her most was the behaviour of the village dogs.

As the car entered a village, the dogs would come sauntering lazily into the street, wearing expressions of unutterable boredom, of complete indifference to everything in the great, wide world. They might even yawn, or sit down to search for fleas. But the moment the car reached the domain of any of these dogs, the creature would suddenly feign the most dreadful fury. Hoarsely barking and growling, it would race along beside the car, just out of reach of the wheels. Then, having seen the intruders safely out of its territory, it would just as suddenly subside into its former indifference, and limp back to its gateway with the old air of unutterable boredom.

Speckled sunlight, dancing on green leaves—swirling white dust and mischievous gusts of wind—the barking of dogs and the shouts of children, merged with the even roar of the racing motor.

That day the barometer in Gabunia's room said "fair".

Gabunia and Mikha could not conquer their anxiety. Mikha kept peering up at the sky for signs of rain. But there was not a hint of cloud. It was a day of crystal azure, hushed and windless. The only sound was the tapping of hammers and axes under the trees on the bank of the canal, where carpenters were preparing a great, long table and benches.

The Mingrelian workers were all in their barracks, shaving. Sima was busily stuffing paper cartridges with mysterious powders. He had been whistling and grunting all morning—a sign of the greatest good humour.

The guests began to arrive at noon. Kakhiani came first, with Pakhomov and Vano Akhmeteli. Then came Chup and Nevskaya, then Grisha, at the head of the militia band.

Red banners were reflected in the water of the canal. Lianas hung from the trees over a table set for a hundred.

The old *duhan* keeper fretted because there were not enough tablecloths. The smell of roast lamb rose from the camp kitchen, mingling with the fragrance of crisp cakes and purple Isabella wine.

A narrow red ribbon was stretched across the canal, from bank to bank, just above the surface of the water.

Kakhiani and Gabunia, with Artem Korkia—the oldest of the local people—descended from the pier into the waiting motor launch.

Sima stood at the helm, steadying the launch with a boathook. He was freshly shaved, and very trim. He stood at attention, as though on parade. Sima knew well enough what was fitting, and when, of the old ship discipline.

The workers gathered along the banks.

Kakhiani raised his hand. Sima started the engine.

The idea was to direct the launch so that its nose would snap the red ribbon stretched across the canal. That was not easy. Sima squinted down at the water, driving straight for the ribbon. The launch rushed forward, faster and faster.

Its nose struck the ribbon fairly. The red line stretched taut and snapped, and the torn ends flew free. The launch chugged furiously down the canal.

"Hip, hip, hurrah!" cried Sima, waving his hand.

He was chorussed loudly from the shores. The band struck up the *Internationale.* The workers waved their hats. Sima stopped the motor, and his passengers rose to their feet.

For the first time, the virgin forest rang to music and song.

Nevskaya glanced at Chup. He stood with his hand to his cap in salute. His suntanned fingers looked black against the dazzling whiteness of his uniform. He made a figure of great strength and calm. It occurred to Nevskaya that people do not so often hear the *Internationale*; that its grand strains enter people's hearts as the crowning measure of achievement, as the music of victory, of completed labour. Perhaps that is why cheeks grow pale with suppressed emotion.

When the music ended, Kakhiani shouted:

"*Gamarjoba*, comrades! Joy to the victors!"

"*Gaguimarjos!*" the workers responded.

"Comrades," said Kakhiani. "The canal is finished, and we may allow ourselves one evening for rest and celebration. You have done a grand job, comrades, every one of you, from the oldest worker down to the young, Soviet-trained engineers. I thank you, in the name of the Bolshevik Party. You have gained a victory over swamps and forests, over rain and fever.

"You have not only drained the land. You have done much more. I should like to tell you of two incidents. There is nothing poetic about them. Just bare fact.

"This old man here, Artem Korkia. All his life he wore around his neck an empty nutshell, with a dried spider inside it. His father wore such a shell, and his grandfather before him. In the old days, as you all know, the people of the swamp country believed that dried spiders were the best cure for fever. Old women whispered prayers over them, and people believed that the spiders and the old women's prayers would protect them from sickness.

"But Artem Korkia took out his nutshell, just now, and threw it into the water. 'What do I need nuts and spiders for,' he said, 'when the engineers will kill malaria better than spiders?' So you see, your labours are teaching men to get rid of their superstitious beliefs.

"And there's one more thing I must tell you about, comrades, a thing that some of us may see in the wrong light. I mean the statue of the Phasian woman that has been found in the swamps. I'm no judge of sculpture. I'm a land reclamation expert, not a Michelangelo or an Antokolsky. But the very fact that men like Gulia, a simple hunter, and this very same old Artem Korkia, should realise, not too clearly, perhaps, but they did realise the cultural value of things like this—that fact makes me rejoice, comrades, even though I'm no judge of the fine points of a statue.

"We shall take the very best, comrades, of every culture and civilisation. We shall add it all to the furnace of our socialist ideals, and we shall create the greatest culture humankind has ever known.

"Long live the Soviet subtropics! You are creating them by the labour of your hands. Rest, now, comrades, and enjoy yourselves!"

After Kakhiani's speech, they all gathered around the huge table. The *duhan* keeper bustled about, red and perspiring. He was torn between horror and rapture. Rapture at this great feast beneath the open sky, just as Becho had painted it, a feast for a hundred, all the work of his hands, for the first time in his life. Horror, because there were not enough tablecloths, and there might not be enough dishes.

Pakhomov looked cheerfully down the table.

"You're Argonauts, all of you," he said to Gabunia. "Jason discovered the Golden Fleece in Colchis, and you've discovered the tropics. Incidentally, have you ever wondered what the ancients meant by a golden fleece? Just an ordinary sheepskin. They'd spread it out at the bottom of a gold-bearing river, and weighed the edges with stone to keep it in place. And the grains of gold collected in the fleece."

"It's very simple," said Kakhiani. "No poetry about it. A primitive method of gold washing, that's all."

"There's lots of poetry about the simplest things," Pakhomov retorted amicably. "Legends contain the seed of the future. It's man's aspiration to lofty ideals that gives rise to legend. The most beautiful of all is the Icarus myth. Every flyer, today, is a new Icarus. The myth of Jason tells how he ploughed a field with a yoke of fire-breathing bulls. Now, what are fire-breathing bulls?"

"Tractors," cried Gabunia, chuckling.

Pakhomov nodded. Chup laughed aloud.

"Man must have faith in his own abilities," Pakhomov went on. "And then he will turn the course of rivers, and grow lemons in Siberia. I'm speaking seriously. Man has to believe in the strength and power of his art. When Orpheus sang and played his lyre, the sea grew calm. The Greeks wrote of this in all seriousness. They naively believed in it. They believed in the power of art; and technology is also an art, Comrade Kakhiani. Let's put our faith in it, as the Greeks put their faith in Orpheus' lyre. You are realising the myth of the conquest of Colchis, of the Golden Fleece, of the bold voyage of the Argonauts. Glory be to you!"

"I have the greatest respect for you," mumbled Kakhiani, very much embarrassed, "and so I must believe you. Have it your own way, then."

Nevskaya sat listening to the talk around her. She heard the debate over Jason and legend, tractors and flyers. She heard the merry talk of the workers, and Mikha's piercing laughter; Gulia's hoarse voice, the children's chatter, Chup's quiet jokes.

The band was playing a lively tune she had never heard before. Sunbeams strayed across the table, throwing golden bands across the white cloths, the bottles and glasses, the swarthy hands of the feasters. They peeped into the glasses, and made the red wine glow. They turned the crisp cakes into gold.

It was a simple, noisy holiday, as though in one big, close-knit family.

Nevskaya did not speak. She felt that something had happened, that something had come to her, which she could not grasp—something fine and good. What could it be?

And suddenly she knew.

Friendship! Genuine friendship, the very finest thing that the earth holds. It arises in work and in danger, in conflicts and triumphs, in reverses and impassioned debate: a new emotion of our new epoch, the finest that mankind has known.

Nevskaya turned to the workers. Many smiled at her, and raised their glasses to drink her health. They were proud of her, of this learned woman who had worked shoulder to shoulder with them the whole night through under the pouring rain, when the embankments were in danger. They were proud of her, of this beautiful woman, in her gleaming silken gown.

She turned again to look at Gabunia, Kakhiani, Pakhomov. All friends. They were still deep in their argument about myths and legends.

Her eyes fell on Chup. Christophoridi, Yolochka, and Soso were staring at the captain, open-mouthed. He was telling them a story. He drew a stern face, then suddenly burst into laughter. The children's clear voices joined. Nevskaya laughed too, she could not have said why.

The sun hung low over the treetops. It was sinking rapidly to the west. Its slanted rays turned the foliage into glinting bronze.

The sun was sinking into the sea, far beyond the forest, when a high, almost girlish voice cut through the din of talk and laughter. It was Mikha, singing an ancient Georgian song:

King Iraclya's infinite power
Failed him in one thing, you see,
His lovely queen drove him forth from her
bower,
His beautiful queen spurned his company.

Gabunia bent to Nevskaya's ear, translating the words of the song. Pakhomov bowed his head, shading his eyes with his hand. Kakhiani sat looking out over the clear, dark waters of the canal, where the evening sky lay inverted.

The king wandered in his gardens, dejected,
And wept alone till the golden morn.
Shepherds and huntsmen knew him rejected,
And made bitter mock of their king lovelorn.

Chup toyed with an empty wineglass. His fingers trembled. He knew the language, and understood the song. A cursed thing, the sailor's life! It seemed to him that the song was about Chup, an old sailor to whom love had been denied.

I have nought to my name but my tatters,
I have nought but my dagger and sheath.
But I claim the smiles of the queenly Tamara,
And King Iraclya envies me.

A heavy blossom struck Chup's hand. Dark petals scattered over the table.

The captain lifted the flower and put it in his buttonhole. He knew these black roses, already overripe. They grew only at the experimental gardens.

He peeped sidewise at Nevskaya. The corners of her lips were twitching. She was trying not to smile. She would not return the captain's glance.

"Hullo!" cried Sima suddenly, tapping a swift tattoo with heels and toes. "Hullo! Ladies and gentlemen, the show goes on!"

The workers sprang to their feet. The band broke into the *Lezghinka*, and Gabunia was off at once, whirling in the swift, light national dance. Mikha followed, with a wild shriek, sweeping the glasses from the table with his sleeves.

The drums beat fast and loud. The feasters crowded into a circle around the dancers, clapping their hands in time with the music.

173

Loud shouts acclaimed the efforts of the fat *duhan* keeper, who twirled about like a top, his wide cotton trousers swelling out like sails. He clapped his hands above his head, and flew lightly around the circle.

"*Ash! Ash! Ash! Ash!*" cried the crowd and the dancers.

A light cloud of dust rose over the forest.

The general ecstasy reached its peak when Nevskaya floated out into the circle. Her green dress shimmered in the fading light, and a warm breeze seemed to fan the watchers as she passed.

"Hurrah!" yelled Christophoridi, turning cartwheels round the circle. "Shine 'em right! Shine 'em bright!"

Soso turned cartwheels in Christophoridi's wake.

Artem Korkia waved his staff and coughed. Gulia stamped his feet, but would not go into the circle.

"Joy has come to our swamps, *katso*, it has come at last," cried Korkia.

Chup lifted Yolochka to his shoulders so that she could watch the dancers.

Wildest of all was Vano Akhmeteli. The devil take the nutria, and keep it! Faster, there, faster!

Vano danced with furious enjoyment. Flying past Yolochka, he whooped and rolled his eyes.

"Ugh! It makes me laugh to watch these people dance," cried militiaman Grisha, bursting into the circle. All the dancers had to stop. Grisha twirled so impetuously that he was almost invisible. People shot away from him as though he were a bomb, on the point of bursting.

174

Just then a piercing whistle cut the air. A rocket exploded among the stars, sending down a burst of sparkling spray. Sima's fireworks had begun.

The rockets flew up in bunches, and burst with a deafening din. Only then did the revellers see that night had descended—blue, early night, pungent with gunpowder and wine.

Bonfires were lit along the banks of the canal. The water turned into liquid flame, its glowing crimson slashed by the white arcs of the flying rockets.

Thousands upon thousands of fireflies flitted among the trees, flashing and fading. It was as though the starry sky had descended close to earth, swooping and whirling over the forest—now retreating in terror from the Bengal lights, now brushing the treetops again with its soft blue train.

Yolochka fell asleep in the captain's arms. He took her away to Gabunia's room and laid her down on the narrow cot. Red and white gleams passed, like summer lightning, over the smiling face of the Phasian statue.

"Ah, it's a ten-times cursed thing, the sailor's life!"

He stood at the window, watching the fiery magic in the sky.

Nevskaya came softly into the room. She laid her light, hot hand on the captain's shoulder and stood beside him, watching the fireworks. Chup was afraid to move. Neither spoke.

Then Nevskaya left, as softly as she had come. Chup heard the rustle of her dress. He heard the door close. And suddenly the night began to spin.

Chup clutched at the window frame, and passed a hand over his eyes. It came away wet.

"Fool!" he muttered. "You held out for forty-seven years, and all of a sudden. . . ."

The night was a world of music and song and light, as Chup stood thinking that only now, in his forty-seventh year, had he learned the meaning of complete happiness.

He turned quickly on his heel and left the room.

Barefoot Argonauts

At daybreak Sima brought a motor launch up the pier. They had decided to return to Poti by way of the canal, the Hopi River, and the sea. The day promised to be fair again.

The bonfires were still smouldering along the banks of the canal. Dew dripped from the leaves and hissed on the hot ashes. Birds sang in the forest.

Sima's passengers were Nevskaya, the children, Chup, and Gabunia.

When the launch shot past the barracks, the workers waved their hats and sang out greetings. Then came the forest, slipping by in a green waterfall of foliage. And then the canal was past, and the launch rocked in the mysterious shade of the winding Hopi.

The sun rose, a huge white ball, behind them, casting long shadows over the water.

On and on they chugged, through the warm odours of foliage and river water, until at last the sea came into view, and the wind brought the cool tang of seaweed and wet sand.

The little town of Redout-Calé lay mirrored in

the river, with every detail of pile-built pink and blue houses, like a bright, ragged shawl spread over the surface of the water.

The hum of the motor ran ahead, from house to house, banging at the doors and waking the people. A woman with a baby appeared on a veranda. A cock crowed, and a flock of pigeons circled overhead.

The launch flew out into the sea and turned southward in a graceful curve. It spattered spray against the sides of an old sailing boat at anchor near the river mouth.

Breakers were beating dully, far away.

The barefoot, suntanned crew of the sailing boat sat on the deck, dangling their legs over the water. Smoking their pipes, they looked out, new Argonauts, over the shores of Colchis.

1934

CANES VENATICI

All autumn the wind had been blowing from the ocean. The air quivered and it was very difficult to observe the stars at night.

The astronomer Merot was sick and old. He had not the strength to slide open the observatory's small dome on his own and asked the gardener to help him. Together the two of them pulled the thin cable. The panels of the dome slid apart with a slight creak and the cold starry sky appeared in the inky darkness.

Merot would sit down on the small staircase to have a rest and shake his head sadly: "Wind again, of course! The different densities of air sweeping over the earth are breaking up the light rays again."

Dry oak leaves drifted into the observatory and the trees outside were rustling. The gardener said that if the wind was blowing the leaves off the oak trees it wouldn't die down for a long time.

Merot liked talking to the gardener. There were only eight of them living in the observatory and it was thirty kilometers of difficult, stony road to the nearest small town. His fellow astronomers were a taciturn lot. They had already said all they had to say to each other and now conversations were rare. They evaded questions and pretended to be immersed in their calculations.

The astronomers' simple dinner was cooked for them by an old woman called Teresa, also silent and brusque. Their meals, always taken at the same time and in the same company, became more and more oppressive each month. And with each passing year they grew increasingly accustomed to solitude. So intense was the silence that even the books Merot happened to read from time to time seemed to be full of noises. He did not actually hear any sounds when he was reading, of course, but he imagined them and the more commotion and loud conversations there were in a book, the more irritated he became.

"What a noisy book!" he would say frowning. "The characters shout, argue and cry their heads off.... I can't be bothered to try and follow all this racket."

Several years in the observatory had given him

an extremely acute sense of hearing. He now heard many sounds which he had never noticed before. They were monotonous ones, like the wind whistling through the cables that supported the pole on which they hoisted the flag on public holidays. Then another sound could be heard— the flag flapping cheerfully in the wind. It brought back memories of childhood holidays, when the sound of the flags in their small town had been so loud that Merot's grandmother had got a headache.

When he was a child there had been lots of sunshine, much more than now, and the sun had been different—huge and very bright covering half the sky.

"I think the sun is cooling before our very eyes," Merot would say to the gardener. "It just doesn't shine like it used to, as if someone had put a dusty pane of glass over it."

The gardener always agreed—who was he to argue with an educated man like Merot.

There were other sounds besides the wind. In winter the mistral would carry dry snow through the mountain passes and fling it like sand against the windows of the laboratory. Now and then there was an eagle's cry, and sometimes rain would gurgle in the stone gutters. Very occasionally in summer there was thunder. But its rumbling was down in the valleys, not overhead. The thunder-clouds clustered way below the observatory.

That was about all, except for the bleating of lost goats, and the hooting of the car once a week when the driver fetched food, newspapers and mail from the town.

The newspapers were snatched up by the young

180

astronomer Neusted, a lumbering Norwegian, who took them to his room and never gave them back. At first the astronomers grumbled about the rude Norwegian, but then they got used to it and forgot that the newspapers existed. Occasionally they would ask Neusted what was happening down below in the world, from which you could expect nothing but trouble. Neusted invariably told them that the world was going on in its mad way as usual, and everyone was satisfied by this reply.

It was at the end of autumn, when Merot had been spending many nights at the telescope studying the Canes Venatici constellation, that he first heard the new sounds. They were like the distant rumble of mountain avalanches. At first they were so faint that Merot could hardly detect them. He racked his brains trying to guess what they were, but did not even attempt to tell the other astronomers about them. They already thought he was a bit of a crank. But the sounds grew in volume and one night the repercussions were so intense that the stars swam together and split in two in the mirror of the telescope.

The sounds came from the direction of the coast. Merot went out onto the iron balcony of the observatory and stared for a long time at the mountains.

Everything was the same as usual—snow, moonlight and the stars topping the peaks like beacons —but there was no sign of the white spray that normally accompanied snowslides.

"Matvei," Merot called to the gardener. "Did you hear something? It must have been snowslides in the mountains."

"Not enough snow for avalanches," said the gardener. "We'd better listen hard."

They strained their ears in silence. Behind the garden wall was the steady splash of water as if it were falling on glass. That was the stream which was already covered with patches of ice. The silence stretched on. Then a heavy thud rang out from the east, hit the mountains and echoed back westwards dying away.

"That's no snowslide," muttered the gardener.

"What is it, then?"

"It's long-range guns," the gardener replied uncertainly. "It's that there war down below. But it won't come up here. Too high up. No point in coming up here."

Then Merot remembered Neusted's brusque accounts of the Civil War which was devastating the old towns in the valleys and the peasants' miserable plots. He remembered the driver complaining that the only people left in the town were women and old men and that he was always late because he had to load on the crates himself. He remembered that Teresa's cooking had got much worse, but nobody had taken any notice.

He must find out everything immediately. Merot closed the observatory and went down to the house.

The astronomers were having supper. The chimney in the dining room fireplace was giving a hollow, sleepy murmur as it had for many a year.

"Listen, friends," said Merot panting hard. He stopped at the doorway pulling off his warm scarf. "I can hear the sound of firing in the distance."

The astronomers looked up from their plates.

"Neusted," Merot went on in a loud, excited voice. The astronomers looked round not at Merot but somewhere in the corner, as if they couldn't believe that this loud voice belonged to the sick old man. "Neusted, you must tell us exactly what's going on."

Neusted did not answer. He looked at his watch and went up to the wireless. Everyone watched him in amazement.

He bent over the knobs. The electric valves lit up with a red glow and a man's voice began to talk sadly about street fighting in Madrid, air raids, hundreds of children mutilated by shells and the destruction of the Alba Palace where paintings by Velazquez and Ribera were burning.

The astronomers listened in silence. The voice suddenly broke off as abruptly as it had begun.

"What do you think of that?" said Merot in the silence that followed, and realised that his question had been somewhat out of place.

Neusted lazily returned to the table. He sat stretched out as if listening to something, gripping the table with his large hands.

A fusty old man in a grey suit, the seismologist Dufour who was noted for his refined speech, was the first to break the silence.

"Ever since we came to the observatory," he said with an ironical smile, "each of us has had the feeling of being in a besieged fortress. We are surrounded by mountains without wood, ore or coal. We are besieged by the wind and snow. The world has no time for us, and we have no time for the world. The people in the valleys are running wild, but there is no reason for them to come up here. Here there is nothing but the stars. They can't be melted down for weapons or used to make poisonous gases. Rational mankind has no use for them. Consequently we have nothing to fear."

"Don't play the fool, Dufour," said Neusted. "The war has been on for five months now."

"Nonsense, nonsense," came the grating voice of Hervé who had been silent up to now. It was impossible to guess his age—he could easily be anything from forty to sixty. "I'd like to know something else. How can anyone be upset about a piece of canvas getting burnt even if it was covered with pretty paint? I mean Velazquez' pictures. I've spent all my life studying the stars and it's taught me not to get worried by trifles. What could be more transient than a piece of canvas? People torment themselves, go into ecstasies and even die over it. It's quite incomprehensible. I just don't understand how anyone can bother with such things when there is human thought and the heavens."

He was interrupted by Dufour, who had gone out and returned with a thin strip of paper.

"There," he said proudly. "More proof of the accuracy of my seismograph. It has recorded nearly two hundred minor earth tremors in the last few days. Obviously these are shell explosions. I've only just realised it."

The astronomers bent over the strip of paper, on which the pencil had traced a jagged line showing the tremors in the earth's crust.

Neusted ran his finger along the line, his eyes screwed up and a cigarette clenched between his swollen, nicotine-stained teeth. He was angry.

"Each curve represents an explosion," he said. "Your apparatus is excellent at registering murders, Dufour."

Before Dufour had time to retort there was a distinct thud outside. The mountain echo turned it into a roll and cast it down into the rocky precipices. All fell silent again.

Merot kept quiet. He didn't want to take part in this futile conversation. All his life he had believed that studying the sky, like the discovery of all the other secrets of the Universe, bound man closer to the earth. Merot was old and kind and was not storing up all his knowledge for himself alone. He had even started writing a book about the sky for those carefree, boisterous youngsters far away in the deep valleys down below, who would envy him, an old man.

Strange thoughts and memories had been crowding into his mind recently. He recalled his childhood, and old men never like dwelling on this period of their life. He remembered the Christmas tree. Before it was lit up, it had lived secretly in the next room behind locked doors, and only the faint smell of its needles stirred the child's imagination. Then the door was flung open and he walked in timidly and saw the sparkling tree. He could look at it, touch its needles and golden nuts, glass decorations and crackers, and smell the oranges and figs hanging on its branches. He could study the fir tree, but nevertheless the sensation of mystery and wonder filling the room never left him for a single moment.

He had the same feeling from studying the Universe.

"Everything exists for man," Merot said. "If people disappear, I'm afraid that I, an astronomer, won't have any use for the starry heavens."

Merot rarely ventured to express these thoughts because they did not meet with approval. He became irritated by the conversation in the dining room. This was the first time that he had noticed how arid the thoughts and feelings of his colleagues were. Coarse, lazy Neusted was perhaps better than the lot of them.

The Civil War in the valleys, the echoes of the fighting and the unpleasant conversation in the dining room did not appear to interfere with the scientists' life. The astronomers worked at night, slept in the morning and spent the evening in the laboratories. There they would compare photographs of the starry heavens on the lookout for the slightest changes. Any change in the familiar jumble of stars was a discovery which gave rise to interesting speculation.

Life went on as usual, but nevertheless the scientists were troubled by a strange unease which only a sharp eye could detect.

Merot would sit by the telescope muttering something to himself angrily. Neusted was twice seen in the daytime turning the telescope onto the distant mountains. The others pretended not to have noticed, since it is accepted among astronomers that only fools use a telescope for observing the earth.

Dufour occasionally said that the sense of the war being so imminent and yet without danger for him steadied his nerves. Formerly when the snow began to fall and the overcast sky stopped their work, the astronomers became moody. Hervé was the most irritable of the lot. But now, after a heavy fall of snow, he remarked that fortunately it would make the road to the observatory impassable for armed detachments. Dufour smirked maliciously.

Bauden, the librarian, had begun to take the newspapers from Neusted and read them all the way through, frowning as if the reports were causing him gnawing pain.

One night in December Neusted came into the observatory while Merot was working. This was against the rules, as the astronomers were not supposed to disturb each other during observation time. Merot looked round and got up.

Neusted stood still, feet apart and hands thrust into his trouser pockets. Both men were silent.

Merot noticed a faint smell of wine. That really was going too far. The young Norwegian's behaviour was becoming provocative.

"I've come to help you close the dome," said Neusted loudly as if he were addressing someone hard of hearing, "because it will hit us all of a sudden."

"He's drunk," thought Merot. This was the first time he had ever seen anyone drunk in the observatory. "What's he talking about?"

"It'll hit us all of a sudden," Neusted repeated angrily. "Do as I say. Come out and look for yourself."

Neusted closed the dome, took Merot by the elbow and led him out onto the iron balcony. Merot did not demur for he had sensed the alarm and threat behind Neusted's words.

"There," said Neusted nodding towards the mountains. "What a magnificent sight."

A sheer bank of cloud lit by a dim, eery light was rising above the jagged mountain tops. It stretched right across the horizon, and you could see it growing and swelling, obscuring the stars and emitting a weird glow.

"A hurricane," said Neusted with a short laugh. "It'll be here in ten minutes. Just as soon as the wind breaks through the mountains."

"Why is it so quiet?" Merot asked.

"It's always like that just before a hurricane breaks."

The silence was so tense that the sound of their own voices seemed harsh and unpleasant. They could not even hear the familiar sound of the stream. The mountains were already wreathed in grey smoke.

"Here it comes," Neusted whispered.

Merot strained forward listening intently. Far off in the unbearable silence was the faint sound of an engine.

"There's someone out there," he said pointing at the mountains.

Snowy whirlwinds were already leaping convulsively up to the black sky.

"Where?" asked Neusted.

Merot clutched him by the shoulder.

"There, there!" he cried pointing to the mountain tops where Neusted could now see nothing but the swirling hurricane streaming down into the ravines. "I can hear an aeroplane."

"You. . .," Neusted started to shout but a sudden blast of wind drove the hoarse cry back down his throat. The earth shuddered and the fierce, unbroken howl of the hurricane drowned everything else. The wind whipped Merot from the rail of the balcony and threw him against the observatory wall. Snow was driving into his eyes and mouth choking him. Neusted grabbed him by the arm and dragged him down the steps. The Norwegian was already white with snow from head to foot.

They forced their way to the house through the leaden current of wind, clinging to trees and bushes, staggering and using their hands to protect their eyes from the flying gravel that was stinging their faces. Everything around was shaking and howling at different pitches: the moaning flag pole, the bare garden whistling like hundreds of shrill flutes, a clattering loose tile, the rattling windowpanes and the constant clanging of the iron roofs.

The lamps were not swaying on their posts. The force of the wind had held them nearly parallel to the ground and at any minute they were likely to be ripped off and swept away.

Neusted dragged Merot into the dining room and only then did he finish the sentence that had been interrupted by the wind.

"You're wrong," he said taking off his jacket and shaking the snow off it. "There wasn't a plane. And even if there was, it's nothing but a pile of firewood now."

Merot did not argue.

Soon all the astronomers had gathered in the dining room. Storms bring people together. They inspire the imagination. Even the most boring person manages to find words to convey the excitement that he feels when the wind is beating wildly outside.

It was very late before they went off to bed. Merot couldn't get to sleep. He lay on his narrow bed listening to the wind howling and a terrible feeling of loneliness came over him. Surely he wouldn't have to spend the rest of his days here in the mountains, in this white room like a hospital ward? Would no one ever come and stroke his grey hair and say: "Go to sleep. I'll sit and read to you until you drop off."

He lay curled up and felt as if he were a little boy again. He remembered Hervé saying that astronomers shouldn't have anyone who is close to them. "Neither should old men, I suppose," he thought.

He got up, raised the blind and went back to bed. He wanted to be closer to the hurricane and the lowered blind had seemed like an iron curtain. Now the hurricane was right next to him outside the double-glass of the windows. It screeched and sang in the rocks, whipping snow against the glass, and emitting a faint bluish light reflected from the snowflakes. It was as if someone had lit large spirit burners outside.

"Why should I bother about sleep?" he muttered and began to think about the aeroplane which had come flying over the mountains ahead of the storm. Steep cliffs were towering up in front of the pilot and he dared not look round. Only his back, his defenceless back sensed the hurricane driving him on like a hound pursuing a hare.

The shutters rattled in the wind. Merot's anguished thoughts became more confused until he eventually dozed off.

He had a strange dream. He was getting into a dusty grey car to drive to the south of Spain. A tall thin old man with a shaking grey goatee beard got in beside him. There was a strange clanking sound from the old man's shabby creased suit and Merot suddenly noticed with alarm that his companion was wearing rusty old armour beneath his jacket.

"We'll drive there and back," said the old man, his armour grinding in the small car, "and you will see everything. But try not to weep."

They raced along the narrow road through the mountains and each time they came to a pass vast expanses spread out below like the sea, some brown and parched by the sun, or dark with the foliage of lemon trees, others burnished with ripe corn, or blue with the haze over the forests. And with each new valley the old man in armour stood up, flung out his arm with a mighty ring and hailed it solemnly with the word:

"Spain."

They raced past towns where there was so much sun that it overflowed from the tiled roofs and walls of the houses and crept into the far corners of the cellars where Merot and the old man sat drinking wine and eating cheese that smelt of cloves.

They raced past ancient cathedrals that seemed to be covered with the grey dust of the heat, past rivers where patient bulls were lazily drinking the clear water, past schools with children singing, past palaces where the paintings of the great masters were gleaming in the shadows behind linen drapes, past orchards and fields where each clod of earth was weighed in the hand and crumbled by the firm palm of the peaceful peasants, past parks and factories humming like bees with the wheels of the hot machines, past the whole country rushing forward to hail them in the wind, laughter, songs, greetings and many other sounds of happy toil.

In a small deserted town they sped past a statue of a tall old man with a grey beard. Merot recognised this bronze figure as his companion and managed to read the inscription on the statue which said: "Miguel Cervantes de Saavedra".

"So you are Cervantes?" he shouted to the old man, who took off his hat and replied vaguely:

"Yes, I once lived in this town."

Then they turned back and began to speed past the same towns, lying in ruins, full of the heavy stench of dead bodies, past the schools where dead children with pitiful open mouths lay by the doors, past women crazed with grief running along the roads with unseeing, staring eyes, past people who had been tied to doorhandles and shot, past orchards gutted by fire, past signs scrawled in soot on the white garden walls: "Death to all who talk of freedom and justice! Death to all who are not with us!", past palaces turned into heaps of charred rubbish.

An infantry detachment stopped the car. The soldiers wore heavy boots like buckets and had red faces with ginger moustaches. The officer in charge was fair-haired with pointed ears and a dry pate.

"Who are you?" he shouted.

The old man in armour got up, his eyes dark with anger and his hands trembling.

"Curs!" he shouted. "Hired assassins covered with a bloody coat. Begone from my country! I am Cervantes, the son and poet of Spain. I am a soldier and an honest man."

The old man stretched out his arms to halt the soldiers.

"Fire!" shouted the officer, his voice shrill with anger. The soldiers fired and Merot heard the bullets hitting the old man's rusty armour. The old man fell face down in the dust and stroked the gravel of the road with his thin, warm arms as he lay dying.

"Spain!" he said fervently and a few precious tears fell onto the baking ground. "Spain, mother, land of my children!"

Another spray of bullets hit his armour, more quietly this time.

Merot woke up. Wasn't that someone at the door? He listened intently. The wind could still be heard, but not like yesterday. The hurricane was dying down. A shutter banged and someone knocked more loudly at the door.

"Who's there?" Merot asked almost in a whisper.

"It's me, sir," came the voice of the gardener.

"What's the matter?"

"There's firing in the ravine on the other side of the stream," said the gardener. "Perhaps you wouldn't mind getting up and we could listen together. I think something terrible has happened."

Merot began to dress hurriedly. Surely the war could not have reached them up here in these useless mountains. He remembered his dream and felt as if someone were slowly squeezing his throat.

"It must be the shutters banging, Matvei," he whispered afraid of waking Hervé who was sleeping next door. He wanted to believe that the gardener was wrong and that there was no firing. Why on earth should anyone be firing in this wilderness?

The gardener made no reply and they went out. The snow had stopped, the wind was dying down and huge banks of dark cloud lingering on the mountains were just visible in the east. The sun was beginning to rise. It filtered through the breaks in the heavy sky, and you could already make out the trees with their caps of snow and the green water of the pool where small scaleless fish were swimming.

The gardener took Merot up to the wall behind which the deep ravine lay in mist with the mountain stream rippling below. The bottom of the ravine was not visible—darkness always lingers longest in the gorges reluctant to leave them, like the snow.

"Here," said the gardener pointing over the wall.

Merot peered down but could not see anything.

"My eyesight's poor," he said miserably. "I can't see anything. Perhaps you'd better have a look."

"Looking down there gives you the willies," replied the gardener. "Let's keep quiet for a minute and see if we can hear anything."

They listened hard and Merot detected something like a weak groan or a short hoarse shout. It came like a bolt from the blue. Then two hollow shots rang out in the darkness on the bank of the stream.

Merot shrank back from the wall and then set off quickly for the house, followed by the gardener who was confused and baffled by what was happening. Two short shots rang out again.

Still followed by the gardener, Merot went into the laboratory and opened a niche in the wall.

His hands were shaking. He pressed a button and five bells began to ring furiously in various parts of the house and observatory. This was the alarm signal which was reserved for extreme emergencies or for summoning all the inhabitants urgently.

The bells made a deafening noise like machine-guns.

Lights switched on and doors slammed. In a few minutes the excited astronomers had gathered in the laboratory.

Only Neusted remained calm. He went up to Merot, grabbed him firmly by the shoulder and shook him lightly.

"What's happened?" he asked in a very loud voice. No one paid any attention to his rude behaviour.

"There's an injured person in the ravine signalling for help," Merot replied.

"What makes you think so?" said Dufour angrily. "Is he shouting?"

"He's shouting and firing at regular intervals."

There was silence.

"Who's coming with me?" asked Neusted unexpectedly. "If he's injured four of us will have to go, otherwise we won't be able to get him out."

"I'll go gladly," said the gardener.

"We need two more."

"What about me then?" said Baudin quietly.

"One more. There must be four of us," Neusted repeated.

Merot kept quiet. He knew he couldn't climb down the ravine. He even got tired going up the mountains by car, just from feeling the straining of the engine.

"Oh, well," said Hervé. "I'm pretty tough although I look like an old man."

"That's not important," said Neusted. "Let's be going."

By the time they had got ready and left the house it was light though misty. Neusted was the first to climb over the wall and begin the descent. He was carrying a rope. After him came the gardener with Baudin and Hervé bringing up the rear. They sent loose stones rumbling loudly down the steep sides.

Merot and Dufour waited by the wall. The sun had risen and the snow was beginning to melt. Large drops of water were dripping from the trees.

Neusted and his companions were swallowed up by the mist. For a while the only sound that could be heard was the stones clattering down the precipice. Then there was a shout from Neusted.

"Halloo there. Halloo," which was answered by a shot from somewhere nearby.

Neusted shouted:

"Shoot upwards, not at the cliffs, blast you! They might ricochet."

An unfamiliar voice repeated several times:

"Over here, over here! On the other side of the stream!"

All the voices were as audible as if they were in the room next door.

"Ricochet," Merot repeated with surprise. He knew what the word meant but this was the first time in his life that he had actually used it. "Ricochet—what an unpleasant word."

"I imagine we shall hear worse," said Dufour coldly.

The sound of voices could still be heard through the mist, but they were much more muffled than before.

"Give us a knife to cut the ropes. He's got all tangled up," came Neusted's voice. "All right, the shears will do. But make it snappy."

"What's happening?" shouted Merot, but there was no reply.

Then came a clatter, a faint cry and an angry shout from Baudin:

"For heaven's sake, watch you don't slip!"

"Let him have a rest," came the gardener's voice from somewhere quite nearby.

"Never mind about that. Carry on," said Baudin.

Merot could now see a black smudge moving slowly up the cliff.

"Hold on, Matvei," said Hervé.

"Don't worry," the gardener replied. "I won't let go. My hands are all sticky with blood."

They reached the fence at last and Merot saw that they were carrying a man covered with blood in blue tarpaulins. His face was obscured by a mass of tangled, clotted hair. Neusted's grey trousers were spotted with patches of blood.

They carried the man quickly up to Hervé's room and lay him on the bed. Baudin, who acted as the observatory doctor as well as librarian, undressed the stranger, bathed his wounds and bandaged him up. Neusted helped him.

The rooms smelt of medicine and there were pools of melted snow on the floor from the men's boots.

The observatory inhabitants gathered in the dining room. They looked at the thick drops of

197

blood trailing across the carpet and waited for Neusted and Baudin to appear. It was a long time before they came.

Merot's hands were shaking.

"We ought to have a fire, Teresa," he said. But the old woman was sitting in a corner muttering something under her breath as though she were praying, and did not hear what he said.

The first to appear was Neusted who walked up to the fireplace and began to warm his hands although there was no fire in the grate. Realising this he gave a forced smile and started to fill his pipe.

"So the war's finally reached us, too," he said. "Congratulations everybody."

"What's the matter with him?" Merot asked.

"It looks as though he's had it," Neusted replied. "He's broken just about everything that is breakable in a man's body. Parachuting in the mountains is always hopeless. He was flying from France to Madrid."

"Is he a soldier?" Dufour asked.

"No. A poet."

"I'm not exactly in the mood for joking," said Dufour in an icy voice.

"I told you. He's a poet," Neusted flared up. "The hurricane threw the plane into a spin and he managed to bail out. The rest should be obvious."

"The main point is not obvious to anyone," drawled Dufour. "You mentioned something about the war."

Baudin came in, took off his glasses and looked round at everyone with his red, short-sighted eyes.

"We need a doctor," he said distractedly. "I don't know enough to be able to save him."

It was decided immediately to send the car to the town for the doctor. Neusted would go along with the driver. Baudin and Merot would keep watch over the man helped by Teresa. For the time being all astronomical observations would be carried out by Dufour and Hervé.

"A true scientist would never have acted so hastily as Merot and Neusted," Dufour said to Hervé after the car had left. "I'm not at all convinced that we should allow this useless fussing to interrupt many years of observation. The man's not going to live in any case."

Hervé did not reply.

"War," he said finally, with a deep sigh. "I know astronomers will never shoot each other, and I'd rather not think about the rest."

"But one should bear in mind that our French observatory is on Spanish soil," said Dufour.

Neusted was driving along. The snow had melted and the wet mountains glistened in the sun. Streams of ice-cold water ran down the cliffs. The sky rose higher and higher, losing its colour. Heat was creeping up from the empty valley.

The driver braked sharply and pointed to the red cliffs, at the foot of which Neusted saw a pile of twisted metal and wood.

"His plane," said the driver.

Neusted got out and cleaned the brown blood stains off his trousers with a handful of snow which he found in the shade of the cliff.

"Let's go," he said to the driver. "Or else the old men up there may fuss him to death."

They whizzed down as if the car had suddenly taken wings, the brakes had gone and they could not stop until they reached the town. It skidded at bends sending great showers of gravel into the ravine.

Neusted was in fine spirits. He sang as the earth grew nearer. He could already smell the smoke from the poor hearths. A small herd of goats was grazing on the bare mountain side, tended by a tall old woman in a black scarf, standing by the roadside, who did not even bother to look round when the car raced past.

The town's narrow streets were deserted. A noisy bunch of thin women gathered round the car as soon as it stopped, all speaking at once. Neusted did not know Spanish at all well, but he managed to gather from what they were saying that the scoundrel of a doctor had made off with his family to Huesca leaving no one but the chemist.

One of the women was holding a little girl by the hand who was wearing the same black headscarf as all the women and the old woman tending the goats. The girl looked up at Neusted fearfully while the woman kept asking him for something wiping her eyes with her dirty apron.

"What does she want?" Neusted asked the driver.

"She wants us to take the girl with us. The girl's father has just been killed by the fascists— near Huesca. She says it's not so dangerous in the mountains. They won't go up there."

"Who's 'they'?"

The driver shrugged his shoulders:

"Who do you think?"

"We can't take her with us," said Neusted. "Who would look after her? We've got a badly injured man on our hands as it is."

The driver said nothing.

"Who would look after her?" Neusted repeated.

"I do the driving—the rest is up to you."

"Oh, so that's how it is."

Neusted opened the car door and pulled the girl in. Her mother laughed, smoothing her greying black hair, and shouted something to her daughter.

The driver started up the car and it leapt forward up the street to the chemist's. Neusted looked round and saw the women waving their black scarves, like a flock of thin birds silently flapping their wings. The little girl stared hard at the driver's back, her eyes brimming with tears.

"Tell her not to be afraid," Neusted said to the driver. "We'll take her back when it's all over."

The driver nodded.

The chemist was asleep and Neusted asked them to wake him up. A sallow hunchback appeared, greeted them sleepily and stepped onto the platform behind the counter to be higher up.

Neusted did not know what he should buy to treat the injured man, so he explained briefly what had happened and asked for advice. The chemist stared at him in amazement suppressing a yawn.

"I haven't got anything. Honestly, I haven't. All I can give you is a little plaster of Paris, some gauze and six ampules of morphine. You won't be able to manage without a doctor. You've got iodine at the observatory. Mr. Baudin bought enough iodine last year for the whole Republican army, not just one of them."

"What makes you think he's a Republican?"

"Who else would be flying from France at night? Did you find the plane?"

"No," Neusted replied. He didn't feel like chatting.

"You should be worrying about the plane, not the pilot," muttered the chemist and went into the backroom. He searched around, still mumbling something under his breath, and finally came back with a small packet.

Neusted said goodbye and the chemist saw him out onto the stone porch. A grey light hung over the town and the snow on the mountains looked very dreary.

"Where's the fighting now?" Neusted asked.

"Everywhere," answered the chemist with a smirk.

They drove back slowly as the road became steeper and steeper. The little girl sat hunched up, with her round, tear-filled eyes fixed on the driver's back. Not knowing how to comfort her, Neusted whistled and said nothing.

Once more they met the tall old woman with the small herd of goats. She turned round frowning to look at the car.

Above them stretched the faded sky. The mountains were a gingery-brown covered with bare oak bushes, and the valley had become enveloped in a greyish mist.

For the first time Neusted realised how tired he was of life in the observatory, even though it was so close to the sky and the stars. If only he were in Madrid where people were full of vigour and drive, fighting for things that were clear and straightforward. Perhaps all this would not last for long, but so what?

"So what?" he repeated out loud. The girl sat, motionless as ever, and did not look round.

"Poor little thing," he thought looking at her. He would have liked to pat her on the shoulder but didn't dare.

Now that he was down in the valley the inhabitants of the observatory seemed like corpses who were just pretending to be alive and who argued, talked, ate and observed the stars like clockwork toys. That walking clockwork mechanism with the refined ring, Dufour, was particularly irritating. Quiet old Hervé didn't seem a bad chap, but life at the observatory had mummified him.

"There's only Merot, but he's so old that a strong gust of wind might be the end of him," Neusted muttered to himself.

As they turned round a bend and the observatory came into view the driver stopped the car.

"No point in hurrying now," he said. "Look at the flag pole."

Neusted screwed up his eyes and saw that the flag had been lowered to half-mast. He knew all about this tradition. As the son of a sea captain with an interest in astronomy, Neusted was familiar with sea customs and the sight of a flag at half-mast—a sign of mourning—always made him shudder apprehensively. This sea custom had been observed by many European observatories for a long time.

Neusted realised that they were too late.

The observatory gates were closed and nobody came out when they hooted. The driver got out and opened them himself.

Neusted took the little girl's hand and set off to find Teresa.

"What's your name?" he asked her on the way.

"Si," she whispered.

"Cecile?" Neusted queried.

"Si," the little girl repeated, her eyes brimming with tears.

Neusted did not ask her any more questions.

Teresa, her eyes swollen with weeping, accepted the girl as if she had been expecting her all along. She wiped her hands on her apron, squatted down, and began to unwind the torn black kerchief round the girl's head, speaking to her in her gruff, mannish voice. The girl whispered back, but did not cry. Neusted went off bewildered—he just couldn't understand the devilish knack of getting on with children.

He went through to Hervé's room where the dead man was lying. The mirror in the dining room was covered with old sackcloth. In the passage he met Matvei carrying some freshly cut branches of pine and yew with dark leaves. They went into the room together.

The man was lying stretched out on the bed covered by a sheet. His hair had been combed revealing a deep scar on his forehead.

Matvei scattered the branches over the floor. Two wax candles were flickering on the small table. The shutters had been lowered.

"Teresa lit them," said the gardener in a hushed voice. "Women always know how to look after the dead."

Neusted looked at the stranger's face which bore the imprint of suffering in spite of its youth. His cheeks were cut by two deep furrows like scars, and his mouth looked as if he were calling softly to someone.

"So death has visited us, señor," said Matvei. "Professor Hervé has ordered a grave to be dug by the fence under the old yew tree."

"Where's Merot?" Neusted asked.

"In his room. He's very upset. The man died in his arms."

Neusted took his time before going to see Merot. Hervé came in.

"Well, Neusted," he said with a bitter smile. "Life has invaded our abode at last, even though it took the form of death."

"That's not all," Neusted replied. "I brought a little soul in need of help back from the town."

"Does someone else really need us?" Hervé asked in genuine amazement.

Merot was sitting at his desk with his weak hands pressed against his temples to restrain the tears.

The cold laquered top of the desk was bare. He had never written a single line here to anyone dear to him, only calculations and respectful letters to other astronomers. There was no one whom he loved or who loved him. There had been long ago, but Merot had forgotten about them. They had probably died long ago like that young man. "Never forget those who love you. It's better to kill than forget," his mother used to say, and now Merot realised that she was right.

The young man had died while Merot was on duty. He had been groaning all the time and had scarcely said a word, calling to Merot only once.

"Father," he said and Merot shuddered at this forgotten word. "Take the letter and papers from my case. . . . Read them. . . . Send them off. . . . If she comes, tell her . . . I am thinking of nothing but her, nothing else matters . . . nothing else. . . ."

Merot found the letter and the papers. The man fell silent and then became delirious. He sang in his delirium, and it was so terrifying that Merot called Baudin.

The man had died by the time Baudin appeared.

Merot took the letter and papers to his room, but try as he did he could not finish reading them. A host of other thoughts crowded into his brain with every line he read.

They buried the stranger in the evening, standing round silently with bared heads while the gardener and Neusted filled in the grave with wet gravel. On the grave they planted a small stick with a board on which Baudin had written the words:

"Victor Frichard, poet, Frenchman. Crashed whilst flying from France to Madrid. May the name of this stranger in our midst be added to the list of those who have distinguished themselves by their valour.

"The astronomers and staff of the French observatory Sierra del Campo (Pyrenees)."

After the burial the astronomers gathered in the laboratory. Neusted had called them all to be present at what he referred to as his emergency announcement. Everyone was exhausted and silent, for the day had cost them as much as several years of their former smoothly running life.

"Professor Merot," began Neusted, standing up to emphasise the importance of what he was about to say, "has handed me papers and a letter left by the dead man. Before his death he asked that they should be read out and dispatched to their destination. It gives me great pleasure to carry out the wishes of this man, all the more so because the contents of these papers," Neusted placed his heavy hand upon them, "compel me to give up my work at the observatory temporarily and go down to the valley where, as you know, the Civil War has been raging for five months now."

"I always knew you were a philanthropist," Dufour remarked.

"That's a tribute to your perspicacity," replied Neusted calmly. "The man whose life we tried to save and whom we have just buried was a French poet. Astronomers and poets are blood brothers. The beauty of life which surrounds us is to be found not only in the laws governing the firmament but also in the laws of poetry."

"Quite so," Dufour murmured. "What about reading the letter?"

"If you understood that," Neusted continued, "you wouldn't be spending your time now calculating the orbit of planet No. 1,212 which is not more than a kilometre in diameter. I consider such work to be as useless as counting specks of dust on the ground."

"Thank you very much!" Dufour exclaimed with a forced laugh. "And after that you still think of yourself as a scientist, do you?"

"Yes," Neusted replied rudely. "You're Dufour and I'm Neusted and we'll never swop brains. But

I haven't finished yet. The poets and writers of France pooled their resources to purchase a few aeroplanes and arms to help the Spanish People's Army. Frisher volunteered to deliver these aeroplanes to Madrid. We know the cause of his death. There are arms in the wrecked aeroplane —rifles, cartridges and machine-guns."

"That's all very well," said Hervé, "but we're not going to use them."

"The letter is addressed to a woman in Briec," continued Neusted as if he had not heard their remarks. "There's little point in mentioning her name. I'll read it to you."

"This letter will be sent to you if I die. Do you remember that last day in Briec when I was leaving, the black cliffs and the smell of the old fishing nets? A piercing wind was blowing from the ocean and your dear little hands were cold. We were alone in the poor town. You and I were quite alone together and you were not only the woman I loved, but my mother, sister and my closest friend.

"In an hour's time I shall be starting for Spain. I carry with me your words that you could not love an unworthy person. It is difficult for some to preserve their dignity in our days when baseness armed with machine-guns and phosgene gas is assaulting all that is good in life and men. Some prefer to flee to far corners and hide in warm burrows on the excuse that we only live once and that each must live his life for himself. But because we only live once, because life is unique and wonderful, I find it easier to look danger openly in the face and win this life for myself or die for it, rather than to write pretty words and suffer from the stench of my own conscience.

"I know that you will understand. I am unable to comfort you. I love this earth because you live on it. I love the air because it touches your face. I love each blade of grass that your eye lights upon, each of your footprints on the wet sand, and the night silence because I can hear the sound of your breathing. And yet I am flying to my death. I am almost certain of it.

"Farewell! Tell the fisherwomen of your grief, if you have the strength to tell. Nobody can understand it better than these simple women grown old before their time. For none of them have a family which has not known grief."

Neusted finished reading and shuffled his papers on the desk, head bowed. Nobody said a word. Hervé began to cough and pulled out a handkerchief convulsively to blow his nose.

"It's a good thing that you read the letter," said Merot quietly. "But now, if you don't mind, I will go. I can't stay any longer."

Merot left and Dufour sat with a cigarette that had gone out in his mouth.

Merot locked himself in his room, went up to the window and began to cry. A sharp heaviness in his chest hurt him. Merot thought that it would dissolve with the tears which were streaming down his sallow cheeks, but it became sharper until he could not see anything through the window. The stars were swimming about on the glass in blurred blotches.

He was filled with sorrow for the dead man, for the young, bereaved woman, for himself, Hervé and all those who were lost without refuge in this vast, pitiless world.

Late that evening Merot went to see Neusted. The Norwegian was standing by his desk tearing up some papers.

"Neusted, I'm leaving," said Merot. "I want to take the letter to Briec myself. I'll give up my work at the laboratory for a while like you."

"Why not," Neusted replied. "You haven't a son or a daughter. I see why you want to go."

Merot gave him a glance full of gratitude, and Neusted put his arm round the old man's shoulders saying:

"We must never forget each other."

"Of course not," Merot replied.

Back in his room Merot noticed his latest astronomical calculations on the desk and carefully put them away in the drawer.

The faint light of the Canes Venatici was glimmering through the window and as he glanced at it Merot suddenly realised that Briec lay in that direction.

Neither Neusted nor Merot left next morning. A distraught woman from the town rushed into the observatory at dawn. It was the little girl's mother. Her voice hoarse with alarm she told them that the town had been taken by a small detachment of fascists, that the chemist had told their commander about an injured man hiding in the observatory who had been flying from France to Madrid, and that a platoon was going to set off for the observatory that morning.

"They think he was carrying secret documents and they want to shoot him," said the woman. "That's what the soldiers were saying."

"The only secret document is with me," said Merot, "and I won't hand it over to anyone."

The woman stared at Merot in amazement. She hadn't understood what the old man was saying.

Another council of war was summoned.

"What are we going to do?" Baudin asked.

"We won't hand him over, even though he's dead," Neusted replied.

"We'll have to defend the stars against them," Dufour said with a wry laugh abandoning his aloof attitude. "Are there many of them?" he asked the woman.

"Thirty."

"Never mind," said Neusted. "Let's get down to some action."

"Of course," Dufour agreed. "Defeating this military detachment won't present any problem for us astronomers. Particularly as it does not include any of our colleagues, so even Hervé can take part in the fighting."

An hour later the driver and Neusted drove back with twenty rifles, cartridges and a machine-gun which they had salvaged from the wreckage of the aeroplane. Some of the rifles were broken, as well as the machine-gun. The driver managed to repair it by midday and wanted to try it out, but Neusted would not allow him to because the firing might put the troops on their guard too soon.

Neusted was fully in command of the situation. By tacit consent he was put in charge of the fortified observatory. Contrary to his expectations nobody questioned the necessity of offering resistance to the detachment marching up from the valley. A strange gaiety took hold of the inhabitants of the observatory, clearly the excitement which people show in moments of great danger.

The plan of defence was simply to take the enemy unawares and catch them in cross-fire. Neusted was convinced that this would be successful.

They sat up the machine-gun on a rock not far from the observatory, which was a good point for covering the bend in the road. The driver lay at the machine-gun, with the gardener and Neusted keeping watch nearby armed with rifles. The gardener had camouflaged the machine-gun and the rock with dead oak branches.

Dufour was keeping watch on the road through the small telescope. Its deserted white bends were clearly visible at a distance of fifteen kilometres. The main entrance to the observatory had been barricaded with heavy boxes of instruments.

Baudin, Hervé and Merot were sitting on a bench near the wall. From their position they could see the same bend in the road as Neusted ensconsed on the rock. Hervé was smoking his first cigarette for many years. The three old men chatted quietly and only the dry glitter in their eyes revealed that they were excited.

Their rifles were standing against the wall a little way off. It was a sunny day, with a cool wind blowing from the mountains. A white cockerel hopped onto the fence and crowed, flapping its wings. They could hear Teresa talking loudly to the woman from the town in the kitchen and saying that the old men looked as if they could still stand up for themselves.

None of the astronomers really believed that there would be any fighting. Merot was watching the shadow from the flag pole. First it lay on one rifle, then the next and now it was creeping towards the third.

"Perhaps they've turned back?" said Baudin with a note of alarm in his voice.

"Ho, ho. Be patient, you old Napoleonic guardsman!" said Merot. "You won't be disappointed."

Merot watched the shadow of the flag pole. It was now lying full on the third rifle. Something black crept up beside the shadow. Merot looked up and saw the flag being hoisted, unfurled and fluttering. This was Dufour's signal to Neusted that the detachment had been sighted on the road.

"Thank goodness, the old boy has picked out the right thing at last," said Baudin.

He was shivering with excitement. Soon Dufour appeared.

"Twenty-five!" he exclaimed animatedly. "Twenty-five royalist cut-throats led by their commander with a fiery shock of red hair."

"How do you know he's the commander?" Merot asked.

"Since when have you doubted the accuracy of our instruments? I saw the stripes on his collar."

"Well, in that case we won't argue with you," said Hervé smiling.

"They'll reach the bend in twenty minutes," said Dufour.

"If I'm not mistaken," Baudin murmured, "that

method of firing which Neusted proposed is known as flanking fire?"

"Quite correct," Dufour affirmed. "They will fall into an ambush. But have you thought about what to do if they manage to break into the yard?"

"They won't," Merot said. "Over our dead bodies."

"We must provide for all contingencies," Hervé objected. "We could withdraw to the observation towers. There are three of them and they are all made of granite. Just look—there's a staircase, a small balcony and an iron door. The two narrow windows will do for loopholes."

"Excellent defence points!" Baudin exclaimed. "Why didn't we think of them like that before?"

"That will be the best solution," said Merot. "At least we shall fall, as they say in military dispatches, at action stations next to our spectrographs and mirrors."

They all laughed. None believed that there would be any real fighting.

"It's time to get Teresa," Dufour said.

He called Teresa and her appearance silenced their jokes. She was dressed in a short skirt with a dark kerchief wound crosswise over her chest. She examined the rifles and picked the newest one saying:

"When I was a little girl my father taught me to shoot kites. They often used to steal our chickens."

"Well friends," said Baudin. "Let's get ready."

The old men picked up their rifles. Each of them had already chosen his own firing point by the wall.

Dufour looked at his watch.

"Not long now," he whispered.

They all took up their positions except Merot who had decided not to do so until the last moment because it was difficult for him to stand for long.

"That looks like a cloud of dust," said Baudin meaningfully.

"Look, Teresa."

"The snow's only just thawed," Teresa replied in the same hushed tones. "How could it be dust."

Merot patted his pocket and the letter to Briec rustled in it. He had told everyone he had the letter and this put his mind at rest.

"Ah," Dufour exclaimed quietly.

Merot hurried up to his firing point. Everyone was watching the road without stirring. The soldiers emerged slowly round the bend. Their rifles were slung over their shoulders and they were walking out of formation.

"Try not to breathe when you pull the trigger," Teresa warned.

"You're a real trooper, Teresa," said Dufour. "But why is Neusted keeping quiet for so long?"

"Our driver used to be in the army. He knows the right moment to open fire."

The road was full of the dark shapes of the soldiers by now. They stopped to let the officer through to the front and at this moment Neusted's machine-gun opened fire with a bursting howl. The yellow oak leaves whirled into the air, and the mountain echo flung the sound of the machine-gun from one cliff to the next. It recoiled from the sheer rockface, plunged down into the depths of the ravines, and soared up again, with a hollow ring which would swell into a deafening crash like steel hammers beating against empty ship's boilers. Gravel and bullets whistled along the road. The soldiers flung themselves behind a stone parapet. The officer shouted something, clutching his head, then fell and lay motionless. Dufour counted ten bodies lying on the road, but then the first bullet cracked against the wall and ricocheted over the garden with a quiet whine knocking some branches off the old pine tree.

"Wake up there, friends," shouted Baudin.

Neusted could not see the soldiers lying behind the parapet, but it was easy to shoot at them from behind the wall. Baudin was the first to fire. Teresa screwed up her eyes. A lock of grey hair kept slipping out from her kerchief and she tucked it back angrily with an impatient gesture. Dufour fired calmly taking aim very carefully. Hervé was aiming for the parapet and his successful shots sent white wisps of dust rising from it. After Merot's first shot his shoulder began to ache from the impact of the butt, but he continued firing scarcely bothering to take aim.

Some of the soldiers had begun firing at the wall and the crack of their bullets became more and more frequent. Frightened by the shooting the white cockerel flew up to the pine tree cackling, fell off and hit the ground with a thud. He had been ripped open by a bullet.

The shooting increased. Merot heard the sound of breaking glass behind him as bullets hit the windows on the first floor. He reflected that it was a good thing the laboratory was on the ground floor because all the instruments would remain intact.

Machine-gun bullets spattered along the top of the wall sending showers of dust into their eyes.

"Everyone aim for the machine-gunner!" Baudin ordered. "They've only got one machine-gun. How on earth did they manage to set it up!"

Merot fired barely conscious of what was happening. It was difficult loading the cartridges into the rifle. He knicked the skin of his palm painfully several times and his finger was bleeding.

He saw the soldiers crawling off slowly down the slope, hiding behind boulders. Judging by the expressions on their faces they were shouting and cursing. He could see the machine-gunner's legs clearly, very thin and bandy in dirty puttees. Then he saw the man jerk up, fall sideways and roll down the steep slope like a green sack until he got tangled in an oak bush.

The machine-gun was quiet now. There was only Neusted's gun going. The soldiers jumped up and ran for their lives crouching low and leaping from rock to rock, some of them throwing away their rifles.

Merot saw Neusted and the driver move the gun down quickly to the road, roll it at the run up to the bend and lie flat. The gun shuddered and barked again, sending long ribbons of dust ripping along the road. Neusted waved.

"Congratulations, old men," said Dufour. "They're retreating."

"So that's the end, is it?" Hervé asked.

The machine-gun stopped firing. A last solitary

shot rang out from Teresa. Hervé shook her by the shoulder. The road was clear except for a few soldiers who soon disappeared round a bend.

Merot threw down his rifle and stretched. The sun was shining overhead and silence lay on the mountains. He filled his lungs with air and felt the rich tang of leaves and roots.

The sound of the stream at the bottom of the ravine could be heard again. The amphitheatre of the mountains, drenched in sunshine, sparkled in an ever-changing array of late autumnal shades. Merot smiled. He knew that he had a daughter down there in Briec, someone immensely close to him, and friends, the astronomers, who were old men but courageous ones. He felt as if he had just won the right to be alive and possess the whole vibrant world below in the valleys which had once been alien to him.

Teresa smiled at Merot. He embraced her and the two old people kissed one another like brother and sister. They could hear Neusted singing a Norwegian song along the road.

The rest of the fascists were driven out of the town the same day by a detachment of Basques. Merot and Neusted left immediately. They were given a noisy farewell, but no one could conceal their sorrow at this parting.

Silence fell on the observatory once more, and the starry sky shone over it at night as usual, listening gravely to the quiet voices of the astronomers, the slow steps of the gardener and the ripple of the old stream at the bottom of the ravine.

1936

ISAAK LEVITAN

The artist Savrasov's skinny hands were shaking. He could not drink a glass of tea without spattering it over the dirty unbleached table-cloth. His grey unkempt beard stank of rye-bread and vodka.

Steaming like a samovar Moscow lay under a pall of March mist. It was getting dark. The packed ice in the drainpipes was beginning to thaw. Thundering through the pipes it would crash onto the pavement leaving glassy blue mounds which the crunch of boots soon transformed into dungwash. The Lenten chimes from the churches boomed drearily over the woodyards and cul-de-sacs of old Moscow—a Moscow of the eighteen eighties.

Savrasov was drinking vodka from a glass dulled with age. His pupil Levitan, a skinny lad in grey short trousers and a patched check jacket, sat at the table listening to him.

"Russia hasn't got its own spokesman," Savrasov was saying. "We're still ashamed of our country like I always used to be ashamed of my old beggar of a grandmother. She was a quiet old soul with her blinking red eyes, and when she died she left me her St. Sergei of Radonezh icon. Her last words to me were: 'Here, my lad, you just learn to paint like this, so that everyone will weep at the beauty of heaven and earth.' On the icon there was wild grass and the simple wayside flowers that grow along quiet country paths and by lakes surrounded by aspen. What an artful old girl she was! At that time I used to sell my watercolours to the small traders on Trubnaya Market. I'm ashamed to think of it. Ornate palaces with towers and pink swans on the lakes. Disgraceful rubbish. Right up to my old age I never painted the things that were dear to me."

The boy sat shy and silent. Savrasov lit the oil lamp. The fur-cleaner's canary began to warble and trill in the room next door. Savrasov pushed aside his empty glass uncertainly.

"You'd never dream how many views of the Peterhof and Oranienbaum I painted. We beggars worshipped all this splendour, astounded by the imagination of those who had created these magnificent palaces and gardens. After that how could we possibly begin to love our own damp fields, ramshackle cottages, our copses and lowering skies."

He shook his head and poured out some more vodka. For a long time he twirled the glass between his dry fingers. The liquid trembled as the iron rims of a heavy cart went trundling past the house. He drained his glass shiftily and then continued, choking slightly.

"That wonderful painter Corot in France. He's managed to discover beauty in mists, grey skies and deserted water. And what beauty it is! But we.... Our eyes can't stand the light. We must be blind or something. Owls! That's what we are, night owls," he said viciously standing up. "As blind as bats. Disgraceful rubbish!"

Levitan realised that it was time to go. He was hungry, but the half-drunken Savrasov had got so heated that he had forgotten to give his pupil any tea. He left the house. Draymen were trudging alongside their carts cursing and treading the snow into slush. Snowflakes clung to the bare branches of the trees along the boulevards. The taverns billowed steam across his face like laundries.

In his pocket he found thirty kopeks from his fellow students at the School of Painting and Sculpture who took pity on his poverty now and then, and went into a tavern. A music box was jingling "On the old Kaluga Road". A dishevelled waiter rushing past the counter opened his mouth wide and yelled to the owner:

"Sausage and currant loaf for the Jew-boy."

A penniless, hungry lad, grandson of a rabbi from the Kibart shtetl in Kovno gubernia, Levitan sat hunched over a table in this Moscow tavern thinking about Corot's paintings. The bedraggled customers filled the tavern with their dreary noise and the acrid smell of cheap tobacco. They wailed maudlin songs and slopped up yellowish water with sucking noises from well-licked saucers. Wet snow stuck to the black windowpanes and outside the bells continued their reluctant chiming.

He had nowhere to go and sat in the tavern for a long time. He used to spend the night in the cold classrooms at the School in Myasnitskaya Street, dodging the caretaker who was nicknamed Satan. His only relative was a sister in service who occasionally fed him and darned his old jacket. He could never understand why his father had left the shtetl to come to Moscow and why both parents had died so quickly leaving him and his sister destitute. Life in Moscow was difficult and lonely, especially for him, a Jew.

"More currant loaf for the Jew-boy," a waiter with limp legs like a rag doll said to the owner. "Looks like their god don't feed them proper."

Levitan bowed his head low. He was worn out and on the verge of tears. The heat made his legs ache. Outside the night was plastering layer after layer of wet March snow on the windows.

In 1879 the police evicted Levitan to Saltykovka where Muscovites had their summer cottages. A tsarist decree had been issued prohibiting Jews from living in the "time-hallowed Russian capital". He was eighteen at the time.

Levitan was later to recall that summer in Saltykovka as the most difficult in his life. The heat was intense. Almost every day storm clouds darkened the sky, there was a rumbling of thunder and the tall dry weeds under the windows rustled in the wind. But there was never a single drop of rain. The evenings were particularly oppressive. Lamps would be lit on the neighbouring balcony. Crowds of moths beat against the oil lamps. The click of croquet balls could be heard from the green, where grammar-school boys and girls were laughing and squabbling as they finished the game. Then late in the evening a woman's voice sang a wistful romance in the garden:

For you my voice is gentle and languid.

At that time the poetry of Polonsky, Maikov and Apukhtin was better known than Pushkin's simple refrains, and Levitan did not even realise that the words of this song had been written by Pushkin. Every evening he listened to the voice of this unknown woman behind the fence and the words of this and another song about "love's lament" became imprinted in his mind.

He wanted to see this woman with the ringing plaintive song, and the croquet-playing girls and boys chasing the wooden balls right up to the railway track with triumphant cries. He wanted to sit on the verandah drinking tea from a clean glass, stirring the slice of lemon with his spoon and watching leisurely as a clear stream of apricot jam trickled off the spoon. He wanted to laugh and fool around, to play catch, to sing until midnight. He wanted to leap about with giant strides and listen to the schoolboys whispering excitedly about Garshin whose story "Four Days" had been banned by the censor. He wanted to look into the eyes of the woman as she sang—eyes that would be half-closed and full of melancholy charm like those of all singers.

But Levitan was poor, almost destitute. He had grown much too large for his threadbare check jacket and his skinny, birdlike hands, covered with oil paint, stuck out of the sleeves awkwardly. All summer he went about barefoot. How could he possibly join the jolly crowd of holidaymakers dressed like this.

So Levitan hid himself away. He used to take a boat and paddle away into the reeds on the lake, where he would sketch without anyone disturbing him. It was more dangerous sketching in the forest or the fields. Here you might suddenly be confronted by the bright parasol of an elegant young lady reading a slim volume by Albov in the shade of the birch trees, or a governess cackling over her brood of children, and no one had such contempt for poverty as governesses.

Levitan hid away from the holidaymakers, pining for his singer in the night and sketching. He had completely forgotten that back in the School of Painting and Sculpture Savrasov had predicted that he would become another Corot, and his friends, the Korovin brothers and Nikolai Chekhov, had constantly started up arguments about the beauty of the real Russian landscape over his paintings. Corot's future fame disappeared without trace in his bitterness about life, worn elbows and tattered soles.

That summer Levitan did a lot of painting in the open air as Savrasov had instructed him. One spring day Savrasov had arrived drunk at the studio in Myasnitskaya. He smashed the dusty window in a fit of temper, cutting his hand.

"What's this you're painting!" he shouted in an anguished voice, wiping away the blood with a dirty handkerchief. "Tobacco smoke? Dung? Grey porridge?"

Clouds were scudding past the broken window, patches of hot sun lay on the cupolas and the air was full of dandelion fluff. At that time all the courtyards in Moscow were overgrown with dandelions.

"Bring the sun onto your canvas!" Savrasov shouted. The old caretaker, Satan, was already casting disapproving glances into the room. "You're blind to the warmth of spring. The snow has melted rushing down the slopes in streams of icy water—why haven't I seen that in your sketches? The lime trees are in bud and the rain has been streaming down in torrents of silver, but there's not a trace of all this in your painting. Disgraceful rubbish!"

After this harsh reprimand Levitan had begun working in the open air. At first he found it difficult to get used to the new sense of colour. Everything that had seemed pure and bright in the tobacco-laden air of the studio turned dim and lustreless outside for some strange reason.

He tried to convey a vivid sense of the transparent air embracing each blade of grass, each leaf, each haystack. Everything around him seemed to be enveloped in a tranquil, blue brilliance which Levitan called air. But it was not the air that we breathe and smell and feel its heat or cold. For Levitan it was a medium of limitless transparency which endowed his canvases with a captivating softness.

The summer came to an end. The voice of the unknown woman was gradually heard less frequently. One evening as dusk was falling Levitan met a young woman by the gate of his house. Her slender hands gleamed white under the black lace which edged the cuffs of her dress. The sky was covered with soft cloud and a fine rain was falling. A pungent smell of flowers wafted from the front gardens and the lamps had been lit on the railway points.

The woman was standing by the gate trying to open her small umbrella. Eventually she succeeded and the rain began to patter on its silk top. She set off slowly towards the station, her face hidden from Levitan by the umbrella. She could not see his face either, only his dirty bare feet. When she raised the umbrella to avoid bumping into him he caught a glimpse of her pale face in the half-light. It struck him at once as being familiar and beautiful.

Levitan went back to his small room and lay down. The candle was smoking and he could hear the drumming of the rain and the maudlin cries of drunks at the station. From that moment onwards until the end of his days he was possessed by longing for maternal, sisterly, womanly love.

That autumn Levitan painted his "Autumn Day in Sokolniki", the first of his pictures to show a grey, golden autumn, as melancholy as Russian life at that time and Levitan's own life, full of subdued warmth which went straight to the heart of all who saw it.

A young woman in black was walking along a path in Sokolniki Park among piles of fallen leaves—the unknown woman whose voice Levitan could never forget. "For you my voice is gentle and languid." She was alone in the autumn groves and her solitude gave her a melancholy, pensive aura.

"Autumn Day in Sokolniki" is the only landscape by Levitan in which a human figure appears and even then it was painted in by Nikolai Chekhov. After this we never see people in his pictures. Their place is taken by forest and mead, by the misty floods and poor izbas of old Russia, as mute and isolated as its people in those days.

Levitan's studies at the School of Painting and Sculpture finally came to an end. His last piece of work there, the painting for his final diploma, showed a field with stacks of corn under a cloudy sky. Savrasov took one look at it and chalked on the back "Large Silver Medal".

The other teachers at the School were a bit afraid of Savrasov. Constantly drunk and provocative, he would treat the students as equals and when really drunk he attacked everything, raging on about the lack of talent in most of the famous painters and demanding fresh air and open spaces in art.

The teachers transferred their dislike of Savrasov to his favourite pupil—Levitan. Moreover certain teachers were directly irritated by the talented Jewish boy himself. In their opinion a Jew had no right to meddle with the Russian countryside—this was the province of true Russian artists. The painting was pronounced unworthy of a medal and Levitan left the School with a certificate for teaching calligraphy instead of an artist's diploma. It was with this wretched certificate that one of the most sensitive artists of his time, the first budding bard of the Russian countryside, destined to be a close friend of Chekhov's, went out into the world.

The Chekhov brothers had hung up a sign on the barn in the small village of Maximovka where Levitan lived in the summer. It read: "Merchant I. Levitan's Credit Bank".

Levitan's dreams of a carefree life had finally come true. He had made friends with the artist Nikolai Chekhov and his family and lived near them for three summers running. At that time the Chekhovs spent the summer in the village of Babkino near New Jerusalem. They were a rowdy, irreverent and talented family. There was no end to their clowning. The most ordinary activities like carp fishing or picking mushrooms in the forest would develop into a riot of fun. The wild stories, fantasies and laughter would begin round the breakfast table and never die down until late at night. They would seize on every comic human trait or silly phrase and use it for joking and leg-pulling.

Levitan had to bear the brunt of this. They would constantly accuse him of all sorts of ludicrous crimes and ended up by organising his trial. Anton Chekhov, made up as prosecuting counsel, presented the case against Levitan and had everyone doubled up with laughter. Nikolai played the idiot witness, getting all mixed up in his confused evidence and taking fright, very like the character from his brother's short story "The Malefactor" who stole a nut from the railway line to make a plummet for catching pike. Alexander Chekhov gave a high-flown stagey speech as the defending counsel.

Levitan's handsome Arab features were a favourite target for them. In his letters Anton Chekhov often referred to Levitan's handsome appearance. "I will come to you as handsome as Levitan," he wrote, or "His face was as sensitively languorous as Levitan's."

But Levitan's name began to stand for the peculiar charm of the Russian countryside as well as masculine beauty. Chekhov coined the word "Levitanistic" and used it very aptly. "The countryside here is much more Levitanistic than yours," he wrote in one of his letters. He would even compare Levitan's own paintings according to how Levitanistic they were.

At first it was taken as a joke, but as time went on it became clear that this amusing adjective had a very precise meaning. It expressed the unique charm of the Central Russian countryside which Levitan alone among all his contemporaries was capable of conveying on his canvases.

Strange things would sometimes happen in the meadow by the house in Babkino. Levitan rode out dressed as a Bedouin on an old donkey at sunset. Getting off the donkey, he squatted on the ground and began to pray to the East. Wailing piteously he raised his arms and bowed to Mecca in Moslem prayer.

Anton Chekhov was crouching in the bushes with an old Berdan rifle loaded with paper and rags. He took aim at Levitan with a murderous expression on his face and pulled the trigger. Clouds of smoke poured out and there was an agitated croaking from the frogs in the river. With a piercing scream Levitan fell to the ground like a corpse. They placed him on a stretcher with a pair of old felt boots on his arms and began to carry him round the park. The Chekhov choir sang any old rubbish that came into their heads to the tune of melancholy funeral dirges until Levitan, heaving with laughter, jumped down and ran off into the house.

He would go fishing in the Istra at dawn with Anton. They chose steep banks covered with bushes and quiet still pools with water lilies and shoals of red perch in the warm water. Levitan would whisper Tyutchev's poetry with Anton glaring at him and cursing him, also in a whisper, for frightening the fish away.

So everything that Levitan had longed for in Saltykovka had come true: games of catch, the silver of the moon shining above the overgrown country garden at twilight, heated disputes over tea in the evening, smiling young women, their tender words and make-believe quarrels, the stars quivering above the groves, the cry of birds, the squeaking of carts in the night fields, the company of talented close friends, well-earned recognition and ease of body and spirit.

In spite of this life full of the joys of summer Levitan was working very hard. The walls of his barn, which used to be a hen-house, were covered from top to bottom with his sketches. At first glance they appeared to contain nothing new: the same familiar twisting paths losing themselves in the sloping hillsides, copses, broad vistas, the shining moon over the edge of a village, paths trodden across the fields by peasant feet, clouds and lazy rivers.

His canvases showed a familiar world, but there was also something special about it which cannot be conveyed by limited human speech. His paintings evoked the same poignant nostalgia as enticing memories of a dim and distant childhood.

Levitan was a master of the melancholy landscape. Landscapes are always melancholy where people are living melancholy lives. For centuries Russian literature and art portrayed dull skies, poor fields and crooked izbas.

> *Russia, paupered Russia,*
> *your black izbas, the song of your winds,*
> *are like the tears of first love to me.*

Generation upon generation had looked at nature with eyes dulled by hunger. It had seemed as bitter as their own fate, as a hunk of dank rye bread. Even the brilliant sky of the tropics would look inhospitable to a starving person. Thus the poison of despair was generated, engulfing everything and robbing paint of its colour, interplay and splendour. The gentle variety of the Russian countryside was defamed for centuries as being melancholy and gloomy. Painters and writers lied about it unintentionally.

Levitan was descended from the ghetto deprived of all rights and prospects, from the Pale of Settlement, a land of shtetl, consumptive artisans, black synagogues, congestion and poverty. This lack of rights was to pursue him all his life. He was evicted from Moscow for the second time in 1892, although his fame as an artist had now spread all over Russia, and was forced to take refuge in Vladimir gubernia until his friends succeeded in getting the order revoked.

There was a lack of joy in Levitan which reflected the sad history of his people and ancestors. He would fool around in Babkino, engrossed in young women and painting, but somewhere deep down lurked the thought that he was a pariah, an outcast, the son of a race subjected to humiliating persecution. Sometimes this thought would take complete possession of him and he would have fits of deep depression which were exacerbated by dissatisfaction with his work and the knowledge that he was not capable of conveying in his painting things that his fertile imagination had created long ago.

At such times he would shun people, feeling them to be his enemies. He became boorish, rude and impatient, scraping the paint viciously off his canvases, hiding away or going off to hunt with his dog Vesta, when he would wander aimlessly around the forest doing no hunting at all. On days such as these his only close companion was nature. It would comfort him, caressing his forehead with its breezes like a mother stroking her child. He found peace from human stupidity and inquisitiveness in the nocturnal silence of the fields.

He tried to shoot himself twice during these fits of depression and on both occasions it was Chekhov who saved him.

The moods would pass and Levitan would regain contact with people and begin to paint, love and believe again, becoming involved in the complexities of human relationships until a fresh bout of depression overcame him. Chekhov thought that this depression was the first stage of a mental disease. But perhaps it was that incurable disease which afflicts all great men who make high demands on themselves and life.

Everything he had painted seemed wrong. He would look at the colours on the canvas and see clearer, richer ones behind them. These were the ones he wanted to use to show the Russian landscape, crystal clear as the September air and as festive as autumn leaves falling in the forest, not the dull factory vermilions, cobalts and cadmiums.

But his low spirits guided his brush while he was working and it was a long time before he could bring brightness and clarity into his paintings. His canvases were shrouded in dull light. The paint stared out sullenly and, try as he would, he could not make it smile.

In 1886 for the first time in his life Levitan went south to the Crimea. He had spent the whole winter in Moscow painting opera scenery and this left its mark on his work. He began to use paint more boldly, his strokes became freer and the first signs of another attribute of true artists appeared—the imaginative use of materials. This quality is essential to all those who are engaged in giving expression to their thoughts and ideas. A writer must be able to handle language and his store of observations competently, in the same way as the sculptor must handle clay and marble, and the artist colour and line.

The most valuable thing that Levitan gained in the south was a sense of pure colour. For him the whole period of his stay in the Crimea was one long morning when the air, which had settled in the night like water in the gigantic reservoirs of mountain valleys, was so clear that you could see the distant dew falling off the leaves, and the white crests of waves rolling towards rocky shores were visible for miles around. The vast expanses of air lay over this southern landscape throwing its colours into sharp relief.

It was in the south that Levitan became fully aware that the sun alone determines the nature of colour. Its rays possess tremendous artistic force. The greyness of the Russian countryside is beautiful only because it is the same sunlight in subdued form, penetrating through layers of damp air and a thin membrane of cloud.

The sun is incompatible with black, for black is the dead corpse of colour. Levitan realised this and decided to banish all dark tones from his painting after his visit to the Crimea, although he did not always succeed in doing so.

Thus began the long struggle for light which was to continue for many years. At this time Van Gogh was working in France trying to capture the fiery sun which turned the vineyards of Arles into a crimson gold. About the same period Monet was studying the play of light on the walls of Rheims Cathedral. He was struck by the fact that in a hazy light this massive bulk looked ethereal as if it were made from masses of air in different pastel shades instead of stone. The only way to return to reality was to go up and touch the stone.

Levitan was still experimenting hesitantly, while the French painters struck out boldly in new directions. They were supported in their work by a feeling of personal liberty, by cultural traditions and a friendly atmosphere of understanding, all of which were denied to Levitan. He had never known what it felt like to be free.

All he could do was dream about it helplessly, furious with the stupidity and tedium that pervaded Russian life at that time. For him there was no friendly atmosphere of understanding either.

After his visit to the Crimea Levitan's customary depression was reinforced by the constant memory of dry sharp colours and a sun which could transform the most ordinary day into a great festival.

There was no sun in Moscow. He lived in a block of furnished rooms called "Angliya" on Tverskaya Street. The town was so densely shrouded in cold mists at night that it did not manage to cast them off in the brief hours of winter daylight. An oil lamp burned away in his room, its yellow glow mingling with the murky gloom and leaving grey smears on people's faces and his unfinished canvases.

Again Levitan found himself without money, but this time not for long. He was driven to paying the rent with sketches, and felt deeply ashamed whenever the landlady put on her pince-nez and peered at the "little pictures" trying to calculate which would sell best. The worst thing of all was that her muttered remarks coincided with the views of the newspaper critics.

"M'sieu Levitan," she would say. "Why don't you put a nice thoroughbred cow into this meadow and a pair of young lovers under this lime tree? It would make such a pretty picture." The critics said more or less the same. They wanted Levitan to liven up his landscapes with flocks of geese, horses, shepherd boys and maidens. While the critics were asking for geese Levitan was thinking of that glorious sun which would one day flood the Russia of his paintings and give every birch tree the substance and lustre of precious metal.

After the Crimea it was the Volga that was to play an important part in Levitan's life for a long time. His first trip there was not a success. The water became turbid in the drizzling rain. The wind whipped up dismal ripples on its surface. Rain trickled monotonously down the windowpanes of the house in the village on the banks of the Volga where Levitan was staying. Mist covered the horizon and everything around was swallowed up in greyness. Levitan suffered from the cold, the slippery clay banks of the river and the impossibility of painting in the open air.

He began to lie awake at night envying his old landlady who was snoring behind the partition. He described his envy in a letter to Chekhov. The rain was drumming on the roof and every half-hour Levitan would light a match to look at the clock.

The dawn would be lost in the black impenetrable wastes of night where the inhospitable wind held sway. He became terrified at the thought that the night would go on for weeks, that he had been exiled to this dirty village and was doomed to spend the rest of his life listening to the wet birch branches lashing against the log wall.

Sometimes he went out onto the porch at night and the branches beat against his face and arms. He got angry, lit a cigarette and then threw it away immediately—the acrid smoke gave him jaw cramp. He could hear the persistent, servile knocking of a paddle wheels on the Volga where a tugboat with winking yellow lights was dragging a trail of stinking barges up the river to Rybinsk.

The great river appeared to Levitan like the gateway to a gloomy underworld. Dawn brought no relief. The clouds scudded along from the north-west in senseless huddles, dragging their watery hems of rain across the earth. The wind whistled through the crooked windows turning his hands red with cold, and cockroaches scuttled out of his paint box.

Psychologically Levitan was not very robust. He was easily driven to despair by the contrast between what he wanted and what he saw in reality. He longed for the sun which never appeared. Blinded with fury he did not even notice at first the subtle shades of grey that the bad weather brought with it.

But in the end the artist triumphed over the depressive. Levitan discovered the charm of the rain and painted his famous "rain studies"—"After the Rain" and "Above Eternal Rest". "After the Rain" was painted in four hours. The clouds and the pewter colour of the Volga radiated a gentle light. Fearing that it might disappear at any minute, Levitan had to paint quickly.

Levitan's pictures must be looked at slowly. They do not make an immediate impact. Like Chekhov's stories they are unpretentious and precise and the longer you look at them the more they reveal the quiet charm of old provincial towns and the familiar rivers and cart tracks.

"After the Rain" conveys the peculiar beauty of a rainy twilight in a small town on the Volga. The puddles are glistening, and clouds are floating low over the Volga like a trail of smoke. The steam from passing boats is settling on the water and dampness has darkened the moored barges.

On such dusky summer evenings it is a delight to come into the dry passage and low rooms with freshly scrubbed floors where the lamps have already been lit, with the patter of the rain and the pungent fragrance of the overgrown garden drifting through the open windows. It is a delight to hear the sound of an old grand piano, its loose strings twanging like a guitar. A dark aspidistra is standing in a tub by the piano. A schoolgirl is sitting in an armchair reading Turgenev with her legs tucked under her. An old cat wanders about the room, one ear twitching nervously to catch the sound of knives should they start cutting up meat in the kitchen.

There is a smell of bast matting from the street. Tomorrow there is going to be a fair and the wagons are assembling in Sobornaya Square. A steamboat is disappearing down the river overtaking a rain cloud which covers half the sky. The schoolgirl is watching the boat and her eyes widen and grow misted as she watches it go downstream to towns where there are theatres, books and exciting encounters.

Day and night the scruffy rye fields around the small town lie soaking in the rain.

"Above Eternal Rest" conveys the poetry of bad weather with even greater force. It was painted on the bank of Lake Udomlya in the Tver gubernia. The view of a deserted distant river, meadows dulled by the bad weather and a vast cloudy sky is seen from a hillside with dark birch trees bending under the gusts of wind and a dilapidated wooden church in their midst. Thunder clouds heavy with cold moisture hang over the earth. The distant expanses are concealed by coarse slanting curtains of rain.

No artist before Levitan managed to convey with such melancholy force the vastness of rain-drenched Russia, magnificent in its peace and solemnity.

Levitan's second visit to the Volga was more successful. This time he went with a fellow artist Kuvshinnikova. Chekhov described this naive woman with her touching love for Levitan in his story "The Grasshopper". Levitan was so deeply offended by it that their friendship broke up for a long time. Reconciliation was slow and painful, and Levitan could never quite forgive Chekhov for this story.

They travelled first to Ryazan and then by steamboat down the Oka to the small settlement of Chulkovo where Levitan decided to stay for a while. The sun was setting in the fields beyond the clay banks of the river. Young boys were chasing doves crimson in the setting sun. Fires were burning along the meadowed bank and the morose booming of the bittern echoed in the marshes.

Chulkovo embodied everything for which the Oka was renowned, that river:

...welling her wooded banks with spring floods,
Who shining queen-like glides with ease
Among the vastness of our Murom sands
Enfolded all around by honoured shores.

Nothing conveys the charm of the lazy Oka better than these lines by Yazykov.

On the quayside at Chulkovo a short old man with only one eye came up to Levitan, grabbed hold of the sleeve of his tussore jacket and kneaded the material for a long time with his coarse fingers.

"What do you want, dad?" Levitan asked.

"Nice bit o' cloth," said the old man and hiccuped. "Just admirin' this nice bit o' cloth. Silky as a wench's hair. Who's that then, beggin' yer pardon? Yer wife?" He pointed at Kuvshinnikova with a malicious look in his eye.

"My wife," Levitan replied.

"Is that so?" said the old man malevolently, moving away. "Devil only knows what yer up to, why you're gaddin' about."

This encounter did not bode well. When Levitan and Kuvshinnikova found a spot on the hillside the following morning and opened their paint boxes, a great commotion started in the village. Women rushed about from one house to the next and a crowd of sullen-looking peasants with straw in their hair and unbelted shirts began to gather on the hillside and sat down a little way off from the artists glowering at them. Small boys breathed noisily behind Levitan, pushing each other and squabbling.

A toothless old woman crept up on one side, took a long look at Levitan and suddenly gasped:

"Lord Jesus Christ, what's that you're a-doin', you wretched sinner?"

A murmur broke out among the peasants. Levitan sat tight-lipped and pale, but tried to laugh it off.

"Don't look, missus, or your eyes'll pop out,"
he said.

"Ee, the shameless thing!" the old woman cried
and went off to join the peasants, blowing her
nose on her hem. There leaning on a staff, was a
frail, lachrymose monk who had wandered into
Chulkovo one day from goodness knows where
and attached himself to the local church.

"Godless lot," he shouted not very loud. "What
are they up to? Interferin' with God's meadows.
There'll be a fire, brothers. There'll be disaster."

"Call a meeting," shouted the old man with
one eye. "We don't have no time for folk that
come drawin' pictures with women. Call a meeting!"

They had to pack up their paints and go. They
decided to leave the township the same day. As
they walked towards the quay they could hear
the incoherent babble of the mob by the church
and the shrill cries of the monk.

"Godless lot. Unchristened sinners. The hussy's
got nothing on her head."

Kuvshinnikova was not wearing either a hat
or headscarf.

They went down the Oka as far as Nizhny
Novgorod and from there on another boat to
Rybinsk. All the time they sat on deck scanning
the banks for a suitable spot for sketching, but
there were none. Levitan grew more and more
gloomy and complained of being tired. The river
banks glided past slowly and monotonously with
no picturesque villages or smooth pensive bends
to gladden the eye.

At last in Plyoss Levitan saw a tiny old church
made of pine logs, darkling against the greenish

16–1648

sky with the first evening star twinkling brightly above it. The church, the evening hush, and the sing-song voices of women selling milk on the quayside gave Levitan such a deep feeling of calm that he decided immediately to stay in Plyoss, a stay which was to prove one of the happiest interludes in his life.

The small town was hushed and deserted. The silence was broken only by the gentle lowing of cattle, the ringing of the church bells, and the warning tapping of the nightwatchmen. Burdock and goose-foot grew along the sloping streets and gullies. Lime blossoms lay drying on the window-sills behind the muslin curtains.

The dry, sunny weather held out. As it approaches autumn the Russian summer becomes increasingly infused with ripe colour. As early as August the leaves on the apple trees begin to flush, the fields glimmer with a silvery grey and the clouds over the Volga of an evening are touched with a hot red.

Levitan's depression disappeared and he was ashamed to recollect it.

Each day brought something unexpected and touching. A half-blind old woman dropped a worn five-kopek piece into his paint box, taking him for a beggar, young children nudging each other in the back asked him to paint them, then burst out laughing and run off, or else a neighbour, a young woman from the Old Believers, crept in to lament her unhappy lot. Levitan called her Katerina after the heroine of Ostrovsky's play *The Storm*. He and Kuvshinnikova decided to help Katerina to escape from Plyoss and her hateful family. They would discuss her flight in a wood outside the town, the two women whispering together while Levitan lay on the edge of the wood and gave a low whistle to announce approaching danger. Katerina did actually manage to escape.

Before his stay in Plyoss Levitan had loved only the Russian countryside, whilst the people inhabiting this vast country had remained a mystery to him. Whom had he met apart from the rude school caretaker, Satan, the tavern waiters, the crafty attendants in furnished blocks and the uncouth peasants in Chulkovo? He had seen a great deal of spite, filth, blind submission, and contempt for him as a Jew.

Until his visit to Plyoss he had not believed that people could be affectionate, sensible and capable of deep understanding. It was Plyoss that made him realise his kinship not only with the Russian countryside but with its people, its talented, unfortunate people who now seemed to be hushed in expectation of either fresh calamity or the great moment of liberation.

Levitan painted a great deal during this second visit to the Volga and Chekhov told him: "Your pictures are finally beginning to smile."

Brightness and light appeared for the first time in Levitan's work in his "Volga paintings" such as "Golden Plyoss", "A Fresh Breeze" and "Evening Bells".

Almost all of us have retained childhood memories of forest clearings strewn with leaves, lush, melancholy corners of our native land gleaming under the mild sun amid a blue haze, the hush of unruffled waters and the cries of migrating birds. In our mature years these memories sometimes flood back with amazing power at the slightest association. A fleeting glimpse of the countryside through a train window, say, will fill us with a deep inexplicable sense of excitement and happiness, and the desire to cast aside town life, all our problems, our familiar circle of friends, and fly away to these remote spots, to the shores of unknown lakes and forest paths where each sound, whether it be the hoot of a distant train or the twitter of birds fluttering about in the rowan tree, rings out clear and long as if from a mountain top.

Looking at Levitan's "Volga" and "autumn" paintings you have the same feeling of nostalgia for precious places belonging to the past.

Levitan's life was not an eventful one. He did not travel much. He loved only Central Russia and considered visits to anywhere else a sheer waste of time, including his one trip abroad, when he went to Finland, France, Switzerland and Italy.

The granite rocks of Finland, its black rivers, jelled sky and sombre sea made him despondent. "I have become intensely depressed again," he wrote to Chekhov from Finland. "There's no real countryside here."

He admired the Alps in Switzerland but for him they were just like cardboard models painted in garish colours.

The only thing he liked in Italy was Venice where the air was full of silver undertones from the dim lagoons.

He saw Monet's paintings in Paris, but was not particularly impressed by them and it was only towards the very end of his life that he began to appreciate the Impressionists and realised that he was to a certain extent their Russian counterpart.

During the last years of his life Levitan spent a great deal of time in Vyshny-Volochok on the banks of Lake Udomlya, staying with the Panafidins on their estate. Here he again became involved in the complexities of human relationships and once more tried to shoot himself unsuccessfully.

As old age approached Levitan became more and more absorbed with autumn. He painted several magnificent spring scenes, it is true, but in nearly all of them the spring has an autumnal quality about it. "Spring Flood" shows a submerged wood of bare autumnal trees without the slightest hint of young green leaves. In "Early Spring" a deep black river stands still and lifeless between steep banks still covered with loose snow. "March" is the only painting which shows the true brilliance of a spring sky over thawing snowdrifts, with the yellow light of the sun and the crystal flash of the melted snow dripping from the doorway of a log house.

The most gentle and moving Russian poetry, novels and paintings are all about autumn. Like Pushkin and Tyutchev, Levitan would look forward to autumn as the most precious, fleeting season of all. Autumn would strip the deep colours from the forests and fields, the whole of nature, and wash the greenery away with its rains. The groves would thin out. The dense colours of summer gave way to shy golds, scarlets and silvers. The air itself changed as well as the colour of the earth. It became cleaner, colder and seemed to recede more deeply into the distance than in the summer, just as the rich colours and florid language of great artists and writers in their early years give way to a more subdued, dignified style in maturity.

Levitan's autumn studies are immensely varied, and it would be impossible to describe their diversity. He left about a hundred "autumn paintings" not counting his sketches.

They showed the familiar objects of childhood: haystacks dark with damp, small rivers with fallen leaves gyrating slowly in their waters, solitary golden birch trees not yet stripped by the wind, a sky of spun ice, ragged streams of rain over forest glades. But no matter what these landscapes depicted, the thing that they conveyed best of all was the poignancy of these last days, the drifting leaves, the rotting grass, the quiet hum of bees as the cold approached, and the late autumn sun barely warming the earth.

As the years passed Levitan gradually developed a serious heart disease of which neither he nor his friends were aware until the first acute attack. He refused to see any doctors for fear that they would pronounce his death sentence. Obviously they would have forbidden his trips into the country and for him that was tantamount to death.

He felt even more melancholy than in his youth and began going off into the forest more and more frequently, where he used to be found, tearful and distraught. He spent this last summer near Zvenigorod. He knew that nothing, neither doctors, nor a quiet life, nor his frenzied communion with nature could ward off approaching death.

In the winter of 1899 his doctors sent him to Yalta, where Chekhov was living at the time. The two old friends met, now ageing and estranged. Levitan walked with difficulty leaning heavily on a stick, short of breath and telling everyone that he was going to die soon. He was afraid of death and made no attempt to conceal this. His heart pains were almost unremitting.

Chekhov was longing for Moscow and the North. In spite of the fact that the sea was "big", to quote him, it compressed the world. There seemed to be nothing left in life except the sea and the winter quiet of Yalta. Somewhere far beyond Kharkov, Kursk and Orel there was snow and the lights of poor villages winking blindly into grey snowstorms. The snowstorms seemed closer and more precious to him than the cypresses and the balmy sea air, which often made his head ache. Everything seemed precious to him: the forests and little rivers with such homely sounding names as Pekhorka and Vertushinka, the haystacks in deserted evening fields, standing isolated in the dim moonlight, as if they had been abandoned by man for ever.

The ailing Levitan asked Chekhov for a piece of cardboard and within half an hour he had done a sketch in oils of haystacks in a field at evening. Chekhov put it on the fireplace by his desk and often looked at it while he was working.

It was a dry, sunny winter in Yalta with warm winds blowing from the sea. Levitan remembered his first visit to the Crimea and wanted to go into the mountains. He was haunted by the memory of this first journey when he had seen the deserted cloudy sky lying at his feet as he stood on the top of Ai-Petri. The sun shining overhead had seemed much nearer to the earth than usual and its yellow light cast sharp shadows. The cloudy sky swirling below in the ravines crept slowly up to his feet, obscuring the pine forests. The sky moving below him had frightened Levitan as much as the eery mountain silence, broken only by the occasional clatter of loose stones. The slate would slide off the slope and bounce into the dry prickly grass.

Levitan wanted to go into the mountains and asked to be taken to Ai-Petri, but his request was refused. The rarified mountain air might have proved fatal for him.

Yalta did not help him and so he returned to Moscow. During his last months he rarely left his house in Tryokhsvyatitelsky Alley. He died on the twenty second of July, 1900. It was late evening, the time when the first star appears over Moscow at a terrifying height and the leaves on the trees are bathed in yellow dust and the glimmering of the dying sun.

The summer had come late. Lilac was still in bloom in July and its heavy bushes filled the front garden by the house. In the studio where Levitan lay dying there was a smell of leaves, lilac and oil paints, a smell which had constantly followed the artist who expressed the sadness of the Russian countryside in his paintings—that countryside which, like its people, seemed to be waiting for happier times.

These times came very shortly after Levitan's death and his pupils were able to see what their teacher had not—a new land whose countryside had changed because man had changed, a bountiful sun and magnificent expanses, the pure sky and the sparkle of colours which Levitan had never known. Levitan could not see all this because the countryside can only be joyous when man is free and happy.

Levitan had wanted to laugh but could not bring even a faint smile to his canvases. He was too honest to ignore the suffering of the people. He became the bard of a vast, poor land and its countryside, and saw the countryside through the eyes of the suffering people. This explains his power as an artist and, to a certain extent, the secret of his great appeal.

1937

MESHCHORA COUNTRY

A Simple Land

There is nothing particularly beautiful or striking about Meshchora country apart from its forests, meadows and translucent air, but all the same these parts have a kind of magical charm. Like Levitan's landscapes they are unassuming and yet contain all the hidden fascination and variety of the Russian countryside.

Your eye is greeted by flowering or newly-mown meadows, pine forests, meadow or forest lakes overgrown with black water-weed, and stacks of pungent hay that stays warm all through the winter. I remember spending the night in a haystack one October when hoar frost covers the grass like salt in the early morning. Burrowing deep into the hay I slept there all night as snugly as if I were behind locked doors, although a cold rain was lashing the fields and the wind was blowing in slanting gusts.

There are pine forests so quiet and brooding that you can hear the sound of the "dangler" bell on a lost cow from almost a mile off. But in windy weather the forests murmur like vast oceans and the pines bow their tops in the wake of the drifting clouds.

There are dark forest lakes, broad stretches of marshland covered with alder and aspen, lonely woodmen's izbas blackened with age, sands, juniper, heather, flocks of cranes and the familiar pattern of stars at night.

Apart from the murmuring of the pine forests there is the cry of quail and hawk, the flute-like song of the oriole, the busy tapping of the woodpecker, the howl of wolves, the rustle of rain on the fallen russet needles, the plaintive strains of an accordion in small villages of an evening, and the dissonant song of cocks mingled with the tapping of the village night watchman.

At first this is all that strikes the eye and ear. But then each day these parts grow richer, more varied and dearer to the heart, until the time comes when each willow bending over the sluggish river becomes so familiar that it seems to belong to you and you can tell wonderful stories about it.

I have not conformed to usual practice. Geographical accounts almost invariably begin with one and the same sentence: "This area is situated between longitude so many degrees east and latitude so many degrees north, bounded by such and such region to the south and such and such to the north." I do not propose to give Meshchora's latitude and longitude. Suffice it to say that the area lies between Vladimir and Ryazan, not far from Moscow, and is one of the few remaining stretches of forest in the "great coniferous belt" which used to stretch from Polesie to the Urals, including the forests of Chernigov, Bryansk, Kaluga, Meshchora, Mordvinia and along the Kerzhenets. It was in these forests that old Russia sought refuge from the Tatar raids.

First Encounter

I first arrived in Meshchora country from the north, travelling from Vladimir and changing onto a narrow-gauge line at the secluded station of Tuma near Gus-Khrustalny. The train with its engine puffing like a samovar and its shrill "peep peep" belonged to the days of Stevenson. It had the unfortunate nickname of "gelding" and really did look like an old gelding. It groaned to a halt at bends and the passengers got out for a smoke. Then the forest silence surrounded the puffing and panting "gelding", and the carriages were invaded by the scent of white pinks warm from the sun.

Passengers with luggage sat on the platform leading into the carriage because there wasn't enough room for their things inside. Now and then in the course of the journey, bundles, baskets and carpenter's saws came flying from this platform onto the track, followed by their owner, frequently in the form of a very old woman. The less experienced passengers looked on in terror, but the others explained, rolling themselves a cigarette and hawking, that it was the best way of getting off the train near your village.

This narrow-gauge line in the Meshchora forests must be the laziest railway in the Soviet Union. The stations, piled high with freshly chopped timber, smell of resin and wild forest flowers.

At Pilevo an old man with a shaggy beard got into the carriage. Crossing himself before the corner where a rattling bulbous iron stove stood, he gave a weary sigh and began complaining into empty space:

"So they takes me by the beard and says—lace up yer boots and off ter town. 'Course it don't come into their 'eads that it be all a waste o' time. Sendin' me to that there museum where the Soviet government be collectin' cards, price-lists and the like. Got me chitty, too, I has."

"What you on about, then?"

" 'Ere you are. Take a look at this."

The old man fished out a crumpled piece of paper, blew the tobacco off it and showed it to the woman sitting next to him.

"Read it out, Manka," she said to the little girl with her nose pressed against the window.

Manka pulled down her dress over her scratched knees, tucked her legs under the seat and began to read in a hoarse voice:

"This is to inform you that there are three large striped birds of great size living in the lake.

Not known where they came from. Should be captured alive for the museum, for which purpose send bird-catchers."

"There you are," said the old man bitterly. "That's the sort o' thing they're plaguin' old men with nowadays. It's that Komsomol lad Lyoshka. A real pest, 'e is. Blast 'im."

The old man spat and the woman wiped her fat mouth with the end of her scarf and sighed. The engine pooped nervously and the forest murmured right and left, rippling like a lake. The wind was blowing from the west and the train had some difficulty in forcing its way through the wet gusts. It was hopelessly behind time and panted hard at the small, empty stations.

"Such is life!" said the old man. "Year afore they sends me off to the museum and this year again."

"Wot they find year afore, then?" asked the woman.

"A bit of old bone. Stuck in the mud, it was. Deer or somethin'. Horns the size of this carriage, swelp me. Took 'em a month to dig it out."

"Wot they do with it, then?" the woman asked.

"Young 'uns goin' to learn from it."

This find is described in the Research and Publications of the Local Museum as follows:

"The skeleton was firmly entrenched in the quagmire, which gives no foothold for the diggers. They were compelled to undress and descend into the quagmire, which was extremely difficult due to the freezing temperature of the spring water. The enormous horns, as also the skull, were intact, but extremely fragile as a result of extensive maceration (softening caused by steeping in liquid) of the bones. The bones crumbled in the hand, but hardened as they dried out."

It was the skeleton of the gigantic fossil deer known as the Irish elk with antlers two and a half metres long between the tips.

This meeting with the old man marked the beginning of my Meshchora days. I was to hear a great many stories about mammoth teeth, buried treasure and mushrooms the size of a man's head. But it was this first story in the train which I remembered most clearly.

An Old Map

After a great deal of trouble I managed to get hold of a map of the Meshchora area, with a note to the effect that "This map was compiled in accordance with old surveys conducted before 1870". I had frequent occasion to correct it myself. The course of the rivers had changed, or patches of young pine forest had appeared where the map showed marshland, or quagmires had taken the place of lakes.

All the same it was safer to use this map than to ask the local people. It's a well-known fact in Russia that nobody will give you such confused directions as a local person, particularly if he happens to be a talkative soul.

"Don't you listen to anyone else, my lad," he'll say. "They tell you such a load of rubbish that you'll be sorry you ever saw the light of day. Just you listen to me. I know these parts like the back of my hand. Go to the edge of the village and you'll see large wooden house on your left.

Turn right at the house along the path between the sands as far as the Prorva and then go straight on until you get to a burnt willow tree. Bear slightly to the forest past Muzga and make straight for the big hill. Then it's over the marshes to the lake. You can't miss it."

"How many kilometres is it?"

"Goodness knows. Ten or maybe a good twenty. There's no measurin' distance here, lad."

I used to try and follow these directions, but there always turned out to be more than one burnt willow tree or no big hill. So finally I decided to do without this advice and rely solely on my own sense of direction which rarely let me down.

The locals delighted in telling the way and could talk animatedly for hours on end. This used to amuse me at first, until one day I had to tell the poet Simonov how to get to Lake Segdan, and caught myself describing the landmarks along this complicated route with the same gusto.

Whenever you tell someone the way, it's as if you are actually traversing it yourself, all those wild open spots, the forest tracks dotted with immortelle, and you suddenly feel light-hearted again. The light-heartedness which we feel when the road is a long one and we have no cares in the world.

A Word About Signs

If you don't want to lose your way in the forests you must know something about signs. Finding or making them yourself is a delightful pastime. The world of signs is endlessly rich. It's such a pleasure when the same sign remains in the forest year after year; each autumn you find the same bush of flaming mountain ash beyond Larin Pond or the same notch which you cut in that pine tree three years ago, and which oozes more and more thick golden resin each summer.

Path signs are not the main signs. The real signs are those which indicate the weather and time. There are so many that you could write a whole book about them. We have no need for them in the town. The flaming mountain ash is ousted by the blue enamelled plate bearing the name of the street. The time is told by clocks, not by the height of the sun, or the position of the stars, or even by the cock crowing. Weather forecasts are broadcast on the radio. Most of our natural instincts go into hibernation in the town. But after a night or two in the forest our hearing, sight and sense of smell become perceptibly more acute.

The whole of Nature, the colour of the sky, the dew and the mist, the cry of birds and the brightness of the stars, is full of signs.

They contain a great deal of accurate knowledge and poetry. They may be simple or complex. The simplest sign is the smoke from an open fire. It may rise straight up to the sky in a quiet column higher than the highest willows, or drift low in the grass like mist or whirl round the fire. So in addition to the delights of a night fire, the slightly acrid smell of the smoke, the crackling of the dry branches, the flickering tongues of flame and the feathery white ash, we have the pleasure of knowing what tomorrow's weather is going to be like.

By watching the smoke it is possible to predict whether there will be rain or wind tomorrow, or whether, like today, the sun will rise in profound silence and cool blue mist. The evening dew can also be a sign of calm, warm weather. It is sometimes so heavy that it reflects the stars, and the heavier the dew the hotter it will be the following day.

These are all very simple signs, but there are others which are more complex and very accurate. Sometimes the sky suddenly seems very high but the horizon appears to contract as if it were only a kilometre or so away. This is a sign that clear weather is on the way. Or again it sometimes happens that the fish stop biting on a cloudless day and the rivers and lakes grow motionless as if all life had retreated from them. This is a sure sign that a long spell of bad weather is not far off. Another day or two and the sun will rise in an ominous crimson haze and by noon black clouds will almost touch the ground, accompanied by gusts of damp wind and the monotonous, somnolent rain will come pouring down.

Back to the Map

I let myself get carried away by the subject of signs and forgot all about the map of Meshchora.

The best way to get to know a new area is by studying a map—a pastime which is just as interesting as the study of signs. You can roam around a map just as you can an area, and as soon as you actually find yourself in the spot you have been studying you feel the benefit of your newly-acquired knowledge which prevents you from wandering around blindly and wasting time.

At the bottom of the Meshchora map in the farthest corner there is the loop of a large river, the Oka. North of the Oka is a wooded, marshy depression and south lies the well-cultivated and populated countryside around Ryazan. Thus the Oka forms the boundary of two entirely different and very dissimilar stretches of land.

Ryazan country is an area of cereal crops, yellow rye fields and lush apple orchards. One village frequently spills over into the next and they come in thick clusters. Wherever you look you are sure to find at least one, and perhaps two or three belfries still intact. The slopes here are covered with rustling birch groves instead of forest.

Ryazan country is a land of fields and south of the town of Ryazan the open steppe begins. But take the ferry to the opposite bank of the Oka and you will find the dark wall of the Meshchora pine forests rising beyond the broad stretch of meadows by the river. These forests with their round blue lakes stretch both northwards and eastwards, and they conceal vast peat bogs in their depths.

In the west of Meshchora there are eight old lakes among the pine forests. There are no paths or tracks to them and they can be reached only by following a map and compass through the forest. These lakes share a most peculiar feature: the smaller the surface the deeper they are. The large Lake Mitinskoye is only four metres deep, whereas the smaller Lake Udemnoye is seventeen metres deep.

East of these forest lakes lie the Meshchora bogs or *mshari* as they are called. These are lakes which have become overgrown over the centuries. They cover an area of 300,000 hectares. Standing in the middle of such a bog you can see in the distance what used to be the high bank of the lake, the "mainland", with its dense pine forest. Sandy hillocks are visible here and there on the bog, with pines and fern. These hillocks used to be islands and the local inhabitants still refer to them as "islands". They serve as a resting-place for elk at night.

One late September we set off across the bogs to Poganoye Lake, or Poison Lake. This lake was veiled in mystery. The village women said that there were cranberries the size of nuts growing on its banks and poisonous mushrooms "bigger 'n a calf's head". It was from the latter that the lake had got its name. The village women were afraid of going to Poison Lake because of the "awful green quagmires" near it.

"You takes one step," they said, "an' the whole earth gasps like and trembles. The alder quivers all unsteady and the water squelches under yer feet and squirts up into yer face. Honest it do. It don't bear talkin' about. But the lake itself ain't got no bottom, it's all black like. An' if a young girl look at it she goes as weak as jelly."

"Why's that?"

"For fright. You gets an eery feeling down yer spine, 'orrible it is. If we 'appen on the lake by chance, we runs for our lives to the nearest island and don't have a breather until we gets there."

The women had fired our curiosity and we became determined to go to Poison Lake. On the way we spent the night on Chornoye Lake, or Black Lake, with the rain pattering on our tent and water gurgling quietly among the knotted roots. Somewhere in the rain and the pitch black darkness wolves howled.

All night the *mshari* exuded the smell of damp moss, bark and black snag. By morning the rain had stopped and the grey sky lay low. It was quiet and warm from the clouds which were almost touching the birch tops. The layer of cloud was thin and the sun seeped through it.

We packed up the tent, heaved on our rucksacks and set off. Walking was difficult. The summer before a fire in the undergrowth had burnt the birch and alder roots bringing down trees, and every other minute we had to scramble over heaps of fallen trunks and branches. We were walking from hummock to hummock and birch roots protruded like sharp spears out of the stagnant rust-coloured water between the hummocks.

The *mshari* were overgrown with bog moss, cowberries, bog bilberry and haircap moss. Our legs sank into the green and grey moss right up to our knees.

In two hours we had covered only two kilometres. Seeing an "island" ahead of us we put on a spurt, clambering over the fallen trees, and eventually reached the tree-covered hillock, collapsing heavily scratched and bleeding onto the tangle of lilies-of-the-valley. The lilies had hard orange berries between their broad leaves. The pale sky shone through the branches of the pines.

We had the writer Gaidar with us, who decided to make a tour of the "island". It turned out to be a small one surrounded by *mshari* on all sides, with two other "islands" in the distance.

Gaidar shouted and whistled to us from some way off. Unwillingly we got to our feet and went to him. He pointed to the damp earth where the "island" merged into the *mshari* and we saw the fresh imprints of a huge elk which had clearly been running in great bounds.

"This is the path to his watering place," said Gaidar.

We followed the elk's tracks, because we were thirsty and had nothing to drink with us.

A hundred paces from the "island" the tracks led us to a small "window" with clear, cold water smelling of iodine. We drank our fill and went back.

Gaidar went off to look for Poison Lake. It was quite near, but like most lakes in the *mshari* it was difficult to find. The lakes are surrounded by such dense undergrowth and tall grass that you can be within a few steps of one and still not notice the water.

He said he would find the way back by the sun and went off without taking the compass. We lay on the moss listening to the old pine cones dropping from the branches. A hollow trumpeting sound of some large animal reached us from far off.

An hour passed and Gaidar did not return. But the sun was still high and we did not worry. Gaidar was bound to find the way back.

Another hour passed, then the third. The colour drained from the sky above the *mshari* and a grey smoke-like wall crept up slowly from the east. Low clouds covered the sky and in a few minutes the sun had disappeared, leaving a dry gloom floating over the bog.

It would be impossible to find one's way in this mist without a compass. We remembered the stories we had heard of people wandering round the same spot for several days in dull weather.

I climbed up a tall pine and began to shout. There was no answering call. Then I heard a very distant cry. I listened intently and shivers ran down my spine. It was the mournful howling of wolves out there in the *mshari* in the same direction as Gaidar had taken.

What could we do? The wind was blowing in the direction Gaidar had taken. We could light a fire and hope that Gaidar would find his way back to the "island" by following the smell of the smoke. But that wasn't a very good idea. We hadn't agreed on it in advance with Gaidar. Fires were common in the bogs and Gaidar might think the smoke was a sign of an approaching fire and run off in the opposite direction.

There is nothing more terrible in these parts than a fire in a dried-up bog. The flames travel so quickly that it is impossible to escape from them. And where can one escape to, with the dry moss stretching like gunpowder as far as the eye can see. The only hope of safety is on the tree-covered "islands" which the fire sometimes by-passes for some reason.

We all shouted together, but the only answering call was from the wolves. Then one of us went off into the *mshari* with the compass in the direction which Gaidar had taken.

Dusk was falling, and we could hear the startled, ominous cawing of crows circling over the "island".

We kept shouting desperately and then lit a fire all the same. It was getting dark quickly and now Gaidar would be able to see the flames.

No human call answered our shouts, and the only sound we could hear was a car horn which suddenly started to squawk like a duck in the dense gloom near the second "island". It was strange and absurd. How on earth could a car have appeared in these bogs which could only be reached with great difficulty on foot?

The car was obviously coming closer, hooting persistently. Half an hour later we heard a rustling in the fallen branches and the car gave a last hoot nearby. Then out of the *mshari* scrambled a smiling, wet and exhausted Gaidar followed by our friend who had gone off with the compass.

It turned out that Gaidar had heard our shouts and called back all the time, but his cries had not reached us because the wind was blowing against him. Then he had got fed up with shouting and started to hoot like a car horn.

He had not got as far as Poison Lake. On the way he had found a solitary pine tree, climbed up it and caught sight of the lake in the distance. He gave one look at it, cursed and set off back.

"Why, what's the matter with it?" we asked.

"It's a very frightening lake," he answered. "Blast the wretched thing."

He told us that even from a distance he could see that the water in Poison Lake was as black as pitch. A handful of miserable pine trees stood on its banks, bent over the water and ready to fall at the first gust of wind. A few pines had already collapsed into the water. The lake looked as though it were surrounded by impassable quagmires.

The autumn dusk fell quickly. We did not want to spend the night on the "island" and set off across the *mshari* in the direction of the "mainland", the wooded shore of the bog. It was extremely hard going over the fallen logs and branches at night and every ten minutes we stopped to check our way by the compass. It was nearly midnight before we hit the overgrown path which took us to Lake Segden where our friend Kuzma Zotov lived, a mild-tempered, sick man who fished and worked on the local collective farm. We arrived at his place in the early hours of the morning.

I have described this episode, which does not contain anything remarkable, simply to give an idea, however remote, of the Meshchora bogs— the *mshari*.

Peat winning has already begun in some of the bogs (Krasny Bog and Pilny Bog). The peat in these parts is old and thick and there is enough of it to last for centuries.

But I must finish my story about Poison Lake. The following summer we reached it after all. It turned out to have floating banks—not ordinary firm ones, but a dense tangle of wild calla, marsh tea, grasses, roots and moss. They swayed underfoot like a hammock. Beneath the scraggy grass lay a bottomless pool of water. A pole would break through the floating bank easily and disappear into the quagmire. Each step sent warm water squirting out from under your feet. Once you stopped your legs were sucked down, and as soon as you took a step forward your footprint filled up with water.

The water in the lake was black and bubbles of bog gas were rising from the depths.

We fished here for perch, tying long lines to the marsh tea bushes or to young alder saplings and then sitting back against fallen pines and smoking until the bush began to strain and rustle or the sapling bent over and cracked. Then we would get up lazily, tug at the line and pull the fat, black perch out onto the bank. So that they would not die we put them in the deep water-filled troughs left by our footsteps, and the perch thrashed about in them unable to escape.

A storm began to gather over the lake at noon before our very eyes. A small storm cloud changed into a menacing thunder cloud shaped like an anvil, which remained on the same spot as if it did not want to leave.

Flashes of lightning lashed the bog close by and we began to feel apprehensive.

We never went to Poison Lake again, but we won the reputation among the village women of being reckless characters ready for anything.

"Ee, but they're dare-devils," they would say in a sing-song voice. "Such dare-devils, you know. It takes yer breath away."

Forest Rivers and Canals

I have forgotten about the map again. To finish with it I must mention the mighty stretches of forest (which flood the whole map with a dull green), the mysterious white spots in the heart of the forests and the two rivers—the Solotcha and the Pra—which flow south through woods, marshland and stretches of burnt forest.

The Solotcha is a shallow, winding river. There are shoals of ide in the still pools by its banks. Its water is red. Along the whole of its course there is only one point where a road going goodness knows where approaches the river with a solitary inn by the wayside.

The Pra flows from the lakes of northern Meshchora into the Oka. There are scarcely any villages on its banks. Many years ago the Old Believers settled in the dense forests on the Pra. An old wadding factory in the town of Spas-Klepiki in the upper reaches of the Pra discharges cotton combings into the river depositing layer after layer of wadding on the river bed, which turns black with time. This must be the only river in the Soviet Union with a bed of wadding.

Meshchora country has a great many canals. As far back as Alexander II, General Zhilinsky decided to drain the Meshchora marshes and create a vast new area suitable for colonisation not far from Moscow. An expedition was sent to Meshchora and worked there for twenty years, managing to drain only 1,500 hectares. Even this land turned out to be infertile and nobody was eager to settle on it.

Zhilinsky constructed a large number of canals in Meshchora. Today they are overgrown and choked up with marsh grass. Ducks nest in them and they are also the home of the lazy tench and darting loach. The canals are extremely picturesque. They flow away into the depths of the forests with a tangle of vegetation forming dark arches over them. Each canal seems to be leading to somewhere mysterious. You can travel along them for dozens of miles in a light boat, especially in the spring.

The sweetish scent of the water lilies mingles with the smell of resin. Dense patches of high rushes occasionally dam the waters. Wild calla grows on the banks. Its leaves are somewhat like those of the lily-of-the-valley, but each one bears a broad white stripe and from a distance they look like enormous snowy blossoms. Fern, brambles, mare's tail and moss sway over from the banks. If you touch the tangled moss with your hand or an oar it gives off a thick cloud of bright green dust—spores of haircap moss. Pink willow herb grows in low clumps. Olive-coloured water tigers dive in and out of the water pouncing on shoals of fry. Occasionally the water becomes so shallow that you have to get out and drag the boat with the water tigers biting your legs and making them bleed.

The silence is broken only by the humming of the mosquitoes and the plop of fish.

Your trip on the canal will always lead you to an unexpected destination—forest lake or forest river with its clear water flowing over gnarled bed.

Water rats live in deep burrows along the banks of these rivers, some of them quite grey with old age. If you watch quietly you may see one catch a fish. It creeps out of its burrow, dives deep, surfaces with a great noise, making the water lilies tremble in the widening ripples, and swims to the bank with a silvery fish in its mouth.

When the fish is bigger than the rat the battle lasts for a long time and the rat crawls out of the water exhausted, its little eyes red with anger. To make swimming easier they gnaw off a long stem of water weed and swim with it between their teeth. The stem is full of air bubbles and can easily support even heavier objects than a water rat.

Zhilinsky tried to drain the Meshchora marshes, but little came from his attempt. The soil is mostly peat, podsol and sand. The only crop that grows well on sand is potatoes. Meshchora's riches are not in her soil, but her forests, peat and the water meadows on the left bank of the Oka. Some scientists have compared these meadows to those of the fertile Nile valley. They yield excellent hay.

Forests

Meshchora is part of a former ocean of forest. The Meshchora forests are as majestic as great cathedrals. Even an old professor, not in the least inclined to be poetic, wrote the following in a study of the Meshchora area: "Here, in the mighty ancient pine forests, it is so light that you can see a bird in flight at a hundred paces."

Walking through the dry pine forest is like treading on a thick, expensive carpet. The ground is covered with soft, dry moss for miles on end. Oblique patches of sunlight lie on the ground. A flock of birds wheels out in different directions with shrill cries and a light rush.

When there is a wind the forests murmur and the sound ripples like waves across the pine tops.

A solitary aeroplane flying at a dizzy height looks like a torpedo-boat observed from the bottom of the sea. You can see the powerful air-currents with the naked eye, rising from earth to sky. The clouds melt on the spot. It seems as though the dry breath of the forest and the scent of juniper must drift up to the aeroplane as well.

Apart from pine forests, which provide timber for masts and ships, there are fir, birch and scattered patches of lime, elm and oak.

The oak coppices have no paths. They are impassable to traffic and dangerous because of the ants. On a boiling hot day, your whole body from head to heels becomes immediately covered with malevolent reddish-brown ants with strong jaws. Harmless ant-eating bears roam around splitting open old stumps and licking away the ant eggs.

Nothing can be so relaxing and delightful than walking in the dense Meshchora forests along unknown paths leading to a distant lake.

A walk in the forest is miles of silence without a breath of wind. It is the smell of mushrooms and the cautious flitting of birds. It is coarse grass, large mushrooms, wild strawberries, pale bluebells in the glades, the quiver of aspen leaves, the solemn, slanting rays of light and, finally, the forest dusk when dampness rises from the moss and glow-worms shine in the grass.

The sunset flares heavily on the treetops burnishing them with an ancient gold. Down below at the foot of the pine trees it is dark and dense. Bats wing their silent flight and seem to peer into your face. The forests are ringing with a strange sound—the sound of evening and the dying day.

In the evening the lake finally flashes into sight like a slanting mirror. Night stands over it gazing into the deep water—a night full of stars. The sunset still lingers in the west. A bittern cries in a tangle of spurge laurel and the cranes, disturbed by the smoke from the fire, squawk and fidget in the marshes.

All through the night the flames flare up and die down again. The birch leaves hang motionless and the dew trickles down their silvery trunks. In the far distance, in the back of beyond, an old cockerel in the woodman's house gives a throaty cry.

A strange hush heralds the approach of dawn. A greenish glow appears in the east and Venus blazes up in an icy blue light. This is the best time of all. Everything is still fast asleep—the water, the water lilies, the fish and the birds. Only the owls circle the fire slowly and silently like balls of white down.

The kettle mutters and grumbles on the fire. For some reason we all speak in whispers, afraid of startling the dawn. Heavy ducks sweep past with a metallic whoosh. Clouds of mist begin to form above the water. We pile mountains of dry twigs on the fire and watch the vast, white sun rising up to herald an endless summer day.

We camp like this by forest lakes for several days. The smell of smoke and cowberries on our hands lingers for weeks afterwards. We exist on two hours sleep and hardly ever feel tired. Two or three hours sleep in the forest must be worth many more in stuffy town houses and the stale air of the asphalted streets.

Once we were spending the night by Black Lake in high thickets near a big heap of old brushwood.

We had brought an inflatable rubber dinghy with us and went out in it at dawn to fish beyond the carpet of water lilies by the bank. The bottom of the lake was lined with a thick layer of decayed leaves, and branches were floating about in the water.

Suddenly the enormous humped back of a black fish with a dorsal fin as sharp as a kitchen knife surfaced right next to us. It dived again and swam under the boat making it rock. The fish surfaced again. It must have been a gigantic pike. If its fin brushed against the rubber it would rip the dinghy apart like a razor.

I thrashed the water with an oar. The fish replied by lashing its tail with tremendous strength and disappearing under the dinghy again. We dropped our fishing rods and began to row for the shore with the fish swimming along beside us.

We rowed into the tangle of water lilies by the bank and prepared to pull in to the shore, when we suddenly heard a shrill yelping and a pitiful tremulous howl. There on the flattened grass where we had lowered the dinghy into the water stood a she-wolf, her tail between her legs, and three cubs. She howled long and plaintively, her mouth open to high heaven, and cubs yapped and hid behind their mother. The black fish again swam close to the dinghy and caught its fin on an oar.

I threw the heavy lead plummet at the wolf, which made her jump back and trot away from the bank. We saw her and the cubs crawl into a round hole in the heap of brushwood not far from our tent. Then we came ashore and kicked up a great din driving the wolf from the brushwood. After that we moved camp to another spot.

Black Lake gets its name from the colour of the water which is clear and pitch black. Nearly all the lakes in Meshchora have their own particular shade of water, although most of them are black. Some lakes, like Chyornenkoye for example, have water like sparkling Indian ink. It is difficult to imagine this full, dense colour if you have not seen it. And yet the water in this lake, as in Black Lake, is absolutely clear.

This colour is particularly beautiful in autumn when the yellow and red leaves of the birch and aspen, falling onto the black water, cover the surface so thickly that your boat rustles as it moves along leaving a shining black trail behind it. It is also beautiful in summer when the white lilies float on the water as if on a magical sheet of glass. Black water gives a magnificent reflection, and it is difficult to distinguish the real banks and thickets from their reflection.

The water is violet in Lake Urzhenskoye, yellowish in Segden, the colour of tin in Lake Velikoye and slightly bluish in the lakes beyond the Pra. The water in the meadow lakes, which is crystal clear in summer, turns to sea green in autumn and even seems to smell of the sea.

But most of the lakes are black. The old men say this is because the bottom of the lakes is lined with a thick layer of fallen leaves and brown leaves steeped in water give off a dark infusion. This is not entirely the case. It is the peat at the bottom of the lakes which explains the blackness of the water. The older the peat, the darker the water.

I mentioned Meshchora boats. They are similar to Polynesian canoes, carved out of a single piece of wood and riveted at the prow and stern only by forged iron nails with big heads. They are narrow, light and manoeuvrable making it possible to travel in the shallowest waters.

Meadows

There is a wide belt of water meadows between the forests and the Oka. At dusk these meadows look like the sea. The sun sets in the sea of grass and the beacons on the banks of the Oka shine like lighthouses. Fresh breezes blow over the meadows and the sky above looks like an overturned pale green chalice.

An old bed of the Oka, called the Prorva, meanders for many a mile through the meadows. It is a deep, sluggish, overgrown river with steep banks. These banks are covered with old black poplars whose trunks are so large that it would take three men to encircle them, ancient willows, dog rose, tall herbs and brambles.

We gave the name of "magical Prorva" to one of the reaches on this river, because none of us had ever seen such high burdock, twice a man's height, such tall lungwort and sorrel and such giant puffballs as here.

The grass by the banks of the Prorva is sometimes so thick that it forms an impregnable, resilient wall preventing you from landing on the shore. It is entwined with a tangle of treacherous bramble shoots and hundreds of other dangerous, prickly snares.

The Prorva often has a light haze over it which changes in colour depending on the time of the day. In the morning it is a pale blue, in the afternoon a milky white, and only at dusk does the air above the river become as clear as spring water. The leaves of the black poplars, glowing red in the sunset, hardly stir. Pike thrash about loudly in the still waters.

In the morning, when you can't take more than a dozen steps through the grass without getting drenched in dew, the air over the Prorva smells of bitterish willow bark, fresh grass and sedge. It is dense, cool and bracing.

Each autumn I spend many a day camping by the Prorva. In order to give you a faint idea of what the river is like I shall have to describe at least one of these days.

I arrive by boat with my tent, axe, oil lamp, rucksack with food, small spade, a few pots and pans, tobacco, matches and fishing tackle, and, most important of all, a jar of worms which I have collected in an old garden under heaps of fallen leaves.

I have my own favourite spots on the Prorva, which are always the least frequented. One of them is at a sharp bend in the river where it widens into a small lake with very high banks covered with willow bushes.

This is where I put up my tent. But first of all I go and fetch some hay. Yes, I confess that I actually go and forage hay from the nearest stack. But I do it so carefully that not even the sharpest eyed old farmer could see that there was anything missing. I strew the hay under the tarpaulin floor of the tent and then return it when I am about to leave.

The tent must be pegged so tightly that it reverberates like a drum. Then you must dig round it so that the rain will run down the sides of the tent into the trench and not make the floor wet.

Now the tent is up. Inside it is warm and dry. My oil lamp is hanging on a hook. I light it in the evenings and even do a spot of reading—not for very long because there are too many distractions on the Prorva. A landrail will begin to call in the bush nearby, or a whopping great fish gives a tremendous splash, or else a willow branch cracks violently like a pistol shot in the fire and send sparks flying, or a crimson glow begins to spread above the thicket and the sombre moon rises over the vast evening earth. The landrails immediately fall silent and the bittern stops booming in the marshes. The moon rises in watchful silence. It appears as the mistress of these dark waters, ancient willows and long, mysterious nights.

A canopy of dark willows lies overhead. Looking at them you begin to understand the meaning of old words. For some reason on nights like this you think of the Orion constellation as "Stozhari" ("a hundred bright lights") and the word "midnight", which is perhaps a literary concept in the town, assumes its true meaning here. The darkness above the willows, the shining September stars, the bitter tang of the air, and the distant fire in the meadows where young lads are keeping watch over the horses grazing at night—all this is midnight. Somewhere far off the night watchman is ringing out the time in the village belfry in twelve long rhythmic chimes. Then the dark silence returns once more, broken only by the occasional sleepy voice of a steam tug on the Oka.

Night stretches on slowly as if without end. You get a sound, refreshing sleep in your tent on these autumn nights even though you wake up every two hours and go out to look at the sky—to find out whether Sirius has risen or whether the dawn is creeping up in the east.

The night gets colder with every passing hour. Towards dawn the air is already stinging your face and the slightly sagging tent is covered with a thick layer of crunchy hoarfrost. The grass outside is turning silver.

Time to get up. The first faint flush of dawn appears in the east and the vast dim outlines of the willows loom overhead. The stars are fading. I go down to the river and wash from the boat. The water is warm as if it has been slightly heated.

The sun rises, the hoarfrost melts and the sandy river banks darken with the dew.

I make strong tea in a charred tin kettle. The thick layer of soot looks like enamel. Floating inside the kettle are a few burnt willow leaves from the fire.

I spent the whole morning fishing. I test the seines which I had cast from the boat the evening before. At first all the hooks are empty—the bait has been eaten by tiddlers. But then the line goes taut, cutting the water, and a darting flash of silver appears deep down—this is a flat bream thrashing about on the hook. Behind it is a fat, struggling perch and then a pike finch with piercing yellow eyes. I fish them out and they are as cold as ice.

What could be a better description of these days spent on the Prorva than the following words by Aksakov:

"On a flowering green bank, above the dark depths of a river or lake, among shady bushes, under the canopy of a giant black poplar or leafy alder, its leaves shaking quietly in the bright mirror of water, vain passions are stilled, vain conflicts are resolved, vain ambitions and hopes vanish without a trace. Nature comes into its own. And breathing the fragrant, free, invigorating air you gain breadth of vision, a gentle heart, and a feeling of compassion towards your fellow-men and even towards yourself."

A Slight Deviation from the Subject

There are all sorts of fisherman's tales associated with the Prorva and I would like to tell you one of them now.

The great tribe of fishermen inhabiting the village of Solotcha by the Prorva was in a state of great excitement. A tall old man with long silver teeth had arrived there from Moscow to do some fishing.

He used a spinning rod—an English rod with an artificial bait in the form of a small nickel fish. We scorned the spinning rod and used to watch with glee as the old man wandered patiently along the banks of the water meadows, casting his line like a whip, and invariably winding in the empty bait.

And there was Lyonka, the shoemaker's son,

right next to him pulling out fish not with an English spinning rod that cost a hundred roubles, but with a plain piece of string. The old man sighed and grumbled:

"Ah, the cruel injustice of fate!"

He spoke very politely even to the little village boys and used old-fashioned, long-forgotten words in his conversation. The old man was unlucky. We knew that all fishermen are either extremely unlucky or lucky. The lucky ones get a bite even with a dead worm. Then there are the envious ones and the artful ones. The artful ones think that any fish can be out-witted, but I have never seen this kind of fisherman outwit the smallest tiddler, to say nothing of a roach.

It's best not to go fishing with an envious one because he'll never get a bite in any case. Finally, when he has wasted away with envy he will start casting his line near yours, bobbing the plummet about in the water and frightening the fish away.

The old man was unlucky. In one day he broke no less than ten costly spoon-baits in the snag and got covered with scratches and mosquito bites. But nothing deterred him.

Once we took him with us to Lake Segden. All night he stood half asleep by the fire like a horse, frightened of sitting on the damp ground. At sunrise I fried some eggs with lard. The sleepy old man decided to step over the fire to get some bread from his bag, slipped and trod right in the fried eggs. Pulling out his yoke-covered foot he shook it around in the air knock-ing over the jug of milk. The jug cracked and broke into smithereens, with the delicious baked milk sinking softly into the wet ground before our eyes.

"I beg your pardon," he said, apologising to the jug.

Then he went to the lake, put his foot in the cold water and wiggled it about for a long time to wash the fried egg off his boot. We stood there for two minutes unable to utter a single word and then roared with laughter all the morning in the bushes.

Everyone knows that if a fisherman is unlucky sooner or later he will have such a big stroke of bad luck that it will be talked about in the village for the next ten years at least. And this is what finally happened.

We set off for the Prorva with the old man. The meadows had not yet been mown and daisies as big as the palm of your hand beat against our legs.

The old man walked along, tripping over the grass and exclaiming from time to time:

"What an aroma, my friends! What an intoxicating aroma!"

The air was quite still over the Prorva. Not even the willow leaves so much as stirred showing their silvery underside as they do even in a faint breeze. Bees were buzzing about in the warm grass.

I was sitting on a broken raft, smoking and watching the feather float. I waited patiently for it to give a jerk and dive into the green depths of the river. The old man was walking along the sandy bank with his spinning rod and I could hear his sighs and exclamations through the bushes:

"What a heavenly, delightful morning!"

Suddenly I heard grunting, scrambling, puffing and a sound like a cow mooing with its mouth tied up. Something heavy thrashed about in the water and the old man squealed out:

"Goodness, gracious. What a beauty!"

I leapt off the raft, waded waist-deep in water to the bank and run up to the old man. He was standing right by the water, and in front of him on the sand lay an old pike gasping heavily. It looked all of forty pounds.

"Drag it away from the water!" I shouted.

But the old man hissed at me and drew his pince-nez out of his pocket with trembling hands. He put it on, bent over the pike and began to examine it with the rapture of an expert looking at a rare picture in an art gallery. The pike did not take its malevolent, narrowed eyes off him.

"It's just like a crocodile, ain't it," said Lyonka.

The pike squinted across at Lyonka and he leapt back. It seemed to be croaking: "Just wait, you rascal, and I'll give you a good box round the ears!"

"My angel!" cried the old man bending even lower over the pike.

It was then that the accident happened which they talk about in the village to this day. The pike took aim and before you could say "Jack Robinson" landed the old man a hefty swipe across the cheek with its tail. The slap rang out above the sleepy water and the pince-nez went flying into the river. The pike gave a wriggle and plopped loudly back into the water.

"Alas!" cried the old man, but it was too late.

Further off Lyonka was doing a jig and shouting gleefully:

"Ha, ha! Serve you right! Them that can't fish should leave well alone."

The old man packed up his spinning rods and left for Moscow that day. Now there was nobody to disturb the silence of the streams and rivers, or tear the cold water lilies with his spoon-bait, or admire aloud those things which are best admired in silence.

More about the Meadows

The meadows have lots of lakes with various strange names: Tish, Byk, Khotets, Promoina, Kanava, Staritsa, Muzga, Bobrovka, Selyanskoye and, finally, Langobardskoye.

Black oak trees lie on the bottom of Khotets. It is always quiet on Tish (Quiet Lake) because the high banks protect the lake from the wind. At one time beavers used to live on Bobrovka (Beaver Lake) but now perch chase the young fish. Promoina is a deep lake with such capricious fish that only a person with very good nerves can catch them. Byk is a mysterious lake stretching for many a mile. It is full of shallows and still waters, but we avoid it because there is not much shade on the banks.

Kanava has wonderful gold tench each of which takes a good half hour to make up his mind to bite. As autumn approaches the banks of the lake become covered with patches of purple, not from the autumn leaves, but from the mass of large berries on the dog-rose.

On the banks of Staritsa there are sand dunes overgrown with mugwort and marigolds and a plant called marsh-elder. This consists of little greyish-green balls packed close together like a tightly folded rose. If you pull one of these balls out of the sand and lay it down with its roots facing upwards, it will begin to wriggle slowly like a beetle upside down, stretching its petals out in one direction, then leaning on them and turning over onto its roots again.

The water in Muzga reaches a depth of twenty metres. In the autumn flocks of migrating cranes rest on its shores. Selyanskoye Lake is completely overgrown with black water-weed and is a favourite nesting place for ducks.

How names catch on! There was a small lake without a name in the meadows near Staritsa. We called it Langobardskoye in honour of a bearded watchman, "langobard", who lived on the bank of the lake in a hut and kept watch over the cabbage patches. A year later the name caught on, to our amazement, except that the farm workers changed it a little to suit themselves and began to call it Ambarskoye (*ambar* meaning barn).

The meadows have an incredible number of different grasses. Before they are mown their unaccustomed fragrance gives you a dizzy, heavy feeling. There are miles of dense, tall thickets of daisies, chicory, clover, fennel, pinks, coltsfoot, dandelions, gentians, plantain, bluebells, buttercups and dozens of other flowering plants. The wild meadow strawberries begin to ripen just before mowing time.

Old Men

Talkative old men live in the meadows in dugouts and huts. They are either watchmen for the collective-farm vegetable patches or ferrymen, or basket-makers. The basket-makers set up their huts near the osier thickets by the river.

You usually make their acquaintance during a storm or a heavy shower, when you take refuge in their huts until the storm passes beyond the Oka or into the forests and a rainbow appears over the meadows.

This first acquaintance always proceeds according to a strictly set pattern. First of all we have a smoke and then they strike up a polite, artful conversation designed to reveal who we are. This is followed by a few vague remarks about the weather ("rain won't give over" or conversely "nice drop o' rain at last, after that there dry spell"). Then you can pass on to any subject under the sun.

The old men prefer talking about unusual things: the new Moscow sea, the "water hairy-planes" (hydroplanes) on the Oka, French food ("they makes soup out o' frogs and sups it wi' silver spoons"), badger racing and a collective-farm worker from somewhere near Pronsk who, the story goes, earned so many work-days that he bought himself a motor car with music.

The one I used to come across most often was a grumpy old basket-maker who lived in a hut by Lake Muzga. He was called Stepan, but his nickname was "Bearded rake". He was a skinny old boy, with legs as thin as an old horse's. You couldn't make out what he was saying for his beard.

On one occasion I was spending the night in Stepan's hut. I had arrived late. The dusk was grey and warm and the rain was falling in fits and starts. It pattered in the bushes, died down and then started to patter again as if it were playing hide-and-seek.

"Playin' about just like a bairn, this rain," said Stepan. "Just like a bairn—scrabblin' about 'ere and there, and then hidin' away listenin' to us."

By the fire sat a quiet bright-eyed girl of about twelve. She was frightened and spoke only in a whisper.

"This silly lassie lost her way from Zaborye!" said the old man affectionately. "Went on lookin' for her calf in the meadows till it got dark. Then she sees a light and comes runnin' to grandad. What'll we do wi' her, eh!"

Stepan took a yellow cucumber out of his pocket and gave it to the girl:

"Eat up, then. Don't be shy."

The girl took the cucumber and nodded, but did not start to eat it.

The old man put a pot on the fire and began to cook some hash.

"There you are, me dears," he said lighting a cigarette, "you goes a-wanderin' round these meadows and lakes with never a thought that they was once monastery land—and the forest too. Right from the Oka to the Pra, a good hundred versts, all forest belonged to t' monks. But now it belongs to the people, that forest. It's proper workers' forest now."

"But why did the monks own the forests, grandad?" asked the girl.

"Darned if I know. Silly women used to say it was because they were holy. Prayed for our sins. What sins! We didn't have no sins at all. Ee, higgerance, nowt but higgerance!"

The old man gave a deep sigh.

"And I used to go to their churches, too," he muttered in embarrassment. "What were the use of it? Just wore me soles out for nothin'.'"

He stopped for a moment to crumble some black bread into the soup.

"Them were hard times," he said sadly. "Men and women alike had a hard life. The men still got around a bit an' could always turn to their drop of vodka. But the womenfolk had nowt to comfort them. Bairns went hungry. Womenfolk spent their life, toilin' by the stove until they got worms in their eyes. Don't you go laughin'. That be true what I said about worms. They used to grow in a woman's eyes from the fire."

"'orrible!" sighed the little girl quietly.

"Don't you worry, though," said the old man. "You won't get no worms. Now our young lassies have a good life. People used to think like happiness lived in warm waters and deep-blue seas, but then they finds out that it's right here in our 'eads." He tapped his forehead with a gnarled finger. "Take Manka Malyavina, now. Lassy with a bonny voice. In the old days she would 'ave wailed it away, quick as a flash. But now look what's 'appened to 'er. Life's one big holiday for her old dad—plays t' accordion and pies in t' oven every day. And why shouldn't he have a good time with Manka sendin' him two hundred roubles a month, the old devil!"

"Where from?" the girl asked.

"Moscow. She sings in the theatre. Sings like an angel, they say, and has them all sobbin' their 'earts out. That's 'ow our womenfolk lives today. Manka came home last summer. Hardly recognise her, you would. Real little lady. Brought me a present, she did. Sang in t' village club. I've seen a lot in my time but I tell you straight: it right moved me, it did. Don't know why. Why do a person 'ave such power, I thinks. And why have we let it go waste for thousands of years, fools that we be! Now you wanders about with an ear here and an eye there and it always seems too early to be dying. Just can't get round to it somehow."

The old man took the hash off the fire and went into the hut for spoons.

"You just wants to go on and on livin'," he said from the hut. "We was born a bit too soon. We wasn't clever enough."

The girl looked into the fire with her bright, shining eyes absorbed in her own thoughts.

A Land of Talent

On the edge of the Meshchora forests, not far from Ryazan, is the village of Solotcha well-known for its climate, dunes, rivers and pine forests. Solotcha has electricity, and the peasants' horses put out in the meadows to graze at night, stare wildly at the white stars of the electric lights hanging in the distant forest and snort with fear.

My first year in Solotcha I lived with a gentle old woman, who was an old maid and the village dressmaker, Maria Mikhailovna. She was called the Old Maid and had lived quietly all her life without a husband and children.

Inside her spick-and-span doll's house of an izba there were several pendulum clocks ticking on the walls and two old pictures by an unknown

Italian painter. I wiped them over with a raw onion and the quiet house was filled with the Italian morning, the full sun and the reflection of the water. An unknown foreign artist had left the pictures with Maria Mikhailovna's father in lieu of rent for a room. He had come to Solotcha to study the local icon painting. He was almost completely destitute and a strange person. When he left he got them to promise that the pictures would be sent to him in Moscow in return for the rent. He died suddenly in Moscow never sending the money.

At night in the cottage you could hear the sound of the neighbouring garden. In the garden stood a two-storey house surrounded by a stout fence. I had wandered into this house when I was looking for a room, and spoken to a handsome grey-haired old woman. She looked at me severely with her deep blue eyes and said she could not let me a room. Over her shoulders I could make out walls covered with pictures.

"Who's house is that?" I asked the Old Maid.

"Why, it belongs to Academician Pozhalostin, the famous engraver. He died before the Revolution and the old woman is his daughter. There are two old women living there—the other one is very old, all hunched up."

I was amazed. Pozhalostin, one of the greatest Russian engravers, whose work can be found everywhere, Russia, France, England, suddenly turns up here in Solotcha! But then one day I heard farm workers arguing about whether the artist Arkhipov would be coming to Solotcha this summer, while they were digging up potatoes. Pozhalostin was a former shepherd. The two artists, Arkhipov and Malyavin, and the sculptor Golubkina, were all from this part of Ryazan. There is hardly a house in Solotcha without paintings. When you ask who the artist is, it turns out to be a grandfather, father or brother. The village of Solotcha used to be famous for its icon painters.

Pozhalostin's name is still spoken with respect. He taught the villagers to paint and they used to slip in to see him on the quiet bringing their canvases wrapped in a clean piece of cloth for his praise or criticism.

For a long time I could not get accustomed to the thought that next door, in the dark rooms of the old house there were extremely rare books on art and copper-plates. Late at night I would go out to the well for a drink of water. There was hoarfrost on the woodpiles and the cold bucket scalded your fingers. Icy stars shone over this dark, silent land and the only dimly lit window was in Pozhalostin's house, where his daughter would read until dawn. Occasionally she pushed her spectacles up to her forehead and listened, guarding the house.

The following year I settled in with the Pozhalostins, renting the old bathhouse in the garden. The garden was overgrown with lilac, a riot of dog rose, apple trees and maples covered with lichen.

The walls inside the house were hung with wonderful engravings—portraits of old-fashioned people. I could not seem to avoid their glance. Whether I was mending a fishing rod or writing, a host of women and men in tightly buttoned up frock-coats, a host from the seventies, stared attentively down at me from the walls. Looking up I would catch the eye of Turgenev or General Yermolov and feel uncomfortable for some reason.

Solotcha and its surroundings have produced many people of great talent. Not far from Solotcha Yesenin was born.

One day an old woman in a homespun woollen skirt dropped into the bathhouse to see if I wanted to buy some sour cream.

"If you should ever need any just you come round and see me," she said kindly. "Ask at the church where Tatiana Yesenina lives. Anyone will show you the way."

"Was Sergei Yesenin a relative of yours?"

"The poet?" the old woman enquired.

"Yes, the poet."

"My nephew," she sighed wiping her mouth with the end of her scarf. "He was a good poet, but a real strange lad. So if you should want any sour cream, just drop round and see me, my love."

On one of the forest lakes near Solotcha lives a certain Kuzma Zotov. Before the Revolution, he was nothing but a poor, wretched peasant and has still retained the habit of speaking in a quiet, self-effacing way and in general prefers to hold his peace. But the years of poverty also inspired him with the burning desire to make his children "decent people" at all costs.

There have been a lot of new additions in the Zotov's house over the last few years—a wireless, newspapers and books. The only thing that remains from the old days is a decrepit old dog who seems to go on living forever.

"No matter how well you feed him he gets thinner and thinner," says Kuzma. "I reckon being poor has got into his system. He's afraid of anyone who's well-dressed and hides away from them under the bench. Thinks it's gentry."

Three of Kuzma's sons are in the Komsomol. The fourth, Vasya, is still too young to be a member.

Misha, the elder son, is in charge of an experimental ichthyological station on Lake Velikoye, near the town of Spas-Klepiki. One summer Misha brought home an old violin without any strings which he had bought from an old woman. It had been lying in her house in a trunk and used to belong to the Shcherbatov family, who had owned land in these parts. The violin had been made in Italy and Misha decided that in winter, when there wasn't much work at the station, he would take it to Moscow and have it examined by specialists. He didn't play the violin himself.

"If it turns out to be a valuable one, I'll give it to one of our best violinists," he told me.

The second son, Vanya, teaches botany and zoology in a large forest village about one hundred kilometres from his native lake. In the holidays he helps his mother and spends the rest of the time wandering round the forests or wading waist deep in the lake looking for rare water plants, which he has promised to show his bright, eager pupils.

Vanya is a shy lad with his father's gentle disposition, interest in people and liking for heart-to-heart talks.

Vasya still goes to school. The lake does not have its own school—there are only four houses there altogether—and so Vasya has to walk seven kilometres through the forest to school.

He is an expert on the neighbourhood. He knows each forest path, each badger's burrow and can tell any bird by its feathers. His darting grey eyes never miss a thing.

Two years ago an artist arrived from Moscow and took Vasya along to help him. Vasya used to row him across to the other side of the lake, fetch him fresh water for his paints (the artist used French water colours) and hand him the leaden tubes from the box.

One day the artist and Vasya got caught on the bank in a storm. I remember it well. It was not so much a storm as a treacherous roaring hurricane, which sent clouds of dust, pink with the flashes of lightning, sweeping over the ground. The forests were howling as if great oceans had burst their dams and were flooding Meshchora. Thunder shook the ground.

Vasya and the artist just managed to make it home. Then the artist discovered that he had left behind his tin box with the water colours. The wonderful French paints had been lost! He spent several days looking for them in vain and then left quickly for Moscow.

Two months later he received a letter written in a large, uneven hand.

"Dear Sir," wrote Vasya. "Please tell me what to do with your paints and how to send them to you. When you left I spent two weeks looking for them all over the place until I found them. But I caught cold badly because there was a lot of rain and couldn't write to you before because I was in bed. I nearly died, but I'm up now, although I'm still a bit weak. So don't be angry with me. If it's not inconvenient, please send me a book on trees and some coloured pencils—I want to draw. We've had the first fall of snow, but it's melted. And if you're lucky you may see a hare sitting under a fir tree in the forest! Yours, Vasya Zotov."

My House

The small house where I live in Meshchora is worthy of description. It is a timbered cottage panelled with grey boarding and used to be a bathhouse. It stands in an overgrown garden separated from it for some reason by a high fence. This fence is a snare for the local cats, who are all fish-lovers. Every time I come back from fishing the house is besieged by cats of all shades and sizes—ginger ones, black ones, grey ones and white ones with ginger markings. They are all over the place, sitting on the fence, the roofs and the old apple trees, howling to each other and waiting for the evening. Each one's gaze is fixed on the string of fish, hanging from the branch of an old apple tree just high enough to make it almost out of reach.

When evening comes the cats crawl carefully over the fence and gather under the string. Standing on their back paws they aim deft swipes at the fish trying to knock it down. From a distance it looks as though they are playing volleyball. Then some crafty one will leap up and sink its claws in a fish swaying from it and trying to tear it off. The other cats give vent to their irritation by biffing each other on their bewhiskered faces.

I put an end to all this by coming out of the bathhouse with a lamp. Caught unawares the cats bolt for the fence and get stuck trying to squeeze through the stakes, upon which they flatten back their ears, close their eyes and begin to yowl desperately, begging for mercy.

In the autumn the house is surrounded by a carpet of leaves and the two small rooms and garden are lighter.

The stoves crackle and there is a smell of apples and scrubbed floors. Bluetits sit on the branches, sifting little crystal balls in their throats, warbling, chirping and looking at the windowsill where there is a chunk of black bread.

I rarely spend the night in the house. I spend most nights on the lake and when I do stay at home I sleep in the old summerhouse tucked away in the garden and overgrown with wild vines. In the morning the sun's rays pierce into it through the purple, lilac, green and lemon foliage and I always feel as if I am waking up inside a lighted up Christmas tree.

Sparrows peep into the summerhouse in amazement. They are fascinated by the watch ticking on the round table planted firmly in the bare earth. They go up to it and listen to its ticking first with one ear, then with the other and, finally, give the dial a good peck.

It is particularly pleasant in the summerhouse on quiet autumn nights with a leisurely shower of rain pattering quietly in the garden. The cool air barely stirs the flame of the candle. Angular shadows from the vines fall on the floor. A moth settles on an open book like a scrap of grey raw silk, leaving the finest bright dust behind it on the page. There is a smell of rain and the gentle, pungent odour of moisture and grey garden paths.

I wake up at dawn. The mist in the garden is rustling with the sound of falling leaves. I haul up a bucket of water from the well and a frog hops out of it. Then I wash myself down in the water, listening to the shepherd's horn in the distance on the edge of the village.

I go into the empty bathhouse and make some tea. There is a cricket chirping away on the stove very loudly, not taking any notice of my footsteps or the clatter of cups.

It is getting light. I pick up my oars and set off for the river. Divny, the watchdog, is sleeping by the gate. He thumps his tail on the ground once or twice but does not bother to raise his head. Divny is used to my early departures. He merely yawns after me and gives a noisy sigh.

I cast off from the shore in the mist. A pink glow is spreading in the east and I can no longer smell the smoke from the village stoves. Now there is nothing but the silence of the water, the thickets and the old willows.

A deserted September day stretches out before me. A day of wandering in this vast world of fragrant foliage, grass, autumn fading, calm waters, clouds and low sky—this is my idea of happiness.

Unselfishness

There is a great deal more which I could write about Meshchora country. I could tell you that it is rich in forest and peat, hay and potatoes, milk and berries, but I have deliberately omitted to write about this. Surely we do not love our land only because it is rich, because it yields good harvests and because its resources can be used to create our well-being!

These are not the only reasons why we love our native parts. We love them also because, even though they may not be rich, to us they are beautiful. I love Meshchora because it is beautiful, though its charm is not immediately apparent, but unfolds slowly and gradually.

At first sight it is all so quiet and ordinary under a cloudy sky. But the more you get to know it, the more you begin to love this simple country. And if I should ever have to defend my country, somewhere deep down in my heart I will know that I am defending this plot of earth as well, which has taught me to see and understand beauty however plain it may appear, this pensive forest country which always remains in your heart just as your first love never fades.

1938

PRECIOUS CARGO

Stern had read in some book or other that eccentrics add a colourful touch to our lives, but nevertheless nobody liked the one who had appeared on his boat. He wore excessively baggy, yellow check trousers. Their colour irritated Stern intensely, perhaps because everything around, the water in the Gulf of Finland and the sides of his boat, the *Borei*, was a soft grey. The *Borei* was the colour of wet linen, except for a few spots of vermilion where the paint had been scratched off. The eccentric thought it very pretty, but the skipper considered that it was high time for the boat to be given a fresh coat of paint.

The eccentric walked with the gait of an ostrich around the deck piled high with crates. In his deep-blue jacket, green cap and russet-brown tie he looked like a long-legged, tropical bird with bright plumage. His luggage consisted of a suitcase and a violin.

He was on his way to Great Britain with a cargo of toys. Loading the boat with timber, leather or sacks of grain was one thing, but carrying toys was downright humiliating. The old captains from the boats moored nearby simply shrugged their shoulders. The eccentric had demanded that the greatest precautions should be taken in handling the toys, and they were lowered into the hold as if they were high explosive.

The first mate, Chokh, a superstitious soul with a grudge against life, expressed the view that these "wretched playthings will lead to no good". When Stern asked him what he meant, Chokh mumbled that the cargo was too light to be firmly strapped down in the hold and if there were a storm—you know yourself—the crates would slide over to one side, the *Borei* would list and that would be that. Having expressed his considered opinion Chokh went ashore for some cigarettes.

"Keep your opinions to yourself," Stern shouted after him. "You're ordered to load pigs' trotters, you load it. What difference does it make?"

The irritation on board did not abate. In the morning as they were leaving port a sailor from the *Land of the Soviets* hailed them through the megaphone:

"Everything in order with the cargo of teddy bears?"

Stern felt relieved that there was a mist at sea, as if it would conceal his frivolous cargo. He imagined being greeted with the polite enquiry from passing ships at sea:

"Where are you bound for and what is your cargo?"

"Toys to Belfast," the watch would reply.

This would create a great stir on the passing ships and their decks would be lined with the grinning faces of the sailors. A chorus of jeers would greet the crew of the *Borei*. "Ma-ma" the other sailors would cry mockingly and their captain would shout from the bridge:

"Safe voyage with the dollies."

Chokh called the eccentric a clown and it was true that he commanded little respect. Sailors are normally indifferent to their passengers and cargo, but now their pride had been hurt. They would openly make fun of him by pointing at his red, sharply pointed shoes and asking him:

"What did you pay for those pumps?"

And the more impertinent ones phrased the question differently:

"How much are those clod-hoppers?"

The eccentric never took offence answering readily that he had paid twenty roubles in the big Moscow department store GUM.

He was in an ecstatic mood. Marvellous things would happen as evening approached. Clouds loomed up like gigantic balls of pink cotton wool, lighthouses winked through the dark sea mist, and the shores of Denmark seemed to smell of fresh herring and whipped cream. The eccentric would go below to the messroom and announce to Stern:

"I'm most satisfied."

Stern would raise his eyebrows at this, for there was little cause for satisfaction. They were entering the North Sea and the barometer was falling steadily like the weights on a clock.

"Storm rising," he replied and went off to his cabin.

On the fifth day after dinner in the messroom the eccentric tapped his glass of mineral water with a knife and asked for permission to speak. A grey drizzle was falling outside and the lamps in the mess were burning brightly. The lamps and the eccentric were reflected in all the four mirrors at once. Stern was watching the eccentric's reflection and could see his profile with the crooked pince-nez on the soft, good-natured nose.

The request put Stern in an awkward position. As captain he could stop the eccentric by telling him that speeches were out of keeping with strict sea customs. He could remind him that sailors were men of the few words who despised verbosity (unless a fellow had had one over the eight of course). But he disregarded the displeased glances of the mates with a resigned wave of his hand:

"Let him speak."

The eccentric addressed them as follows:

"An annoying misunderstanding has taken place. The cargo which I am accompanying has given you a lot of trouble for the simple reason that you know very little about toys. Your professional pride has been hurt. Of course, taking part in an expedition to the North Pole is much more impressive than carrying a cargo of toys. I had not realised that sailors were so fond of the spectacular and so thoughtlessly hostile to things about which they are simply ignorant."

These words rang out like a declaration of war. The eccentric proceeded to get down to the heart of the matter. He argued that the art of toymaking was just as noble as the art of navigation. He stunned Chokh by announcing that a certain German toymaker had become a millionaire through making tin soldiers. He declared that Soviet toys were the best in the world and that the *Borei* was at this moment carrying the best of the best to an exhibition in Belfast. He infuriated Stern by mentioning casually that he had noticed a small canary coloured sailing boat in the captain's cabin. Toys were a precious cargo. The only people with the right to break them were children, certainly not the dockers or the crew. He challengingly described Chokh's fears as sheer rubbish. Ask any sailor whether a ship could keel over from a cargo of toys and he would laugh in your face.

Chokh protested. He recalled an incident in Leningrad when a porter had been crushed by a bale of cotton-wool. He countered the attack by asking whether the eccentric would get a laugh in the face if he went up to someone and told him that a man had been crushed to death by cotton-wool. The argument got heated, until Stern stopped it by asking with barely concealed curiosity:

"What sort of toys are they?"

"Two classes," the eccentric replied.

He dragged his case into the mess and tipped

a pile of red-cheeked *matryoshkas*, sailing boats, rabbits and teddy bears onto the table.

"This is the second class," he explained. "The English customs officials will have a pleasant surprise when they open the cargo of Bolshevik toys and hundreds of dolls with beautifully arched brows and bright artificial smiles tumble out to greet them. These smiles will conceal the real cargo, the first class toys. Here they are."

He shook the case and there was a shower of papier-mâché Komsomol dolls and Pioneers, Budyonny on a grey horse, Red Army soldiers with ruddy cheeks, blacksmiths hammering ploughs, policemen with comical faces, spinners at the wheel, miners doubled up in the shafts, crowds of children on May Day floats and, finally, a comical king with white eyes, who gave a hoarse bark at the slightest touch.

The toys were passed round from hand to hand. The junior mate sat a policeman on the sugar bowl, gave him a flick on the nose and stuck a cigarette into his mouth. The policeman swivelled his wicked beady eye angrily. Stern started to argue with Chokh about the model sailing boats. Chokh said that they were tea clippers, but Stern angrily insisted that they were brigs. They got out a book on old ships. Then the wireless operator sat down at the piano and a Pioneer doll began to do a tap-dance under the expert guidance of the mechanic.

The sailors kept popping their heads through the door with a grin. The bosun came to report on the speed, picked up a toy whistle and piped all the songs of the nightingale.

The excitement spread to the crew's quarters.

The helmsman Shiryaev boasted that he could carve a torpedo-boat with masts, funnels and a conning-tower out of a single piece of bark. Nobody believed him. He gave his word of honour and demanded a piece of bark, but there was none to be found on the *Borei*. The air rang with the names of famous ship model builders from Hamburg, Odessa and London.

Chokh remained true to his superstitious beliefs, regarding the toys, especially the fluffy teddy bears, as a protection against acts of fate.

Stern told them how he had seen workers' children in Le Havre playing in the deserted, refuse-filled spots in the harbour where the port watchmen did not bother to chase them away. Their toys were simple. They used planks of wood for boats and rusty nails for anchors. They played very quietly and there was something very sad about their pleasure because it was so fearful.

The eccentric interrupted him to say that a lot of skill and affection goes into toys, possibly because their makers had an unhappy childhood. A child without toys has nothing but the stuffy adult world around him. He cannot talk to steam trains and rabbits, or have the wonderful experience of unscrewing a policeman's head and looking inside into the hollow plaster ball.

"I quite understand how insulting it must be to carry a load of dolls in lace knickerbockers and rubber nigger boys who are going to get knocked about in rich children's nurseries," he continued. "But our cargo's quite different. You can see for yourselves. We are transporting toys for those parts of the town where the children play with old tins and dried herring tails. It is difficult to imagine how much tears and laughter lie in those crates in the *Borei*'s hold, which you hate so much. But you wouldn't mind taking a cargo of salted tripe, would you?"

The noise did not die down until midnight when four bells sounded particularly melodiously in the dark, windless night.

Stern went up onto the bridge. He took a look at the barometer and cursed. There was a storm approaching from the Atlantic. The stars were blinking in confusion through long trails of mist.

The tender strains of a violin floated up from the eccentric's cabin. Stern listened. The sound of a violin on the ship at night was as unusual as the cargo lying in the holds. He lifted his whistle to his lips, hesitated and then blew. A sailor came running up.

"Tell Chokh to make sure the cargo is secure," he ordered. "There's a storm approaching."

"Aye aye, sir," said the sailor, running off.

When Stern went below there were lamps covered with thick nets shining in the hold and Chokh was shouting:

"Careful there! It's not soap, you know."

They were hard at it until morning, but the cargo was secured beautifully, as only Chokh could secure it when he was in good spirits.

The eccentric went on playing the violin until the early hours.

The thick gloom struck against the ship's lanterns and crept behind the stern. The barometer was falling in leaps and bounds.

The eccentric had dropped off to sleep with a book on his chest—*David Copperfield* by Dickens.

He dreamt about old England with its yellow post chaises, pale-faced young girls, attorneys with checked frock coats, and glasses of grog drunk on an empty stomach. . . .

His sleep was unexpectedly interrupted at six in the morning, when the book slipped to the floor and the *Borei* dived into the abyss.

The eccentric woke up and grabbed his pince-nez to find out what was happening. He could see nothing except a yellowish fog and a raincoat hanging perpendicularly on the wall and flapping against his face. A black monster crawled out slowly from under the bed and began to slither round the room—it was his old leather suitcase.

It felt as if the *Borei* was in an enormous bottle and someone was blowing into it as hard as they could. He did not realise immediately that there was a storm. At first he thought that the *Borei* was tossing about like a chip of wood at the bottom of a giant waterfall. The nails creaked in the overdry timber and the iron hinges screeched, but the worst sound of all was the steady, clear howl of the hurricane outside in the rigging.

He threw on a few clothes quickly and went to the mess where he was greeted by the dawn. The scene reminded him of a winter's day in an army hospital: the forgotten lamps were burning with an egg-like flame and the unpleasant light oozed in to form puddles by the windows. He opened the door and went out on deck. The green, turbid morning was roaring and tossing at the ship's sides. The ocean moved like a wall and the moaning in the rigging made his flesh creep. He crawled his way up to the bridge, but the view here was even gloomier. Here you could see the *Borei* twirling like potato in an icy cauldron.

Stern's oilskins were soaked through, and so were the junior mate's. Stern gave the eccentric a wry smile and pointed downwards. The eccentric's blood ran cold. This must mean that the *Borei* was about to sink at any minute now. Then he realised that he was being politely requested to go below to his cabin. He shook his head stubbornly and stayed on the bridge.

Stern ceased to pay attention to him. He was staring ahead, frequently pulling the handle of the ship's cabling machine. Torrents of water bore down on the boat, whipping up gigantic mounds of foam before them. There was one moment when the eccentric was certain that the *Borei* was finished. The boat had plunged into the waves and for a few minutes there was nothing but the red funnel and the bridge with Stern sticking out of the lathery ocean. Then the boat rose up reluctantly and water streamed from its deck as if it were pouring out of a bucket with holes in it. The eccentric could see from Stern's taut back that the moment had been a very dangerous one.

He was sobered up by an angry shout through the megaphone, which was almost drowned by the storm. Stern's voice croaked:

"How about the toys in the hold, Chokh?"

"So far so good," replied the echo from the brass tube.

Stern grabbed the eccentric by the collar and shouted in his ear:

"We've got to break through into the North Channel!"

The eccentric nodded in reply, but thought privately that breaking through was out of the question. The *Borei* was jerking like a man whose face is being hit, first right, then left, by a mob of lynchers. He was struck by the fact that the prow did not seek to avoid the blows, but sailed head-on into the most towering waves. This was either the courage of despair or sheer insolence.

Stern opened his lips wide as if they were made of rubber and shouted hoarsely:

"Force eleven! Can you hear me? Yes. At night. We'll deliver the cargo all right. Down, down...."

His lips stretched into a smile.

The eccentric crawled below. A steward was lying on a divan in the messroom. He was upset because the galley was out of order and they would have to serve cold food. The very idea of eating seemed absurd, and the eccentric put the man's words down to an unbalanced state of mind.

At three o'clock the horn sounded gloomily above deck. The eccentric pressed his nose against the icy porthole and saw a rusty boat with its stern rearing out of the water and scraps of a flag flying on its mast. The boat dived into the water and disappeared in the rain. Although he was not a sailor, the eccentric noticed one strange thing: the *Borei*'s flag was on its stern, but on the other boat it was at half-mast. He asked the steward about this.

"What's strange about that," replied the steward annoyed. "They're asking for help."

Even the eccentric realised that asking for help was pointless to say the least. The other boat was carried away in a swirl of foam. After that there were only a few glimpses of its red hull in the breaks between the waves.

The eccentric was shaking. He had lost faith in the soundness of the *Borei* and the omnipotence of Stern. The radio operator picked up two SOS calls. The ocean was like a raving lunatic.

The storm grew. Night was approaching but sleep was out of the question. The only thing to do was smoke and wait. Wait for what? The eccentric avoided thinking about the possibility of death, but then the *Borei* keeled violently over on its side and plunged down, its decks pounded by thousands of tons of water.

A desperate whistle came from the bridge. The white-faced steward cried to the eccentric:

"We're passing the Rock! On deck!"

The eccentric jumped out and recoiled at the sight of white death roaring ahead of him. He did not notice the cliffs, only the powerful jets of water spurting high into the sky. Faint with nausea he crawled onto the bridge. The *Borei* was keeling violently from side to side water pouring over its deck. It was sailing parallel with the breakers.

"What? What's up?" shouted the eccentric to Stern, but the wind stopped up his mouth like a cork and whistled like a flute on his teeth.

Stern did not even give him a glance. His eyes were fixed on the blindingly white jets, all the more terrifying because the dense gloom of night was advancing rapidly from the east.

The junior mate looked at the eccentric with his tired eyes, seized his hand and traced these words on his palm:

"We're passing the Rock."

The eccentric realised that the most difficult moment had come. The *Borei* was fighting with all the remaining strength it could muster. It was being swept passed the cliffs. The turbid waves were as steep as the cliffs themselves.

The eccentric squatted down and closed his eyes, holding on tightly to the rail. He was suddenly seized with the overwhelming desire to go deaf and blind. Then he felt a tug at his shoulders, got soaked to the skin and jumped up: a swirling wave had passed just below the bridge sweeping the lifeboat from the deck, which now bobbed about in the water with its keel sticking up. The *Borei* lifted its bows sharply and then plunged down past the last cliff. Waves beat against the stern and the engines gave a light shudder.

Stern wiped his face on his sleeve and spat. He turned heavily to the eccentric, squeezed his elbow and took him down to the messroom. There he sat in silence and the eccentric did not dare to ask him anything.

"Yours is a lucky cargo," said the skipper at last. "It's almost impossible to pass the Rock in this weather. All the boats crash on it. But we had no choice. We'll be protected by the shore in an hour's time."

The eccentric asked why they had needed to pass the Rock. He knew that in heavy storms boats sail against the wind and waves until the weather has calmed down, and never change course so as not to expose themselves to mortal peril.

"If I'd been carrying a cargo of salted tripe, I would never have changed course," Stern muttered. "Now go to bed."

The eccentric meekly went off to his cabin, changed his clothes and lay down. The swell had become regular and pleasant. He got warm and fell asleep.

He dreamed of a town where the snow was falling thickly and quietly, covering the tiles of the houses and the bridges of the ships. The wintry air off the sea was as fresh as spring and quite unforgettable. Millions of lights were flickering in the dusk.

Stern came out onto the bridge in a new jacket with gold chevrons. His clean-shaved face looked young. The *Borei* gave a solemn hoot. Huge torches were lit and they began to unload. A smell of fresh paint wafted from the crates of toys.

The eccentric went ashore and roamed around the alleys soft with snow. He met old men like characters out of Jules Verne and savoured the strong smoke from their pipes. The town smelt of old ships. In the streets jolly, rosy-cheeked nannies told their children, how the *Borei* had fought its way through a storm as frightening as the end of the world and as cold as an icy compress, to bring them toys. The children's eyes shone with delight at the words which they did not understand.

The snow and the flames from the open hearths evoked magical scenes from Hans Christian Andersen. The eccentric noticed the dainty footprints of Cinderella. She had very warm tiny feet and the snow melted as she trod on it. He followed the footprints and they led him to the *Borei*. Cinderella was standing on the boat talking to Stern, whose face was wreathed in smiles. The

310

eccentric stepped back a pace as she turned to him. Her eyes shone and her face was radiant with joy. Small snowflakes nestled in her dark hair and her dress, the colour of sea water, shone with changing colours in the light of the fireworks leaping up over the town. The fireworks were to mark the beginning of a big winter festival.

The eccentric woke up. It was quiet. He went on deck and before him in the silent light of dawn lay Belfast—an old city with its lights still burning, tucked away in a thistledown mist. There was a scent of autumn grass. The *Borei* steamed along rocking gently on the water in a slow greeting to the town.

1926

THE GROVES OF MIKHAILOVSKOYE

A poet whose name I forget once said: "Poetry is all around us even in the wild grass. All you have to do is bend down and pick it up."

It was early morning, and a fine rain was falling as the cart entered a forest of ancient pines. There was a flash of white in the grass by the roadside. Jumping off the cart I bent down and saw a small board overgrown with bindweed. Something was written on it in black paint. Pulling aside the wet strands of bindweed I read the almost forgotten words: "Many a time did I linger under your canopy, groves of Mikhailovskoye."

"What's this?" I asked the driver.

"Mikhailovskoye," he answered with a smile. "This is where Pushkin country begins. You'll find signs like that all over the place."

After that I would come across these boards in the most unexpected places—the unmown meadows by the River Sorot, the sandy slopes along the road from Mikhailovskoye to Trigorskoye, the banks of Lake Malenets and Lake Petrovskoye. Pushkin's simple lines echoed all around from the grass, moss and a dry earthen hut, to be heard only by the leaves, the birds and the sky, that pale, timid Pskov sky. "Farewell Trigorskoye, where joy was mine so oft." "I see the azure plains of two lakes."

One day I lost my way in a nut grove. The faint track disappeared among the bushes. A barefooted girl perhaps came once a week with a bag of bilberries here and nobody else. But here too I found a white board in the undergrowth with a quotation from Pushkin's letter to Osipova: "Couldn't I buy Savkino? I would build myself a hut, move my books there and come to spend a month or two among my dear old friends."

At first I could not fathom out why this inscription belonged here, but the path soon led me to the little village of Savkino. Waves of ripe oats reached right up to the roofs of the low wooden houses. There was not a soul to be seen in the village; only a black dog with grey eyes barked at me from behind a wattle fence and sturdy pines murmured quietly on the hills around.

I had been nearly everywhere in my country

313

and seen many wonderful places that left you speechless with emotion, but not one of them made such an immediate lyrical impact as Mikhailovskoye. It was quiet and deserted. Clouds drifted overhead and their shadows moved across the green hills, the lakes, and the paths of the ancient park. The silence was broken only by the humming of bees.

The bees were gathering honey in the avenue of tall lime trees where Pushkin met Anna Kern. The limes were already losing their blossom. A lively little old woman was often to be found sitting here with a book on a bench. Pinned to the collar of her blouse was an old turquoise brooch. The old woman was reading Fedin's *Cities and Years.* She was Anna Kern's granddaughter, Aglaya Pyzhevskaya, a former provincial actress.

She remembered her grandmother well and readily talked about her. She hadn't liked the old girl. And indeed who could be expected to like this ancient senile old woman who used to quarrel with her granddaughters about the best helping at dinner. The granddaughters were stronger than she was and always took the best helping away from her. Then she would weep at the horrid girls' behaviour.

I met Kern's granddaughter for the first time on the sandy slope where the three famous pines once stood. Now they are no longer. Two of them were struck by lightning before the Revolution and the third was cut down one night by a thieving miller from the small village of Zimari.

The workers on the Pushkin estate decided to plant three new young pines on the same spot, but it was difficult to establish where the old trees had stood, since all trace of them had disappeared, even the stumps. So they summoned the old locals to calculate the exact spot.

The old men spent the whole day arguing. Their decision had to be unanimous, but three old boys from Deriglazovo refused to agree with the rest. When the three had finally been talked round, the old men began to pace out distances on the slope and make calculations. It wasn't until evening that they finally said:

"Here! This is the spot all right! Go ahead and plant them."

When I met Anna Kern's granddaughter near the three recently planted young pines, she was mending a fence that had been broken by a cow.

The old woman told me, laughing at herself, that she had made herself a niche in Pushkin country and found it hard to leave for Leningrad, although it was high time for her to do so. She was in charge of a small library on Kamenny Island in Leningrad and she lived alone, having no children or relatives.

"No, no," she said, "don't try to dissuade me. I shall definitely come here to die. These places have such a hold on me that I don't want to live anywhere else. Each day I think up some new excuse for postponing my departure. Now I'm going round the villages writing down everything the old men say about Pushkin." "But they're awful liars," she added sadly. "Yesterday one of them was describing how Pushkin was called to a meeting of state powers and asked whether they should fight Napoleon or not. Then Pushkin ups and says: 'What's all this about fightin' then, noble state powers, when your peasants are wearin' nothin' but the same pair of bags day in day out. You b'aint strong enough!'"

Anna Kern's granddaughter was indefatigable. I used to come across her in Mikhailovskoye, Trigorskoye, the graveyard at Voronichi and on the outskirts of Trigorskoye where I lived in a chilly empty wooden house. Rain or shine, dawn or dusk she wandered everywhere on foot.

She told me about her earlier life, about famous provincial producers and tragedians who had taken to drink (her stories left one with the impression that the only people with talent in the old days were tragedians) and finally about her love affairs.

"All you can see now is a fussy old woman," she said. "But I used to be gay, independent and beautiful. I could leave some interesting memoirs behind me, but somehow I never get round to writing them. When I finish writing down the old men's tales I'll start preparing for the summer festival."

A summer festival is held each year in Mikhailovskoye on Pushkin's birthday. Hundreds of carts decorated with ribbons and little Valdai bells drive up to the meadow on the other side of the Sorot opposite Pushkin's park.

In the meadows they light fires and dance the *khorovod*. They sing old songs and new chastushki:

> *Oh, how beautiful they are*
> *All our lakes and pine trees.*
> *We are doing all we can*
> *To preserve Mikhailovskoye.*

All the local peasants take pride in their fellow countryman Pushkin and tend the estate as carefully as their own gardens and fields.

I was living in Voronichi with Nikolai, the keeper of Trigorsky Park. The lady of the house did nothing but clatter about with the dishes and nag her husband: a fine husband he was, stuck day and night in that there park, nipping back home for an hour or two, and even then sending his poor old father-in-law or the young boys to the park to keep an eye on things while he was away.

One day Nikolai had just popped home for a cup of tea. Before he even had time to take off his cap the lady of the house rushed in dishevelled from the yard.

"Go back to the park, you old skiver!" she shouted. "I was just rinsing my washing in the river when I saw some whipper-snapper from Leningrad nip straight into the park. Goodness only knows what he's getting up to!"

"What could he be getting up to?" I asked.

Nikolai was already at the door.

"Anything under the sun," he said on his way out. "Give him half a chance and he'll go breaking a branch off or something."

But everything was alright in the end. The "whipper-snapper" turned out to be the known artist Natan Altman and Nikolai calmed down.

The Pushkin estate contains three enormous parks—Mikhailovsky, Trigorsky and Petrovsky—all as different from each other as their owners were.

Trigorsky Park is drenched in sunlight. For some reason it gives this impression even on cloudy days. The light lies in golden pools on the bright grass, the foliage of the limes, the sloping banks of the Sorot and Eugene Onegin's bench. These patches of sunlight give an appearance of mystery and unreality to the heart of the park enveloped in a summer haze. The park seems to have been made for family celebrations, friendly chats and dancing by candlelight under the black canopy of leaves with laughing young girls and playful declarations of love. It is full of the spirit of Pushkin and Yazykov.

Mikhailovsky Park is the haven of the recluse. Made for solitude and reflection it is not a place for jollity. It is tall, silent, and somewhat gloomy with its old fir trees and runs imperceptibly into ancient deserted forests as majestic as the park itself. Only on the edge of the park through the twilight that always reigns under the canopies of the ancient trees, do you suddenly glimpse an open glade covered with shining buttercups and a quiet pond with swarms of leaping little frogs.

The park's main attraction lies in the high bank of the River Sorot and the small house where Arina Rodionovna, Pushkin's old nurse, lived. This is the only house dating back to Pushkin's time that is still standing. It is so sweet and tiny that you feel afraid to walk up the steps to the rickety porch. From the bank over the Sorot you can see two blue lakes, a forest-covered hill and the simple, age-old Russian sky with its slumbering clouds.

Petrovsky Park is where Pushkin's grandfather, the gloomy, self-willed Hannibal, used to live. There is a good view of this park from Mikhailovskoye on the other side of Lake Kuchane (also called Lake Petrovskoye). It is black, damp and overgrown with burdock. Entering it is like walking into a cellar. Hobbled horses graze among the burdock. The flowers are choked by nettles and in the evening the park groans with the croaking of frogs. Squawking jackdaws nest in the dark treetops.

On my way back from Petrovskoye to Mikhailovskoye I once happened to get lost among the forest dells. Little streams were gurgling among the roots and at the bottom of the dells there was a flash of small lakes. The sun was setting. The motionless air was reddish and hot. In one of the forest glades I suddenly caught sight of a storm rising above Mikhailovskoye on the evening sky in steep banks of coloured cloud, like a huge mediaeval town surrounded by white turrets. Then came a hollow boom of thunder and the wind swished over the glade dying down in the undergrowth.

It was difficult to imagine Pushkin's horse carrying its silent rider lightly along these simple paths marked by the tread of bast sandals, over the anthills and twisted roots.

I can still see the forests, lakes, parks and sky. These are almost the only things that have remained here since Pushkin's time. The countryside has been completely untouched and is very carefully preserved. When electricity was to be installed in Mikhailovskoye it was decided to lay it underground to avoid putting up poles which would have ruined the essential charm of these parts.

In Voronichi where I was living there was a tumbledown wooden church which everyone called the "old church". It stood morosely, overgrown up to the roof with yellow lichen, barely visible through the elder thicket surrounding it. It was in this church that Pushkin ordered a memorial service to be held for Byron.

Now the church porch was covered with resinous pine shavings. A school was being built alongside it.

Only once during all the time I spent in Voronichi did the hunch-backed priest in a torn straw hat hobble up to the church. He carefully propped his fishing rods up against a lime tree and opened the heavy lock on the church doors. That day a very old man had died in Voronichi and they had brought his body to the church for a funeral service. After the service the priest picked up his rods again and plodded off to the Sorot to fish for chub and roach.

The joiners building the school watched him go and one of them said:

"The clergy's come down a bit in the world! When Alexander Sergeyevich was alive Voronichi had a priest who was as important as a brigadier-general. And a nasty piece of work he was too. No wonder Alexander Sergeyevich nicknamed him 'Bully'. But this one's a sorry sort of bloke in his tatty old straw hat."

"What's happened to their power now?" muttered another. "Where's all their silks and velvet gone?"

The carpenters wiped their sweaty brows, the blows of their axes rang out again, and another shower of fresh, pungent shavings flew onto the ground.

Several times in Trigorsky Park I came across

a tall man wandering along the deserted paths. He would stop by a clump of bushes and spend a long time examining the leaves. Sometimes he would pick a blade of grass and study it through a small magnifying glass.

One day I got caught in a heavy shower near the pond not far from the Osipovs' house. It suddenly began to pour down and I took shelter under a lime tree. The tall man walked up slowly to where I was standing and we fell into conversation. It turned out that he was a geography teacher from Cherepovets.

"You must be a botanist as well as a geographer," I said to him. "I've seen you examining the plants."

The tall man gave a smile.

"No. I just like trying to find something new in my surroundings. This is my third summer here, but I don't know a fraction of all there is to know about these parts."

He spoke quietly and diffidently. With this the conversation ended.

Our second meeting was on the banks of Lake Malenets, at the bottom of a wooded hill. The pines were murmuring dreamily and beneath their tops the semi-darkness of the forest swayed with the wind. The tall man was lying in the grass examining a blue jay's feather through his magnifying glass. I sat down beside him and he gave me a slightly ironical, halting explanation of why he was so attached to Mikhailovskoye.

"My father was a book-keeper in a hospital in Vologda," he said. "He was a pretty wretched person—always drinking and showing off. Even when we were desperately hard up he wore a carefully ironed and starched shirt front and boasted about his background. He was a Russian Lithuanian from a family called Yagellon. He used to beat me mercilessly when he was drunk. There were six of us children. We all lived in one filthy, untidy room, quarrelling and being beaten all the time. I had an awful childhood. When father got drunk he used to begin to recite Pushkin's poetry and burst into tears. The tears fell onto his starched shirt front and he would crumple and rend it, and shout that Pushkin was the only ray of sunshine in the lives of miserable beggars like us. He couldn't remember any of his poems all the way through. He would begin reciting them, but never once got to the end. This always made me angry, even though I was only eight and could hardly make out printed letters. So I decided to read Pushkin's poems to the end and went to the town library. I stood at the door for ages until the librarian called me over and asked me what I wanted.

" 'Pushkin,' I said rudely.

" 'Do you mean the fairy stories?' she asked.

" 'No. Not the fairy stories. Pushkin,' I repeated stubbornly.

"She handed me a thick volume. I sat down in a corner by the window, opened the book and burst out crying. I was crying because I had only just realised, that I couldn't read the book, that I couldn't read at all and that there was a whole magical world concealed behind these lines, which had made my drunken father weep. The only two lines of Pushkin which I had learned by heart from him were 'I see a distant land, the magic shores of southern climes', but this was enough for me to be able to picture a different life from ours. Just imagine a man who has been in solitary confinement for years and years. At last he is helped to escape and given the keys to the prison gates. But as he walks up to the gates with freedom, people, forests and lakes on the other side, he suddenly realises that he doesn't know how to open the lock with this key. There is a vast world vibrating only a few inches away behind the iron gates, but to unlock them you must know a stupid little secret which this runaway doesn't possess. He hears the alarm sounding behind him and knows that they will soon grab him and that everything will be just the same as it was until he dies: the dirty window under the ceiling of his cell, the smell of rats and the despair. This is what I went through with the volume of Pushkin in my hands. The librarian saw I was crying, came up to me and said, picking up the book:

" 'What's the matter, my lad? Why are you crying? Didn't you notice you'd got the book upside down?'

"She laughed and I went away. Since then I have been in love with Pushkin. This is my third year running in Mikhailovskoye."

The tall man fell silent. We went on lying on the grass for a long time. You could just hear the faint sound of a shepherd's horn in the meadows on the other side of the curving Sorot.

A few kilometres from Mikhailovskoye is the Svyatogorsky Monastery standing on an elevated piece of ground with Pushkin's grave by the monastery wall. The village round the monastery is called Pushkin Hills.

The village is packed with hay. Night and day the hay carts creak over the large cobblestones, bringing dry hay into Pushkin Hills. There is a smell of bast matting, smoked fish and cheap cotton from the shops and stalls.

The one and only teahouse rings with the constant clinking of glasses and teapots. The steam reaches up to the ceiling and in this steam sit farm workers and shrivelled old men from the time of Ivan the Terrible, unhurriedly drinking their tea and eating hunks of grey bread. Where these old men come from with their parchment skin, piercing gaze and hollow, croaking voices no one knows. But there are lots of them and there must have been even more in Pushkin's day when he wrote *Boris Godunov* here.

To get to Pushkin's grave you have to walk through the empty monastery courtyards and go up a flight of weathered stone steps which lead to the top of the hill and the wind-eroded walls of the main church.

At the base of the wall over a steep slope you can see Pushkin's grave in the shade of lime trees, the earth sprinkled with yellowed lime blossom.

The brief inscription "Alexander Sergeyevich Pushkin", the solitude, the creaking of the carts on the hillside below and the clouds brooding in the low sky—this is all you will find. This spot marks the end of the brilliant, turbulent life of a great man. Here is the grave known to all mankind, the "sweet bourn" of which Pushkin spoke during his life. There is a smell of weeds, bark and settled summer days.

And here on this simple grave from which you can hear the hoarse crowing of cocks in the distance it becomes particularly obvious that Pushkin was the first poet of the Russian people.

He is buried in the backwoods of Russia, in the coarse sandy earth where only flax and nettles grow. From his grave you can see the dark forests of Mikhailovskoye and the distant storms which roll in a stately dance over the bright river Sorot over Savkino, Trigorskoye and the simple vast fields bringing his beloved, refreshed earth peace and prosperity.

1936

LUMP SUGAR

One northern summer I arrived at the small town of Voznesenye on Lake Onega.

It was midnight when the boat drew into the harbour and a silver moon was shining low over the lake. There was no need for it here because we were well into the season of the white nights with their colourless lustre. There was scarcely any difference between the long days and the short nights. Both day and night the whole of this low-lying forested landscape seemed to be melting away in the half-light.

The northern summer always provokes a feeling of uneasiness. It is very unstable. At any moment its precarious warmth may suddenly disappear. For this reason you begin to treasure the slightest breath of warm air and the gentle sun which transforms the lake into a sheet of shining, quiet water. This northern sun does not shine, but seems rather to glimmer through a thick pane of glass. It is as though winter had not yet disappeared and was only hiding away in the forest or at the bottom of the lake still giving off a tingling scent of snow.

The birch trees in the gardens were losing their blossoms. Fair-haired, bare-footed boys were sitting on the landing stage fishing for smelt. Everything seemed to have turned white except for their large black floats. The boys' eyes were fixed on them in frowning concentration and they would ask each other in a whisper for a cigarette.

A militiaman with freckles and a cap stuck on his tousled hair was fishing with the boys.

"Now then. No smoking on the landing stage. No messing about there!" he would shout from time to time, and immediately several lighted cigarettes would flash into the white water, hiss and go out.

I set off for the town to find somewhere to spend the night accompanied by a fat, apathetic man with a crew cut who had tagged on to me. He was bound for the River Kovzha on business and carried a large worn briefcase full of reports and calculations about timber. He talked clumsy officialese like a rather incompetent business man, using such expressions as "curbing travelling expenses", "checking accounts", "organising a bite to eat", and "overfulfilling the timber rafting norms".

The sky grew pale with boredom from his very presence.

We walked along the planked footways with the smell of bird cherry wafting from the cold, nocturnal gardens and pale lights gleaming behind the open windows.

A quiet, bright-eyed little girl was sitting on a bench by the garden gate in front of a wooden house singing her rag doll to sleep. I asked her if it would be possible to spend the night there. She nodded silently and then led me up a steep, creaking flight of steps into a clean room. The man with the crew cut persisted in following me.

An old woman in steel-framed glasses was knitting at the table and a thin dusty old man was sitting, eyes closed, leaning back against the wall.

"Grandma, here's a traveller who wants a bed for the night," said the little girl pointing at me with her doll.

The old woman rose and bowed low to me.

"You're welcome, my dear," she said in a singsong voice. "You're welcome as an honoured guest. But we haven't much room, I'm afraid. We'll have to make you up a bed on the floor."

"So things here are a bit primitive, citizen," said the man with the crew cut censoriously.

At this the old man opened his eyes—they were almost white like those of a blind man—and replied slowly:

"Some people never learn. Be thankful for small mercies."

"Now you just mind who you're talking to, my man," said the man with the crew cut.

The old man said nothing.

"Don't take offence at what the old man said," the old woman quavered pitifully. "He's got no home of his own, the poor old wanderer. You can't hold him to answer."

The man with the crew cut became animated. His eyes narrowed into a hard expression and he hit the table loudly with his briefcase.

"The old man's certainly an alien element," he said pompously. "You should be more careful who you let into your house. We'll soon find out who he is. Now then, you there. What's your name and where were you born?"

The old man gave a wry smile. The little girl dropped her doll and her lip began to quiver.

"The world's my home and I'm at home everywhere in it," replied the old man calmly. "And my name is Alexander."

"Occupation?"

"I reap and sow," said the old man in the same calm voice. "When I was a young man I would reap and sow the crops. Now I sow a kind word and reap other wonderful words. The trouble is that I can't read or write, so I have to take everything in by ear and rely on my memory."

The man with the crew cut said nothing for a while, puzzled.

"Any papers?"

"Yes, I have papers. But they're not intended for the likes of you, my lad. Them's valuable papers."

"I see," said the man with the crew cut. "Then we'll find the person they are intended for."

And he went out slamming the door behind him.

"There's a right thick 'un for you," said the old man after a pause. "Nothin' but fuss and bother from the likes of him."

The old woman set the samovar going, apologising contritely in her wavering voice for not having a lump of sugar in the house because she had forgotten to buy it. The samovar provided a mournful accompaniment to her lament. The little girl lay the table with a clean tablecloth of unbleached linen which smelt of rye bread.

Outside the open window a single star was shining. It was misty and very large and looked strange on its own in the vast gloaming sky.

This tea-making in the middle of the night did not surprise me. I had discovered a long time ago that northerners stay awake until very late in the summer. Outside by the gate of the house next door two young girls were standing with their arms round each other gazing into the dim waters of the lake. As always on a white night, the girls' faces looked pale with emotion, sad and beautiful.

"That's the two Komsomol lassies from Leningrad," said the old woman. "Captains' daughters. Always spend the summer here."

The old man was sitting quietly with his eyes closed as if he were listening for something. Suddenly he opened his eyes and sighed.

"He's bringing him!" he said sadly. "Forgive me for being such a fool and a nuisance, Grandma."

The steps outside creaked and there was a sound of heavy footsteps. The man with the crew cut came in without knocking, followed by a worried, tousle-haired militiaman in a cap—the one who had been fishing on the landing stage. The man with the crew cut nodded in the direction of the old man.

"Now then, Grandad," the militiaman said sternly. "Come on and establish your identity. Let's have your papers."

"I'm a simple enough person," the old man replied. "But it's a long story. Sit down and I'll tell you all about it."

"Mind you're quick, then," said the militiaman. "I haven't got time to sit around. I've got to take you down to the station."

"There's plenty of time for us to get down to the station, my lad. They don't waste any words there. No one to have a good talk to. I've turned sixty and I might pop off any day now in a strange place. So you just listen to what I have to say."

"Come on then," the militiaman agreed. "But don't you go making it all up, mind."

"Why should I? My life is a simple one and there's no getting away from it. All of us Fedosievs were coach drivers and singers from way back. My grandfather Prokhor was a great singer. His mighty voice would ring out and weep all along the highway from Pskov to Novgorod. A person should look after his voice. It's not given to a man for nothing. My grandfather looked after his well until one sad day when he forgot and that was the end of it. Happen you know that our famous countryman Alexander Sergeyevich, the poet Pushkin, lived in Pskov gubernia."

The militiaman grinned.

" 'Course I knows that."

"Well, it was because of him that my grandfather ruined his voice. One day they met at the fair in the Svyatogorsk monastery. My grandfather was singing and Pushkin stood there listening to him. Then the two of them went into a drinking house and sat there all night. Nobody knows what they were a-talking about, but my grandfather returns home as merry as a lord altho' hardly a drop of wine has passed his lips. Later on he told my grandmother: 'I got drunk from his words and laughter, Nastyusha. He spoke so beautifully—much more beautiful than my singing.' There was one song my grandfather knew that Pushkin was real fond of."

The old man paused for a moment and then suddenly burst into song in a powerful, anguished voice:

Over the plains so broad and white
The snow our bitter tears hath buried.

The girls walked up to the window and listened, their arms round each other. The militiaman sat down cautiously on a bench.

"Aye," the old man sighed. "A fair time after that my grandfather died at a ripe old age and bade his sons and grandsons sing that song after him. But that's not what I meant to tell you about. One winter's night grandfather was woken up by knocking on the window and ordered to harness the horses on urgent state business. He comes out on to the steps and sees the place a-swarming with policemen, walking about and rattling their broadswords. So we're taking off another bunch of convicts, he thinks. But instead of prisoners

there's a black coffin lying there bound with rope.
Who can that be, he thinks, carried to his grave
in fetters? God have mercy on him. Who is it
that the Tsar fears even after death? He goes up
to the coffin, brushes the snow off the black lid
with his sleeve and asks the policeman: 'Who
are we taking?' 'Pushkin,' says the policeman.
'He's been killed in St. Petersburg.' Grandfather
started back, flung off his cap and bowed low
before the coffin. 'Did you know him then?' said
the policeman. 'I sang to him.' 'Well, you won't be
singing to him any more!' The night was so bitter cold, that you could hardly breathe. Grandfather tied the bells so that they would not ring,
climbed up to the coachman's seat and set off.
There was silence all around except for the swish-
ing of the runners and the sound of the broadswords knocking against the coffin. His heart was
heavy, his eyes smarted with tears and he burst
into song at the top of his voice:

Over the plains so broad and white....

"The policeman struck him on the back with his
scabbard, but grandfather went on singing, paying no heed to him. He got home and went to
bed in silence—the cold had ruined his voice.
From that day onwards he could speak only in
a hoarse whisper."

"He really put his heart into his singing, then,"
murmured the militiaman in a moved voice.

"No use doing anything unless you put your
heart into it," said the old man. "And here you
are going on at me about who I am and what I
do. I sing songs. That's what I do. Just go about
singing to people. And when I hear a new song

I try to remember it. For example, it's one thing to say something, but if you sing it that's quite a different matter. Then the words go straight to the heart. We must cherish the power to sing. People who don't like singing are not worth a farthing. They don't understand the meaning of life. And don't you go worrying about my papers. I'll show you one."

The old man put his shaking hands inside his shirt and drew out a grey pouch from which he took a piece of paper.

"There. Read this."

"Why should I?" said the militiaman offended. "I don't need to read it now. I can see who you are without that. You just stay where you are and have a good rest, Dad. And as for you, citizen," he said turning to the man with the crew cut, "you'd better go and spend the night at the hostel. That will suit you better. Come along and I'll show you the way."

They left. I took the piece of paper from the old man and read the following:

"This is to certify that Alexander Fedosiev is a collector of folk songs and stories for which he receives a pension from the government of the Karelian Republic. Local authorities are requested to render him all necessary assistance."

"Dear me," said the old man. "There's nothing worse than a person who has dried-up soul. They make life wither like grass from the autumn dew."

We sat drinking tea. The girls with their arms round each other went down to the lake, and their simple cotton dresses showed white in the light nocturnal twilight. A pale moon was descending into the water and somewhere in the garden among the birch trees a night bird called.

The bright-eyed little girl went into the street and sat down again by the gate to sing her rag doll to sleep. I could see her through the window. The tousle-haired militiaman in the cap came up to her and pushed a bag of sugar and biscuits into her hands.

"Take these to the old man," he said blushing hard. "Tell him it's a present. I haven't got time myself—got to get back on duty."

He went off quickly and the little girl brought the bag of lump sugar and biscuits to the old man who burst out laughing.

"Ee, but I'd like to go on living for a long time yet," he said wiping his wet eyes. "It's such a pity to die and leave such good people behind. Such a pity. And when I look at the forest, the bright water, the young lads and the wild grass, I just haven't got the heart to die."

"You just go on living, my dear," said the old woman. "Why should you do anything else with a life as easy and simple as yours."

The following afternoon I left Voznesenye for Vytegra. The small *Svir* sailed along a canal, its sides brushing against the willow-herb which grew along the banks in profusion.

The little town gradually disappeared into the sunny haze, the silence and the distance of the summer day, and the low-lying forest enveloped us in a dark circle. Around us lay the pale northern summer, as shy as the bright-eyed local children.

1938

LYONKA FROM LITTLE LAKE

We were following a map which had been compiled in the eighteen seventies from "information obtained from the local inhabitants" as a footnote in the corner explained. We were not overjoyed by this note in spite of its frankness, for we too had obtained information from the local inhabitants and it was almost invariably inaccurate.

They would shout long and heatedly, contradicting each other and referring to a lot of landmarks. Their directions were usually something like this: "As soon as you get to the ditch make

336

a sharp turn across to the forest, then just go on and on across burnt clearings until you reach the badger's hole. From there you make straight for the big hill that you can just see in the distance, and once you've reached the hill it's just a matter of crossing the tussocks to the lake. You can't miss it."

We would follow these instructions to the letter and never find the place we were looking for.

So today we were using a map, but had got lost all the same among the dried up marshes overgrown with small sparse trees.

The autumn day was rustling with crisp leaves. Then a fine rain began to fall which felt like cold dust on our faces. About three o'clock we found ourselves on a sandy bank covered with dry fern in the middle of the marshes. The light was fading fast, and dusk was gathering under the unfriendly sky, heralding the approach of night— a bleak night in the marshes, with nothing but the cracking of dead branches, the pattering of rain and an unbearable feeling of loneliness. We shouted and listened hard. The wind moaned back at us through the lifeless thickets bearing the harsh cawing of crows.

Then suddenly we heard a long, faint answering call in the far distance. The calls grew nearer and there was a cracking sound among the aspen trees. A boy with a freckled face emerged from the thicket. He looked about twelve years old and was picking his way carefully over the dead branches barefoot carrying a pair of old boots. He came up and greeted us shyly.

"I heard this shouting," he said and added with a laugh. "Got a bit scared, because you don't expect to find anyone here at this time of year. You get women picking berries in the summer, but it's not the season for berries any more. Are you lost?"

"Yes," we said.

"You wouldn't last long here," said the boy. "A woman got lost last summer and they didn't find her until spring. Just a heap of bones."

"What are you doing here?"

"I live here. By Little Lake. I'm looking for a lost calf."

The boy took us to Little Lake. It was almost night by the time we got out of the marshes onto hard ground and reached the overgrown path. The wind had driven the clouds southwards and the stars were blazing over the pine trees, but the familiar constellations looked different through the tangled branches and it was even difficult to find the Great Bear.

"I made that up about the calf," said the boy after a long silence. "I wasn't looking for a calf at all."

"What were you after in the marshes then?"

"A falling star. Saw it fall the night before last behind the big hills. Woke up and heard Manka the cow mooing and tossing about. Thought there must be a wolf outside, so I went to have a look. I stood in the yard listening and then something blazed across the sky, sailed low over the forest and fell somewhere behind the hill. It was a meteor. Made quite a noise, like an aeroplane."

"What do you want a meteor for?"

"I'll take it to school and we'll examine it. Do you know what stars are made of?"

We began a nocturnal discussion about stars and spectral analysis. It was almost midnight when we arrived at the forest lake with the starry autumn sky reflected in its black waters. There were several cottages on the bank and the boy knocked at the door of the far one where an oil lamp was still burning in the window.

"Where on earth have you been, you little rascal," said a woman's voice angrily behind the door. "Wearing out your boot leather."

"I took them off, Ma," said the boy.

There was a rattling of bolts being drawn and we groped our way into the little passage smelling of hay and fresh milk. We spent the night in the boy's cottage—his name was Lyonka Zuyev—smoking a cigarette with his father, an elderly quiet man with steel-rimmed glasses, and then going to sleep on the straw near the warm stove. A cricket was chirping and sleepy hens were clucking in the passage.

I was woken in the middle of the night by the sound of a powerful woman's voice giving a passionate rendering of the well-known aria from *The Queen of Spades* accompanied by a host of high pitched violins. Stars were shimmering through the misted windowpanes and the cricket had stopped chirping to listen to the singing.

"That there radio's disturbing you," said Lyonka's mother from her bed above the stove. "Lyonka made it himself. It'll prevent you from sleeping, but I don't know how to stop it. Haven't got the education. I'll wake up the lad."

"No, don't bother. Let him have his sleep."

"But we love listening to Moscow singing, we really do," she went on in the dark, her voice hushed and wistful. "Somehow it's so strange and sad and gay, all mixed up together. You can go on listening to it until the cock crows even though you were ready to drop after a hard day's work."

She paused for a moment.

"And it's all our Lyonka's doing," she continued, obviously smiling to herself in the dark. "He's a right one for finding out about things. Takes after his father."

"What does his father do then?" I asked her.

"Semyon? He's been in the Party since nineteen eighteen. Never a thought for himself. Give away his last crust, he would, and live on his books."

The next morning we found out all about Semyon Zuyev. He had started off as a tailor's apprentice in Ryazan. The Lysov firm where he worked was considered to be the best tailors in the town and was patronised by the governor, the military and the legal profession. Semyon had ruined his eyesight sewing silk braid by hand onto the trousers of lawyers' dress coats. It was very painstaking work.

Lysov, a devout old fogy with a face as green as a frog, spent all his time reading religious books or Karamzin's *History of the Russian State*. He spent a thousand roubles on beautifying the town's dusty streets by having steel plates with quotations from Karamzin put up on houses. Each extract had a footnote saying: "See Mr. Karamzin's *History*", volume so-and-so, page so-and-so.

"So I began with Karamzin and finished up reading Lenin," said Semyon. "Lenin's voice penetrated right into the most remote backwaters. You'd read at night and then go out into the street in the morning to be greeted by dust everywhere, geese waddling about among the puddles and scraps of red sealing wax all over the shop where they sold vodka. The bells were ringing in the church and the beggars beating each other with their staffs for the sake of a farthing. In other words, primeval Russia in all its glory. And the stirring words would be ringing in your head like the dawning of a new life."

After the Revolution Semyon went to live by the lake, built himself a cottage and began the hard job of reclaiming the land from the dense forest. There were already five families living there now.

In the morning Lyonka took us to the main road. A white sun was shining through the thinning branches and its cold light picked out each leaf as it fell from the aspen and birch into the lake. Occasional gusts of wind would send the leaves showering and rustling down, tickling our faces.

A few days later Lyonka appeared in our village with a piece of "falling star" in the form of a pointed burnt-out fragment covered with soot and rust, which he had discovered in a twisted old tree stump behind the hill. From then onwards he and I became great friends. I liked wandering round the forest with him. He knew every path, every nook and cranny. He could name all the plants, bushes, mosses, mushrooms and flowers and tell all the birds and animals by the sound they made.

Lyonka was the first of the many hundreds of people I had met to tell me how and where fish sleep, how dry marshes putrefy under the ground for years, how old pine trees bloom and how tiny spiders, as well as birds, migrate in the autumn. They hang suspended from their cobwebs and get carried along by the wind dozens of miles southwards. Lyonka had two books by Kaigorodov which he had read until they were falling apart. He had searched through them in vain to find an explanation of the spiders' autumn flight.

"The one thing I don't understand is how such tiny spiders can weave so much cobweb. If you were to wind it all into a ball it would be forty times their size."

Each day Lyonka went ten kilometres to school and he had only stayed away twice in the whole winter. This was when a strong snowstorm had covered their house in snow right up to the eaves, but Lyonka didn't like talking about it. He was ashamed of having missed school. In the winter he would leave the house when it was still dark. The spiky stars were shivering in the bitter cold, the pine trees creaked, and the snow crunched underfoot. Lyonka was terrified that he might be heard by the wolves, who used to come right up to the lake in winter and live in the haystacks. The worst time of all was late autumn, November, when the paths were covered with a slushy mixture of snow and rain, and gusts of wind from the lowering sky lashed your face and froze you to the marrow.

In the summer Lyonka and his mother would plough the fields, dig up the vegetable garden, sow and mow the hay. Semyon could not do that sort of work any more. He suffered more and more from his weak heart that made his face sallow and puffy, and was racked by fits of dry coughing.

"I'm more dead than alive," he would say spreading out his hand on his thin chest. "That dog's life ruined my system. The Revolution must have come too late for me. Never mind. Lyonka will finish the job off for me."

So Lyonka and I became friends and I used to send him lots of books from Moscow. I got into the habit of coming to the lake every autumn. I would always arrive unexpectedly, walking through the quiet autumn forest, deserted except for the birds, and recognising the familiar tree stumps, the twists and turns of the overgrown path and the bright forest clearings. I knew every pine tree on the edge of the forest and it was Lyonka who had taught me to love them.

I usually arrived in late twilight when the pale stars were heralding a cold night and the smell of smoke seemed to be the most delicious odour in the world. It conjured up the nearness of the lake, the warm house, lively conversations, Lyonka's mother complaining in her sing-song voice, and beds of dry hay. It reminded me of the chirping cricket and the endless nights when I would wake up to a torrent of strings playing Beethoven or Verdi, drowning the tremulous howls of hungry wolves.

Each time Lyonka would leap out of the house to greet me. He was too shy to show how pleased he was and just gave me a firm handshake. Then we talked for a long time about the books he had read, the harvest, winter in the Arctic, an eclipse of the sun and loach fishing. We were never at a loss for interesting topics of conversation. Semyon used to tell us tales about his young days and the students who had brought revolutionary leaflets to Ryazan.

We became really close friends. Wherever I was, I knew that I would return to the lake in the late autumn and see Lyonka and Semyon. And that my contact with these people would make me increasingly certain that life was getting better all the time. There seem to be more and more days when you are suddenly aware of the rushing sound of the wind in the forest, the cold springs gurgling in the moss, and you realise the tremendous value of books, quiet meditation and friendship with a country lad who has been dreaming for three years of coming to Moscow and seeing the metro, the Kremlin and a live elephant at the zoo.

This year Lyonka saw me off as usual. The funny little local train, which the inhabitants call "The Old Gelding" was puffing along through the forest. Each clearing revealed gold and crimson copses. In one of the clearings Lyonka was standing right by the railway track, waving his father's old cap. The kettle-like steam engine gave an angry whistle at him, but he just laughed and shouted:

"We'll be waiting for you. I'll write you a letter about everything. Don't forget to send me Brem!"

It was a long time before the ruddy-faced lad running after the train through the wet, stinging branches of the autumn copses, disappeared from view. He ran waving his satchel of books and smiling his shy, open smile to me, the forest, the sun and the whole world.

1938

SNOW

Old Potapov died a month after Tatyana Petrovna moved into his house. Tatyana Petrovna remained alone there with her daughter Varya and the child's old nurse.

The little three-roomed house stood on a hill at the town limits, overlooking the northern river. Beyond the house and the now naked garden gleamed a white birch grove. Jackdaws cawed there from morning to night, soaring in swarms over the bare treetops and calling down gloomy weather on the town.

After Moscow it had taken Tatyana Petrovna some time to grow accustomed to the deserted little town with its tiny houses and creaking garden gates, to the evenings when it was so still that you could hear the flame spluttering in the paraffin lamp.

"What a fool I was!" Tatyana Petrovna had thought. "Why did I leave Moscow, why did I give up the theatre and my friends! I could have sent Varya out to her nurse's place in Pushkino—there weren't any air raids there—and remained behind in Moscow myself. Goodness me, what a fool I was!"

But now it was too late to return to Moscow. Tatyana Petrovna decided to give performances in the army hospitals—there were several of them in the town—and stopped worrying. She even began to grow fond of the town, especially when winter came and smothered it in snow. The days were mild and grey. The river did not freeze for a long time; mists kept rising from its green waters.

Tatyana Petrovna had grown used both to the little town and to the stranger's house. She had grown used to the piano that was out of tune, and to the yellow photographs of cumbersome armoured battleships of the coastal fleet pinned up on the wall. Old Potapov had once been a ship's mechanic. On the faded green baize of his desk stood a model of the cruiser *Gromoboi*, on which he had served. Varya was not allowed to touch it. As a matter of fact she was not allowed to touch anything.

Tatyana Petrovna knew that Potapov had a son, a naval officer now serving in the Black Sea Fleet. There was a picture of him on the desk, next to the model of the cruiser. Sometimes Tatyana Petrovna would pick it up, and frown thoughtfully gazing at it. She felt she had seen that face somewhere long, long ago, before her unsuccessful marriage. But where? And when?

The sailor gazed back at her with calm, slightly mocking eyes, as though he were chiding her: "Well, how about it? Can't you remember where we met?"

"No, I can't," Tatyana Petrovna would reply very quietly.

"Mummy, who are you talking to?" Varya would call from the next room.

"To the piano," Tatyana Petrovna answered laughing.

In the middle of the winter letters addressed to Potapov began to stream in, all written in the same hand. Tatyana Petrovna stacked them up on the desk.

One night she suddenly awoke. The snow was emitting a faint glow outside the window. The grey tomcat Arkhip, Potapov's legacy, was dozing on the couch.

Tatyana Petrovna slipped on her dressing gown, went into Potapov's study and stood there at the window. A bird swept some snow off a bough as it flew out of a tree. The snow floated down in a fine white dust and filmed the window.

Tatyana Petrovna lit the candle on the desk and sank into an armchair. She gazed at the flame for a long time—it was burning without even the slightest flicker. Then she carefully picked up one of the letters, opened it, and, glancing round, began to read.

"Dear old Dad," Tatyana Petrovna read. "I've been in hospital a month now. My wound is not a very serious one, and it's healing well. But for goodness sake don't you start worrying and smoking cigarette after cigarette. Please!

"I often think of you," Tatyana Petrovna read on, "and of our house and our little town. It all seems far, far away, at the other end of the world. I close my eyes and see myself opening the gate and walking into the garden. It is winter and there is snow on the ground, but the path has been cleared to the arbour overlooking the river. The lilac bushes are all covered with hoarfrost. Inside the house the stoves are crackling. There is a smell of birchwood smoke. The piano has been tuned at long last and you've put the yellow candles—the ones I brought from Leningrad—in the candlesticks. The same music lies on the piano: the overture to *The Queen of Spades*, and *For the Shores of My Distant Country*. Does the doorbell work? I didn't get a chance to fix it before I left. Will I really see it all again? Will I really wash myself in water from our well out of the blue jug when I get back? Remember? Ah, if you only knew how I have grown to love all this from afar! Don't be surprised when I tell you in all seriousness that I used to recall it all during the most difficult moments of battle. I knew that I was defending not only my country but also that little corner of it dearest to my heart—you, our garden, our mischievous little village boys, the birch groves beyond the river, and even our tomcat Arkhip. Please don't laugh and don't shake your head.

"I may be able to come home for a short leave

after my discharge from hospital. But I don't know yet. Better not to count on it."

Tatyana Petrovna sat at the desk for a long time, staring fixedly out of the window at the dawn spreading over the dark blueness outside. She was reflecting that any day now a strange man, evidently a calm, courageous person, might arrive from the front, and that it would be difficult for him to bear the sight of strangers living in the house and to find everything quite different from what he had been looking forward to.

In the morning Tatyana Petrovna told Varya to take a wooden shovel and clear the path to the arbour overlooking the river. The arbour was a ramshackle affair. Its wooden columns had turned grey and were overgrown with lichen. Tatyana Petrovna mended the doorbell herself. It bore the amusing inscription: "I hang at the door, so ring some more!" She rang the bell. It gave a high-pitched tinkle. Arkhip twitched his ears with displeasure, and, taking this as a personal affront, stalked out of the entrance hall. To his mind the merry tinkle was obviously nothing short of outrageous.

Later in the day Tatyana Petrovna, flushed and vivacious, her eyes sparkling with excitement, brought an old piano tuner in from town, a Russianised Czech who tuned pianos when he wasn't repairing primus and oil stoves, dolls and accordions. When he had finished, the Czech said that it was an old piano but a very good one. Tatyana Petrovna was aware of that herself.

After he had gone she looked carefully into all the drawers of the desk until she found a package

of thick yellow candles. She put two of them in
the candlesticks on the piano. In the evening she
lit the candles and sat down at the piano, and the
house became filled with sound.

When she finished playing and blew out the
candles, the same sweet smell that one associates
with Christmas trees spread through the rooms.

Varya could not contain herself any longer.

"Why do you touch other people's things?"
she said. "You won't let me, but you touch them
yourself! You've touched the bell, and the candles, and the piano. And you put somebody else's
music on the piano."

"Because I'm a grown-up," said Tatyana Petrovna.

Varya pouted and glanced at her with disbelief.
Just then Tatyana Petrovna did not look at all
like a grown-up. She was all pink and radiant
and looked more like the girl with the golden
hair who lost her glass slipper in the palace.
Tatyana Petrovna herself had told Varya about
the girl.

While he was still in the train Lieutenant
Potapov had calculated that he could not spend
more than twenty-four hours at home. His leave
was very short, and the journey took up almost
all of it.

The train arrived in the afternoon. At the station the lieutenant learned from the stationmaster,
an old acquaintance, that his father had died a
month before and that a young Moscow singer
and her daughter were living in his house.

"Evacuees," the stationmaster explained.

Potapov said nothing. He gazed through the

window at the passengers in padded jackets and felt boots scurrying up and down the platform with teapots. His heart sank and he grew dizzy.

"Aye," said the stationmaster. "He was a good soul. Didn't live to see his boy come home."

"When can I get a train back?" Potapov inquired.

"At five in the morning." The stationmaster paused and then added, "You can spend the night with me. My old woman will give you some supper. There's no need for you to go home."

"Thanks," said Potapov. He went out.

The stationmaster shook his head as he gazed after him.

Potapov walked through the town to the river lying under a soft grey sky. A light snow was slanting down between sky and earth. Jackdaws hopped about the dung in the road. Twilight was deepening. A wind blew from the woods on the opposite bank whipping tears into his eyes.

"Well!" said Potapov. "I'm too late. And now I don't belong here any more—the town, and the river, and the forest, and the house."

He turned and gazed at the distant hillside above the river. There they stood—the frost-covered garden and the house. Smoke was curling up from the chimney. The wind carried the smoke to the birch grove.

Potapov walked slowly in the direction of the house. He decided not to go in but only to walk past it, and perhaps enter the garden and stand for a moment in the old arbour. He could not bear the thought that strangers who cared nothing for him and his father were living in his father's house. It would be better not to see any-

351

thing, not to torment himself—to leave and to forget the past.

"Well," thought Potapov, "you grow older as time passes and learn to see things with harder eyes."

He reached the house at dusk. He opened the gate carefully, but it creaked just the same. The white garden seemed to give a start. Snow fell rustling from a bough. Potapov turned round. The path leading to the arbour was cleared of snow. He went over to the arbour and put his hand on the rickety rail. In the distance, beyond the forest the sky was tinged pink—the moon must have been rising behind the clouds. He took off his cap and passed his hand through his hair. It was very quiet. Only below, at the foot of the hill, women were clattering their empty pails as they went to the ice hole for water.

Potapov leaned his elbows on the rail and clasped his head between his hands.

"I just can't accept it," he murmured.

He felt a light touch on his shoulder and turned to face a pale, grave young woman with a warm kerchief on her head. She looked at him with her dark, attentive eyes. Snow was metling on her cheeks and eyelashes—it must have slipped from a branch onto her face.

"Put on your cap," she said softly. "Or else you will catch cold. And come into the house. You mustn't stand here."

Potapov said nothing. The woman took his hand and led him along the cleared path. Near the porch he stopped. He felt a sudden lump in his throat and could not breathe. The woman said in the same soft voice:

"It's all right. And please don't take any notice of me. It'll soon pass."

She stamped her feet to shake the snow off her boots, causing the little bell to tinkle and resound through the entrance hall. Potapov took a deep breath.

He entered the house, muttering something in his confusion, and took his coat off in the hall; a smell of birchwood smoke assailed his nostrils. He saw Arkhip sitting on the couch and yawning. Near the couch stood a little girl with pigtails, gazing with delighted eyes at Potapov; she was not looking at his face, though, but at the gold stripes on his sleeve.

"Come along," said Tatyana Petrovna. She ushered Potapov into the kitchen.

There was the blue jug filled with cold water and the familiar linen towel embroidered with green oak leaves.

Tatyana Petrovna went out. The little girl brought Potapov a cake of soap and watched him while he washed. Potapov still felt embarrassed.

"What does your mummy do?" he asked the girl, reddening.

He had asked the question just for the sake of saying something.

"She thinks she's a grown-up," the girl said, in a mysterious whisper. "But she isn't at all. She's even more of a girl than I am."

"Why?" asked Potapov.

The girl did not reply. She laughed and ran out of the kitchen.

All evening Potapov could not shake off the strange sensation that he was living in a gossamer, but very sound, dream. Everything in the house was just as he had hoped to find it. The same music lay on the piano. The same yellow candles spluttered as they illuminated his father's small study. Even the letters he had written from the hospital lay on the desk—under the same old compass, where his father had always placed his letters.

After tea Tatyana Petrovna took Potapov to his father's grave, beyond the grove. A hazy moon had risen high in the heavens. The birches gleamed in its light, casting soft shadows on the snow.

Then, late in the evening, Tatyana Petrovna sat down at the piano. Running her fingers lightly over the keys, she turned to Potapov and said:

"I have a feeling that I've seen you somewhere before."

"So have I," answered Potapov.

He looked at her. The candlelight slanted down, lighting up half her face. Potapov rose, paced the room and came to a stop.

"No, my memory fails me," he said in a husky voice.

Tatyana Petrovna turned and shot an alarmed glance at Potapov, but she did not say anything in reply.

Potapov's bed was made up on the coach in the study. He could not fall asleep. Each minute in this house was precious, and he was loth to lose a single one. He lay listening to Arkhip's stealthy steps, to the ticking of the clock, to Tatyana Petrovna whispering something to the nurse in the next room. Then the voices died away and the nurse went out, but the strip of light under the door remained. Potapov heard the rustle of pages—Tatyana Petrovna was evidently reading. He guessed that she was sitting up so that she could wake him in time for the train. He wanted to tell her that he was not sleeping either, but he did not dare to call out to her.

At four o'clock Tatyana Petrovna quietly opened the door and called him. He stirred.

"Time to get up," she said. "I do hate to wake you up so early!"

Tatyana Petrovna saw Potapov to the station through the sleeping town. They said good-bye after the second bell. Tatyana Petrovna held both hands out to him.

"Write to me," she said. "We are almost relatives now, aren't we?"

Potapov said nothing. He only nodded.

Several days later Tatyana Petrovna received a letter from Potapov, written on the journey back:

"I hadn't forgotten, of course, where we met, but I didn't feel like talking about it back there, at home. Remember the Crimea in the autumn of 1927? And the old plane trees in the park in Livadia? A dimming sky, a pale sea. I was walking along the path to Oreanda. On the way I came upon a girl seated on a bench by the path. She must have been about sixteen. She saw me, got up and walked towards me. As we came to a level I glanced at her. She passed by quickly and lightly, holding an open book in her hand. I stopped and gazed after her for a long time. That girl was you. I could not have been mistaken. I gazed after you and suddenly felt that a woman who could either ruin my whole life or make me ecstatically happy had walked past me. I felt that I could have loved that woman to distraction. I knew then and there that I must find you at all costs. This is what I thought, standing there, but I did not move from the spot. Why—I do not know. Ever since then I have loved the Crimea and that path where I saw you for only a fleeting moment and lost you forever. But life has been kind to me. I met you again. And if everything ends well and you should want my life, it is yours, of course. Oh yes, I found my opened letter on father's desk. I understood all and can only thank you from afar."

Tatyana Petrovna put away the letter and stared misty-eyed at the snow-covered garden outside the window.

"Oh dear!" she murmured. "I've never been to the Crimea in my life, never! But can that make any difference now? And is it worth disillusioning him? Or myself!"

She laughed and then covered her eyes with her hand. Through the window a dim sunset glowed faintly; somehow its light could not fade away.

1943

GLASS BEADS

Dawn in a peasant cottage is much the same wherever you may be—in the parts where I come from near Kostroma, in the Ukraine, or in the little Gutsul village in the foothills of the Carpathians. There is a sourish smell of bread and the sound of an old man sighing, sleepy hens clucking in the yard and the rapid ticking of the clock on the wall.

The darkness outside begins to turn blue and you can see from the misted panes that there is a spring frost and dew on the grass outside and it is a clear day. You gradually begin to make out the black crucifix over the door, the sheepskin jerkin on the stool, covered by a faded felt hat, and then you remember that you are not near Kostroma. You are on the extreme western border of the Soviet Union in Gutsul country. And those remote blue clouds through the window are not clouds at all. They are the Carpathians. Far off in the mountains, beyond the forest and mist, there is a protracted sound of cannon fire. Another day of battle is beginning.

You go into the yard to wash. The cold water clears your head and everything that happened yesterday comes back to you vividly.

There are so many daisies in the clearing in front of the house that the soldiers are reluctant to trample on them and go round the edge instead. A solitary briar bush is flowering in the clearing. Its scent is more powerful in the morning coolness than in the heat of day. The sun is still behind the mountains but the treetops on the western slopes are already glowing russet in its early rays.

This cottage is the home of Old Ignat and his granddaughter Ganya. Ignat is old and sick. He used to be a woodcutter but has been unable to wield his heavy axe for a year now. "Thank God I still had the strength to cross myself when I saw the Russian guns," he says. Even walking as far as the church is difficult for him, so Ganya helps him along. He kneels in front of the altar which is decorated with blue paper flowers. His grey shaggy hair quivering, he whispers thanks for his daily bread, for the liberation of his country from the cursed Swabians, and for the joy of living to see another spring in his native land.

What a magnificent land it is, swathed in light mists which seem to rise above its gentle hills from the breathing of the early spring grass, flowers and leaves, the ploughed earth and the green shoots.

Small rainbows shimmer over the splashing water wheels, spraying the dark willows on the bank.

One line of hills follows the next and they ripple in waves of greenness and light from one end of the horizon to the other. The sky is so pure and solid that you cannot help wanting to use its old name, the firmament. The sun is shot with yellow. With every breath you inhale a bracing infusion of pine bark and the vestiges of snow still left on the mountain tops.

It was only yesterday that we occupied the village. It was empty except for old women, children and doddery old men. The rest of the inhabitants were still hiding in the woods from the Germans, who had now retrenched not far away on the other side of the gorge overlooking the only mountain road. We needed a guide to take us to the cliff called Cheshske Lono above the German's position. This was the only point from which we could dislodge the Germans and clear the road.

Instead of a guide they brought a ten-year-old girl to our lieutenant. She was wearing new leather mocassins, a long maroon skirt edged in white, a sleeveless yellow jacket with lots of pearl buttons and a silk head scarf. The little thing stood there with downcast eyes in her Sunday best twisting the hem of her blue apron.

"Surely you can find someone older?" said the lieutenant, taken aback.

The old men standing nearby exchanged glances, took off their felt hats, scratched their heads and explained that this girl was the granddaughter of Old Ignat, a famous hunter and woodcutter in these parts, and that unfortunately no one knew the way to Cheshske Lono better than she did. Ignat himself knew it, of course, but he was very weak now and hadn't been into the mountains for a year or so.

The lieutenant shook his head doubtfully.

"Will you get us there? You do know the way?"

"Yes," said the girl blushing.

"So not even a bird will notice us?"

"No," she said, blushing even deeper.

"Aren't you afraid?" the lieutenant asked sternly.

His men were standing around frowning. What sort of guide was this? It didn't sound like a serious conversation.

The girl did not reply. Instead she looked up at the lieutenant with her big grey eyes, smiled and looked down again. The lieutenant involuntarily smiled too, and then the soldiers. No one had expected to see such a shy, happy smile under these dark eyelashes.

There was a silence broken only by the envious cry of "Ee, Ganka" from a shock-headed lad with shifty eyes who was looking round the wattle fence. The girl scowled, the soldiers looked round and the boy disappeared. The old men shook their heads. Yes, the lad really had something to be jealous about, I'll say he did.

The little girl led the soldiers up to Cheshske Lono and the road was cleared of Germans. She came back in the evening with a soldier called Maleyev who had been wounded. He was a fine, brave lad and the only criticism you could make of him was that he tended to be somewhat talkative.

That evening he was sitting on a stone near Ignat's house, drinking milk and chatting with the old men, resting his bandaged right arm. They listened to him with respect and affection, but probably understood very little of what he said. Maleyev was from Ryazan and it was difficult for the old Gutsuls to make head or tail of his conversation.

"Our high-ups will reward her for this. Indubitably. For being a canny, brave lassy. We know how to reward bravery. So don't you have no doubts on that score, citizens."

The old men nodded and smiled.

"But leavin' aside the high-ups," he went on, "our lads are right grateful to that lassy. Can't praise her enough. And she ought to have something from the lads for what she's done. The trouble is what! A soldier doesn't carry anything round with him except iron rations and cartridges, as you well know. But she ought to have a doll or something like that."

While he was expounding on these aspects of a soldier's life, Maleyev kept giving sly winks and glances at the embarrassed girl and jingling something in his pocket, but no one understood his subtle hints. He was jingling a string of glass beads which the lieutenant had given to him and asked him to present to Ganya next morning. If possible it should be a surprise. He wasn't just to pull it out and thrust it into her hands with a "here you are, take this!" The whole thing must be handled with more delicacy.

Maleyev understood what he was being asked to do and agreed enthusiastically although he thought it a difficult, ticklish job.

The old men went their separate ways into the night. The stars blazed on over the Carpathians and the rushing of the waterfalls grew louder. A smell of dampness and wild plants wafted from the evening forest.

Old Ignat, Maleyev and Ganya sat on for a long time outside. Maleyev stopped talking for a while and Ganya asked him timidly:

"Are your rivers near Moscow like ours, or are they right different?"

"They're different," Maleyev said. "Yours are nice and so are ours. Our rivers are wide and clear with lots of flowers and grasses. They flow into the Crimean seas a long way away. White boats with red silk flags sail along them and there are hundreds of shining, twinkling towns on their banks."

"And is the forest different?"

"Yes, that's different too. Our forests are full of mushrooms. Stretch for thousands of miles, they do. The mushrooms are all different kinds. There's a clever old bird in our forests called the woodpecker. He goes round tapping the trees with his beak and when he finds one that's dead or rotten he leaves a mark on it that means: "Chop this one down. It's no good.""

Maleyev stopped talking, but when Ganya did not ask him any more questions he went on again.

"Why don't you ask me anything about the people, then? What our people are like?"

"I know what they're like already," answered Ganya smiling.

"So you do!" said Maleyev. "It's real fun talking to you."

In the morning Maleyev woke up very early and went outside. Looking round, he took the beads out of his pocket and hung them on the fence by the house, then hid behind a corner and began to wait. Ganya had gone to fetch water from the river and should pass the fence on her way back. Maleyev was sure that she would notice the beads. He had spent a long time breathing on them and rubbing them on his greatcoat, and now they were sparkling in the sunshine like a handful of diamonds.

She appeared walking along the path. Maleyev's eyes were glued to her. Suddenly she noticed the beads, stopped short smiling and put her buckets down on the ground. Then she began to walk slowly towards the fence with one thin hand stretched out hesitantly for the beads. She was walking carefully as if she were afraid of frightening a bird.

Suddenly she screamed, grabbed hold of the ends of the scarf tied round her head and began to sob. Maleyev dived out of his hiding place in surprise and saw the shock-headed boy rushing along by the fence with the shining beads clutched in his hand.

"Thievin' rascal!" thought Maleyev and thundered:

"Drop it, I say. Or you'll be sorry."

The boy looked round, flung the beads into

the grass and made off faster than ever. Then everything happened just as the lieutenant hadn't wanted it to. Maleyev picked up the beads, walked over to the tearful Ganya and thrust them into her hand, mumbling gruffly:

"Here. These are for you."

So it was all done very crudely and there was no surprise. But Ganya gave him such a look with her beaming, wet eyes that he stepped back in confusion and could only mutter:

"The high-ups do things their own way. But this is from the lads."

Old Ignat was standing in the doorway grinning. When they came up to him he took the beads from Ganya and shook them so that they tinkled and flashed in the sun. Then he hung them round her neck and said:

"This necklace is more beautiful than gold. Ee, my little darlin', your pretty eyes will live to see happiness with folk like these."

Ganya put her buckets on the ground and looked shyly down at the beads with shining eyes. The water in the buckets splashed reflecting the sun onto the beads and they sparkled on the little girl's brown skin in a myriad of twinkling lights.

1944

A NIGHT IN OCTOBER

Personally, I find it far easier to write in the country than in town. In the country everything helps you to concentrate: even the sputtering of the small paraffin lamp and the moaning of the wind in the garden—and then, in between these sounds, there is that complete hush when the earth seems to have come to a standstill and hang soundlessly in space.

And so, late in the autumn of 1945, I left town to work in a village near Ryazan. There was a country house there, with a garden that was completely overgrown. Its mistress was an old lady named Vasilisa Ionovna, a retired Ryazan librarian. I had been there previously, and upon each new visit had found the garden wilder and the house and its mistress more aged.

I left Moscow on the last boat of the season. Rust-coloured banks drifted past outside the windows of my cabin, and grey little waves sent out by the paddle wheels lapped up against them. In the saloon a small red bulb burned all night long. I felt as though I was alone on that boat; the passengers seldom left their warm cabins. Only a lame army captain with a weather-beaten face wandered around on deck and gazed smilingly at the banks. They were ready for winter: the leaves had long since been shed, the grass lay flat, the potherbs had turned black, and little white wisps of smoke curled over the cottages of the villages—the stoves were already being heated everywhere. The river, too, was ready for winter. Almost all the quays had been shifted to the back waters. The buoys had been removed, and it was only thanks to the grey moonlight sheathing the earth that our boat was able to proceed at night.

I struck up a conversation with the sapper captain to our mutual delight and satisfaction. It appeared that Captain Zuyev was also getting off at Novoselki and that he, like myself, intended to cross over to the other bank of the Oka and walk to the village of Zaborye over the meadows. Our boat was due to arrive at Novoselki that evening.

"I'm not stopping at Zaborye, though," the captain told me. "I'll push on a bit farther to the forestry office out there; but we can go together as far as Zaborye. I've fought at the front and have seen a thing or two in my life, but I don't quite fancy plodding through those deserted places at night by myself. Before the war I was a forester, and now that I've been demobbed I'm going back to the old job. It's a wonderful job— looking after those forests! I'm a graduate silviculturist. Come and visit me. I'll show you some spots that will take your breath away. At the front I dreamt about them almost every night."

He laughed, and his face grew visibly younger.

When the boat reached Novoselki late in the evening, there was nobody on the quay except the watchman with his lantern. Zuyev and I were the only passengers to go ashore. No sooner had we stepped off the damp gangplank than the boat got under way, enveloping us in a cloud of steam. The watchman with the lantern departed at once, leaving us to our own resources.

"Let's not hurry," said Zuyev. "We might as well sit down on a log, have a smoke and work out what to do next."

Judging by his voice, the way he drew in the smell of the river water, glanced about him and laughed when the boat gave a short whistle as it rounded a bend, and the night echo picked up the sound and rolled it on and on until it drifted away into the forests beyond the Oka—judging by all this, I could see that Zuyev was in no special hurry for the simple reason that he was experiencing an extraordinary and unexpected joy at finding himself in this familiar place to which he had almost lost hope of returning.

We had our smoke and then made our way up the steep bank to the lodge of the beacon-keeper

Sofron. I tapped on the window. Sofron came out so quickly that I doubted whether he had been asleep. He recognised me and we shook hands.

"The water's been rising today," he said. "All of two metres during the last twenty-four hours. Looks like it's raining higher up. Did you hear anything about it?"

"No."

Sofron yawned.

"Autumn, nothing to be done about it. Well, shall we cross?"

At night the Oka seemed to be very broad, much broader than by day. The current was strong along the entire width of the river. Fish were splashing about here and there, and in the faint moonlight we could see how the rings formed by the splashes were swiftly carried along by the current and stretched out of shape.

At length we reached the opposite bank. The meadows gave off the smell of withered grass and the sweetish scent of willow leaves. We walked along a barely visible path and soon came to a country road. It was very quiet. The moon was sailing earthward; its light was already on the wane.

We next had to negotiate a meadow island about six kilometres wide, cross an old bridge spanning a second, very still and overgrown, bed of the Oka, and there, beyond a stretch of sand lay Zaborye.

"I recognise it all," said the captain excitedly, "every little landmark. It seems I haven't forgotten a thing. See that cluster of trees? Those are the willows on the Prorva. Am I right? I told you so! Look at the mist over Lake Selyanskoye! And not a bird to be heard. I've come too late, of course—the birds have all flown off. And the air! Just smell that air! It's infused with the smell of the grasses. I've never breathed such air anywhere else. Can you hear the cocks crowing? That's in Trebutino. Lusty devils they are! You can hear them four kilometres away!"

The farther we went, however, the less we spoke, and soon we stopped talking altogether. An opaqueness lay over the creeks, the black hay-stacks and the clumps of bushes. The silence of the night had communicated itself to us.

On our right spread a reed-choked lake whose surface gave off a dull gleam. Zuyev found it hard to walk because of his bad leg. We sat down to rest on a willow that had been blown down by the wind. I knew that willow well—it had been lying there for several years now and was all covered with low-growing dog rose.

"Life's pretty good, when you think about it!" sighed Zuyev. "I've been intensely aware of it ever since the war ended. You can laugh if you like, but now I could spend the rest of my life grow-ing pine trees. Absolutely. Am I talking non-sense?"

"On the contrary," I said. "Not at all. Have you a family?"

"No, I'm an old bachelor."

We continued on our way. The moon disap-peared behind the steep bank of the Oka. Dawn was still a long way off. In the east the darkness was as dense as in the other parts of the sky. We found walking more and more difficult.

"There's one thing I can't understand," said Zuyev, "and that is why they've stopped bringing the horses out for night grazing. They used to keep them out at night all the way up to the first snowfall. And now there isn't a single horse in the meadows."

I had noticed this also but had not attached any significance to it. The meadow all around was so desolate that there seemed to be no other living creatures on it but ourselves.

Presently I made out a broad strip of water ahead of us. It hadn't been there before. I peered into the darkness and my heart sank—was the old bed of the Oka flooded as badly as that?

"We'll soon see the bridge," Zuyev said gaily. "And beyond that lies Zaborye. We've practically arrived."

On the bank of the old channel the road led right into the black water. The water lay there at our feet, lapping against the low bank. There were dull splashes here and there as lumps of the bank collapsed into the water.

"Where's the bridge?" Zuyev asked anxiously.

There was no bridge. It had either been washed away or flooded by water. Zuyev switched on his torch. We saw muddy waves and the swaying tops of bushes jutting at least two metres of them.

"We-e-ll!" said the puzzled Zuyev. "We're cut off. By water. Now I understand why the meadows are so deserted. It looks like we're the only ones here. This wants some thinking over."

He felt silent.

"Shall we try shouting?"

But it was no use shouting. Zaborye was still quite a distance away. And in any case nobody would have heard us. Besides, I knew that there was not a single boat in Zaborye to take us off the island. The ferry had been set up about two kilometres downstream, by the Pustinsky forest.

"I suppose we'll have to go down to the ferry," I said. "Of course—"

"Of course what?"

"Oh, nothing. I know the way."

I had been about to say, "Of course, if the ferry is still there." But I had thought better of it. If the meadows were already deserted and they were being flooded by the autumn waters, then it stood to reason that the ferry had been removed. And Vasily the ferryman, that stern and sensible old fellow, would not be sitting in his little hut for nothing.

"Oh well!" agreed Zuyev. "Come along, then. Look how dark the night's become, curse it!"

He switched the torch on again and let out an oath—the water had already covered the tops of the bushes.

"This is getting serious!" Zuyev muttered. "We'd better hurry."

We set out for the ferry. A wind blew up out of the darkness; it came slowly, with a hum, sweeping snowflakes before it. The splashes made by the collapsing bank grew more frequent. We plodded along, stumbling against hillocks and clumps of old grass. There were two small gullies which had always been dry. Now we waded across them up to our knees in water.

"The gullies are filling up," said Zuyev. "I hope we don't get caught in this. I just can't understand why the water is rising so fast!"

Not even during the heaviest autumn rains had the water risen so rapidly or flooded the island.

"I don't see any trees here," Zuyev remarked suddenly. "Nothing but bushes."

There was a cart-track leading to the crossing. We found it thanks to the mud and the smell of manure. The bank on the other side of the old channel was steep and covered with pines now moaning in the wind.

The night kept growing darker and colder. The water was hissing. Zuyev switched his torch on again. The river was now on a level with the bank, and narrow tongues of water were already darting out over the meadow.

"Fer-r-ry!" Zuyev shouted. He listened. "Fer-r-ry!"

Nobody responded. The pines moaned.

We shouted for a long time, until we became hoarse, but nobody answered. The snow gave way to rain. Scattered drops began to thud heavily on the ground.

Again we shouted. The pines continued to moan indifferently.

"The ferryman's gone!" Zuyev said crossly. "That's clear enough! And why the devil should he be here when the island's being flooded and there's not a living soul on it? How ridiculous! A stone's throw from home...."

I realised that nothing but pure chance could save us: either the water would suddenly stop rising, or we would find an abandoned boat. Most terrifying of all was the fact that we did not know why the water was rising so rapidly. It was hair-raising to think that only an hour ago there had been not the slightest sign of this night predicament of ours, and that we had walked into it ourselves.

"Let's follow the bank," I suggested. "We might come across a boat."

We groped our way along the bank, skirting the flooded places. Zuyev used his torch, but it was growing dim. Finally he turned it off to save it for an extreme emergency.

I stumbled against something dark and soft. It turned out to be a small haystack. Zuyev put a match to it. The stack blazed up in crimson, lurid flames. The fire lit up the turbid river, the now flooded meadows stretching ahead as far as the eye could see, and even the pine forest on the opposite bank. The forest was swaying and moaning indifferently.

We stood at the burning haystack staring into the fire. Disconnected thoughts flashed through my mind. At first I felt sorry that I had not done a tenth of what I had intended to do in life. Then I reflected that it was stupid to perish of one's own folly at a time when life promised many more days like this, bleak and autumnal perhaps, but fresh and dear to the heart, when the first snow has not yet fallen but everything already smells of snow—the air, the water, the trees and even the cabbage leaves.

Zuyev must have been ruminating along the same lines. He slowly drew a crumpled pack of cigarettes from his coat pocket and held it out to me. We lit them from the burning hay.

"It'll go out in a moment," Zuyev said softly. "The water's at our feet already."

I did not say anything. I was listening. Above the moaning of the forest and the splashing of the water I could hear faint, intermittent sounds. They came nearer and nearer. I turned to the river and called out:

"He-e-ey, you in the boat! This way!"

A boyish voice responded at once from the river:

"Co-o-ming!"

Zuyev quickly poked the hay. A column of flame burst forth, shooting sparks into the darkness. Zuyev began to laugh softly.

"Oars!" he said. "Those are oars creaking. How could we have suspected for a moment that we might perish in this dear spot of ours?"

I was particularly stirred by that responsive cry of "Coming". I'm coming to your aid! I'm coming through the darkness toward the smouldering light of the campfire! The call awakened memories of the ancient customs of brotherhood and aid, which had never died out among our people.

"Hey you, come down to the sand! This way!" a voice rang out from the river, and I suddenly realised that it was a woman's voice.

We hastened down to the water's edge. A boat suddenly drifted into the dim light of the fire and grounded its bow on the sand.

"Don't climb in yet, I've got to bail out some of this water," the voice said.

A woman jumped out of the boat and dragged it up on the bank. We could not see her face. She was wearing a padded jacket and boots, and her head was wrapped in a warm kerchief.

"What on earth are you doing here?" she asked brusquely, without looking at us, as she began to bail.

She listened rather indifferently to our tale and then said in the same brusque tone:

"Why didn't the beacon-keeper tell you? They opened the sluices on the river yesterday. For the winter. The whole island will be flooded before morning."

"And what are you doing in the forest at night, dear lifesaver of ours?" Zuyev asked playfully.

"I was on my way to work," the woman answered somewhat reluctantly. "From Pustini to Zaborye. I saw the fire and you people on this island here. So I guessed what had happened. The ferryman's been gone two days already; there was no reason for him to stay here any longer. It took me some time to find the oars. They were under the hay in his hut."

I sat down at the oars and rowed as hard as I could, but it seemed to me that the boat, far from moving ahead, was being carried along toward a black waterfall down which all this muddy water and the gloom and the whole night were falling.

At last we reached the other bank. We climbed up the slope and did not stop for a smoke until we had reached the forest.

The forest was very still and warm, and smelled of rotting leaves. Way above us there was a steady, majestic roar—the only reminder of the gloomy night and our recent danger. Now the night seemed wonderful and beautiful. And the face of the young woman seemed to me very pleasant and familiar in the brief glimmer of the match as we lit up. Her grey eyes regarded us shyly. Wet strands of hair slipped out of her kerchief.

"Is that you, Dasha?" Zuyev suddenly asked in a very soft voice.

"Yes, Ivan Matveyevich." The woman burst into a light laugh, as though amused by something known to herself alone. "I recognised you at once. Only I didn't feel like telling you. We've been waiting for you all this time, ever since victory! We didn't want to believe that you wouldn't return to us."

"That's how it is!" said Zuyev. "I was at the front for four years and came close to death many a time. And now it is Dasha who actually saves me from death. She's my assistant," he told me. "She works in the forestry office. I taught her the job. She was a weak little thing, as slim as a stalk. And now look at what a beauty she's become! And she's grown strict, too."

"Oh no! I'm not at all strict," Dasha replied. "It's just the suddenness of it all. Are you going to Vasilisa Ionovna's?" Dasha suddenly asked me, apparently to change the subject.

I answered yes, that I was going to Vasilisa Ionovna's, and invited the two of them to come along with me. We all wanted to dry ourselves and to rest in the warm old house.

Vasilisa Ionovna was not in the least surprised by our nocturnal arrival. She had reached the age when nothing surprised her any longer, and she gave her own interpretation to everything

that happened. Now too, after hearing the story
of our misadventure, she said:

"Great is the God of the land of Russia. And
as for that Sofron, I always said he was a block-
head. I just can't understand how you, a writer,
didn't see through him! It only means that you
have a blind spot for people too. Well," she said,
turning to Dasha, "and I'm very glad for you.
Your Ivan Matveyevich has finally come
back."

Dasha reddened, jumped up, grabbed an empty
bucket and ran out to the garden, forgetting to
close the door behind her.

"Where are you going?" cried the startled
Vasilisa Ionovna.

"To fetch water—for the samovar!" Dasha
cried back.

"I can't understand the girls nowadays," said
Vasilisa Ionovna, paying no heed to Zuyev, who
somehow could not light his match. "You say
something to them, and they blow up like fireworks. A wonderful girl, she is, though. In fact,
she's my only comfort."

"Yes," agreed Zuyev, who had finally lit his
match. "She's a wonderful girl."

Of course, Dasha dropped the bucket down the
well. I know how to extract buckets from that
well—with a pole. Dasha helped me. Her hands
were ice-cold with agitation, and she kept repeating:

"Oh, how could Vasilisa Ionovna! How could
she!"

The wind had blown away the storm clouds,
and a starry sky was now flickering over the
black garden. I pulled up the bucket. Dasha

began to drink straight from it, her wet teeth gleaming in the darkness.

"Oh, goodness me," she said, "how can I go back now?"

"It's quite all right, come along."

We went back in. The lamps had already been lit and a clean cloth laid on the table. From his black frame on the wall Turgenev gazed down tranquilly upon the scene. A rare portrait, engraved on steel with the finest needle. It was Vasilisa Ionovna's pride and joy.

1946

THE TELEGRAM

That October was especially cold and rainy. The wooden roofs turned a slaty black, the tangled grass lay flattened in the garden and a solitary small sunflower bloomed by the fence. unable to shed all its petals. Thick shaggy clouds dragged over the meadows from beyond the river, catching on the leafless willows, and shedding a dreary constant drizzle.

The roads were completely impassable and the herdsmen had ceased driving the cattle out to the pastures. The shepherd's horn had fallen silent till spring.

Katerina Petrovna found it more painful than ever getting up in the morning, to the same unchanging scene: the rooms with the stagnant acrid smell of unheated stoves, the dusty "European Herald", the yellowed cups on the table, the long-unpolished samovar, the pictures on the walls. Perhaps the rooms were too dark and Katerina Petrovna's sight was failing, or the paintings may have faded with time, but the fact remained that she was unable to make out any of the details in them. It was only from memory that Katerina Petrovna knew that the one over there was a portrait of her father, while the small one in the gilt frame was a gift from Kramskoi, a sketch for his "Unknown Lady in a Velvet Jacket".

Katerina Petrovna was living out her days in the old house built by her father, a well-known painter, who had left St. Petersburg in his old age to return to his native village, where he could take life easy and potter about in the garden. He could not paint any more as his hand shook, and besides, his sight was failing and his eyes often ached.

The house was a "memorial", as Katerina Petrovna put it, being under the protection of the regional museum. But what would happen to it when she, its last inmate, died, she could not imagine.

There was no one in the village—it was called Zaborye—with whom Katerina Petrovna could discuss paintings, St. Petersburg life or that summer when she had lived with her father in Paris and seen Victor Hugo's funeral.

After all, she couldn't talk about this to Manyushka, the daughter of her neighbour, the cobbler, who came every day to fetch water from the well, sweep the floors and get the samovar going.

In return for her services Katerina Petrovna gave the girl presents, such as a pair of crumpled gloves, some ostrich feathers, or a black beaded hat.

"What good is this to me?" Manyushka would ask in a hoarse voice, sniffing loudly. "Take me for an old-clothes woman?"

"Sell it, my dear," Katerina Petrovna said in a whisper. For a year now she had been so weak that she could not speak aloud. "Sell it."

"I'll give it to the junkman," Manyushka decided, swept up the things and departed.

Once in a while Tikhon would drop in, the very thin, red-headed watchman from the fire-engine shed. He could still remember Katerina Petrovna's father coming from St. Petersburg, building the house and laying out the grounds.

He had been only a boy then, but he retained his awed respect for the artist all his life and would gaze at his pictures and say with a sigh, "Real work, that."

Tikhon often pottered about aimlessly out of a feeling of pity, but all the same he did help by cutting down dried trees in the garden, sawing and chopping them up for firewood. On leaving he would invariably stop in the doorway and inquire, "Katerina Petrovna, have you heard from Nastya lately?"

Katerina Petrovna said nothing, sitting on the divan, small and hunched, and went through some papers in a brown leather reticule.

Tikhon shuffled uneasily in the doorway, taking his time to blow his nose. "Well," he said after waiting in vain for a reply, "I'll be going, Katerina Petrovna."

"Yes, certainly, Tisha," Katerina Petrovna would whisper, "go on. God bless you."

He went out, carefully closing the door behind him, and Katerina Petrovna began to cry softly. The wind whistled in the bare branches outside, tearing off the last leaves. A paraffin night lamp flickered on the table. It seemed the only living thing in the deserted house: without that weak flame Katerina Petrovna would not have known how to survive till morning.

The nights were long and oppressive as insomnia. The dawn came later and later, seeping unwillingly through the unwashed windows where last year's yellow autumn leaves turned mouldy and black still lay on the cotton wool between the frames.

Nastya, her daughter and only relative, lived far away in Leningrad and it was three years since she had last visited her mother.

Katerina Petrovna understood that Nastya had many more important things to think of than her old mother. Nowadays the young folk had their own affairs, their own strange interests, their own happiness. Better not to interfere with them. That was why Katerina Petrovna rarely wrote to Nastya, though she thought of her every day, sitting on the edge of the sagging couch so quietly that a mouse, deceived by the stillness, would scuttle out from behind the stove, stand up on its hind legs and twitch its nose for a long time, sniffing the stale air.

Nastya did not write either, but every two or three months the cheerful young postman Vasili would bring Katerina Petrovna a money order for two hundred roubles. He carefully guided Katerina Petrovna's hand so that she did not sign in the wrong place.

Vasili would leave and Katerina Petrovna would sit distraught with the money in her hands. Then she put on her spectacles and read the few words scribbled on the back of the order. They were always the same: so busy, that there wasn't time even to sit down and write a letter, let alone come for a visit.

Katerina Petrovna carefully fingered the roll of money. Old age made her forget that these were not the notes Nastya had held in her hands, and she imagined that they smelt of Nastya's perfume.

One night towards the end of October someone knocked persistently at the wicker gate at the far end of the garden, which had been nailed up several years before.

Worried, Katerina Petrovna spent some time tying a warm kerchief round her head, then put on her old coat and, for the first time that year, went out of the house. She walked slowly, groping her way along. The cold air made her head ache, the forgotten stars gazed earthward piercingly, the fallen leaves impeded her progress.

At the gate Katerina Petrovna asked softly, "Who's there?"

But no one replied from the other side.

"Must have imagined it," said Katerina Petrovna, and shuffled back to the house.

She stopped at an old tree to catch her breath, clutching a cold, wet branch, and recognised it as the maple she had planted many, many years ago when she had been a sprightly, giggling girl. Now it stood cold and leafless, with nowhere to escape to from this windy, shelterless night.

Katerina Petrovna felt sorry for the maple, touched its rough trunk, shuffled home, and that same night wrote Nastya a letter.

"My dearest," Katerina Petrovna wrote, "I shan't survive this winter. Come for at least one day. Let me look at you and hold your hand. I've grown so old and weak that it's a burden for me to even sit or lie down, to say nothing of walking —death has forgotten the way to me. The garden is drying up, it has changed completely—but I can't even see it now. This autumn is terrible. So gloomy—it seems longer than the rest of my life put together."

Manyushka, sniffing loudly, carried the letter to the post office, stuck it into the letter box and peered through the slot to see what was inside. But there was nothing except a tinny emptiness.

Nastya was a secretary at the Artists Union. She had so much to do what with arranging exhibitions and competitions and the like.

She received Katerina Petrovna's letter at work and put it into her bag without reading it: she'd do that after work. Letters from Katerina Petrovna drew a sigh of relief from Nastya: they meant her mother was alive. But at the same time they awakened a smouldering uneasiness in her, as though each letter were a silent reproach.

After work Nastya had to go to the studio of the young sculptor Timofeyev to inspect his living conditions, so as to report on them to the Union board. Timofeyev complained that his studio was cold and that in general he was being overlooked and prevented from showing all he was worth.

On one of the landings Nastya got out her compact, powdered her nose and smiled at herself in the mirror, pleased by the image that looked back at her. The artists called her Solveig because of her fair hair and large cold eyes.

The door was opened by Timofeyev himself, a resolute, angry little man. He was wearing a coat, his neck was wrapped in a huge scarf, and on his feet, Nastya observed, he wore a pair of lady's felt boots.

"Don't take your coat off," Timofeyev barked. "You'll freeze even in all your furs! Come in."

He led Nastya down a dark passage, walked up several steps and opened a narrow door that led into his studio.

The air was thick with oil fumes. A paraffin stove was burning on the floor next to a cask of wet clay. On several benches stood pieces of sculpture covered with wet rags. Outside the window snow streaked obliquely across the sky, obscuring the Neva and melting in its dark water. The wind moaned in the windowpanes and rustled old newspapers littering the floor.

"Goodness, how cold it is!" Nastya exclaimed.

The white marble bas-reliefs scattered over the walls made the room seem even colder.

"Here you are," said Timofeyev, moving over clay-spattered armchair. "It's a wonder I'm still alive at all in this den. But in Pershin's studio the radiators blast out heat like the Sahara."

"You don't think much of Pershin?" Nastya inquired guardedly.

"An upstart!" Timofeyev said angrily. "A manual labourer! His figures have coat hangers instead of shoulders. His kolkhoz woman is a granite squaw with her apron pulled up. His workman looks more like a Neanderthal man. He sculps with a wooden shovel. But he's crafty as well, my dear, as cunning as a fox."

"Could I see your Gogol?" Nastya asked to change the subject.

"Go over there," the sculptor ordered gruffly. "No, not there. In the other corner!"

He took the wet rags off one of the figures, looked it over critically from all sides, squatted down next to the paraffin stove and, warming his hands over it, said, "Here he is, Nikolai Vasilyevich, if you please."

Nastya started. A sharp-nosed, round-shouldered man was looking at her quizzically as though he knew her through and through. She could even see a thin sclerotic vein pulsing on his temple.

"And the letter's unopened in your bag," Gogol's piercing eyes seemed to be saying. "Eh, you scatterbrain!"

"Well?" Timofeyev said. "What do you think of him?"

"Why, it's marvelous," Nastya gasped. "A real masterpiece!"

Timofeyev laughed bitterly. "A masterpiece," he mimicked her. "That's what everyone says: a masterpiece. Pershin too, and Matyash, and experts from all kinds of committees. But what's that to me? Here it's a masterpiece, but over there, where my fate as a sculptor is decided, that same Pershin will only snort equivocally—and that's all. And when Pershin snorts it's the end! I can't sleep at night!" Timofeyev shouted, and began to pace rapidly up and down the studio, stamping his felt boots. "I've got rheumatism in my hands from the wet clay. Three years I've spent reading every word about Gogol. I see pigs' snouts in my dreams!" Timofeyev lifted a pile of books from the table, shook them in the air and hurled them back. A cloud of gypsum dust rose from the table. "All this is about Gogol!" he said, and suddenly calmed down. "What? Have I startled you? I must apologise, my dear, but honestly, I'm spoiling for a fight."

"Well, we'll do your fighting together," said Nastya and stood up.

Timofeyev shook her hand with a firm clasp, and she left with the firm resolve to spare no effort to lift this talented man out of oblivion.

Nastya returned to the Union and immediately went to see the president. She spent a long time in his office, arguing and insisting on the importance of organising an exhibition of Timofeyev's work without delay. The president tapped the top of his desk with a pencil, hummed and hawed for some time but finally agreed.

Nastya went home, to her antiquated room with its gilt stucco ceiling on the Moika embankment, where she at last read Katerina Petrovna's letter.

"I *can't* go now!" she said and stood up. "Nobody'll let me."

She thought of the crowded coaches, changing on to the narrow-gauge train, the jolting cart, the withered garden, her mother's inevitable tears, the weary, unadorned dullness of country life—and put the letter in the drawer of her desk.

For a fortnight Nastya was busy organising Timofeyev's exhibition.

During this time she alternately quarrelled and made it up with the irascible sculptor. Timofeyev packed his sculptures for the exhibition with the air of one preparing them for the rubbish heap.

"Nothing'll come of it, ducky," he said to Nastya spitefully, as though she were arranging her own show and not his. "I tell you, I'm only wasting my time."

At first Nastya was piqued and offended, but then she realised that Timofeyev's capriciousness was nothing but pretence and that in his heart of hearts the man was delighted at the prospect of his exhibition.

The opening ceremony was held in the evening. Timofeyev objected angrily, declaring that sculpture could not be viewed in electric light. "Dead light," he grumbled, "deadening! Even a paraffin lamp would have been better."

"What kind of light do you need, you impossible man?" Nastya flared up.

"Candlelight, I tell you, candlelight!" Timofeyev groaned dismally. "You can't place Gogol under an electric bulb! It's preposterous!"

The opening was attended by sculptors and painters. The uninitiated listening to the sculptors' comments would have found it difficult to decide whether they were praising Timofeyev's work or criticising it. Timofeyev, however, could see that the exhibition was a success.

An excitable grey-haired painter came over to Nastya and patted her hand. "Thank you," he said. "I hear that it's you who brought Timofeyev out of the shadows. An excellent accomplishment! You know, we've so many people who babble about concern for the artist, sensitivity and what not, but when it comes to doing things all you encounter is a blank wall. Once again, thank you!"

Then the discussion began. Many speeches were made with praise and impassioned words, and the idea mentioned by the old artist about concern for this young and undeservedly forgotten sculptor, was repeated in every speech.

Timofeyev sat hunched up staring at the parquet floor, but he kept stealing sidelong glances at the speakers, not sure whether they could be trusted, or whether it was still too early to tell.

A messenger from the Union, kind, muddle-headed Dasha, appeared in the doorway. She made signs to Nastya, who went over to her, and with a grin Dasha handed her a telegram.

Nastya returned to her place, unobtrusively slit the telegram open, read it but could not grasp it's contents: "Katya dying. Tikhon."

"Who's Katya?" Nastya thought confused. "Who's Tikhon? It must be for someone else."

She looked at the address: it was certainly for her. Only then did she notice the thin printed letters on the paper tape: "Zaborye".

Nastya crumpled the telegram and frowned. Pershin was speaking.

"In our time," he was saying, swaying slightly and adjusting his spectacles, "concern about man is becoming a splendid reality which helps us in our work and development. I am happy to note a manifestation of this concern in our midst, in the midst of sculptors and painters. I have in mind the exhibition of Comrade Timofeyev's work. We are wholly indebted for this exhibition—and I do not mean this as a slight on our board members—to a rank-and-file employee of the Union, our dear Anastasia Semyonovna."

Pershin bowed to Nastya and everyone clapped their hands. The applause lasted for some time and Nastya was moved to tears.

Someone touched her arm from behind. It was the excitable old artist. "What's that?" he whispered glancing at the crumpled telegram in Nastya's hands. "Something unpleasant?"

"No," Nastya whispered back. "Just ... from an acquaintance."

"Oh," the old man mumbled and began listening to Pershin again.

Everyone was looking at Pershin, but all the time Nastya was conscious of someone's heavy, piercing gaze upon her and she was afraid to lift her head. "Who could it be?" she wondered. "Could someone have guessed? How foolish. My nerves are in a bad way."

With an effort she raised her eyes and then quickly looked away again: Gogol was looking at her mockingly. The thin sclerotic vein seemed to be pulsating heavily in his temple, and Nastya imagined that he muttered quietly through clenched teeth, "Well, what have you to say for yourself?"

Hastily Nastya got up, left the hall, hurriedly put on her coat in the lobby and ran out into the street.

A slushy snow was falling. Grey hoarfrost decked St. Isaac's Cathedral. The overcast sky sank lower and lower over the city, over Nastya, over the Neva.

"My dearest," Nastya recalled the last letter. "Dearest!"

Nastya sat down on a bench in the park near the Admiralty and sobbed bitterly. Snow melted on her cheeks and mingled with the tears.

She shivered with cold, and suddenly realised that no one had ever loved her as much as that decrepit old woman, forsaken by everybody out there in dull Zaborye.

"It's too late! I'll never see Mummy again," she said to herself, and realised that this was the first time in the past year that she had uttered that childishly endearing word, "Mummy".

She jumped up and walked off swiftly into the driving snow which lashed at her face.

"What is this, Mummy? What is it?" she thought, seeing nothing before her. "Mummy! How could this have happened. I haven't got anyone else. There's no one dearer to me and never will be. If only I'm in time for her to see me and forgive me!"

Nastya turned into Nevsky Prospekt in the direction of the city railway station.

She was too late. There were no tickets left.

Nastya stood by the booking office, her lips trembling. She could not speak, feeling that as soon as she opened her mouth she would burst into tears.

The elderly woman in the booking office peered out of the window. "What's the matter?" she inquired grumpily.

"Nothing," said Nastya. "My mother. . . ." Nastya turned and walked rapidly to the exit.

"Wait a minute!" the woman called out. "You should have said so at once."

Nastya left the same evening. The Red Arrow express seemed to be hardly moving, whereas in fact it was hurtling along through night-shrouded forests, blowing white steam over them and piercing the air with its warning shriek.

. . . Tikhon came to the post office, held a whispered conference with the postman Vasili, took a telegram form, turned it over and then spent a long time scrawling a message in tottering letters, wiping his moustache every now and then with his sleeve. Then he carefully folded the form, stuck it in the lining of his hat and shambled off to Katerina Petrovna's.

It was Katerina Petrovna's tenth day in bed. Nothing hurt her, but a terrible weakness bore down on her chest, head and legs, and it was hard for her to breathe.

For six days Manyushka had been at her bedside. At night she slept without undressing on the sagging couch. Sometimes she thought that Katerina Petrovna had stopped breathing. Frightened, she would whimper and call out, "Granny? Hey, Granny? Are you alive?"

Katerina Petrovna moved her arm under the blanket and Manyushka calmed down. A November twilight clung to the rooms all day long, but it was warm, for Manyushka heated the stove regularly. When the merry fire played on the log walls Katerina Petrovna sighed carefully: the fire made the room cosy and inhabited, just as it had been long, long ago when Nastya still lived there. Katerina Petrovna closed her eyes and a single tear slipped out of them, rolled down the yellow temple and got tangled in the grey hair.

Tikhon came in. He coughed and blew his nose, evidently agitated over something.

"What is it, Tikhon?" Katerina Petrovna asked weakly.

"Got colder, Katerina Petrovna," Tikhon said briskly, with an anxious glance at his hat. "Snow'll be coming soon. So much the better, if you ask me. The frost will harden the road, make it easier for her to get here."

"For whom?" Katerina Petrovna opened her eyes, and her dry old hand began to stroke the blanket convulsively.

"Why, Nastasya Semyonovna, naturally," said Tikhon with a crooked smile, taking the telegram out of his hat. "Who else?"

Katerina Petrovna tried to rise, but she could not and fell back on the pillow again.

"Here you are," said Tikhon, carefully unfolding the telegram and holding it out to her.

Katerina Petrovna did not take it however and kept looking at Tikhon entreatingly.

"Read it to her," Manyushka said in a hoarse voice. "She can't read no more. Her eyes are bad."

Tikhon looked about apprehensively, adjusted his collar, stroked his sparse red hair and read in a hollow, shaky voice: "Coming immediately. I remain your ever loving daughter Nastya."

"Don't, Tikhon," Katerina Petrovna said softly. "Don't, dear. God bless you. Thank you for your kindness, for your goodness."

Katerina Petrovna turned with difficulty to the wall and seemed to fall asleep.

Tikhon sat on a bench in the cold hall, smoking with bowed head, spitting and sighing, until Manyushka came out and beckoned him to Katerina Petrovna's room.

Tikhon tiptoed in and wiped his face with his hand. Katerina Petrovna lay there pale, small, as though peacefully asleep.

"So she didn't live to see her," Tikhon muttered. "Poor suffering soul. Look here, you silly girl," he said turning angrily to Manyushka, "see that you repay kindness with good. Sit here while I go to the village Soviet and report."

He went off leaving Manyushka sitting perched on a stool, her knees drawn up, shivering and staring intently at Katerina Petrovna.

They buried Katerina Petrovna on the following day. It was freezing and a light snow had fallen. The day was brighter, the sky was dry and light, but grey as though a newly washed frozen strip of unbleached linen had been stretched out overhead. The distances beyond the river were dove-grey and they wafted up the pungent, joyous smell of snow and willow bark gripped by the first frost.

Old women and children attended the funeral. The coffin was carried to the cemetery by Tikhon, Vasili and the two Malyavin brothers, two old men who looked as if they were overgrown with clean tow. Manyushka carried the coffin lid with her brother Volodya and stared unblinkingly before her.

The cemetery was just outside the village

overlooking the river. Tall willows covered with yellow lichen grew there.

On the way they met the schoolmistress. She had come to Zaborye from the regional centre only a short while ago and did not know anyone there yet.

"The teacher, the teacher," the boys whispered.

She was young, shy and grey-eyed, hardly more than a girl. She saw the funeral procession, halted timidly and looked fearfully at the little old woman in the coffin. Prickly snowflakes fell on the old woman's face without melting. Back in the regional centre the schoolmistress had left her own mother, just as small, eternally worried about her daughter, and just as grey.

The schoolmistress hesitated, then slowly followed the coffin. The old women glanced at her and whispered among themselves that she looked like a quiet girl and that she would find it hard at first with the children—they were a mischievous lot in Zaborye.

The teacher finally forced herself to ask one of the old women, Grandma Matryona, "She must have been all alone?"

"Well, my dear," Matryona sang out readily, "you could just about say she was. A dear, compassionate old soul she was, if there ever was one. And there she'd be sitting all day long on her coach without a soul to say a word to. It was pitiful! There is a daughter in Leningrad, but she seems to have gone up in the world. Passed away here all alone with none of her kin."

In the cemetery the bearers set the coffin down at the freshly dug grave. The old women bowed to the coffin, reaching down to the ground with dark hands. The teacher approached the coffin, stooped and kissed Katerina Petrovna's yellow withered hand. Then she straightened up swiftly, turned away and walked over to the tumble-down brick wall, beyond which, sprinkled with light drifting snow, lay her beloved, slightly melancholy native land.

The teacher stared at it for a long time, listening to the old people exchanging words behind her back, to the earth hitting the coffin lid and the cocks discordant crowing in the distance, forecasting clear days, light frosts and winter stillness.

Nastya arrived in Zaborye on the second day after the funeral. She found the fresh grave mound in the cemetery with the earth frozen on it in chunks, and Katerina Petrovna's cold, dark room from which, it seemed, all life had gone long, long ago.

In that room Nastya wept the whole night through, until the dull, heavy dawn paled the windows.

She left Zaborye stealthily, so that no one should see her or ask her anything. It seemed to her that no one but Katerina Petrovna could absolve her of her irreparable guilt, her unbearable burden.

1946

IN THE HEART OF RUSSIA

Once in a while every writer feels like writing a story without bothering about any of the "iron" or "golden" rules set out in handbooks on composition. These rules are excellent, of course. They channel the writer's hazy ideas into a current of precise thought and guide them along to their final conclusion, the completion of a book, just as a river carries its water to the broad mouth.

Obviously not all the laws governing literature have been neatly tabulated. There are many effective ways and means of expressing ideas which have not yet been formulated.

An experimental film about rain appeared some twenty years ago in Moscow. It was shown exclusively to people connected with the film industry because it was felt that the ordinary public would be bored by such a picture and leave the cinema wondering what it was all about.

The film showed rain from every imaginable sort of angle. Rain on the black asphalt of the town, in the leaves, during the daytime and at night, heavy rain, rain absolutely pelting down, drizzling rain, rain with the sun out, rain on a river and rain on the sea, air bubbles in puddles, wet trains racing through the fields, a host of different rain clouds, and a great deal more as well which I will not go into here.

This film remained fresh in my mind for a long time and made me much more acutely aware of the poetry of ordinary rain than I had been before. Like many other people I had noticed the fresh smell of a dusty road after a fall of rain, but I had never listened carefully to the sound of rain nor perceived the dull, pastel colouring of rainy air.

What could be better for a writer, and every writer must always be a poet as well, than the discovery of new fields of poetry right beside him enriching his perception, understanding and memory of things?

All this is simply a way of justifying myself for departing from the strict demands imposed on me by the subject of this story.

The morning on which this story opens was cloudy but warm. The broad meadows were drenched with night rain, so that there was a glistening drop of water on each corolla, and the whole great host of plants and bushes gave off a sharp, bracing odour.

I was walking over the meadows to a rather mysterious little lake. To the sober eye there was nothing at all mysterious about it, but it always left people with a feeling of something enigmatic. Try as I did, I could not put my finger on the reason for this.

For me the air of mystery lay in the fact that the water in the lake was crystal clear but at the same time had the colour of wet tar with a faint greenish tinge. According to the accounts of ancient, garrulous old men, carp the size "of a samovar tray" lived in this watery blackness. Nobody had ever succeeded in catching them, but occasionally there would be a flash of bronze disappearing with a flick of the tail deep down in the lake.

A sense of mystery comes from expecting something unknown and out of the ordinary. And, indeed, the height and denseness of the vegetation round the little lake made you think that there must be something unusual concealed in them: a dragonfly with red wings, a blue ladybird with white spots, or the poisonous flower of the oleaster with a juicy stalk as thick as a man's arm.

And all this really was there, including huge yellow irises with sword-like leaves. They were reflected in the water and, for some reason, their reflection was always surrounded by shoals of minnow like pins drawn to a magnet.

The meadows were completely empty. There

were still two weeks to go before hay-making. In the distance I saw a small boy in a faded, artilleryman's cap obviously too large for him. He was holding a bay horse by the bridle and shouting. The horse was jerking its head and lashing its coarse tail at the boy trying to shake him off like a horsefly.

"Hey, Uncle!" cried the boy. "Uncle! Come here!"

It was an insistent call for help. I turned off the path and went over to the boy.

"Uncle," he said, gazing at me boldly with an imploring glance. "Give us a hand onto the gelding. I can't make it on my own."

"Who do you belong to?" I asked.

"The chemist," he replied.

I knew that the village chemist, Dmitri Sergeyevich, had no children and was somewhat surprised at the boy's reply.

I lifted him up, at which the gelding immediately took fright and began to shy away from me with mincing steps trying to keep an arm's length between us.

"Ee, yer wicked devil!" said the boy reproachfully. "Bundle o' nerves. Let me grab hold of the reins and then give me a lift up. He'll never let you like that."

The boy grasped the reins and the horse calmed down immediately, almost as if it had snoozed off. I lifted the boy onto its back, and it just went on standing, head bowed, looking as though it intended to remain on the same spot all day. It even gave a faint snore. Then the boy gave it a sharp kick in its bloated, dusty flanks with his bare heels. The gelding hiccuped with

400

surprise and broke into a lazy, swinging gallop in the direction of the sandhills beyond Beaver stream.

The boy kept on bobbing up and down, waving his elbows and digging his heels into the gelding's flanks. I realised that all this hard work was obviously the only way of keeping the gelding on the go.

A green, silt shadow lay on the lake, tucked away in the steep banks, and in this shadow the broom, itself silver, sparkled with silvery dew. A small grey bird in a red jacket and yellow tie sat on a branch of broom making a short, pleasant rattling sound without opening its beak. I stood for a while marvelling at this bird and its enjoyable pastime, then made my way down to the water.

A town girl called Masha who was very fond of plants had come to stay with us from Moscow after her school exams, and I had decided to pick her a bunch of nice flowers. But since there are no nasty flowers I was faced with the difficult task of choosing which ones to give her. In the end I decided to take one flower and one branch of all the plants which made up the dense, sweet-smelling, dew-covered thickets round the lake.

I looked around me. The meadowsweet was already blooming in fragile, yellowish clusters. Its flowers smelt like mimosa. It was almost impossible to carry them all the way home, especially in windy weather, but I cut a branch all the same and lay it under a bush to keep it from wilting quickly.

Then I cut some swordlike leaves of sweet flag which gave off a strong, spicy smell. I remembered that in the Ukraine the women strew sweet flag over the floor before big holidays and its pungent aroma lingers in their homes almost until winter.

The first green cones had appeared on the arrowhead covered all over with soft needles. I took a branch of this as well.

Then I managed, with some difficulty, to hook a strand of frog's-bit out of the water with a dry branch. The petals of its white flowers with reddish centres were as thin as cigarette paper and wilted at once, so I had to throw them away. Using the same branch I hooked some flowering water buckwheat. Its pink panicles stood above the water like little round thickets.

I could not manage to reach the white lilies and did not fancy undressing and wading into the lake, because your legs sank into its silty bed up to the knees. Instead I decided to take a flower on the bank with the somewhat crude sounding name of *susak*, whose flowers were like tiny umbrellas blown inside out by the wind.

Large patches of innocent blue-eyed forget-me-nots peeped out from the banks of mint. Further on behind the hanging loops of brambles a wild young mountain ash with tight clusters of yellow blossom was blooming on a slope. Tall red clover mingled with cow vetch and bedstraw and above this happy union of flowers rose a giant thistle. It stood firmly up to its waist in grass looking like a knight in armour with thorny plates at the elbows and knees.

The warm air vibrated and swayed over the flowers, nearly all of which revealed the striped belly of a wasp or bee buried in their petals.

Butterflies fluttered about like obliquely falling white and lemon-coloured leaves.

Further still was a dense wall of hawthorn and eglantine. They were so closely twined together that it looked as though the bright red flowers of the eglantine and the white, almond-smelling blossoms of the hawthorn were miraculously growing on the same bush. The eglantine stood proudly, arrayed in its best attire and covered with a large number of sharp buds. Its blooming coincided with the shortest nights—our Russian, northern-like nights, when the nightingale sings in the dew all night long, a greenish glow never leaves the horizon, and at the darkest time of all it is so light that you can see the craggy tops of the clouds clearly in the sky. Here and there on their snowy steepness glimmer flecks of pink from the sun. And a silver aeroplane flying at a great height sparkles above the night like a slowly flying star, because at that height the sun is already shining.

When I arrived home scratched to death by eglantine and stung all over by nettles, Masha was pinning a piece of paper to the gate, on which was written in printed letters:

> *Oh, there's dust along the roadside*
> *And there's must along the way.*
> *If you wish to come inside now*
> *Kindly wipe your feet first, pray.*

"Ho ho!" I said. "So you've been to the chemist's shop and seen that notice on his door?"

"Ooh, what lovely flowers!" Masha exclaimed. "Really smashing! Yes, I did go to the chemist's.

And I met someone really nice there. His name is Ivan Stepanovich Kryshkin."

"Who's he?"

"A boy. Really different from the rest."

I grinned. If there's anyone I know inside out it's the local village boys. I can confidently say, after many years of experience, that these noisy, restless compatriots of ours all possess one really unusual feature. A physicist might define it as "all-penetrability". These boys are "all-penetrating", or in archaic, highfalutin language "omnipresent".

In the most god-forsaken corner of a forest, lake or marsh I would always find these boys engaged in the most multifarious and sometimes startling activities.

This is to say nothing of the time when I met them on a freezing, misty September morning at sunrise, shivering with cold in the wet alder thickets on the bank of a remote lake twenty kilometres from the nearest house. They were sitting, concealed in the bushes with their home-made fishing rods, and the only thing that betrayed their presence was the familiar sound of snuffling noses. Sometimes they hid so well that I did not notice them at all and would give a start when I suddenly heard a hoarse, pleading whisper behind me:

"Give us a worm, Uncle!"

The boys' inexhaustible imagination and curiosity brought them to all these remote parts where, as the writers of adventure stories like to put it, "man's foot has rarely trod".

I am quite certain that if I arrived at the North Pole or, say, the Magnetic Pole, I would be sure to find a young lad with a fishing rod sitting there by a hole in the ice snuffling and watching for a cod to appear, or hacking a piece of magnet out of the ground with a broken knife.

As this was the only remarkable feature of theirs with which I was acquainted I asked Masha:

"What's so really different about your Ivan Stepanovich Kryshkin?"

"He's eight," she answered, "but he goes around collecting all sorts of medicinal plants for the chemist. Valerian, for instance."

From the rest of her account it transpired that Ivan Stepanovich Kryshkin bore a remarkable resemblance to the boy I had helped onto the old gelding. Any remaining doubts on this point disappeared when I heard that the said Kryshkin had appeared outside the chemist's with a bay gelding and that on being fastened to the fence this gelding had promptly fallen fast asleep. But Ivan Stepanovich Kryshkin had gone into the chemist's and handed him a sack of valerian picked beyond Beaver stream.

The only point which remained obscure was how Ivan Stepanovich Kryshkin had managed to pick the valerian without getting off the gelding. But then I discovered that he had arrived leading the horse by the reins, and realised that he had ridden as far as the valerian and returned on foot.

It is now high time for me to turn to the subject of my story, the chemist Dmitri Sergeyevich or, perhaps, not so much to him as to the subject of a person's attitude towards his work, which has been occupying my mind for some time. Dmitri Sergeyevich was entirely devoted to pharmacy.

Talking to him convinced me that the popular assumption that certain occupations are uninteresting is a prejudice born of ignorance. After that I began to find pleasure in everything in the village chemist shop, from the clean smell of the freshly scrubbed floor boards and the juniper to the misted bottles of fizzy Borzhom mineral water and the white pots on the shelves, bearing the lable "venena"—poison!

According to Dmitri Sergeyevich nearly all plants contain either medicinal or poisonous juices. The problem was to extract these juices, determine their properties and the use to which they can be put. A great deal, of course, has been discovered a long time ago, for instance, the action on the heart of infusions obtained from lilies of the valley or foxgloves and such like. But there were still thousands of plants which had not been studied and Dmitri Sergeyevich saw this task as the most fascinating occupation in the world.

That summer he was engaged in extracting vitamins from young pine needles. He would make all of us drink a scalding green infusion prepared from them and although we grimaced and protested we were compelled to admit that it was most effective.

One day Dmitri Sergeyevich brought me a heavy tome to read—a pharmacopoeia. I cannot remember its exact name. This book was as absorbing as the most brilliantly written novel. It contained a description of the properties of a multitude of plants—not only herbs and trees, but moss, lichen and mushrooms—which were at times really amazing and unexpected. It also gave detailed instructions on preparing medicines from these plants.

Each week Dmitri Sergeyevich contributed a short article to the local district newspaper on the medicinal properties of plants, such as some perfectly ordinary plantain or mushroom. These articles, which he referred to for some reason as essays, were printed under the general heading "In the World of Friends". I used to see them cut out of the newspaper and pinned up on the wall in people's houses and was able to recognise from them the specific ailment which an inhabitant of that particular house was suffering from.

There was always a crowd of little boys in the chemist's shop. They were Dmitri Sergeyevich's main suppliers of herbs. They spared no efforts, going off to the most remote parts, such as Khvoshchi bog, for instance, or even beyond the distant Kazyonnaya stream where hardly anyone ever went and those who did returned with tales of waste ground covered with shallow silted lakes and tall thickets of sorrel.

The boys asked nothing in return for gathering the herbs except babies' rubber dummies, which they would blow up, straining hard and going red in the face, and then tie with a piece of tape so that they looked like "flying bubble" balloons. The "balloons" did not fly, of course, but the boys carried them around all the time, sometimes tying them to their fingers with pieces of string and making a sinister buzzing sound, or simply bonking each other on the head with them enjoying the delightful popping sound which accompanied this pastime.

It would not be fair to think that the boys spent most of the day idling around enjoying themselves. It was only in the summer holidays, and even then by no means every day, that they were free to play around. Most of the time they spent helping the grown-ups graze the calves, gather brushwood, cut willow, bank up potatoes, mend fences and keep an eye on the younger children when the grown-ups were not there. The worst of it was that the little ones could barely walk and you had to carry them everywhere on your back.

The two people whom the village boys loved most of all were Dmitri Sergeyevich and an old man nicknamed Scrap.

Scrap used to appear in the village once a month, sometimes even less frequently. He would shuffle along lazily in a dusty loose overall beside his old horse and cart, trailing a rope whip on the sandy ground and crying mournfully:

"Bring out your rags, old galoshes, horns and hooves!"

On the front of Scrap's cart there was a magic box made of ordinary plywood, with the lid hanging open. Suspended from nails on the lid there were lots of brightly coloured toys— whistles, yoyoes, celluloid dolls, transfers and skeins of bright embroidery cotton.

As soon as Scrap appeared in the village little boys and girls would rush out from all the houses, jostling each other and tripping over, like young chicks about to be fed, dragging along their younger brothers and sisters, with old sacks, worn-out homemade slippers, broken cow's horns and all sorts of old junk.

In return for the rags and horns Scrap would hand out new toys, the paint on them still fresh, and would conduct long conversations and sometimes arguments about them with his young suppliers.

Grown-ups never brought anything out for Scrap—this was the exclusive privilege of the children.

Dealing with children clearly develops many good qualities in people. Scrap had a severe, even frightening appearance with his shaggy head, bristly cheeks and purple nose peeling from sun and wind. His voice was loud and coarse. But in spite of these menacing features he never sent the children away empty-handed. Only once did he refuse to take two completely decrepit tops from a pair of boots belonging to her father which were brought to him by a little girl in a faded red sarafan.

The girl seemed to shrink up, her head receding into her shoulders, and walked slowly away from Scrap's cart to her house as if she had been beaten. The children gathered round Scrap suddenly fell silent, wrinkling their brows and some of them began to snuffle. Scrap rolled himself a thick cigarette, appearing not to notice the weeping girl or the children who were stunned by his cruel action. He licked down the edge of the paper slowly, lit the cigarette and then spat. The children remained silent.

"What's the matter with you?" said Scrap angrily. "Don't you understand? I'm doin' a job for the state. Don't you go bringin' me a load o' rubbish. I need stuff that can be used in industry. Get me?"

The children said nothing. Scrap took a deep drag on his cigarette and said, without looking at them:

"Bring her back, then. Off you go. Starin' at me as if I was a monster!"

The children flew off like a flock of frightened sparrows to the house of the girl in the red sarafan. She was dragged back flushed and embarrassed, her eyes still brimming with tears. Scrap examined the boot tops ostentatiously, threw them on the cart and handed the girl the best, brightest doll with plump crimson cheeks, rapturously round, deep blue eyes and chubby outstretched fingers.

The girl took the doll shyly, hugged it to her thin chest and laughed. Scrap shook the reins, the old horse flattened back its ears, settling into the shafts, and the cart creaked its way on along the sandy road. Scrap walked beside it, looking as severe and coarse as ever, not saying a word. Only after he had passed a good twenty houses did he cough and start his long drawn-out cry:

"Bring out your rags, horns, hooves and old galoshes!"

Gazing after him I reflected that there were few less attractive occupations than being a rag and bone man, but this person had managed to turn it into a source of delight for the peasant children. Another interesting fact was that Scrap went about his work with a certain inspiration, inventiveness and concern for his boisterous young suppliers. He managed to get a fresh batch of toys from his superiors for each trip round the villages. Scrap's assortment of toys was varied and fascinating.

410

It was a great event in the village when Scrap, at the request of Dmitri Sergeyevich, brought bronze fishing hooks as a form of payment for those boys who collected medicinal herbs for the chemist, ticking them off on a special sheet of quarto paper. Ivan Stepanovich Kryshkin received ten hooks for services rendered. The hooks were distributed in reverent silence. As if in response to some silent command the boys took off their caps that had all seen better days and began to stick the hooks into the lining with tremendous care and concentration. This was the most reliable hiding place for all their treasures.

In Russia we have all grown accustomed to the idea that a person of unassuming, modest appearance may prove to be quite outstanding and unusual. The writer Leskov was particularly aware of this, due to the fact that he knew his country inside out and loved it with every fibre of his being, having travelled its length and breadth and been the bosom friend and confident of hundreds of ordinary people.

Dmitri Sergeyevich's modest appearance which, to put it humorously, was striking for its lack of anything remarkable, concealed an indefatigable explorer in his field, a truly humane person who made high demands on himself and those around him.

Beneath Scrap's unprepossessing exterior beat a warm, kind heart. Moreover here was a person of imagination who applied it to his seemingly trifling occupation.

While I was reflecting on this I remembered an amusing incident which happened in these parts to me and a friend. We had gone to fish on Staraya Kanava, which is a narrow forest stream with swift flowing brown water. This stream is buried deep in the forest far from human habitation and reaching it is quite a difficult business. First you travel forty kilometres on the narrow-gauge railway and then it is another thirty kilometres or so by foot. There are large ide in the eddying pools on Staraya Kanava and this was what we were after.

We returned the following day reaching the station in the quiet forest twilight. There was a strong smell of turpentine, sawdust and cloves. It was August and yellow leaves had begun to appear here and there on the birch trees. These leaves now lit up in turn with the rays of the dying sun.

The small train arrived with lots of empty goods trucks. We got into the truck with the most people—women with baskets of cowberries and mushrooms, and two tatty, unshaven hunters sitting by the open doors of the truck, dangling their legs and smoking. At first the women chatted about village affairs, but soon the magical charm of the forest dusk invaded the carriage and they fell silent with a sigh. The train emerged into the meadows and the quiet sunset became visible in all its glory. The sun sank into the grass, mist and dew and not even the noise of the train could drown the chirping and warbling of the birds in the bushes along the track.

Then the youngest woman began to sing gazing at the sunset with eyes of burnished gold. She sang a simple Ryazan folksong and some of the other women joined in. When they had finished the scruffy hunter with puttees made out of an old army greatcoat said in a low voice to his companion:

"How about us singing, eh, Vanya?"

"Why not," answered his companion.

The two scruffy men began to sing. One of them had a rich light bass. All of us were stunned by the ease and power of this remarkable voice. The women listened to the singers shaking their heads with amazement. The youngest one began to weep quietly, but nobody even turned in her direction because hers were tears of intense admiration, not of pain or grief. When the singers stopped the women began to bless them and wish them long life and happiness for the rare pleasure which they had given.

We asked the singer who he was and he replied that he was bookkeeper on a collective farm. Then we tried to persuade him to come to Moscow so that eminent singers and professors from the Conservatoire could hear him sing. "It's a crime to hide yourself away with a voice like that, letting your talent go to waste," we told him. But the hunter simply smiled shyly and persistently refused.

"Give over!" he said. "How could I sing opera with my untrained voice! Besides I've passed the age to go gallivanting around taking risks like that. I've got my house and garden in the village and a wife with two children at school. Go to Moscow, indeed. Are you joking? I was there three years ago and all the hullabaloo made my head ache from morning to night. I just couldn't wait to get back home to the Oka."

The small engine gave a shrill whistle—we were approaching our station.

"Listen," my friend said firmly to the hunter. "We've got to get out now, but I'll give you my Moscow address and telephone number. You must be sure to come. I'll introduce you to all the right people."

He tore a leaf out of his diary and rapidly scribbled down his address. The train had already stopped at the station and was now puffing hard preparing to resume its journey.

The hunter read what was written on the paper in the fading light and asked:

"You're a writer, aren't you?"

"Yes, I am."

"Of course. I've read your work. Delighted to make your acquaintance. But allow me to introduce myself—Pirogov, soloist at the Bolshoi. Please don't take offence at my little joke. The only thing I can plead in defence of it is that this is a fortunate country indeed when people are so kind and solicitous to one another."

He laughed.

"I'm referring, of course, to your eagerness to help a collective-farm bookkeeper become an opera singer. And I'm sure that if I had really been a bookkeeper you would have stopped me from wasting my voice. Thank you!"

He shook our hands warmly. The train moved off and we were left perplexed on the wooden platform. It was only then that we remembered Dmitri Sergeyevich saying that the singer Pirogov came back every summer to his large native village on the Oka not far from us.

But now it's time for me to finish this story. I can see that I have caught the habit of "going on" from the local old men and got carried away like the ferryman Vasili. Whenever he starts to tell a story it always reminds him of another one which leads on to a third and then a fourth. There's really no end to it.

My aim was a simple one: to relate a few ordinary incidents that reveal the talent and warmth of the Russian character. And we will talk about the outstanding incidents another time.

1950

GOOD FORTUNE FLOWER

One day last summer I was on my way back to the village from Borovoye Lake. The path ran along a cutting in a pine wood. Everything was covered with wild grass fragrant with summer dryness.

Eared grass and wild flowers grew in profusion round the old stumps. At the slightest touch of your foot these rotten stumps would fall to pieces, sending up dark clouds of brown dust like finely ground coffee, and from the maze of secret passages drilled inside the stump by bark beetles there was a sudden scuttling of winged ants, horned beetles and black flat-backed beetles with red stripes like regimental bandsmen.

A sleepy black and gold bumble bee crawled out of a hole under the stump and flew up droning like an aeroplane and taking aim to give the intruder a good bang on the forehead.

The sky was a mass of cumulus. The dazzling white blanket of the clouds looked firm enough to lie on and gaze down at the friendly earth with its forests, cuttings, glades, ripening rye, still, glinting water and herds of grazing cattle.

In a clearing near the edge of the forest I saw some blue flowers nestling together in clumps like small lakes of deep, blue water. I picked a large bunch of them, and when I shook it the dry seeds rattled lightly. I had never seen these flowers before. They looked like bluebells except that their dry cups stood erect not bending down like those of the bluebell.

The path ran out of the wood into the open fields. High above the rye some invisible larks immediately burst into song. It seemed as if they were tossing a string of crystals back and forth, letting it fall only to swoop down and catch it instantly in flight. Its tremulous ringing never ceased for one second.

Two country lasses appeared walking towards me along the path over the fields. They must have come a fair way. Their dusty shoes tied together by the laces were hanging over their shoulders. They were laughing and chatting about something, but fell silent as soon as they saw me, hastily smoothing their fair hair under their head scarves and pursing their lips primly.

One always feels a bit hurt when sunburnt girls with their smiling grey eyes turn stiff and stern at the sight of you. And even more hurt when you hear their smothered giggles behind your back after they have passed.

I was just about to take offence when the girls stopped as they drew level with me and both gave me such a shy, sweet smile that I felt quite at a loss. Nothing could be more delightful than an unexpected smile from a young lass on a quiet country path, when a moist affectionate sparkle appears in the deep blue of her eyes and you stand amazed as if a bush of fragrant, dewy honeysuckle or hawthorn had suddenly burst into blossom before your eyes.

"Thank you," they said to me.

"What for?"

"For crossing our path with those flowers."

The girls suddenly ran off, looking round several times, laughing and repeating warmly:

"Thank you! Thank you!"

I decided that they must have been teasing me in a burst of high spirits. Nevertheless there was something strange and puzzling about that little episode which I could not understand.

On the edge of the village I met a lively, trim old woman with a smoke-coloured goat on a rope. She took one look at me, stopped short, throwing up her hands and letting go of the goat and cried:

"Ee luv! What a piece of luck you crossing my path. I just don't know how to thank you."

"Thank me for what, grandma?" I asked.

"No good pretendin' now," she answered with an artful shake of the head. "As if you didn't know! I can't tell you because you're not allowed to tell. You just keep going slowly, so as to meet as many folk as possible."

The mystery was not solved until I got to the village. It was explained to me by the chairman of the village Soviet, Ivan Karpovich, a severe, business-like man with surprising interest in local lore and historical research "within the boundaries of my district" as he put it.

"You've found a rare flower," he told me. "It is called Good Fortune. There's a popular belief— I don't really know whether I ought to give it away—that this flower brings young girls true love and old people a peaceful old age. And happiness in general."

He gave a laugh.

"And now you've crossed my path with the Good Fortune flower. Maybe it will bring me success in my work. Perhaps we'll finish building the main road from the regional centre to the village this year. And harvest our first crop of millet. It's never been grown here before."

He paused and smiled at a thought that had occurred to him, adding:

"I'm happy for the girls. They're good lassies— our best vegetable growers."

1953

A BASKET OF FIR CONES

The composer Grieg was spending the autumn in the forest around Bergen. All forests are beautiful with their rustling leaves and scent of mushrooms, but those that stretch down mountain slopes to the sea have a particular charm. They ring with the sound of waves breaking on the shore. Mist is constantly rising from the sea and the abundant moisture encourages the exuberant growth of moss. It even hangs down from the branches in green braids that touch the ground.

These forests are also inhabited by a lilting echo, like a mocking bird, that lies in wait to catch the slightest sound and send it cascading down the cliffs.

One day Grieg met the woodman's daughter, a little girl with pigtails and a basket, collecting fir cones in the forest. It was autumn and if you could have collected all the gold and copper in the world and fashioned it into thousands of fragile leaves they would still be only a tiny fraction of the burnished splendour that lay on the slopes, and would look crude beside the real leaves, particularly those of the aspen. A bird's song is enough to make aspen leaves quiver.

"What's your name, little girl?" Grieg asked.

"Dagni Pedersen," she replied in a low voice. It was shyness not fear that made her speak quietly. She could not be afraid of someone with such friendly twinkling eyes.

"What a pity," said Grieg. "I haven't got anything to give you—not a single doll, ribbon or velvet rabbit."

"I've got my mother's old doll," the little girl replied. "Once she used to close her eyes like this."

She closed her eyes slowly and as she opened them again Grieg noticed a flash of leaves in her greenish pupils.

"But now she sleeps with her eyes open," said Dagni sadly. "Old people always sleep badly. Grandad groans all night as well."

"I know what, Dagni," said Grieg. "I'll give you something interesting. But not just yet—in about ten years time."

Dagni threw up her hands.

"That's an awfully long time!"

"The thing is, I've got to make it first."

"What is it?"

"You'll find out."

"Do you mean to say that you can't make more than five or six toys in your whole life?"

Her voice was very stern and Grieg felt embarrassed.

"No, it's not that," he replied somewhat at a loss. "I can probably make it in a few days, but it's not the right sort of thing for little children. I make presents for grown-ups."

"I won't break it, I promise," pleaded Dagni clutching at his sleeve. "Grandad's got a glass boat that I dust and I've never once even chipped it."

"Dagni has put me in a tizzy," thought Grieg and then said what grown-ups always say when they find themselves in a difficult position with children.

"You're still very young and there are lots of things you don't understand yet. Just be patient. Now let me carry that basket. It's much too heavy for you. I'll see you home and we'll talk about something else."

Dagni handed over the basket with a sigh. It really was heavy. Fir cones weigh much more than pine cones because they have a lot of resin.

When the woodman's house appeared between the trees, Grieg said to the little girl:

"You can manage on your own now, Dagni Pedersen. There are lots of little girls with your name in Norway. What's your father's name?"

"Hageroop," she replied, then frowned and asked:

"Won't you come in for a minute? We've got an embroidered tablecloth and a ginger cat and the glass boat. I know Grandad will let you pick it up."

"Thank you, Dagni, but I haven't got time now. Good-bye."

Grieg patted the little girl on the head, then turned and walked off towards the sea. Dagni watched him go, pouting. She had tipped her basket and the fir cones were falling out of it.

"I'll write a piece of music," Grieg decided. "And on the title page I'll ask them to print the words: 'To Dagni Pedersen, daughter of Hageroop Pedersen, the woodcutter, on the occasion of her eighteenth birthday'."

*

Everything in Bergen was just as it had always been. Grieg had got rid of anything that could muffle sound, like carpets, door-curtains and upholstered furniture, a long time ago. Now there was nothing left but the divan. It could seat up to ten guests and Grieg did not dare throw it out. His friends said that his house looked like a woodman's cabin. The only decoration was the grand piano. A person with imagination could hear the most magical sounds within these white walls, from the roar of the Arctic gathering up its breakers in the darkness and the wind whistling its wild saga over them, to a little girl singing her rag doll to sleep with a lullaby.

The piano could sing about love, about people's urge to do great things, about everything under the sun. Rippling under Grieg's powerful fingers the black and white keys would pour out a torrent of yearning, laughter, passion and anger and then suddenly subside. A single faint note echoed on in the silence like Cinderella crying because her sisters had been nasty to her. Leaning back Grieg would listen to this last note until it died away in the kitchen where a cricket had taken up residence some time ago. Then he began to hear the water dripping from the tap, counting off the seconds with the precision of a metronome. It was saying that time waits for no man and that you must hurry to do everything you have planned.

Grieg spent more than a month writing the music for Dagni Pedersen. Winter had come and the town was tightly furled in mist. Rusting boats would arrive from other countries and doze by the wooden quaysides, puffing quietly. Soon the snow came and Grieg would watch it drive past the window and cling to the treetops.

It is impossible to put music into words however rich our language may be. Grieg was writing about happiness and the delight of being a young girl. As he wrote he saw a girl with shining green eyes rushing towards him breathless with joy. She put her arms round his neck and pressed her warm cheek against his grey, unshaven one. "Thank you," she said, not knowing yet what she was thanking him for.

424

"You're like the sun," Grieg would tell her. "Like a gentle breeze and early morning. A white flower has bloomed in your heart and filled the whole of your being with the fragrance of spring. I have seen life. Whatever people may tell you always remember that it is amazingly beautiful. I'm an old man now, but I have given my life, work and talent to the young. I have given away everything and perhaps this has even made me happier than you, Dagni.

"You are a White Night with its mysterious light. You are happiness itself. You are the first glimmer of dawn. Your voice makes the heart leap and tremble.

"May everything that surrounds you be blessed, everything that touches or is touched by you, everything that gives you joy and cause for meditation."

Grieg put all these thoughts into his music. He had the feeling that others were listening to his playing and tried to guess who they were—the tomtits on the tree outside, the carousing sailors from the port, the washerwoman next door, the cricket, the snow falling from the low sky and Cinderella in her patched dress.

All of them were listening in their own way. The tomtits were excited, but no matter how they fidgeted and twittered they could not drown the playing. The carousing sailors sat on the steps below listening with tears in their eyes. The washerwoman straightened her back, wiped her red eyes and shook her head. And the cricket crept out of the crack in the tiled stove and peered at Grieg through a chink in the wall.

The falling snow would hang suspended in the air to catch the rippling strains of music. Smiling Cinderella looked down at the floor where a pair of glass slippers stood by her bare feet. The slippers were jerking and tapping against each other in time with the music wafting out of Grieg's room.

They were all dearer to Grieg than the polite, smartly dressed concert audiences.

*

Dagni left school when she was eighteen and her father decided that she should go and visit his sister Magda in Christiania. Let the girl (her father still thought of her as a girl, although Dagni was now a slim young woman with heavy fair plaits), let the girl have a look at the world and enjoy herself a bit. Who could say what the future held for her? Perhaps a husband, upright and devoted, but also mean, close-fisted and dull. Or a job as shop assistant in the village store. Or work in one of the many shipping offices in Bergen.

Magda made costumes at the same theatre where her husband Niels worked as a wigmaker. They lived in a tiny attic in the theatre with a view of Ibsen's statue and the brightly coloured flags of the ships in the fjord. All day long the boats hooted through the open windows. Uncle Niels had studied them so carefully that he maintained he could recognise all their voices—the *Norderner* from Copenhangen, the *Scottish Minstrel* from Glasgow or the *Jeanne d'Arc* from Bordeaux.

Aunt Magda's room was full of bits and pieces for costumes: brocades, silk, tulle, ribbons, lace, old-fashioned felt hats with black ostrich feathers, gypsy shawls, grey wigs, jackboots with bronze spurs, swords, fans and creased silver shoes. All this had to be sewn, mended, cleaned and ironed.

The walls were covered with cuttings from books and magazines: cavaliers from the age of Louis XIV, beautiful ladies in crinolines, knights, Russian women in sarafans, sailors and Vikings with oak wreaths on their heads.

A narrow staircase led up to the room which always smelt of fresh paint and gilt lacquer.

*

Dagni was fascinated by the theatre and used to go there frequently, but she found it difficult to get to sleep after seeing a play and sometimes even cried lying in bed. This worried Aunt Magda who used to try and comfort Dagni by telling her that she must not believe everything she saw on the stage. On hearing this Uncle Niels would call Magda a "broody old hen" and say that on the contrary you should believe everything in the theatre, otherwise people would not need theatres at all. And Dagni went on believing.

Nevertheless Aunt Magda insisted that Dagni should go to a concert for a change. Niels did not object to this. "Music is the mirror of genius," he said. Niels was fond of making obscure, high-flown statements. He said that Dagni was like the opening chords of an overture and that Magda had a magical power over people, because she made theatrical costumes. Everyone knows that when a person puts on new clothes he changes completely. This explains how the actor who was a foul murderer yesterday can be an ardent lover today, a court jester tomorrow and a popular hero the day after.

"Don't listen to all that awful rubbish, Dagni," Aunt Magda would exclaim on these occasions. "He doesn't know what he's talking about, that garret philosopher!"

It was a warm day in June, the time of the White Nights, and open-air concerts were being held in the City Park. Dagni set off for the concert with Magda and Niels. She had wanted to put on her only white dress, but Niels had said that a beautiful girl should always dress in contrast to her surroundings. His long lecture on this subject boiled down to the fact that it was essential to wear black on White Nights and, conversely, appear in dazzling white on dark nights.

It was impossible to argue with Niels, so Dagni agreed to wear a black dress of soft silky velvet which Magda had borrowed from the theatre wardrobe. As soon as she put it on Magda had to agree that Niels was probably right—nothing could have set off the young girl's pale face and long plaits flecked with tints of old gold better than this mysterious velvet.

"Look Magda," said Niels quietly. "Dagni is as lovely as if she were going to her first rendezvous."

"Quite true. Only I don't remember meeting any dashingly handsome young man when we had our first rendezvous, you old chatterbox!" said Aunt Magda and kissed him on the forehead.

The concert started after the traditional firing of the old cannon in the port at sunset. Although it was evening neither the conductor nor the players switched on the small lamps over their music stands. It was still so light that the lamps in the lime trees had clearly been lit for effect rather than illumination.

This was the first time that Dagni had heard a symphony and it had a strange effect on her. The transitions and crescendoes conjured up a host of dream-like images. Suddenly she started and looked up. It had sounded as if the thin man in tails who was announcing the items had mentioned her name.

"Did you call me, Niels?" she asked her uncle, looking puzzled as she saw the expression on his face. He was staring at her with a mixture of wonder and delight. So was Aunt Magda who had her handkerchief raised to her lips.

"What's the matter?" asked Dagni.

Magda clutched her arm and whispered:

"Listen!"

Dagni heard the man in tails announce the following:

"Ladies and gentlemen! Some members of the audience sitting at the back have requested me to repeat my announcement. The next item in our programme is a song by the celebrated composer Edvard Grieg dedicated to Dagni Pedersen, daughter of Hageroop Pedersen, the woodcutter, on the occasion of her eighteenth birthday."

Dagni sighed so deeply that it hurt her chest. She was trying to hold back the tears which were welling up, but it was no good. She leant forward and covered her face with her hands. At first she could hear nothing because of the turmoil inside her. Then she finally heard a shepherd's horn ringing out in the early morning and the quivering reply of a host of strings. The tune swelled, rose, raged like the wind sweeping over the tree-tops, tearing off the leaves, whipping up the grass and casting cool spray into the face. Dagni felt the wave of fresh air surging from the music and forced herself to calm down.

Yes, it was her forest, her own native land with its mountains, the sound of horns and the murmuring sea. Glass boats foamed the water with the wind whistling in their rigging. Then this sound gave way to the tinkling of bluebells, the trill of birds somersaulting in the air, children's halloos, and the song of a girl whose lover has thrown a handful of sand at her window. Dagni had heard this song in her native mountains.

So that grey-haired old man who had helped her carry the basket of fir cones home had been Grieg, the great musician. And she had reproached him for not being able to work quickly. And this was the present he had promised to give her in ten years time!

Dagni wept without attempting to conceal her tears of gratitude. The music now seemed to fill all the space between the earth and the clouds over the city. Its waves sent a faint ripple over the clouds revealing the stars. The music was now a call. It was calling Dagni to follow it into that realm where sorrow can never quench love, where no one will destroy another's happiness and where the sun shines like a crown on the head of a fairy godmother.

Suddenly a familiar voice rang out in the flood of sound: "You are happiness itself. You are the first light of dawn."

The music died away and the applause began, slowly at first, and then rising to a great crescendo. Dagni got up and made her way rapidly to the exit from the park. Everyone was looking round at her. Perhaps some of the audience had guessed that this young woman was the Dagni Pedersen to whom Grieg had dedicated his immortal work.

"He's dead," she thought. "Why?" If only she could see him! If only he would suddenly appear here! How her heart would beat as she rushed towards him, put her arms round his neck and pressed her moist cheek against his, whispering: "Thank you!" "What for?" he would ask. "I don't know," she would reply. "Thank you for not forgetting me, for your generosity, for showing me the beautiful things that give meaning to our lives."

Dagni walked through the deserted streets, not noticing that Niels was following her trying to keep out of sight. He had been sent by Magda and was reeling like a drunken man, muttering something about the miracle which had happened in their ordinary lives.

Nocturnal dusk still hung over the city, but the northern dawn was touching the windowpanes with a faint gold. Dagni went down to the sea which was slumbering peacefully without the slightest splash of foam. She clutched her hands and let out a cry at the overwhelming sense of the beauty of this world which possessed her and which she herself did not fully understand.

"I love you, life," she said quietly.

Then she laughed looking with wide eyes at the lights of the boats rocking gently in the translucent grey water. Niels, who was standing a little way off, heard her laughter and went off home. He was no longer worried about Dagni. He knew that her life would not be wasted.

1954

ILYINSKY WATERS

People are constantly plagued with regrets of some kind or other—over big things, small things, serious or ridiculous things. As for me, I frequently regret that I did not become a botanist and do not know all the plants in Central Russia. There are absolutely masses of them, of course, more than a thousand at a rough estimate. But just imagine how interesting it would be to know all these trees, shrubs and flowers and their different properties!

Time rushes past with such unjustifiable haste that this must be our greatest regret of all. Before you know where you are summer is fading, that "irretrievable" summer which is associated in nearly everyone's mind with memories of childhood.

In a flash youth has passed, old age is creeping on and you have still not seen the tiniest fraction of the enchantment that life has cast around you. Each day, sometimes each hour, brings with it regrets. They waken in the morning, but do not always subside at night. On the contrary, they sometimes flare up at night and there is no sedative that will quieten them. Together with the strongest regret of all about the rapid flight of time, there is another one, as sticky as pine resin. This is the feeling that one has not been able, and perhaps never will be able, to see the world in all its amazing and mysterious variety.

What am I saying, the world, when time and health do not even permit you to get to know your own country. For instance, I have never seen Baikal, the islands of Valaam, Lermontov's estate in Tarkhany or the flat, broad waters of the Ob near its mouth by the small town of Salekhard which used to be called Obdorsk.

Going over the places which I have seen convinces me that I have seen very little. But if you think of these places in terms of their quality, their essence, and not in terms of quantity, the picture is more encouraging. You can see a lot of marvellous things even if you spend your whole life sitting on the same spot. It is just a matter of having a keen, searching eye. We all know that the tiniest drop of water can reflect a kaleidoscope of light and colour, right down to a multitude of completely different shades of green in the foliage of the elder or the bird cherry, the lime and the alder. Incidentally, alder leaves are like the palms of young children's hands with their plumpness between the thin veins.

A mere ten kilometres from the log house where I live each summer there is one of the greatest, though little-known spots in the whole of Russia. In my opinion the word "great" is just as relevant to some of these places in our country as it is to events and people. We obviously dislike exalted feelings because we do not know how to express them, and put up with dry officialese to avoid the accusation of being sentimental. In spite of this many people, myself included, feel like saying "the great fields of Borodino" not simply the "fields of Borodino", just as people were not afraid of saying in the old days "the great sun of Austerlitz".

Great events naturally leave their mark on the countryside. We are aware of a special solemnity in nature in the fields of Borodino and hear its vibrant silence. It returned here after the bloody battles of the last war and since then no one has disturbed it.

The place I want to tell you about has a simple name, like many other magnificent spots in Russia. It is called Ilyinsky Waters, and to me this name is just inexpressibly attractive. It is not associated with any historical events or famous people, but simply expresses the true nature of the Russian countryside. Thus it is "typical", even "classical" as people like to put it.

Places such as these have an incredibly powerful effect on one's emotions. It is only fear of being accused of sentimentality that stops me from adding that these places are serene, soothing and have a holy quality about them. Pushkin was right when he spoke on the "holy twilight" in the gardens of Tsarskoye Selo. Not because they were consecrated to any events from "Holy Writ" but because they were holy to him.

Such places fill our hearts with joy and reverence for the beauty of our native land, the Russian countryside.

You have to climb down a slope to reach Ilyinsky Waters. No matter how much of a hurry you may be in to reach the waterside, you cannot help stopping several times on the way down to glance at the vast expanses on the other side of the river. I have seen many broad vistas in different parts of the world, but the view over Ilyinsky Waters is something which I never expect to find anywhere else.

This spot with all its charm and the unassuming beauty of common field flowers fills one with a sense of profound peace and the strange thought that if you have to die, let it be here in this patch of mild sunlight among the tall grass. The flowers and herbs—chicory, clover, forget-me-nots and meadowsweet—seem to welcome you, passersby, with a warm smile, nodding under the weight of heavy bees.

But the main charm of these spots was not in their herbs and flowers, or in their stout elms and rustling broom. It was in the magnificent view that opened up, tier upon tier, before one's eyes. Each tier, I counted six of them in all, had its particular blend of colour, light and air, as an artist might put it. It was as if a magician had taken all the colours of Central Russia and set them out in a broad panorama shimmering in the warm air.

Dry meadowland, *sukhodol*, in a riot of green and flowers lay in the foreground. Here and there in the thick grass sorrel rose up in long thin torches, the colour of deep red wine. Closer to the river there were water meadows overgrown with pale pink meadowsweet. It had already faded sending up swirls of dry petals over the quiet dark patches of still water.

The second tier was made up of ancient willow and broom bathed in intense heat and resembling clouds of greyish green mist. The leaves hung lethargically until the odd breeze blowing up from nowhere turned their undersides to the sun. And then the whole riverside kingdom of willow and broom became a seething torrent of foliage.

There were many rocky shallows in the river. The water streamed over the stony bed with a glinting murmur, sending out concentric ripples of river freshness.

Forests stretched up to the high horizon in the third tier. At this distance they seemed completely impenetrable and resembled mounds of fresh grass piled up by giants. By looking carefully at the shadows and the different shades of colour you could make out where the cuttings, tracks and the big dell were. The dell naturally concealed an enchanted lake with dark olive-green water.

Kites wheeled persistently over the trees. And the day sweltered in expectation of a storm.

Here and there the forest gave way to fields of waving rye, buckwheat and corn. They lay like patchwork quilts stretching out smoothly to the very ends of the earth and fading into the haze—the constant companion of remote expanses. The fields of grain shone through the haze like copper. It had ripened and a dry rustle, the endless whisper of the ears, rippled constantly from one vast stretch to the next like the majestic music of harvest.

Beyond the fields nestled hundreds of small villages stretching right up to our western border. You seemed to be able to smell newly baked rye bread, that enchanting, age-old smell of Russian villages. A dove-grey haze hung over the last tier, stretching above the horizon low over the earth. Something would flare up in it, like thin slivers of mica bursting into flame and dying away. The haze glinted and trembled with these slivers and in the sky above blanched with the intense heat, solemn swanlike clouds sailed in a shining procession.

One summer I lived in the steppe beyond Voronezh. I spent all the day either in an overgrown lime park or in a windmill on a dry hillock. The mill was surrounded by coarse violet immortelle. Half of its plank roof had been torn away by blast at the time of the German advance on Voronezh. You could see the sky through this opening. I used to lie on the warm clay floor of the mill reading novels by Ertel or simply looking up at the sky through the hole in the roof, where I could see bank upon bank of billowing white cloud trail past slowly northwards.

The clouds cast their gleaming light down to

earth and it crept over my face, making me close my eyes to protect them from the brightness. I rubbed some thyme flowers between my fingers and savoured their dry, healthy, southern fragrance. Then I had the strange feeling that the sea was just beyond the windmill and that the aroma of thyme was coming from its smooth sands, not from the open steppe.

Sometimes I would doze off by the millstones of pink sandstone and they would carry me back to the days of Ancient Greece.

A few years later I saw the famous head of the Egyptian Queen Nefertiti made out of the same stone and was astonished at the feminine grace expressed with such crude material. The brilliant sculptor had turned the stone into the beautiful head of a vibrant, gentle young woman and presented it to future generations, to us his distant descendants as tireless as he in our search for eternal beauty.

Two years later in Provence I saw the famous windmill of the French writer Alphonse Daudet where he actually lived for a time.

Life in a windmill smelling of flour and old herbs must have been absolutely delightful. Particularly in our Voronezh windmill, since Alphonse Daudet lived in a stone mill, not a wooden one full of the delicious smell of resin, bread and convolvulus, full of fresh steppe breezes, the light of the clouds, the trilling of the larks and the twittering of small birds—yellow buntings or kinglets.

Unfortunately Ilyinsky Waters had neither a windmill nor a watermill. That was a great pity because nothing suits the Russian countryside as well as these mills. Just as a colourful silk shawl on a Russian peasant girl makes her eyes darker, her lips brighter and her voice intimate and gentle.

In the far distance between the dim waves of oats and rye stood a knotted elm, its dark leaves murmuring from the gusts of wind. I had the feeling that the elm was not simply standing amid these hot fields, but that it was guarding some secret as ancient as the human skull washed up by a heavy downpour in the neighbouring gully. The skull was a dark brown. It had been cleft from forehead to crown by the stroke of a sword and must have been lying in the ground since the time of the Mongol invasion. It must have heard the calling of the wood sprites, foxes yelping at the blood-red setting sun and the wheels of Scythian chariots creaking slowly over the steppe.

As well as going to the mill I often spent a lot of time sitting in the shade of this elm tree. Patches of shy short-stemmed clover were growing on the border between the fields. An angry old bumblebee made a threatening dive at me in an effort to banish man from its unfrequented realm. I sat in the shade of the elm, lazily picking flowers and grasses with a deep affection welling up inside me for each blade and petal. I was thinking of my silent friends, all these trusting stems and blades, and of the joy and peace of mind which I got from seeing them each day and living with them in this quiet steppe under the open sky.

. . . You could see the green wall across Ilyinsky Waters. It was the forest on the right bank of the Oka and beyond it nestled the Bogimovo estate with its old park and terraced manor house with Venetian windows. Chekhov once spent the summer here and wrote *Sakhalin Island* and *The House with the Mansard*, that incredibly sad love story about the sweet young girl Missie. Missie left these parts never to return, but Chekhov's sadness remained. It dwells in the dampish avenues and the empty rooms of the large house where moths sleep on the dusty windowpanes. Touch a moth and you will find that it is dead.

The pond is covered with an enormous green carpet of duckweed. Carp champ away quietly at the waterweed turning first one side of dark liquid gold and then the other to the sun. These carp are the descendants of those for which Chekhov used to fish here.

But Chekhov is no more. I was twelve the year when he died and remember how my father's shoulders hunched up and his head shook when he learnt of Chekhov's death. And how he turned abruptly and went off to grieve over this irreparable, hopeless loss in private. None of the Russian writers, apart from Pushkin and Tolstoi, were mourned as deeply as Chekhov, for he was not only a great writer but a person whom we admired and loved. He knew the way to human dignity and happiness and mapped it out for us.

It is difficult to say how habits grow up, particularly unexpected ones. Every time I was about to set off on a long journey I always went to have a last look at Ilyinsky Waters. I simply could not leave without saying good-bye to the Waters, the white willow and the rolling Russian plains.

I used to say to myself: "You'll suddenly remember this thistle when you are flying over the Mediterranean. If you get there, that is. And you'll think of that last blushing ray of sun lost in the vast heavens when you are somewhere near Paris. If you get there too, that is."

And I did too. There I was flying over the Tyrrhenian Sea. Through the small round window I saw the yellow outline of an island looking like a thistle appear in the fathomless blue depths. It was Corsica. Later I learned that seen from above islands take on fantastic shapes just like cumulus cloud. These shapes are the product of our imagination, of course.

The jagged coast of Corsica lashed by the centuries and baked by the intense heat, its castles protecting the islands like spiky thorns, patches of bright red shrubs, a torrent of deep blue Mediterranean light bursting through the invisible weir of the heavens and cascading in all its might onto the island—all this could not distract my thoughts from a small damp hollow on Ilyinsky Waters smelling of hemlock with a solitary thistle that grew up to your head—impregnable, bristling with prickles, its sharp couters and visor.

On the western shore of the island was a small town resembling a handful of carelessly scattered dice. It emerged from the wing of the plane like a honeycomb. This was Napoleon's birthplace, Ajaccio.

"All conquerors are mad," said my neighbour, a fat, jovial Italian in sun-glasses, glancing down at Ajaccio. "How on earth a person who was born and grew up in such beauty could become a mass murderer is completely beyond me!"

He opened his newspaper noisily, looked at a page and then threw it aside, announcing to all and sundry:

"Ho ho. De Gaulle's not a bad Catholic, it seems."

Rome was shining in the distance with the bright reflection of the sun on the glass of new, multistorey blocks. The intercom at the airport kept repeating agitatedly that Signor Parelli's car was waiting for him at the main entrance.

And I suddenly felt an intense yearning to be back in my simple log house, on the Oka, on Ilyinsky Waters where the willows, the misty Russian sunsets on the plains and my friends were waiting faithfully for me.

As for the blushing ray of sun I saw that as well a few days later in the small town of Ermenonville near Paris where Jean Jacques Rousseau spent the last weeks of his life on an old estate. The concierge opened the iron gate for us, took our entrance fee in silence and indicated with an angry wave of the hand where we should begin our look round the park. Then in an equally angry manner she told us that the house was closed and all we could do was look at the park.

The park was deserted. We did not meet a single soul in it. If the ghost of Rousseau had been in the park, no one would have prevented us from communing with it. Yellow plane leaves rustled beneath our feet. They had covered the surface of the misty ponds as well as all the ground. I had never seen such enormous plane trees. Their leaves were falling fast baring the gigantic treetops. The trees seemed to have been cast in light bronze by some great sculptor. Their tops were enveloped in mist and this gave them a somewhat eery appearance.

Everything around was immersed in a grey silence. The park was enveloped in mist. Now and then transparent icy drops would fall off the branches onto our arms. The yellow, spreading leaves fell constantly, their light rustle following on our heels.

A slate grey sky stretched overhead, but it was a light, radiant Paris grey all the same. Rousseau's tomb stood gleaming on an island in the middle of a pond. The only way of reaching it was by boat and there were no boats on the pond. Nor were Rousseau's remains on the island. They had been removed to the Pantheon a long time ago.

Then the rosy light of the sun began to break through the shrouds of mist and the plane trees suddenly seemed to come to life, transformed into burnished copper. I remembered a similar rosy evening on Ilyinsky Waters and was suddenly overwhelmed by the familiar feeling of homesickness, longing for our vast country, for the sunsets, the plantain and the gentle rustle of the fallen leaves.

Beautiful France was magnificent, of course, but indifferent to us. We were homesick for Russia. That day I began to long to get home to the Oka where everything was so familiar, so dear and so open-hearted. My heart sank at the very thought that my return home might be delayed for some reason even by a few days.

I fell in love with France long ago, intellectually at first and then really seriously. But I

444

could not sacrifice even such a small thing as a saffron beam of morning sunlight on the log wall of an old izba for her. You could follow the movement of the sunbeam over the wall, listen to the saucy shrieks of the village cocks and the old familiar words would spring to your lips:

The cocks are crowing over Holy Russia—
Over Holy Russia it will soon be day....

Now and then the leaves drifted down from the plane trees. The gardens of Ermenonville, those sacred gardens imbued with the memory of Rousseau, nestled in the darkling autumn day as short and melancholy as a Russian autumn. Something very close and dear beckoned to us in this silent mist above the pond and in the hush of approaching night.

No! A Man's country is his very life-blood. He cannot live without it.

1964